ON SUCH

A FULL SEA

•

CHANG-RAE LEE

Little, Brown

LITTLE, BROWN

First published in the United States in 2014 by Riverhead Books
First published in Great Britain in 2014 by Little, Brown

Published by arrangement with Riverhead Books,
a member of Penguin Group (USA) Inc.

Grateful acknowledgement is made to Hal Leonard for permission to reprint lyrics
from 'Only the Young' by Steve Perry, Jonathan Cain and Neal Schon

A CIP catalogue record for this book
is available from the British Library.

ISBN 978-1-4087-0547-6

Book design by Gretchen Achilles
Printed and bound in Great Britain by
Clays Ltd, St Ives plc

Papers used by Little, Brown are from well-managed forests
and other responsible sources.

MIX
Paper from
responsible sources
FSC
www.fsc.org   FSC® C104740

Little, Brown
An imprint of
Little, Brown Book Group
100 Victoria Embankment
London EC4Y 0DY

An Hachette UK Company
www.hachette.co.uk

www.littlebrown.co.uk

Chang-rae Lee is the author of the bestselling novels *The Surrendered* and *Native Speaker*, which won the Hemingway Foundation/PEN award. He teaches at Princeton University.

BY CHANG-RAE LEE

Aloft

A Gesture Life

Native Speaker

The Surrendered

On Such a Full Sea

FOR EVA AND ANNIKA

We, at the height, are ready to decline.
There is a tide in the affairs of men,
Which, taken at the flood, leads on to fortune;
Omitted, all the voyage of their life
Is bound in shallows and in miseries.
On such a full sea are we now afloat,
And we must take the current when it serves
Or lose our ventures.
—WILLIAM SHAKESPEARE, *Julius Caesar*

In the shadows of a golden age
A generation waits for dawn
Brave carry on
Bold and the strong

Only the young can say
They're free to fly away
Sharing the same desires
Burnin' like wildfire
—JONATHAN CAIN, STEVE PERRY,
NEAL SCHON, "Only the Young"

ON SUCH

A FULL SEA

IT IS KNOWN WHERE WE COME FROM, BUT NO ONE MUCH cares about things like that anymore. We think, Why bother? Except for a lucky few, everyone is from someplace, but that someplace, it turns out, is gone. You can search it, you can find pix or vids that show what the place last looked like, in our case a gravel-colored town of stoop-shouldered buildings on a riverbank in China, shorn hills in the distance. Rooftops a mess of wires and junk. The river tea-still, a swath of black. And blunting it all is a haze that you can almost smell, a smell, you think, you don't want to breathe in.

So what does it matter if the town was razed one day, after our people were trucked out? What difference does it make that there's almost nothing there now? It was on the other side of the world, which might as well be a light-year away. Though probably it was mourned when it was thriving. People are funny that way; even the most miserable kind of circumstance can inspire a genuine throb of nostalgia.

The blood was pumping, yes?

Weren't we alive!

You can bet that where we live now was mourned, too, in its time, and though it may be surprising to consider, someday this community might be remembered as an excellent place, even by those of us who recognize its shortcomings. But we don't wish to dwell on the unhappier details. Most would agree that any rational person would leap at the chance of living here in B-Mor, given what it's like out there, beyond the walls. In the open counties. And even those relative few who've secured a spot in the Charter villages might find certain aspects of life here enviable, though they would definitely never say so.

We, on the other hand, will offer this: you can rely on the time here, the tread of the hours. If you think about it, there's little else that's more important than having a schedule, and better yet, counting on that schedule; it helps one to sleep more soundly, to work steadily through one's shift, maybe even to digest the hearty meals, and finally to enjoy all the free time available to us, right up to the last minutes of the evening. Then, if the stars are out—and they do seem to be out most every night now—we can sit together in our backyards and wave a hand to neighbors over the fences and view our favorite programs while sitting in the open air and authentically believe that this stretch of sky sings its chorus of light for us alone.

Who would tell us we are wrong? Let them come forward. Let them try to shake our walls. Our footings are dug deep. And if they like, they can even bring up the tale of Fan, the young woman whose cause has been taken up by a startling number of us. She's now gone from here, and whether she's enduring or suffering or dead is a matter for her household, whatever their disposition. They are gone, too, transferred to another facility in the far west, the best scenario for them after the strife she caused.

We can talk about her openly because hers is no grand tragedy, no apocalypse of the soul or of our times. Yes, there are those who would like to believe otherwise; that each and every being in the realm is a microcosm of the realm. That we are heartened and chastened and diminished and elevated by a singular reflection. This is a fetching idea, metaphorically and otherwise, most often enlisted for promoting the greater good. But more and more we can see that the question is not whether we are "individuals." We can't help but be, this has been proved, case by case. We are not drones or robots and never will be. The question, then, is whether being an "individual" makes a difference anymore. That it can matter at all. And if not, whether we in fact care.

Did Fan care about such things? We can't be certain. We know much about her daily life but that still leaves a great deal to be determined. She was perhaps brighter than most, certainly less talkative, but otherwise, in terms of character, not terribly distinctive. Nor would anyone have thought that she could do the thing she did. Such a lamentable action!

She did stand out physically, and not because she was beautiful. She was pleasing enough to look at. She was tiny, was the thing, just 150 centimeters (or not quite five feet tall), and slim besides, which made her the perfect size for her job in the tanks. At sixteen she had the stature of a girl of eleven or twelve, and thereby, when first encountered, she could appear to possess a special perspective that one might automatically call "wisdom" but is perhaps more a kind of timelessness of view, the capacity, as a child might have, to see things and people and events without the muddle of the present and all it contains. Perhaps Fan truly had that kind of clarity, and not just a semblance of it.

But if we may, let us picture her before the trouble, just as she was, clad in black neoprene, only the pale gleam of her bare feet and hands and face to indicate her humanity. Once she pulled on gloves and flippers and her eye mask, she looked like a creature of prey, a sleek dark seabird knifing into the waters. Of course, that's not what she did in the tanks, where her job was to husband and nurture the valuable fish that allow our community to do so well in this mostly difficult world. She was one of the best in her function as a diver, easily able to hold her breath for two minutes or more while she scrubbed and vacuumed and replaced tubing and filters, and patched whatever tears had formed in the linings, a half-weight vest to hold her beneath the surface. Even that was almost too heavy for her and she would have to bend her knees while at the bottom of the two-meter-deep water and propel herself upward to breathe, before descending again, her various tools attached to her work belt.

Once submerged, a diver is not easily seen. Given all the fish in the water—naturally as many healthy fish are raised as possible—she is a mere shadow among them, trained to do her tasks quickly and unobtrusively. That is why she uses no special breathing apparatus aside from a snorkel, compressed gases causing too much of a disturbance. Fearful fish are not happy fish. The diver is not "one of them" but is part of the waterscape from the time they are hatchlings, and they see her customary form and the repeated cadence of her movements and the gentle motor of her flippered feet that must come to them like a motherly lullaby. A dream-song of refuge, right up to the moment of harvest. The diver is there at harvest, of course, and sees to it that the very last of them finds its way into the chute. And it is only then, for the span of the few hours while the tank is being cleaned and filtered before the next generation of hatchlings is released, that the water is clear of activity, that the diver is alone.

How somber a period that must be. The constant light from the grow bulbs filtering through the canopy of vegetables and herbs and ornamental flowers suspended above the tanks throws blue-green glints about the facility walls, this cool Amazonian hue that suggests a fecundity primordial and unceasing. The diver inspects each aquarium, which is roughly the dimension of a badminton court, and by the end she is exhausted not by the work or holding her breath but instead from the strange exertion of pushing against the emptiness. For she is accustomed to the buoying lift of their numbers, how sometimes the fish seem to gird her and bear her along the tank walls like a living scaffold, or perhaps lead her to one of their dead by swarming about its upended corpse, or even playfully school themselves into just her shape and become her mirror in the water. At the pellet drop they are simply fish again and thrash upward, mouths agape, the vibrato of the water chattering and electric, as if bees were madly attempting to pass through her suit. And wouldn't it be truth enough to speak of those bristling hundreds as not only being cared for by the diver but as serving to shepherd her, too, through the march of days?

For who is she, given the many hours she and all the other members of her household spend at their jobs and how generally sparse their conversation is during downtime or when they're having their morning or evening meal while watching a vid or game? All around B-Mor it's much the same, which is happy enough. But maybe it's the laboring that gives you shape. Might the most fulfilling times be those spent solo at your tasks, literally immersed or not, when you are able to uncover the smallest surprises and unlikely details of some process or operation that in turn exposes your proclivities and prejudices both? And whether or not there is anything to be done about it, you begin to learn what you value most.

For Fan, more than the other divers, took to the tanks with a quiet abandon, rarely climbing out at the ending hour to peel herself of the suiting in the changing room with the others. She would appear just as they were leaving for home, or if she didn't and they grew concerned, someone would go to her tanks and check that she was still working. For divers have perished from time to time, as they can believe too well that they are one of the throng. But Fan would be there, simply swimming about, scrubbing or patching, and the other diver would splash the water and wait until Fan surfaced with a thumbs-up. She once told us that she almost preferred being in the tanks than out in the air of B-Mor, that she liked the feeling of having to hold her breath and go against her nature, which made her more aware of herself as this mere, lone body. In the hour or so after the shift, with no more tasks to be done, she would pull her knees to her chest and drift to the bottom and stay there in that crouch until her lungs screamed for forgiveness. She wasn't inviting oblivion or even testing herself but rather summoning a different kind of force that would transform not her but the composition of the realm, make it so the water could not harm her. And we would say, Please, Fan, please, you cannot truly believe this, and she would almost smile and mostly nod but the impression you were left with was that she did, in fact, believe in such a possibility. And if that is an indication of her instability, everything else that happened makes sense and no more needs to be accounted for.

But let's suppose another way of considering her, which was that she had a special conviction of imagination. Few of us do, to be honest. We wish and wish and often with fury but never very deeply. For if we did, we'd see how the world can sometimes split open, in just the way we hope. That it and we are, in fact, unbounded. Free.

Not that this means Fan was wholly in the right. Though we will not say this of her boyfriend, Reg. He was just anybody else, in most people's view, except perhaps that he was tall and had the most beautiful skin one might ever see. This sounds silly, but this was Reg, in a phrase. His skin was the color of a smooth river stone, though one that's lighter than those around it, a wheat-brown, buttery hue that seemed to glow warmer in the pale illumination of the grow facility. That's where they met, as he took care of the deck of vegetables that perched over her tanks. His long arms could easily reach the inner sections to plant and pollinate, prune and harvest, and it's a fetching image of the two of them, he standing high on his ladder that rolled side to side on a track, she paddling in the cool waters below, both at labor for the good of our community like any responsible pair.

Workers in the grow facility regularly become romantically involved, there's no rule or code against it, and there are probably dozens of families in our part of B-Mor originating from such unions; we ourselves derive from two of the first generations of growers, this well before the fish tanks were laid in. Stability is all here in B-Mor; it's what we ultimately produce, day by night by day, both what we grow for consumption and how we are organized in neighborhood teams, the bonds of blood or sexual love relied upon equally to support our constitution. In this difficult era the most valuable commodity is the unfailing turn of the hours and how they retrieve for us the known harbor of yesterday, and in this sense, too, there was really nothing to alarm about Fan and Reg, who were just another estimable couple, if almost comically mismatched in height as they strolled the neighborhood on the more pleasant evenings.

But one day, toward the end of the shift, Reg was told to go speak to the manager. Fan didn't even notice him leaving; there was no reason to. People are called in all the time to be informed of some minor change in schedule or procedures. This is likely what one would assume as you took off your gardener's gloves and ascended the stairs to the manager's mezzanine office filled with screens and controls. For example, there will be a switch-out of this fish or vegetable for another, depending on what's in demand in the Charter villages. Recently there was a call for Japanese knotweed because it supposedly prevents certain blood Cs, so now at each meal every Charter adult and child eats Japanese knotweed, kilos of which anybody can easily pull from the ground beyond the walls but which, of course, being out there, no one would ever touch.

Reg was summoned from his ladder the day before his free-day.

On free-day, Fan was seen sitting by herself in the park, listening to music through her earbuds. She didn't appear distraught; apparently Reg (or else somebody posing as Reg) had messaged her to say that he was occupied, no further explanation, and would see her the next day. His family was unconcerned; Reg was known to wander, sometimes even beyond the walls. It's not that he was reckless or dimwitted, though it must be said that Reg was never going to ace the Exams, not in a millennium. In fact, he didn't even bother to take them. He was the sort of kindly, dreamy boy who is prevailed upon by whim and instinct, and if he sometimes found trouble, it was always the charming kind, such as when a dog gets his muzzle stuck in a jar of peanut butter. We all recall the time he decided to rig his harvest tray directly onto his back rather than filling it and bringing it down and then lugging an empty one back up, and at first it seemed to be working, despite the ungainly appearance, as he'd gently drop the tomatoes over his shoulder while he stood on the ladder, filling it steadily. But it got much heavier than he anticipated, and when he momentarily lost balance on the rung, the fully laden tray tipped him backward. It was a ridiculous mess and the floor forewoman was furious over the ruined fruit and Reg, his kinky head of hair pulp-sopped and dripping, was lucky his neck wasn't broken, for how he landed on that bin. You could only chuckle and think, Reg, you especially are one fortunate young man for being born inside B-Mor!

But when he didn't appear the first workday of the week, people began to talk. As always Fan worked in the tanks, rarely coming up for more than a few minutes straight. At the lunch hour someone went to Reg's row house to see if he was ill, and at first no one answered but then his aunt opened the door just long enough to say that Reg wasn't there anymore. When asked what "anymore" meant, she simply replied that they didn't want to be bothered and shut the door on him like he was any open counties peddler allowed into B-Mor for the day. And when the shift was over, we asked Fan what she knew and all she could say was that she, too, had stopped by his family's house and been brusquely turned away. The following day Fan asked the forewoman what she knew of Reg's whereabouts and she referred her to the manager, who told her that it was now a directorate-level matter and that he had no idea where Reg was. After that, Fan went to the succeeding manager and administrator until there was no one else here in B-Mor to query; for more definitive word from above, she would have to question a Charter person, who (for us) are as rare a sight as honeybees.

A week passed by, then nearly two. There were scattered rumors and gossip and the broader rumblings of what must be called a genuine vexation, if not anger, that echoed about the lofty ceilings of the grow facility and on the stoops of the narrow-faced row houses. In the past few seasons one heard of similar "call-aways" at other facilities, including B-Mor. Sure, some of us had been summoned from work and sequestered for a few days and then had been returned to our posts. But Reg was gone. Had his clan made noises of dissent, there might have been a swell of emotions but they all went about their jobs or studies and did not air a single word of question or complaint, which at first surprised us but soon enough was like a cold quilt thrown over our corpus, snuffing every atom of ill heat. They were magnificently silent. For naturally you then think, If his kin are this placid, well . . .

And you could think Fan, too, was mute on the subject, for whenever one of us would approach her to see if she knew anything, she'd simply affix her mask and disappear beneath the densely populated waters, or if out on the block, she'd raise the volume of whatever she was listening to and take an escaping tack on her scooter. She had a typical cohort of friends and acquaintances from work and the neighborhood but she receded from them after Reg disappeared, or they from her, even though there was no shunning going on, more a realization by all that Fan and Reg had come to belong together and that once unpaired, Fan should be perhaps left alone for a while. No one brought up his or her theories of what happened to him or why. You would expect the directorate of B-Mor to put out word official or otherwise of what he had done in order to stall speculation and focus our attention on some act or crime, but the remarkable thing about a silence so total is that it soon squares your attention not on the subject but on your very self. For you can't help but interrogate your own behavior, actions, tendencies, even the stray skeins of your thoughts, and not wonder how in the course of the days you may have been close to transgressing some unspecified limit. It's like when a toddler has a toy drum or piano and unconsciously taps away at it without a mote of annoyance from his seemingly copacetic father, right up until one random ordinary clang, which instantly dissipates the man's patience and the keyboard ends up smashed.

Did Fan know more than what she let on? She must have known that Reg had done nothing wrong. He was an innocent, through and through, which is why she admired him. And isn't this why we admired Fan, too, this tiny, good girl, who never crossed anyone or went against even a convention of B-Mor, much less a regulation, until the moment she did? And why, despite her present notoriety, we think of her still as one of us, one of our number, even as she left us for the open counties? Some would balk at this, they can hardly utter her name without a stony jaw, unable to forgive Fan for what she did before disappearing of her own accord as much as for the greater troubles that arose afterward. For how unnecessary all of it was. And from a certain perspective this was true. It was unnecessary. She had larger aims for sure, and it can be argued that she attained some measure of them, but why before leaving she had to poison some of the tanks is not fathomable. It makes no sense. The funny thing, the oddest thing, even for those of us who won't eternally condemn her, is that she caused the deaths of only her own fish, the ones she so carefully raised.

Those poor sweet fish.

EVERYONE KNOWS IT IS ROUGH LIVING IN THE OPEN COUN-
ties. In this region, where it can get both very hot and very cold, it's
especially unpleasant. Though it seems that's most places now! Our
elders will say there used to be whole seasons in between of perfectly
glorious days. Now, of course, those days are few, mere intermittent
glimpses of what seems to us a prehistoric world, when the air was
drier and clearer and more temperate, when the scent of turned earth
or wildflowers or crisp dead leaves made one think of time as a kind,
calm clock, rather than a sentence.

Here in B-Mor, along the runway-straight blocks, we can't avoid
enduring the same extremes as in the open counties, but it is a blessing to note that we have numerous places to go for respite, like our
indoor gymnasiums and pools, and the subterranean mall busy with
shops and game parlors and eateries, where people naturally spend
most of their free time. Because it's rarely pleasant out of doors, we've
come to depend on the atmosphere of seasonally perfumed, filtered
air and the honey-hued halo lighting and the constantly updated
mood-enhancing music that all together are hardly noticeable anymore but would likely cause a pandemonium were they cut off for
any substantial period.

Last year, in fact, the very thing happened for several minutes because of a power plant mishap, and while we had air and backup lights, there arose in the dimness a distinct odor of cave, which was not so awful as it was alarming, for you couldn't help but realize that we were lodged in the innards of the realm. Eventually people stopped what they were doing and looked about, their mouths half open, awaiting an announcement. None came. Suddenly some people started running, the trigger unclear, and before you knew it, everyone was racing about, toddlers desperately yanked along, the elderly panting and trying to claw through the scattershot mobs, the young and fit sprinting as if the dogs of hell were chasing them. What panic in those corridors! What knife-in-the-heart terror! But then a great wheeze spewed from the ducts, and they rattled mightily, and then the banks of soft light revived and the old familiar songs that we never quite listened to reset us to the more tranquil rhythms of our souls.

We're no longer fit for any harsher brand of life, we admit that readily, and simply imagining ourselves existing beyond the gates is enough to induce a swampy tingle in the underarms, a gaining chill in the gut. For there's real struggle for open counties people, for in a phrase the basic needs are met but not much else; the power is thready, constantly cycling on and off; housing is rudimentary, with shantytowns the rule; water is plentiful only during the wet seasons, and should be boiled at any time. And talking about smell! The system of sewers in the open counties (ours in B-Mor was redone as recently as ten years ago) dates from nearly two hundred years *before* our people arrived from New China, truly ancient times, such that after there's a heavy rain and the wind blows from the southwest, you can pick up from our very block the sharp rot stink of human settlement, that undying herald: We are here! We are here! We are here!

We know you are there, believe us.

13

Maybe Charters can easily forget what it's like out there, but we B-Mors and others in similar settlements should be aware of the possibilities. We shouldn't take for granted the security and comfort of our neighborhoods, we shouldn't think that always leaving our windows open and our doors unlocked means that we're beyond an encroachment. We may believe our gates are insurmountable and that we're armored by routines, but can't we be touched by chance or fate, plucked up like a mouse foraging along his well-worn trail? Before you know it, you're looking down at the last faint print of your claws in the dirt.

But hold on, you might say. On our street, once called North Milton Avenue and renamed Longevity Way by our predecessors, who saw the nearly three-kilometer run of ruler-straight road and couldn't help but think of wondrously extended, if not eternal, life, the main infractions are spitting or littering or publicly relieving oneself, most always perpetrated by the very old and very young and those who overindulge on nights before their free-day. There hasn't been a property theft in recent memory, and a report of a serious crime, some mugging or assault, would likely halt all work and social activity immediately, for how exceedingly rare such a thing would be, like some solar eclipse.

So, yes, yes, you would be more than right. It's been nearly a hundred years since our originals arrived and fifty plus since the final reconstruction and incorporation of what B-Mor is today, and for all that time we have kept up the community, curbstone by curbstone, brick by brick, we have not let our windows get dingy or our brass knobs spot, we are always after our children to pick up after themselves in the playgrounds, we have not allowed anyone to shirk his or her duties or to become lazy and dependent. B-Mor works because we work, our sense of purpose driving us that extra measure, that extra hour, and then, of course, the knowledge of what's out in the counties and what it used to be like here before the originals landed refueling us whenever we flag.

We know very well how it was because it's central to our schooling, a primary unit of our studies devoted to the history of B-Mor and the conditions that made it possible, and how B-Mor itself and other places patterned after it have in turn been stabilizing elements in this long-struggling land. There are times we need to remind everyone of those conditions, especially people like Fan's boosters who even now would be so misguided as to believe they can follow her example and simply step outside the gates and embark on some journey that will write itself on our houses and walls, like the murals our originals found splashed all over the deserted neighborhoods. Those murals depicted scenes of children dancing in circles, of teams of smiling, joyously laboring adults, of never-setting suns whose rays illuminated only acts of kindness and sharing. For aren't all such murals as bounteous in their hopes as in their scale? Aren't they expressions of the grandest wishes, which by definition will never come true?

Now, from time to time, you'll see freshly painted portraits of Fan and Reg on the side of a row house or fence, hastily done in the night and clearly by different hands, though the eyes of the pair are always rendered so as to look at you squarely, relentlessly, like Fan and Reg never would have in real life, for how shy they both were. Their eyes like beams. And even though it's laughable, and the homeowner or some outraged neighbor immediately paints it over before anyone from the directorate can notice, they keep popping up regularly enough such that you are almost guessing where one will appear next. And if one doesn't, maybe you begin to picture it yourself.

A legend can be made, it turns out, one crude stroke at a time.

But we should pause, for the moment, in the tale of Fan, and of her dear Reg, and of the several others who would figure into the consequences of these travails. We need to remind all boosters, agitators, wonderers, wishers, of what it was like here when the originals landed. What did they first see, before B-Mor was B-Mor?

Perhaps the most telling artifact is a picture that hangs prominently in our historical museum, right by the entrance. It's an enlarged image of one of our characteristic row houses, dating to the very year of arrival. The image shows the front façade of the house, its two narrow first-floor windows and the stoop leading up to the front door. On first view it's all trimmed up and neat, the brick face painted over in daffodil yellow, the sills in creamy white, the iron railing of the stoop a lean, rigorous black. The patch of sky in the upper corner reveals that it's later in the day, a cloud tinged reddish on its wispy belly, the summing impression being that this is yet another fine day in the neighborhood, and you wonder why the curators would display such a picture when the museum is all about the pivotal role of B-Mor, so much so that you're sure you've mistakenly read the date and that it's an image of the present time. What you can easily miss—and many younger B-Mors do—is that there's something odd about the second-story windows, which aren't reflecting the warm hues of the cloud but instead shimmer with an icy white-blue, like the most exotic, fantastical marble; and then you gather that they are not windows at all but plywood sheets painted as such, quite wonderfully executed trompe l'oeil; and on further examination, you can see a slit where one of the plywood sheets has come loose at a corner, and you now realize that the reddish light glowing behind it is only possible to see because this house has no roof, because it is open to the sky.

Now, take this house, and the one next to it, and next to that, and you can see that even though they still have roofs, the continuous run of them on this block are similarly closed up with boards of wood and colorful paint. And as you move through the foyer of the museum into the cavernous main hall where there are banner-sized pictures that show other blocks like it in the same scale and then zoomed out, this block multiplied by scores, if not hundreds, you are struck by the fact that immense sections of this old harbor city are completely abandoned.

Everyone has left, though not for the same reasons our predecessors had to leave their small riverside town in New China. By the time they departed, Xixu City was made uninhabitable by the surrounding farms and factories and power plants and mining operations, the water fouled beyond all known methods of treatment. Although the population of the town was only 300,000, the cars and trucks and scooters and buses easily numbered a million, and so along with around-the-clock coal and rare-earth excavation, the air never had a chance to clear. Then one day the provincial government could not transport in any more fresh water—fresh water was shockingly scarce even in the major cities—and so the town was forced to cease. Those who can remember the tales of the old-timers report that in the heydays it was as if the entire valley and everything in it were slowly scorching, all the rubber and plastic and alloys, all of what little real wood remained, all the rotting food and garbage, the welling pools of human and animal wastes, such that in the end it was as though the people themselves were burning, as if from the inside, exuding this rank, throttled breath that foretold of a tortuous, lingering demise.

When our ancestors were first brought here—the archival vids and pix show them rolling in on fleets of shiny silver company buses—the air was to them fresh and clear, just like in the image of the roofless row house, and when they stepped out, they must have been entranced by the scant briny notes of the harbor waters, breathing them in deep. And think of how startled they might have been by the strange brand of tidiness in this place (once known as Baltimore) and other abandoned cities that settlers were sent to in other eastern and midwestern states, this preservation by dint of absence, such that after they gathered their luggage from the curb and were shuttled by carts to the houses assigned to them, our and your and Fan's forebears among them, their gasps were not of trepidation or disappointment but of gratitude and relief.

Indeed, it's difficult for us to understand how genuinely grateful they were; we glance around B-Mor now and it's impossible to imagine how our people could have felt that way (how time and safety and a filled belly rapidly evolve us!), to be presented with so depleted a cityscape and still have a heart-surge of excitement. The legendary Wen Shurbao, who would be our first and only mayor, reportedly exhorted his brethren by invoking the classic proverb: "Our generation will plant the trees. The next will enjoy the shade."

Surely there were the discontented among those originals, but which of them could deny the promise of this place? Here was an entire community, ready for revitalization. Yes, the houses were basically shells, but in fact many still had roofs and walls and sturdy stairs; yes, few had any boilers, but the majority had salvageable wiring and plumbing; yes, the floors had to be scraped and sanded and refinished, every cabinet and counter scrubbed and disinfected of the leavings of birds and vermin and insects, and yet what activity offers more immediate, honest gratification than shining up a seemingly ruined surface back to the distinctive grain of its essence?

After you tour the museum with the school groups and senior outings and those foreign visitors who come from time to time to study the society we've built, you could only emphatically agree to the leaps we've made. From the utter desiccation of the long-abandoned blocks, and the clearing and emptying of the huge city cemetery, to the early structures they were tasked to construct upon that plot, which would house the first truly uncontaminated grow beds that are now a B-Mor trademark, and the parallel complex of fish tanks that were conceived later once the Charter villages officially organized themselves and boosted demand, we have drawn up the map, as it were, by our daily labors, and we etch it still.

We should concede that unlike the experience of most immigrants, there was very little to encounter by way of an indigenous population. There were smatterings of them, to be sure, pockets of residents on the outskirts of what is now the heart of B-Mor, these descendants of nineteenth-century African slaves and twentieth-century laborers from Central America and even bands of twenty-first-century urban-nostalgics, all of whom settled the intimate grid of these blocks and thrived for a time and, for reasons that history can confidently trace and identify but never quite seem to solve, inexorably declined and finally disappeared. Our predecessors had the unique advantage of being husbanded by one of the federated companies, rather than the revolving cast of governmental bodies that overreached in their efforts or were disastrously neglectful, all of them downright clueless. The originals were brought in en masse for a strict purpose but with their work- and family-centric culture intact, such that they would not only endure and eventually profit the seed investors but also prosper in a manner that would be perpetually regenerative.

And while all this is true, and uplifting, and everyone you might greet on a stroll down Longevity Way will automatically trill *It is fine* or *It is right*, one has to accept that deformations have appeared on the surface of our serene terra, where even the most positive feelings can begin to pool, and seep down through new fissures, and trickle away.

For it's like this: soon after Reg disappeared and Fan departed, other people began to disappear, too. Not many, perhaps one or two a month, certainly no more. The difference was that these people were officially *dispatched*, the notifications, unlike Reg's, both posted in the grow house and also messaged to all of B-Mor. For example, there will be a general notification that James Beltran Ho, forty-four, has been dispatched, or that Pei-Pei Xu-Tidewater, twenty-nine, has been dispatched, or that an unnamed infant of the Reynolds-Wang clan of Bright Diamond Lane is now dispatched, information that we know not to inquire about further. But their relatives, unlike Reg's people, didn't go away. What was unusual, at least at first, was that they simply acted as if their loved one had died, just as if from a disease or unfortunate facility accident or old age, and even held memorial ceremonies in the customary way, inviting us, depending on the age and status of the deceased, to view the bodies, which were, of course, not there, just framed photographs of them. We would don our mourning costumes, wail softly or loudly as appropriate, burn paper offerings, do everything we're supposed to do; there was no difference in this regard. Everything was conducted as though life and death, as always, were ceaselessly trundling on, nothing to indicate that they had been instructed or directed to act the way they did, nothing to suggest they were forced to accede or comply.

Perhaps it was the same with our originals, though in a different circumstance. They went about their first labors, renovating the row houses in the same way, it turns out, that certain antique American communities used to do, the foreman or forewoman of each block marshaling all its residents to converge on one address and revamp, say, the bathrooms or kitchen, the museum clips just like a science class vid of hundreds of ants tugging a sourball-sized rock. You can picture it now. They'd go from one house to the next, right on down the block, this mobile, instantly adaptive assembly line, each person assigned a function, with the children passing beach pails of dust and rubble in a brigade, the elderly offering sips of cool chrysanthemum tea from canteens, even the unwell propped up in chairs close by or even inside the site, so that they might lend moral support or learn by watching.

Painters to the fore! or Tilers will proceed! the forewoman would brightly holler, and the troop would rush forward. Maybe the feeling in the group was reminiscent of the early days back in Xixu, before the river was blighted, before the hills were gouged away, before the province and country and world all discovered they craved a piece of us, when each soul recognized the face of every other and did not think it a belittling fact.

Yet to go back to that moment would be a sentimental journey. We have grown up now, generations deep, generations strong. And have we not lasted long enough to dare say all the hopes of our forebears have come true?

Have we not done the job of becoming our best selves?

THE DAY FAN LEFT WAS SOON AFTER THE LAST BIG FLOOD-
ing. Naturally, there is a record of her departure but no one paid
much mind to it at the time. We have mild floods early each autumn
because of the hurricanes that sweep up from the South Atlantic
and arrive here as somewhat diminished but still formidable storms,
but it was especially bad then, as there were several storms back to
back to back, with the rainwater having eventually nowhere to go.
We remember it well because a number of B-Mors perished during
the third and final storm, including a popular twelve-year-old boy
named Joseph, who died while trying to save his brother's friend from
drowning. It was a tragic occurrence that shook everyone in B-Mor,
and perhaps, it turns out, Fan most of all.

For it had hardly been more than a week since Reg disappeared,
and poor Joseph had been his friend. They weren't "best friends" but
lived on the same block, and Reg had known Joseph from the time
the boy was an infant and they still regularly spent time together. Of
course, Reg was nineteen and the substantial difference in their ages
would have normally precluded any such terming, at least by the
older one, but Reg was young at heart, as they say, and not in the
least self-conscious about hanging out and playing with whoever

happened to be out on the street. On their free-days Fan might scooter over there to pick up Reg but then happily sit and watch for a while as he kicked the soccer ball around with Joseph and his gang, Reg the only non-peer. He was much taller and more maturely built than all of them but they had the advantage of nimbleness and speed (Reg, as has been noted, not being the most agile of fellows), for every shot Reg blocked by simply craning out his pontoonlike foot, Joseph and the others scooted a pass between his legs or deftly maneuvered the ball around his too-upright frame, Fan unable to suppress her giggles whenever Reg stumbled and nearly lost his balance, his lankiness unsuited to quick pivots and reversals.

Naturally there were moments Reg would steam with frustration, as anyone swatting at gnats would, especially if one of the boys got past him with the same old feint or won the ball from him too easily. But there was never any taunting or lingering funny feeling, and when he said he had to go, the boys would plead for him to stay through one more goal and turn with him to Fan and await her signal, sending up a stout cheer when she said Sure, which she always did. When they were finally done, they'd each leap up and double high-five Reg's hands raised high, and in the sharpness of the smacks Fan could hear how pumped they were, how literally uplifted, how much bigger and brighter they must have felt themselves to be by virtue of his wholly generous being.

And maybe, if only in retrospect, we felt that way, too, whenever we saw Reg and Fan riding their electric scooters side by side, often close enough to hold hands (Reg having no balance issues here), their easeful gliding down the long alleys of these streets a demonstration of our good order. For no matter the shadows of an age, the picture of a young couple in love, we are told, speaks most luminously of the future, as the span of that passion makes us believe we can overleap any walls, obliterate whatever obstacles.

In the days between when Reg went absent and the accident with the boys, we would be hoping to see Fan doing okay on her own. As we've already noted, she didn't seem overly concerned, she was quietly biding the time, doing the appropriate things in terms of asking questions and pursuing available avenues, and yet in the mall or at the facility one could see she seemed, ironically, even smaller than before, for not being always next to Reg. He sized her, if this can be said, the way a planet does its moon, the two bodies perhaps much differing within their scale but nothing like they would be once adrift in the profound vastness of space.

Though plenty cozy, B-Mor can be a lonesome place.

And when Reg's young friend, Joseph, was suddenly lost in that last big storm, one could see how it was a lot to take. Here is what happened: Joseph was watching his brother and his brother's friend that afternoon, both sets of parents at work in the grow house, but the Wi-Fi had gone out because of the heavy rains and so they had been stuck inside all day without any gaming or vids; but then there was a sudden break in the cloud cover—it was one of those swirling weather systems that are rapidly changeable—and the younger boys begged to go out. Joseph agreed, and when they got to the park, it started to rain lightly but in a brilliant sun shower and rainbow. When it turned into a full-blown downpour, they decided what the heck, let's have some fun, happily getting soaked to the bone as they played.

Then they apparently came upon a shallow, newly formed pond in a low-lying area near the entrance of the park, the muddied water running off from a nearby swollen stream, and to their glee there were what seemed a thousand fish bristling about the surface. As any boys might, they decided to try to catch some, Joseph wielding a few downed leafy branches to corral them, while his brother and friend tried to snatch them with their bare hands. Of course, they weren't

catching them to eat—these were our fish, but released for an ornamental life in the ponds (only counties people would ever eat wild
fish, plus we have the benefit of purchasing our own prized fish at a
significant discount from what Charters have to pay)—the three
boys just having a blast like boys have since the beginning of time,
shouting in triumph whenever one actually caught a fish, the rain
coming down in sheets but unable to dampen any part of them.

And they were frolicking like that, without a care, because what
dangers could Joseph have anticipated in the thigh-deep water,
which was very slowly rising, other than maybe a jab from the pointy
ends of a dorsal fin? Though even that was not a concern because of
the training all B-Mor children receive, including units in piscine
biology, hatchery operations, and free-diving techniques, this last
area mostly meant to identify future divers. Joseph had, in fact, dived
with Fan on several occasions, as she sometimes demonstrated her
techniques for those classes. Joseph might have become a diver, as he
was a superbly athletic boy with tangles of orange hair (his line no
doubt including some blood from the first European settlers in the
area) and the captain of the only Junior Bs soccer team that ever
made it to the regional quarterfinals, nearly defeating a Charter
squad that ultimately won the championship. In fact, school sporting
contests are the only real extended contacts we have with Charters
and the few better-organized counties areas, as otherwise there would
be a sore lack of new playoff competition. Joseph, in this regard, was
something of our champion, and Reg and Fan would watch him play
matches whenever they could, this boy who had that special ability
to configure himself, dynamically and instantly, to whatever was
at hand.

This was likely his doom, for another boy might not have had the
instinctive confidence to do what Joseph did when the water started
to recede in that impromptu pond. Despite the torrents of rain, the

level was going down, which would have seemed strange if the boys
had even noticed, and they kept on wading after the fish, the schools
of which seemed to be heading toward one end of the pond. The
younger boys were in the lead, hurdling with slowed strides through
the water, when for some reason the fish were turning around and
swimming back through their legs, which delighted them. But Joseph
could see why the fish were turning back: a hidden drainage pipe
that ran beneath the entrance road had opened up. It had likely been
dammed by some branches but it was now free and making a horrible
gulping sound that you could hear even above the threshing rain.

The boys tried to run against the suddenly fierce current but the
friend slipped and fell beneath the surface. And then he was gone.
Sucked into the pipe. Joseph tugged his brother to the shallows and
then without saying another word dove in, letting the strong flow of
the brown water take him.

He can't have known, none of us could, that his brother's friend
had already been shot out the other end of the pipe, to the far side of
the embanked road, coughing and frightened and with a belly full of
dirty water but otherwise fine. But Joseph, three years older, just that
bit wider, got stuck three-quarters of the way through, and though
fighting as he must have to push himself back out, the force of the
water held him in place.

After an hour, emergency services was finally able to extract him,
almost losing one of their own men in the process. Despite the duration, they attempted to revive him, but it was no use. When they
brought Joseph back to his household, they say, he was the most startling shade of blue, transparent but still darkened, as if he'd been
dyed by the cold evening sky.

Oh, the lament on the blocks! The outpouring! As mentioned,
there were others who died during the storm: a couple who drowned
in their vehicle when they tried to ford a submerged intersection; a

man who was electrocuted as he attempted to pump out his flooded basement with a self-modified vacuum cleaner; some people who were inexplicably rowboating in the harbor and whose vessel immediately sank. The observances for these people were suitably somber and modest (and perhaps especially subdued, for the faintly embarrassing circumstances of their deaths), but for Joseph it seemed that every row house in B-Mor emptied onto the streets for his ceremony, all of us gathering outside his family's row house in an awesome silence, the only sound the shushing of hundreds and hundreds of rubber-slipper-shod feet as we waited our turn to view his body.

Fan had a place in the line along with most of her clan, listening to them talk about Joseph's wasted future. Usually this sort of chatter is merely just that, the idle blather of pipe dreams, but it was agreed Joseph really could have been one of those few who end up making a life as a Charter. For there are rare instances of B-Mors being recruited by Charter talent scouts for looks or athletic prowess—Joseph's parents had been contacted after his stellar performance in the soccer playoffs—to be models or actors or professional athletes. The only other way was, of course, to do extremely well on the yearly aptitude Exam that the Charters let our children take at the age of twelve, then allowing those who place in the top 2 percent of Charter scores to be eligible for promotion and adoption by a Charter family. Such performance on the test was even rarer, though members of Fan's clan could brag—and often did—that one of theirs had been promoted, if years ago; a sibling of Fan's, in fact, a boy named Liwei, whom she had never known because of the difference in their ages.

When Fan ascended to the top of the stoop, we could all see her. Maybe some mourner inside was taking an especially long time over the casket because Fan seemed to be perched there forever. It was a sunny day post storm and she wore the wraparound sunglasses she preferred, her bob of black hair curling under ever so slightly at the ends to cup the delicate lines of her jaw, and you could almost imagine her as one of those people who end up doing something that was far beyond what we B-Mors can ever expect, such as being a programs personality or an actor. Again, Fan was not beautiful but rather distinctive in her presence, which was one of more than merely being petite but like a distillation, this purity by way of exquisite scale, and to view her perfect little hand clutching the railing, and the tense purse of her mouth as she awaited her turn inside, was enough to tap a fresh well of admiration in your heart.

For the viewing, everybody was routed through the kitchen and eventually deposited in the shared alley that separates the rear yards of the houses. Fan saw exactly what we saw: there he was, reclined in a heavy cardboard coffin in the cramped front living room, asleep in his death robes, the amazing color of his face courtesy of Tang, the senior B-Mor mortician. And maybe it was to compensate for the stone hue of his subject, or just because he'd lost his touch, but old Tang truly went too far, for poor Joseph looked as though he had just trotted off the field after a hard-fought match. He appeared *too* alive, (perhaps literally) flushed with lifeblood, as if he might pop up at any moment and ask for a sports drink. Then, too, someone had placed a mini soccer ball in his hand and you could see that Joseph had a real grip on it, the soft plastic surface ever slightly deformed, and though it was just a toy ball, the sensation we had as we stood beside him was that he was squeezing *us*, not menacingly or in admonition like the dead normally would, but with the gentlest press of solidarity.

I know, Joseph seemed to say. I know.

Then we shuffled into the adjacent kitchen where one of his aunts ushered people out to the small rear yard. There on long tables they had put out the customary feast, though this time including some homemade delicacies like Shanxi-style smoked pork belly, stuff you hardly ever see these days. The fatty, peppery scent of the dish was absolutely transporting and would have been cause for a wink of wicked glee at another wake, but at Joseph's it was a cloud you kept wishing would blow away, so you could taste only woe. The smell was too good, too luscious, our salty tears an embittering drink for our tingly, watering mouths, and we would have tipped down the whole platter at once to repel the emptiness had his parents and now lone brother not stood right there like totems in their severe mourning costumes and white gloves. His mother thanked each of us for coming and his father, also athletic in youth if not as gifted as Joseph, received our bows with eyes not vacant or blank but very much the opposite; you could see in them how packed full they were of all things Joseph, manifold glints of him on the field and in his tank-diving training, plus whatever else everyone hoped he might have accomplished beyond B-Mor, had he ever gotten the chance.

Only his younger brother was unable to look up, for how miserably he was crying, his tears leaving whitish spots on the surface of the red lacquered offering box he held to his chest, a slide show of pictures of Joseph looping on the screen stretched across the front. It was amazing that the boy could stay on his feet. Though they were in a line of three, his parents seemed separated from him, they in their bubble and he in his, with the box he was holding serving as his partner. No doubt he felt partly responsible for pushing Joseph to take them to play outside, and though no one should ever feel right in blaming him, did more than a few make a point of shoving their envelopes into the slot with an extra-hard pat? Did we? If there was the barest audible *ttok* when we pushed ours in, we regret it now.

We bring all this up about Joseph and his family and our own displays because it makes us mindful of how solemnly composed Fan was as she bowed to his mother and his father, and how she slipped in her own envelope (even as her household's offering sufficed), touching the boy's shoulder for a longish beat. From the food tables—Fan must have been the sole mourner who didn't eat—we couldn't help but notice how she stationed herself an appropriate distance from Joseph's brother but clearly with the intention of standing there *with him,* and though no one spoke to or made eye contact with Fan, we were well aware of her presence. After that, the line seemed to move a bit more slowly, people taking their time with their envelopes and maybe even nodding sympathetically to the boy before hustling over to the tables. The remarkable thing, looking back on it, was that nobody commented on Fan. Not a one of us uttered a word amid the glottal murmurs of chewing and swallowing and the scraping of plastic forks on plastic plates. Maybe it was because we were famished—glimpsing mortality can be a surprisingly appetizing sauce—or because we were being pushed along the buffet by the shuffling throng armed with plates, or because of what had recently happened with Reg, but our hesitance to acknowledge her became itself a part of the meal.

At some point Fan left the boy's side and came down toward the buffet line. Most everyone noticed this and seemed to pause in what they were doing. And in a voice that surprised for its clarity and reach she said, quite oddly:

Where you are.

By now everybody had turned to her. Her hands were curled into loose fists and she said the words again, this time softer, as though she were speaking to herself rather than addressing any crowd. Again no one said a word. She then left via the back gate of the yard with those who had finished eating, leaving us to wonder what she was talking about.

The wake lasted for another hour or so, and probably would have gone on for hours longer had the skies not suddenly clotted up and the winds blown in yet another immense storm system, one that would hover for weeks in a slowly unwinding gyre, the sun blocked out the whole time so that all you could see in your waking and your sleep was not brightness or darkness but a waxen shimmer, as though everything were stuck behind a grimy piece of glass. We B-Mors are accustomed to spending time indoors and underground, but knowing that there was only grayness and mists above the grow houses or subterranean shops proved wearying. And while under this moody, thwarted light, we began to discuss, in the most casual way, what Fan's statement exactly meant. *Where you are.* Some took it as the beginning of a thought that Fan couldn't quite finish, others as mere gibberish, that she had stood too long in the line and should have eaten something. One especially misguided fellow believed she was speaking exclusively to him and was asking that he save her a folding seat!

But most of us agreed it was posed not as a question but as the ending to a phrase. Such as "Everything you desire can be found . . ." and "Look not elsewhere but simply . . ." plus other examples people came up with that, not surprisingly, accorded with their character or current outlook, like the terminally ill man who proposed, "One's destiny lies not in the past nor the future but . . . ," none of which was, of course, uttered by Fan but that somehow in the end became attributed to her, at least in our feeling, which began to bloom with surprising fullness only after she had been long gone from B-Mor, a feeling that she was, in fact, looking after us, perhaps even advising us about something crucial.

It was at this point that the first signs of a collective interest in Fan appeared. Of course, she was not the first B-Mor to have left these kind confines but she was certainly the youngest (and littlest!) to do so on her own. Every other instance was someone who was forced out because of a certain scandal or crime, and only after that person had exhausted all means, official and otherwise, in the hope of being pardoned. Nobody sane would ever do otherwise. Why invite ready hardship or possible doom? And yet Fan was as sane—and comfortably situated—as any young woman in the prime of her B-Mor life. She was quietly admired for her tank skills. For her innate gracefulness and gentility. She was sociable enough, and filial enough, which is as much as anyone can expect. There was not a molecule of wrongness about her.

Which may be why Fan captured our imagination. The very imagination, to be honest, that never seems terribly vital or necessary when things are going right, when we are eating well and sleeping well and lacking only certain exalted luxuries. For doesn't B-Mor as conceived and developed and now constituted obviate the need for such purposeful dreaming?

But now look at all the unusual activity. Someone got ahold of the video archives of the feed at the main gate the day she departed and posted it on the grow-facility page, embedding it in an ad for a take-out *chaat* shop in the underground mall. You clicked it to get your free-drink-with-meal coupon and instead of a beep and a code there was a silent vid of Fan, viewed slightly from above and in three-quarter profile, a small backpack slung over one shoulder, an umbrella in hand, and dressed in a bulky dark-hued counties style, so unlike the colorful loose-fitting pajama-type outfits B-Mors usually wear. Beyond the shelter of the entrance you could see the rain coming down in drenching curtains—yet another storm had blown in—and then being whipped sideways by winds so strong that the sentry very quickly scanned and checked her out, not bothering to see that she wasn't a counties peddler who was having no luck in the miserable weather and was giving up for the day.

And that was it. Merely a few seconds of Fan, standing before the sentry booth, looking nothing like she was about to mount an expedition. Her expression as glum as cold rain. Word spread about the ad—it was a real shop, whose owner contended he knew nothing and that his ad had been hijacked—and until it was removed several hours later, it was the most popular clip on the B-Mor web, outpacing even that night's showing of the boys' and girls' swim championships. And though it made no sense whatsoever, crowds soon descended on that otherwise ordinary snack shop, the long line of people attracting more people to the line, until finally the owner decided to lease a much bigger space in order to offer table service, which for a brief time did a great business, until suddenly it didn't, and he had to shut down.

Another camera showed Fan walking out the main gate and taking the access road out of B-Mor to the main tollway. The official record ends there. But the story of what happened afterward is well-known, or at least it has been recounted by everyone in B-Mor—and maybe beyond—many times over, in messages and postings and vids and songs and, yes, in plain words, too, spoken to one another in the quieter moments of the evening, when the muscles are all used up to the point of near numbness and we feel more as though we are piloting our bodies rather than being at one with them, cooped up at the top and looking outward and uncertain of what is real and what is perceived. And in this state of mind we can't help but build upon what is known, our elaborations not fantastical or untrue but at times vulnerable to our wishes for her, and for ourselves.

SO FAN WENT THIS WAY: INSTEAD OF HEADING NORTH OR
south on the main coastal tollway she veered westward, onto the
olden roads, thoroughfares that once meandered through farmland
and forests and that linked antique-style settlements that the Charter villages are modeled after and you can really only see in movies
now, communities where people strolled with shaggy dogs and children licked ice cream cones and where the benches were occupied by
the contented elderly or smooching lovers and trains came and went
all day, shuttling people back and forth to their jobs.

But what Fan encountered that sodden evening was nothing like
that. It was—and is—a landscape of bushy weeds grown so thick and
high their hollows are often used as rooms by wanderers and thieves.
Weeds are the trees because in most of the inhabited sections the
trees have been cut down and in the warmer months the punky reek
of their pollen overdoses the breezeless air. It seems nearly impossible
to breathe. The derelict houses that anchored the streets have long
been bulldozed and carted away, the once paved streets devolved to
a more elemental state, the asphalt ground down to drifts of blackened dust. The more passable streets are pocked by calf-deep potholes and waves of buckles from the serial deluges and freezes and

droughts, and because of their poor condition, the truckers and Charters move about exclusively on the secured, fenced tollways that few counties drivers can afford, and are often banned from anyhow, for justified reasons of their slower, much older vehicles that are breaking down constantly, hoods up and steaming. So counties drivers travel fitfully on the leftover roadways, swerving and mincing along, and one of these, maneuvering in the blinding gray chaos of that early evening's downpour, squarely struck Fan.

She was knocked into a ditch half filled with rainwater, her temple striking a partly buried chunk of curb. She would have cried out from the pain running from the top of her thighbone to the point of her hip but the blow to her head was a thunderclap and all she could do was numbly move her fingers. The car, an old VW electro-diesel, kept on for twenty meters before stopping. It reversed and the passenger window rolled down halfway and a woman's scratchy voice pronounced, It's no deer.

A dog? a man asked.

Looks like a little girl, she answered.

Silence.

Is she dead?

Not yet. She's moving a little.

Silence again. Then the driver's door creaked open.

No way I'm nursing her back to health, if that's what you're thinking.

The man ignored her. He trudged around the front of the car without an umbrella and stood over Fan, his head and shoulders partly shielding her from the dense warm drops of the rain. She kicked her leg to try to move but could only lamely push mud against one side of the ditch.

Goddamnit, Quig, the woman cursed.

He pressed his foot down upon Fan's ankle, pinning it beneath the water. Fan looked up but in the dimness and rain could just make out the contours of his face under the dark shadow of his baseball cap's bill. He was bearded and had a wide frame to his jaw, and his nose looked like it had been broken multiple times, and the expression in his eyes was that of someone who has seen the worst of this life and would not be disturbed to see whatever measure more.

Let's go! We have another three hours' driving at least, and I'm starving!

Be quiet, Loreen.

Something in his tone silenced her, and when he reached down to Fan with his rough-hewn hands, both the woman in the car and Fan flinched, for what he might do. But instead he cupped her beneath the knees and arms, and lifted her swiftly enough that she didn't have time to resist. With one arm holding her, he lifted the rear hatch of the station wagon and then laid her in beside a greasy tangle of ropes and tools. She tried to kick at him but a shot of pain in her thigh practically choked her and she lost consciousness as he shut the tailgate.

When she came to, it was darkest night. They were still driving, a bump or deep rut having jarred her awake. The car air was humid and smelled of mildew and chain oil and of the two counties people, who didn't wash as regularly as B-Mors, their clothing as well as themselves. Their odor was so keen and alive it was as though they were twinned and sitting on either side of her. Plus, everything was damp where she lay because of her soaked clothes and the steady drip coming from the top of the tailgate. Her right leg felt like a twenty-kilo sack filled with broken glass but it was her head that hurt even more, the whole side of her face clanging with every mar in the road. She told them she was going to be sick and the woman cursed her but the car braked and the man opened the hatch and tugged her by the hair so she could throw up onto the ground. She splashed his boots but he didn't seem to care. When she was done, he shoved her back in and Fan fell again into a daze as they drove on in the steady rain north-westward, up and through the lightless hills, toward where once Maryland had become West Virginia had become Pennsylvania, a huge swath of open counties land where no B-Mors have ever gone.

Their destination was the hilly, sparsely populated "county" re-ferred to as the Smokes. We did not know about it then but of course do now. The origins of the name are unclear, but most say that it derives from the name of a once prominent local family, Smolk, whose people used to own a great deal of the land and many various small businesses; others simply point to the fact that nearly every present inhabitant, whether adult or child, smokes a locally culti-vated weed that is supposedly a powerful antioxidant; the rest will note the prevailing practice of cookery there, which is to smoke everything they eat, and even drink, the favorite beverage being a homemade beer made from smoked grains.

The drive that night took longer than even Loreen had estimated due to their having to take detours around impassable roads, and it felt to Fan, drugged by an injection that Quig administered mid-trip when she could not stop moaning—and then shouting—from the sawing pain in her thigh, that it was a journey of days. For someone born and raised exclusively in B-Mor, there's really no occasion for making trips of such duration, and it's amazing to consider that this was the circumstance of her first true venture beyond the gates: sopped to the core, a ringing in her ears, perhaps a hairline fracture in her hip or leg, and being taken by strangers to a place that prom-ised only hardship, or worse.

And enveloped in the strange, cool oil of the man's drug, Fan must have dreamed. She dreamed hard and vividly, as we have, that the thick ropes on which she lay were the fronds of a sea plant that ensnared her as she drifted to the bottom, this willowy tangle of arms that now cradled and fed her. Kept her alive. There was a taste in her mouth like sour almonds. She nestled herself down even deeper, her leg now right again, and as one will, she had a welling of gratitude for the nurturing, this feeling that erased all thoughts of B-Mor behind her and of the open counties ahead, momentarily erasing even thoughts of Reg, whose voice and images she'd loaded onto the album card she'd sewn inside the pocket of her vest, plus some of his favorite oldies songs, which she would play in the card's tinny voice, just to make out a chorus, "Only the young . . ." In a word, she was alone for the first time in her life, as if she were in a state of nature like the girl who lived by herself on an island in that ancient movie Fan once saw, hunting and fishing and swimming. What was her name? Fan could not remember. Could she have been called Fan? This Fan who could take care of herself, who could wield the spear, dive from the high rock, who could plunge into the deepest waters and hold her breath for as long as she wanted? But beneath her, the kindly fronds suddenly ossified, turning into muscled shoots. Chattering blindly at first, they found her. These ravenous eels. And as they gnawed at the flesh on her back, they lifted her, pushing her up and out of the water, all the weight returning to her and collecting in her leg. She was frantically wrestling the creatures when the woman reached back and hit her in the head with the tail end of a large flashlight. Fan fought some more and she was struck again, hard enough this time to take her breath away.

When Fan came to, she was in the man's arms, being lifted from the car. She may have been drugged again for she could only move her eyes. She could not quite speak. A strong breeze crossed them and, aside from the man's animal odor, the air was damp but smelled green and fresh with what she didn't yet know was the scent of young pines. She could hardly see a thing. There was complete cloud cover and it was as black as night gets, for out in the counties after sunset the settlements go wholly dark, the roads and buildings un-lighted, the few shops shuttered and closed. They had driven up and around the peak of a hill, finally stopping in a cleared patch of flatter land. Around her she could make out the shapes of other vehicles and in the background the outline of a structure, a house built low to the ground and with wings on either side, one of which the man entered after the woman opened a door. The woman lighted the way and he brought Fan inside and laid her on a table.

I'm going to sleep, Loreen said.

Crank on the generator, he told her.

She turned the light on his face and he squinted, his expression one of limited tolerance. She flashed on Fan.

I don't know what you mean to do with her but I'm so fed up and tired I don't care. I'm hungry! So I'm getting myself something and going to bed.

Get the generator on. Then come back.

Get it on yourself!

Do it.

She cursed at him and left. For a while, Fan and Quig were just there in the dark but then a distant whirring could be heard and Quig pulled a chain and a shop light above her flickered twice and then came on. When her eyes adjusted, Fan could see in the penum-bra that they were in a kitchen of sorts, fitted with a short run of cabinets, a freestanding utility sink, a burner plate, a large microwave on the counter. He asked what her name was and she was surprised that she wanted to tell him, though she wasn't able. But he was a frightening-looking man. He was big, much taller and broader than most of the men in B-Mor, probably in his fifties, darkly bearded and mustached but with wild streaks of gray. When he removed his cap, he was balding, the smooth, wide dome of his head bulbous and very pale, as well as tattooed with many fine jagged lines: a pattern of cracks. Her extremities began to itch and prickle, and when he reached for her leg, Fan jumped, bringing on a hot shear of pain. He placed his large hands on her ankles, but gently, his touch oddly pacifying as he removed her wet sneakers, her wet socks. She bucked and tried to twist away when he unbuttoned her trousers but he pressed his hand on her hip and said, Don't move. He then lifted her with the other hand beneath the small of her back as he inched down the soaked, binding fabric. He did not touch her underwear. When her trousers were off, he examined her injury, pressing gingerly as he probed the splotchy, deep bruise on the outside of her thigh. He was as serious and focused as any nurse practitioner in B-Mor. He bound it tightly with a bandage and then left.

Loreen reappeared while he was gone. She scrounged about a drawer and found a quick-eat pouch of pork and beans. It was dim in the room and she looked older than Quig but maybe it was because she was heavier, her hair long and scraggly. She had a mouthful of gray crooked teeth. She cut off the top of the pouch and ate little spoonfuls out of it cold as she stared at Fan, talking to her between chews.

Where the hell did you think you were going?

You can't be more than eleven or twelve.

You shouldn't feel good that he's bothering. He's got plans for you, like he's got for everyone.

Quig returned with a sack of assorted items and tools, including a handsaw, a drill, a length of soft cord, bungees, and then an old rake with mostly broken tines. He unscrewed the rake head from the plastic handle and then held the handle against the inside of her leg, marking its length. He turned it around and did the same with the unmarked end against the outside of her leg. Then he sawed the two pieces to size. These were the splints, which he joined with screws to a short crosspiece at the bottom; her foot would sit on this. With the bungees, he bound the splints to her leg, Loreen holding everything in place while he wound it around. He rigged the cord to secure her foot to the crosspiece and then twisted it until there was a tugging force on her leg; this was the only way, he would tell her later, that it would heal right, keeping it in traction. When it was done, Quig carried her to a small room of shelves and bins that was almost completely filled with random equipment and appliance and car parts, but there was a cot in the corner with a sleeping bag and he placed her on top of it. He hadn't said more than two words to her, nor said anything now, just giving her another injection, this one to make her sleep. She was losing consciousness when Loreen appeared and tugged the sleeping bag out from beneath her, saying it was her son's. She tossed a thin, musty blanket atop her.

Better heal up quick, Loreen said, looming. Her breath smelled of alcohol and was sugar-sweet, from the beans. Or you won't be around long.

FOR ALL OF US HERE, it is difficult not to think often about that first night of Fan's. Even now, after all that's transpired, we still discuss how we might have fared in her place, being maybe seriously injured, stuck in a faraway counties house deep in the Smokes, and not knowing what would happen next. It's an unnerving scenario. In fact, the circumstance is so far beyond what any of us could imagine that it seems like some evening-programs story line dreamed up with the help of one of those edgier young B-Mors you hear about these days, who, of course, still work in our facilities but "consult" for the Charter creators of such shows and sometimes even take a hand in writing them. Maybe Charter people don't ultimately care about what happens outside their gates, but they're certainly curious, and so you see more and more characters like us popping up in the shows, if not in starring roles. We're mostly bystanders or else hardworking service people for Charter heroes and heroines, but sometimes more prominent foils, too, like a recent character in *St. Clair Beach* named Ji-lan, a beautiful woman from D-Troy, the big midwestern facility, who captures the heart of a married Charter executive and causes him much delicious and humiliating trouble. And though suffering plenty, he weathers his self-inflicted misfortune, and it's no surprise that it's Ji-lan who loses all in the end, everyone learning a harsh lesson in what can happen when you stray too far beyond your circle.

It's funny, for although Ji-lan is nothing at all like Fan in either person or her situation (Ji-lan being a tall, statuesque femme fatale, mercurial and passionate, who would not hesitate to wreck the lives of others if it meant her gain), it's almost impossible not to think of our petite, gentle Fan as the inspiration for her character. Perhaps it's the actress's Fan-like hairstyle that's a cue for us, or the similar way she sometimes rides sidesaddle on her scooter (though in Ji-lan's case it's clearly due to the very short cut of her skirts), but whatever it is, the impression is unmistakable. Fan, of course, never knew of these developments in the show, if she ever watched the show at all. Being as modest as she was, she probably would have shaken her head at the notion of any perceived concordances, maybe even chuckled at the huge gap between the sinister sparkle of Ji-lan's exploits and the dismal reality of her situation, what with her profound injury and the ragged conditions and being under the care of the ill-tempered Loreen and the mysterious and seemingly volatile Quig, whose standing in the Smokes, it would turn out, was much higher than he cared to let on.

When Fan awoke the next morning in the room of spare parts, she felt sick to her stomach and leaned over the side of the cot and gagged, though only a slick of spit fell from her mouth onto the dingy, scarred floorboards. It was nausea in the wake of the night's painkillers, and probably some hunger, too, as she hadn't eaten anything since the previous afternoon. Her leg was in the splint Quig had rigged, but she couldn't quite bear to examine it yet and so didn't remove the blanket. Instead she looked around the room. It had a salvaged clerestory pane installed near the top of the wall, which let in a good amount of the morning light; one could see the various plastic and metal and wire-sprouting parts set off by type with an unexpected neatness, stationed in rows rather than jammed in; in fact, the feel was somewhat similar to a parts room the maintenance workers have at the grow facility, though theirs is obviously much larger and cleaner and brighter, the atmosphere scrubbed of any foreign matter or organisms that could taint the planting beds or fish tanks. Here the air was closed off and smelled of dust and chain oil and dry-rotted wood and was laced, as was everything, with a rank counties perfume, but it was the sensibility of order, if only an order masked by roughness and grime, that Fan latched on to and could quell the brunt of her fear with and so attempt to keep her mind composed and steady. For she had to believe what we all would have believed, given our schooling and our shows, which is that she would be used up in hard labor—if not much, much worse—and only after an interminable sentence of such use, disposed of. In fact, one of the sayings B-Mors will sometimes offer to someone on an errand or trip outside the gates is Don't become *xiāng-cháng!*—Don't become sausage!—a bit of black humor that comes from a famous episode of a now classic evening program in which a group of foolhardy B-Mor teenagers goes camping out in the counties before the commencement of their facilities careers and end up having their livers cut out and made into you know what.

That's sensationalized, to be sure, and yet there are all sorts of rumors and anecdotes and semiofficial reports that over the decades have grown into a bank of lore about the counties that each of us adds to whenever we repeat that saying or others with which we admonish our naturally curious children. Thank goodness they are curious! It's a sign of healthy minds. And while it may be obvious, it's our responsibility to educate them to the idea that romancing the unknown is attended by myriad possibilities, too, shepherding them through those heady periods of urge and instinct when they think they can soar, and deliver them, we hope whole, to a place where perspective begins to reign, where they know that the groggy old bear at the zoo will instantly wake the moment you step inside the cage.

But Fan, we have come to learn, was one of our number who was well aware of perils but pushed forward anyway, not rashly or arrogantly but with what might be thought of as a kind of inner faith. And as terrified as she might have been as she lay in that room, perhaps regretting herself to the core, she had already resolved not to show any fear, no matter what was in store for her. So when footfalls approached the other side of the door, Fan tried the best she could to sit up in the sagging cot, propping herself on an elbow and lifting her head so as not to look as feeble and vulnerable as she felt. A padlock was tugged at several times and the door opened and it was Loreen, holding a plastic mug with a spoon stuck in it, which she waved before Fan. Instant oatmeal.

You're supposed to eat.

Fan nodded.

Well, you going to or not?

Fan leaned over and picked up the mug and slowly ate, twisting in the cot so she could take half spoons of the gruel. It was tepid and only partly reconstituted, certain flecks of oats hard-edged and dry, but it had a flavoring, if stale, of maple brown sugar, which made her mouth water and the swallowing easier. Loreen lit a hand-rolled cigarette and stood over Fan as she smoked, her arms crossed over her ample bosom. She wore loose blue jeans and a gray-colored sweat-shirt that matched the long, untidy strands of her graying hair. She was heavier than she had appeared the night before, which was un-doubtedly surprising to Fan, given the fact that all counties people were supposedly underfed, very thick about the hips and thighs, and with a fleshy face that made her look much younger than she was. Her eyes were a pretty marine blue and she might have been pretty generally but her nose was misshapen and pointed well off center and this lent her a skeptical aspect, as it appeared she was literally look-ing at you sideways. And then her harsh, threshing voice made her seem preternaturally irritated, angry.

I told him I wasn't going to feed you. This isn't some fancy facili-ties health clinic, you know. It's not like everyone gets to stay here. I don't know why he's letting you.

Fan couldn't understand what she was talking about but she kept eating anyway, glad now for the food. The nourishment stirred life in her veins and the more she ate the hungrier she got and she finished the oatmeal quickly, scraping out the last gluey streaks until Loreen took the mug from her and went to leave. Fan told her she needed to use the bathroom right away and Loreen said she'd find something Fan could use so she had better not soil the cot, unless she wanted a whipping. The door shut with a bang and was padlocked from the outside, and who could blame Fan for wanting to cry at that mo-ment, being frightened of course by this gratuitous aggression (which is most uncommon in B-Mor) but also now longing for the comfort of her row house, where you were never alone for all the clan occu-pants.

For if she did not long *particularly* for her parents or siblings (or cousins or grandparents or aunts and uncles), she missed them in sum, for their constant and interchangeable array. They never much talked to one another at the table, or while watching their programs, or sitting in the yard on their free-days, but that didn't matter now. Do not discount the psychic warmth of the hive. And Fan finally succumbed and cried, fiercely and silently, half ashamed at herself for doing so, half wanting to devolve into a mere cluster of cells, something simple enough that were she to disappear even she might not notice the moment of demise.

After a while, Fan realized Loreen was not returning anytime soon. She desperately had to pee and she scanned the room for any suitable container. On a shelf near the door were some partly used cans of paint and on top of these was a roller tray that she could probably reach, at least if she stood. Fan drew the blanket aside and examined her splinted leg, undoing the bandages within the structure as gingerly as she could, noting how he had wound them so she could redo them herself. Once exposed, her leg looked horrid with a multihued bruise of muddy purples and reds covering most of her left thigh, its shape very much like Australia as it curled about her limb. In school they had briefly studied the origins of the continents, and while Australia wasn't one of them, the teacher had made a point of likening it to B-Mor, this substantial land that had detached from the rest and become a self-sustaining island, and here it was, tattooed on her leg, this sign of what might as well be a thousand miles away.

She probed the bruise with her fingers, pressing until it hurt, surprised to find that it was not as fragile or tender as she feared. When she twisted her leg, the pain was still searing but she could lift it several inches without too much discomfort. Slowly she swung her legs onto the floor and then bent her good leg and leaned forward and up and onto it, attempting to find her balance. She faltered and had to let herself down on the edge of the cot. She tried twice more before finally being able to stand on her good leg alone. When she tested the other, it was okay, until she tried a normal stance and then it hurt too much; she had to lean on one side of the splint to brace herself, hobbling across the room. She reached as high as she could on the shelf and barely grabbed the roller tray, but it hooked a can of paint, which came down with it as well, nearly landing on her foot. The top popped off and glaring yellow paint—the kind used for marking lines in roads—spewed onto the wood floor. Though it was pointless to be careful now, she crouched as much as she could with a splinted leg, holding the tray beneath her as she pulled her underwear to the side. And in a sweet whoosh she let it all go; it seemed she was relieving herself forever as she stared at the shimmering paint thrown out in the pattern of a seal's flipper, fully extended, racing through the waters, and all at once she was crying again, in what seemed to her an equally ridiculous deluge. She couldn't stop either flow, as hard as she tried she couldn't, even when the padlock chocked and the door swung in to reveal Loreen holding an old green plastic beach pail, her fetching eyes shouting murder. Before Fan could take another breath, Loreen stepped forward and struck her across the cheek with the pail, sending her hard to the floor in a clatter, dismantling the splint and upending the tray and splaying Fan in her own warm, odorous water.

You little bitch! Look at what you've done! What a goddamned mess!

Fan, however, could not look, being momentarily blinded by the attack. And when her sight returned, all she could see were the woman's pudgy, unpainted toes poking out from her rubber sandals, these mini-Loreens traveling pendulously to and fro before they struck, too, in the chest and shoulder and now on her arms, with which she was trying to shield her face. Fan had almost given up, not knowing anymore if she was asleep or awake or dead. But then the blows ceased, and Loreen was down on all fours beside her, and she saw Quig, looming high and wraithlike above them, a long white wand in his hand, its red tip two-pronged. He seemed to have stepped right out of a fantastical movie, like he was one of those warlocks but without a special hat.

I told you, he said softly. Be gentle.

Oh, screw you, Loreen rasped through her teeth. Screw you.

He extended the wand and touched her on the back of the neck. She bucked and stiffened, and then pitched forward, face-first, right in Fan's puddle.

He said, with calm, Be gentle.

THOSE FIRST FEW WEEKS FAN WAS GONE WERE A QUIET period in the neighborhoods of B-Mor. Naturally, as after Reg disappeared, there was the background noise of rumors and gossip, even some mad talk in certain quarters about a conspiracy to make it appear that Fan had willingly left but was actually sent away; of course, the posted video clips dispel that notion, though they say even those can be faked and made to look absolutely real. And we know why some wish to believe it was totally contrived; for it's much easier to subscribe to various outlandish theories than confront the reality of her departure and what that might say about B-Mor and its ways.

But we will note once again: B-Mor is not perfect, nor was it ever meant to be. It was not a promise of anything to anyone. Yes, our women and children can walk about at night without any fear of assault; yes, there is always enough wholesome food to eat and clean water to drink, with our special celebrations, such as weddings and funerals, graced by lavish spreads; yes, we can count on steady employment if we are sound of mind and able-bodied, and expect a reasonable level of care if we are not; yes, we live in a kennel of our own blood, even if thoroughly mixed after numerous generations, which offers, during the fiercest storms, the most reliable shelter.

Yet there are some needling issues, even aside from the case of Fan, such as the fact that the less durable, discretionary-type goods in the shops have become stretches to the typical budget, and are often nearly unaffordable. Even our own products have become much costlier, the price of a single five-hundred-gram perch equal to what two cost just five years ago. Or that the maximum stay period in the health clinics is effectively one work cycle (six days), no matter the condition or needs of the patient, as the family is now responsible for the fees past that time, fees that are well beyond most any B-Mor clan's capacity to pay.

An example of this would be the recent experience of the Rivera-Deng family, who occupy not one but two row houses down near the B-Mor waste treatment plant. They are not an especially large family, but because they run a popular aboveground trinkets and bubble tea shop (the subterranean-level shops are almost without exception owned, if never operated, by Charter investors), they could afford to purchase the leasehold on the adjacent house when it became available. They are considered rich by B-Mor standards, though what else this wealth truly buys them is not at all apparent. Harvey Rivera-Deng might show up at a wake in his flecked suit jacket with a contrasting pocket square but we aren't inclined to offer any notice, much less compliments. He stands stout and flashy in his finery but clutches the same plastic buffet plate as everybody else, jostling to get to the snow-pea shoots before they're all gone. And this is how it should be. But when his wife, a portly, ever-smiling, sweetly damp-necked woman named Ruby, took seriously ill recently, eventually passing, the feeling we had can only be one of steady, drenching sorrow.

Ruby was not the most healthful person in B-Mor, a longtime diabetic who liked her sweet cakes and scallion fritters a bit too well, washing everything down with creamy bubble fruit teas. One afternoon she collapsed in the back of the shop; one of her kidneys had failed, which apparently led to a stroke that paralyzed one side of her body. She was rushed to the clinic but then suffered another stroke before being stabilized, which left her unable to speak. Otherwise her mind was intact, and Harvey and the rest of the Rivera-Deng clan told her not to worry, that they would take care of her at home, but everyone could see that she would need a dialysis machine to bolster her remaining, chronically weakened kidney, a machine that a physician's assistant told her (when she queried him via a weak left-handed scribble of "$$?") would cost an astronomical sum to purchase or else lease for an indefinite period.

No doubt you can imagine what happened next. Harvey made the necessary arrangements to transport Ruby home, machine and all, despite the absurdity of the finances; it would be like some counties peddler buying a Charter condo with only her pedi-bike rickshaw and its junky contents as collateral. There is no leaping of worlds in this world. Except for the rare case, the distance is too great. But of course, Harvey was only thinking about how much he loved his wife. He was only thinking about the details of her care. He set up their tiny bedroom to be hers alone, even rewiring (he was a facilities electrician before retirement) the bedside outlet to be on a circuit that would instantly feed off a generator if the main power cycled down in the middle of the night, as it often does. He requested a change of his children's work shifts at the grow facility and water plant, so that they would stagger instead of align. He was even putting up for sale his and Ruby's fancier shoes and clothes on a B-Mor weblist, even if few of us could ever afford them, when he got word from the clinic that Ruby had died during the night of multiple major organ failure. He was going to bring her home that day and instead had to view her sheeted body already rolled out to the corridor, the tented, plumped mound truly the saddest sight of his life. What had happened? They figured out that she herself shut down the dialysis machine for most of each day's session, only switching it back on just before the nurse returned, ensuring her own doom.

And while self-sacrifice is a hallmark of life here in B-Mor, one of our original and most cherished mores, is there anyone who does not flinch whenever he or she hears of yet another act such as Ruby's, which seem to grow more numerous each quarter, each year? In the old days, with our first generations, people would relieve their households all the time, but those were mostly the very old, ultrastubborn, salty pioneers who were too proud to become any kind of burden, their gestures as much prods to the community as discharges of their respective families.

Yet one looks around, and not just at the more flagrant cases. Visits to the health clinics were once unlimited, a yearly exam for every citizen an option as well, and in this way Charter people had very little on us, save that most of them go to private offices and see the same physicians each time. Our clinics are staffed by Charter doctors (if the youngest ones, often fresh out of residency), who rotate through monthly, but the nurses and physician's assistants are constant and are B-Mor residents, and it's these people who tender the real care. You could stop in and get your thumb stitched up (a regular occurrence for our indomitable fish filleters); you could pick up a bottle of pills for impotence or anxiety; you could get a quick session of chiropractic or acupunctural therapy, and for the most part people availed themselves of these things without abusing the privilege. In fact, we often reminded ourselves of our fortunate circumstance with the saying "Save some noodles for tomorrow's lunch."

Now there are so many new rules that make it all very complicated. The doors are still open twenty-four/seven but for life-threatening emergencies only; the rest of us with broken fingers or kidney stones have to wait it out until the next morning, an emergency-care doctor making the final determination. And when you do check in at the clinic, everything that has happened to you and that you've ever been prescribed or treated with pops up on the screen like always, but now some lines flash when a certain frequency is exceeded, and if you want that particular prescription or treatment, you'll have to pay a fee beyond the usual token fee to receive it, an additional cost that is sometimes not so small.

When did this change? you ask, though of course nobody at the desk knows. It did change, and now *is*, these "reforms" from this point forward in force, and the result is that you may forgo that diagnostic X-ray, you might take only every other blood pressure pill if that's tolerable, you will decide to amble another season on that arthritic hip in the hopes that it will somehow, someday, kindly warm. Really, every person we know has had to make such compromises, most not leading to horrific consequences, but the truth is you can't help but wonder where this will lead, what new reforms will be instituted next year, or in ten, and to what extent the quality of life in B-Mor might someday come to resemble the conditions outside.

They say that with the economy stuck so long in the doldrums, even the Charter villages have had to institute certain cost-cutting measures, like no more free full-body scans each quarter for everyone over age thirty, though some of our more cynical citizens contend this is simply what the directorate and the Charters want us to believe. Even if this is true, what of it? How can it matter what goes on inside those gates? You might as well worry about the life cycle of the nearest star. A twinkling in the heavens, rightful but brief. We must remind ourselves of what the reality is within those lovely confines, that along with the neatly paved streets and the spotless schools and the fancy shops offering uncontaminated goods from all over the globe comes the fact that very little is guaranteed for a Charter person, if anything at all, and that one must continually work and invest and have enough money to sustain a Charter lifestyle or else leave.

This is, in fact, what had befallen certain open counties people. For it is known that a surprising number of them are former Charters. One might ask, Hey, why don't they just come to the gates of a place like B-Mor? But it's not as simple as that, and in practical terms, impossible. They can't quite enter a B-Mor–like settlement because those are oversubscribed already, the row houses or residence halls occupied right up to the rooftops, our children assigned two to a desk at school. Plus, what could any newcomer among us possibly do to make a living? The jobs in the grow facilities and water and power plants are always filled and backed by apprentice attendants, who have been training since youth to step into the positions the moment they come open. The smattering of privately run businesses, like the one the Rivera-Dengs own, have been under family control for generations, and their leaseholds are rarely relinquished.

It's ironic that ex-Charters should have to fall so far so quickly, that there's no middle realm for them and their kin, pushed out as they are into the counties with little practical know-how or clue as to how to get by. It's the reason why so few do get by, at least for very long, in particular those with solely Charter-specific skills, such as real estate speculators, or brokers of insurance or stocks, or the writer/ creators of evening programs, one of whom was a compulsive gambler who squandered his considerable fortune. Needless to say, he did not last.

So when our dear Fan came to after the assault by Loreen, lying again in the cot with the splint redone, she couldn't help but wonder about Quig. Like any of us, she knew the possibilities. Could he in fact be a former Charter nurse, or maybe even a doctor? Though as they say in the Charter villages, that would be quite an "outcome."

Doctors are among the most important and prestigious people around, especially for Charters, and thus often quite wealthy, too.

The messes were gone, her arms and legs and torso sponged mostly clean, the floor cleared except for a faint scrim of yellow paint. Loreen was of course gone, too, and though a panic that the mad woman might soon return sparked through Fan, she had a naturally reciprocal welling of what must be gratitude for Quig's having halted the beating. She was surely wary of him, but the fact remained that he had already rescued her twice.

For the rest of the day Fan kept as still as she could. She tried to quell her hunger and thirst the same way she'd pushed back the need to breathe when she was underwater in the tanks, with the force of pure will, but applying it now like a balm to the jabs in her belly, the dry spots in her throat. She wanted not to need anything, at least as long as she could bear it. She couldn't stand up, so she could not look out the little window set high in the wall, but she listened to numerous vehicles and people who came and went through the compound all day. One of the voices was Loreen's, bossy and annoyed, rudely ordering people about; yet no one seemed to contest her. There were other voices and she listened for Quig's; but none were his.

It was toward the end of the afternoon that someone approached the door, which immediately made Fan brace and sit up. When it opened, it was neither Loreen nor Quig but rather a pale, curly-haired boy of about thirteen or so, wearing a soiled T-shirt and dungarees and decrepit sneakers, and sipping from a drink box of strawberry-flavored soy milk. He had another drink box in his free hand and he offered it to Fan. She poked the straw through the foil hole and they drank without speaking. Fan surely couldn't help but recall the breaks at the grow facility when she and Reg would buy a cup of tamarind juice from the refreshments cart and maybe slip away for a quick hug or even a peck or two before getting back to work. She drank the soy milk slowly in a long, steady draw. It was brackish and artificially flavored but still tasted as good as anything she could imagine. All the while the boy stared at her without a hint of self-consciousness. His sleepy, slightly up-angled eyes, like a goat's, were the color of seawater beneath an overcast sky, and just as blank and murky.

Finally he said, You really from B-Mor?

Fan nodded. It hadn't occurred to her until that moment that she hadn't uttered more than a few words since walking out from the gates. She had not meant to keep such a silence but here she was with a sensation of stitchedness upon her mouth and there was no reason to try to break it until she had to.

They say it's nice there. Someday I'm going to see it.

She finished her drink and held it out, shaking it.

You want another?

She nodded again.

He skipped away and quickly returned, this time with two drink boxes in each hand. This easy bounty surprised her and made her worry for them both, in case he'd done wrong to retrieve them. But she drank two more anyway, one right after the other, while he asked her numerous questions about B-Mor that oddly enough could all be answered with a simple shake or nod of the head, which was perhaps an apt reflection of the workings of his mind but also his instinct telling him that that's all he would get out of her. He asked, Did all the children go to school? Did everyone end up working in the "factories"? Did they ever run out of things to eat? Were the streets and parks as neat and clean as they say? Did people really live to old age? Yes, yes, no, yes, sort of; and then she gave replies to a score of other queries both childish and knowing. He was excited to talk to her and had turned over the large white toilet bucket that had been left for Fan as his own seat and would have gone on querying her indefinitely had Loreen's voice not sawed through the air.

Sewey!

The boy rose slowly to his feet. I give out the numbers, he grumbled.

Sewey! You still in there?

Okay, Ma! he yelled.

Okay nothing! Get your ass out here! Now!

I'll bring more drinks later, he said, a dull grin marking his face. Then he left her alone, locking her in once again.

FOR THE FEW DAYS Fan lived on flavored soy milk and graham crackers and peanut brittle and the odd piece of chicken jerky, Sewey was her sole sustained contact with the world. The injury was more minor than Quig had surmised, for her leg was only moderately painful and already seemed to be healing. She kept this fact to herself, an instinct for discretion overriding any fears she had for what might befall her, good leg or no. Quig came briefly to examine her leg and the splint, but he appeared both times in the middle of the night, his mini-flashlight rousing her from sleep, her heart bounding in a fitful dash; and before she could form any words, he'd have retightened the cord and checked the splint bindings and extinguished the light and left, depositing her back in her dreams. And what were those dreams? They were tableaus of the unknown, naturally, visions of anxiety and miserable solitude, the kind you might have when you are a child and clenched by high fever, when you see your loved ones from the bottom of a salt pit and they are as far off as the moon, when your arms are too heavy to lift, much less wave, and your voice has no carry. Fan's dreams were all this but shot through as well with what surely were figments of a self-doubt characterized in her mind by the silhouette of our row houses set against a blood-orange haze of sky, the line of the roofs deviating by certain centimeters as they spanned the endless street, the segments discernibly shifting but never quite broken.

During those first visits from Sewey, Fan learned about life in the compound. She hardly had to ask any questions; Sewey was a born talker, the kind of talker you meet and have to nod at frequently and right off think about how to slip away from, but of course, Fan was going nowhere and Sewey had the companion he'd always longed for and no adults or older kids around to tell him to shut up. Fan was not just the quiet type but someone with a bountiful store of patience who didn't mind following the endless branches of his thoughts as they reached skyward and backward and around the corner, toward whatever sun he alone felt the warmth of and could see. He brought another old bucket for a seat (she using hers to relieve herself, which he happily emptied and hosed out at day's end), while she ate or drank or mostly just lay there and listened to Sewey talk while playing with something he called a yo-yo, a translucent orange plastic disc with a string wound about its split middle that he made go up and down, up and down, and sometimes would let spin in place, magically suspended a few centimeters above the floor, before flicking it back up.

And he told her more or less this: that they were in Quig's place, and had been for as long as he could remember. Sewey was born here, in fact: Loreen was indeed his mother. She had come to give birth to him and was lucky she had because he needed to be cut out of her to be born and Quig was the only person in the Smokes and within a two-day's drive around who could do it, at least without killing the mother most of the time. Loreen had then stayed on, at first to work off the debt she owed Quig, eventually becoming his main assistant and scheduler. It was the most important job at Quig's because of the dozens of people who showed up every day with injuries from bad accidents like severe cuts and burns and broken bones, not even mentioning the pains from the C-illnesses that pretty much afflicted every adult. Each arrival was an emergency—it had to be, to burn fuel for the winding trek into these hills—and each arrival knew to bring money or gold or jewelry or else some special offer of barter or services. Loreen's job was to assign an order to them determined by injury but mostly by what they could offer to move up a few spots or even to the head of the line. Naturally there were constant renegotiations: if someone came and got a place ahead of you, you could offer something more, or else different. It was your decision, and then Loreen's, and of course, ultimately Quig's, Sewey tasked as the messenger whenever the batteries for the two-ways went out, conveying word of a young man with two fingers crushed and near amputated offering twenty dollars to cut them off cleanly, or a lady with a festering rash covering half her back who will give him a gold wedding band, or an older man with a terrible pain in his side who will leave his pretty daughter for three days in exchange for surgery, four if the "doctor" could also pull a bad tooth, and every once in a while a younger person might be left there, indefinitely, as payment; it went like this all day and every day, Sewey describing it with a much younger child's innocent delight, the terribly sick and injured queued up beneath the ferocious sun or pelting rain to have Quig take a look and say if he could fix them. Most times he could, which is why so many people were journeying to the Smokes, word of his skills having spread across the region over the last fifteen or so years after Quig had left the big Charter village down south where he once lived.

Apparently, Quig had not been a physician in his village, but rather a veterinarian with a large, successful practice. With a few partners, he owned an animal hospital and operated a small fleet of house-call vans, the business thriving until that infamous year of the bird and swine flu epidemics that hit in rapid succession and crossed the species barrier to infect and kill dozens of Charters in a village out west. In the ensuing panic across the Charter Association every last home-raised fowl and toy swine was destroyed and soon after all the dogs and even the cats and ornamental birds, with a permanent ban on all nonmarine pets instituted, and soon thereafter even on pet fish, just to be safe. His profession was gone overnight. He and his wife eventually lost their condo to the bank and were living month to month in a trades- and services-people's dormitory when they were caught in a sting selling animal tranquilizers at a health club. They were arrested, swiftly tried and convicted, their sentence immediate banishment; Quig and his wife had a young daughter and the three of them had to leave behind whatever they couldn't fit into their car, the very same that Fan rode in the back of that first drench-ing night. Apparently, his wife and daughter did not last long.

They got dead like right away, Sewey told her now. And adding as if quoting: How it always goes.

Fan asked him what happened, but he shook his head.

Momma won't say. And she told me to never ask him and to never bring it up. So we shouldn't.

They were quiet for a minute, Sewey unfurling his yo-yo up and down, getting it to hover, skitter across the floor, snap back.

Momma says we got a good thing here, even if B-Mors or Char-ters would never believe it. Is that why you came out here? To see if it was as awful as people say?

Fan didn't answer. While it didn't matter because the rhetorical was Sewey's optimal mode, as he got his wind and proceeded to ram-ble about how sometimes people died before they could be seen by Quig, literally collapsing while waiting, and how if they had come alone it was Sewey's job to go through their clothes for anything of value before summoning certain of Quig's men to haul the body away, it strikes us that Fan must have posed his question to herself again. It couldn't have been just Reg she had gone to search out. She had no real leads as to where he might be, or if he was even alive. So why would any sane person leave our cloister for such uncertainties? He was the impetus, yes, the veritable without which, but not the whole story. One person or thing can never comprise that, no matter how much one is cherished, no matter how much one is loved. A tale, like the universe, they tell us, expands ceaselessly each time you examine it, until there's finally no telling exactly where it begins, or ends, or where it places you now.

SO LET US KEEP OUR ATTENTION ON THE SMALL. WHICH means, for the moment, that we should consider Reg with special focus. To be sure, Reg was unaware of himself as anything but a keeper of Building Six vegetable beds F-8 through F-24, a fourth-generation member of the Xi-Jang household, and the first and only boyfriend of Fan.

Let's not forget he meant the world to her, and even if that speaks more to the limited extent of her experience than his personal qualities, we ought to remind ourselves of how fetching a young man he was in sum. Very tall, as noted, around 180 centimeters not counting the fluffy pad of his hair, which made him seem at least six or seven centimeters taller. We have, of course, described his amazing skin, its hue and hand. He was by nature filial to his household, bringing home whenever he could hard candies for the younger ones and sticky rice cakes for his elders, and then without exception (after maybe playing with Joseph et al.) taking out Fan on their free-days, most often spending the entire afternoon in the subterranean mall shopping for stickers and costume jewelry and other trinkets and splitting a lychee smoothie and basket of spicy-sweet fried chicken wings with her. He always treated for the movies or games or photo-booth images of themselves that each carried in an old-fashioned hand-sized folding album, one of our favorite shots showing Reg having to tilt far down to sip his straw from their shared drink, Fan craning up for hers, their smooth cheeks drawn in. Both are looking at the camera with a mirthful conspiracy in their eyes that is part of the animated moment but also suggests how wonderfully unadulterated their romance was, as yet free of the grit of life that accumulates, inexorably, no matter what you do to screen it out. Call it first love, puppy love, but in this case Fan and Reg didn't just rush away on their free-day to the pillowed compartment of a mini-inn like so many of our youth (and not-youth) now do and on the roaring pyre of their lust self-immolate. Fan and Reg were as keen on each other as any, let us say that. The difference lies in their easeful lingering, in their letting the time simply pass, thereby unbinding themselves from the false insistence of the hours. They were not the only couple, of course, to do this, but it was plainly heartening to see good young people, out in public, enjoying in quiet thrall the company of the other while welcoming the rest of us to draw upon their contentment, the gleam of which broadcasts wider than one can ever believe, which warms from within.

Since they've been gone, B-Mor has not been the same place. We have mentioned the murals featuring their portraits, guerrilla-painted under cover of night, with other less prominent notations around the blocks becoming more and more a part of our everyday life. Does it seem that the streets these days are more frequently blemished, at least between the twice-daily sweepings, by the litter of bottle tops and taco wrappers and, amazing to say, gobs of spit (the habit of expectorating long thought eradicated after countless years of education and social reinforcement!), or that the queues at the movie theaters and school sporting events aren't as orderly as you expect, distinctly more wedge than file, or that even inside the grow facilities, where nothing so much as a few liters of deviation is tolerated in those massive tanks, significant numbers of fry fish have been going missing, presumably to be nurtured in illegal home nurseries.

Just the other week an older fellow and his wife were caught by inspectors of the directorate with a catfish-raising operation set up in their basement; they were visited because of what the inspectors believed was a faulty water meter, and when they were led down to the basement by an unknowing child, they could hardly believe the elaborate thicket of tubs and piping and filters filling the room right up to the ceiling. To spare the rest of their household the old couple took full responsibility, immediately sacrificing themselves, and when asked how they thought they could get away with such a blatant violation, the wife purportedly said, We knew it couldn't last, but who cares anyway.

Who cares anyway?

This is a startling attitude, one that you might not even hear muttered by some preternaturally indolent, thrice-rejected facilities applicant whose only remaining choices are a janitorial position at the shopping mall and a potentially hazardous job at the wastewater treatment plants. But so baldly voiced, and then by a fish tank alumna, whose pension is modest but certainly adequate and forever secure? This amazes. Enough to make one think ahead to a perhaps inevitable epoch, when the character and disposition of this place might have changed so profoundly as to be untenable. Don't sanctuaries become prisons, and vice versa, foremost in the mind?

Reg, of course, was not one to entertain such ideations. It wasn't in his makeup. What he possessed instead, it is now clear, was much rarer, something that occurs in B-Mor and other cousin settlements maybe only a few times in a generation, if at all.

For Reg, the rumor goes, was C-free.

Yes, it is hard to believe.

Our gangly, bumbling, perennially smiling Reg. Free of the curse!

Free of any rogue neoplasms, in either fact or destiny. Naturally, there is a record of every inhabitant's annual blood panel, which unlike the general physicals have not been suspended, protein, sugar, fat, hormone, vitamin, and numerous other levels collected and tabulated to track and identify trends across the B-Mor population, rather than any individual's state of health; but always included are tests for known markers of disease. Eventually everyone will express it, the blood panels show this, unless they're done in by something else, like poor young drowned Joseph or stroke-afflicted Ruby. Our tainted world looms within us, every one.

Most Charters can afford the latest drugs and interventional therapies, such that very few perish directly from a form of the disease; on average they live quite a bit longer than we do, ten or so years. But most will succumb instead to something known as the Crash, a degenerative condition in which the major organs begin to fail, one after another, caused by the accrued ill side effects of the serial therapies, or maybe the therapies themselves (no one really knows, though study has been continuous), until complete shutdown ensues, and there's nothing left to be done. We suppose that there are a few of us who would, given the means, endure the serial treatments and procedures that Charters now consider a natural part of the experience of life, applied measure after measure, each one increasingly heroic. That what remains of our dwindling resources should be devoted by all rights to you, or you.

The rest of us, however, recognize the advantages of not knowing when one's day will come. Better to be fine up to the moment a severe fever or backache or rash flares up and lingers, when it's too late for anything but the quiet room of palliatives, the kind lantern of a picture viewer, and steady visitations from one's kin and closest friends, whose tears flow not so much in sadness as prideful recognition of your role in the legacy of our cadre. For you have done your job, you have labored and nurtured, you have helped secure the foundations of B-Mor in this fraught civilization without heed to your own dreams, ever modest, unfinished.

And you will never die alone, something that even Charters cannot say, what with how intent they are to outlive one another.

But to pass from mere old age! To drift away in one's sleep or pull up a chair at the food court with the not-quite-idle thought, I'll just shut my eyes for a second. What a blessing that must be for one and all. And to think that Reg might have that chance, indeed, makes sense in the way of a karmic embodiment, in that he was an exceedingly ingenuous soul, a true babe of the woods whose striking sandy-hazel eyes cast more broad sheen than sparkle.

In fact, it's funny that Reg should end up being the one who was so cellularly pure. The lines of his family, the Xi-Jang clan, go back right to the beginning of B-Mor, the Jangs among the originals who landed in the destitute city that very first hour. After the initial period of strife with the handful of remaining inhabitants finally died down, one of the Jang boys fell in love with a girl from one of the holdout native families, surname Willis, and married her, producing several children. There's no record of further mixing for the Jangs, just an extensive linking during those early years with the Xi clan of Shining Tomorrow Road, but there are inevitable jokes and snickerings about certain undiluted features that show up in every generation of the clan, like Reg's amazing head of Afro-type hair, which clearly derive from that Willis girl.

How indelible, blood. Which is why, after Reg went missing, the rest of his household was apparently shuttled by special bus to the clinic for a few days of testing and retesting, everyone from the walker-ambling grannies to the swaddled babes scanned and pricked, and closely observed afterward by platoons of purple-jumpsuited Charter researchers seeking to determine whether some clan practice of hygiene or domiciling or even cuisine could somehow explain the perfect anomaly of Reg. They couldn't, though every so often we will hear that the younger Xi-Jangs have been summoned from whatever facility or mall where they might be and bused to the clinic for ultimately fruitless examinations, going so far as to corral other B-Mor clans whose members are believed to have certain genetic filaments woven through their beings. Word of this quickly spread, presumably to the negative, but now one hears that among those of Fan's and Reg's age, in the midst of their prime marrying years, the more "native-looking" young B-Mors have become remarkably popular.

This, needless to say, is an ironic development. It is astounding that one could ever imagine that the dance clubs and tearooms and game parlors would be dotted by young men who visited the ladies' salons to have their hair teased wildly à la Reg, or that there would be a companion run by both sexes on bronzers at the pharmacy, or that the prevailing style of outerwear would feature something called a hoodie, which some enterprising teen discovered in the vid archives and had his mother design and produced in a counties factory (and sold by the dozen, like cinnamon-sugar *malasadas*), and which transforms any respectable, demure person into a shifty, slump-shouldered gnome.

There was a time—not as long ago as one would like to think—when people of Reg's appearance would have been talked about openly, right in their faces, as if they didn't have eyes or ears. Maybe there would be a young mother and her not-purely-from-the-originals kids strolling through the park, and the mere sight of them might elicit a comment by some busybody auntie to her friend, They can still breathe through such flat little noses! or Even the winter sun makes them darker, or And such an attractive woman! Such talk didn't much disrupt the atmosphere of whatever park, or mall, or facility lunchroom, and though not applauded or admired, it was certainly, like some extra measure of mugginess on an otherwise pleasant day, not found to be intolerable.

When we were much younger, and as yet unaware of certain aspects of B-Mor, there was an uncle of ours who lived in one of the clan row houses on the block. His name was Kellen Yip. He and his wife, Virginia, didn't have a family of their own—they wanted children but were unable to reproduce—and for a while he often played with us on free-day or after his shift in our street contests of tag and soccer. Uncle Kellen was our favorite among those uncles and aunts (really they were second and third older cousins) who treated us fondly enough but saw us mostly as a pack of pesky sweaty-heads to be fed and duly shushed off. He was a slight man, perhaps no more than fifty-five kilos fully dressed, but he was fast and athletic, and to view him now is to realize how adept he was at gearing himself down to our skill level. He could coax the ball from foot to knee to shoulder like it was a circus animal, and if we showed mettle and were aggressive and quick enough, he'd leave the ball vulnerable so we could win it. What a feeling that was! What a surge of elation and pride and maybe, too, an arrogance tinged with that slightest instinctual contempt for the defeated, at least until he mussed our hair and trumpeted our names as we streaked away.

Afterward he would sit on the stoop with us and "talk story" about olden times while Auntie Virginia poured cups of iced tea to go with the boiled peanuts she'd bring out in a white plastic bowl. Through the muted crackling of the dampened shells, he'd describe how things were for the originals, who were, of course, before his time but whom he'd heard about from his great-grandparents. His stories weren't exactly the ones you studied in school or watched vids of at the historical museum, the oft-documented stuff about how by dint of their collective will and the discipline of their leaders in keeping everyone focused on the job the originals transformed the desperate nothingness about them.

Uncle Kellen was a truck driver who transported fresh B-Mor goods to Charter villages and from those collected any unsold produce plus second-hand clothing and furniture and other discards to sellers out in the counties. He would take a big gulp of his cold drink and wipe his brow with the back of his hand and you could see the droplets of perspiration sparkling in his close-cropped salt-and-pepper hair, just like one of us but old, and he might begin by asking one of us an ordinary question about B-Mor history such as who was the first original to open a private business, to which we eager-to-please students would shout the answer (Wu Gangshur!), and then what he sold (kitchen and bathroom plumbing supplies!), but then he would remind us that there were, in fact, numerous existing businesses when the originals arrived, businesses run by the smattering of natives who had stayed on, whose deeds and leases to their properties were unilaterally voided and reassigned to the (then nascent) directorate.

But there was no real population to speak of anyway, one of the more stridently confident of us might have said. Those shops were failing!

You should know, he answered, eyebrows rising, that they were failing for a very long time.

We asked what he meant by this, and Uncle Kellen explained that while it was true that the existing city was an impoverished husk of a society, with just enough inhabitants to fill the schools and ride the buses and, indeed, shop in the stores, there *were* schools and buses and small businesses, there was a police force on patrol, with a governmental body overseeing it all (if not terribly well); and that this society, barely clinging to life, was still stubbornly doing so, and might have improved itself if given the opportunity our originals had to retool and create a B-Mor of their own. Where most of them ended up instead were the open counties.

Not all of the native citizens left after the arrival of the originals, Uncle Kellen told us. Living around the old hospital complex was a sizable population who had refused a relocation scheme that would send them out to an abandoned university campus in the western part of the state. An attempt was made to evict them by force, but after dozens of people including children were killed in an apartment building that somehow caught fire during the operation, it was decided to let them remain, though no more public utilities would be provided to them.

The Parkies! we sneered, which is how they were identified in our history class materials, owing to their subsequent annexation of a large city park. For nearly a generation they were entrenched in their flawed Eden. There was a brief but memorable study unit on the period, with close-up footage of the initial protests and ensuing riots and eventually a sprouted tent city. The Parkies contended that because there were no jobs, and they'd been cut off from city services, that they needed the land for growing food and collecting firewood and drilling water wells, though the historical record shows that by the end of their occupation all the trees were felled and the ponds had become craters of muck and the plots were either misused or neglected and were producing nothing. They'd even tried farming shrimp but had the wrong equipment and token assistance from the authorities, and they only succeeded in fouling their water.

Now it is a typical park again, very popular on fair-weather free-days.

But do you realize how difficult it is to grow fruits and vegetables outside? Uncle Kellen said to us. We forget about how ideally engineered our grow facilities are. No pests or bad weather. Uncontaminated, nutrient-rich media. And all of you now trained from an early age in the techniques of maximized production. It is only natural for you to believe that we have achieved mastery.

And you believe we haven't, Uncle?

He snorted, snacking on his peanuts, being quiet in the way he often was, not quite responding to our questions, clearly not for lack of views but because he wanted us to formulate our own opinions rather than automatically inscribe ourselves with his, which we would have done, immediately, happily.

That's not what's important, he said.

All these years later we're still not certain what he meant. Perhaps this is why we remember him so well. You can be affected by a person because of something particular they said or did but sometimes it is how a person was, a manner of being, that gets most deeply absorbed, and prompts you to revisit certain periods of your life with an enhanced perspective, flowing forward right up to now.

A couple of free-days afterward, we knocked on his bedroom door on the top floor (row-house attic rooms are always the smallest, and thus go to couples) and Auntie Virginia answered and told us he was away driving, a rare instance for Uncle Kellen on a free-day; sometimes there were shortages or maybe a big occasion when a village required an emergency shipment of goods, and someone had to go. Like most everybody else, Uncle Kellen was a hard worker and devoted to whatever might benefit B-Mor, so it was no surprise that he volunteered. The next time she said he had a chest cold and was napping, which seemed like bad luck, but when on the following free-day we noticed Auntie Virginia making a cup of tea in the kitchen and we bounded upstairs to their door knocking and calling to no answer, despite sounds of movement within, we had to wonder if we had somehow disappointed or offended him. We accused one another of being rude to Uncle, of haughtiness and overfamiliarity,

of accidentally kicking him too often in the shins, and would probably have gone on berating ourselves had the directorate not posted
a message for certain citizens to report to the central clinic for testing.

A month before, just around the time when Uncle receded, all of
us B-Mors had gone in to be evaluated for a certain marker for liver
disease, but this time it was only certain people being summoned,
the listing of their names by clan flashed on every screen in the settlement, hand and home, facility and mall. Of course, it was casually
known who might be *mixed*, but to that point it had never been
officially designated. It was a very small percentage, in any case, and
we were young and wouldn't have really cared about such things, but
to our surprise there was one person in our extended clan on the list,
and it was Auntie Virginia.

She was the last person you'd think was possessed of native blood.
She married into our clan, yes, but she was very pale, paler, in fact,
than most of us, who tend to be ruddy and darken quickly in the sun.
She was on the short side, too, and spoke with a faint New China
accent (like many older B-Mors did back then), and Uncle Kellen
had known her since their first school days, her parents and siblings
all derived from the originals, or at least appearing like they were. So
what happened? Maybe the directorate has that information somewhere, the evidentiary gel lines. We shall never know. What we do
know is that Uncle Kellen was hardly seen after that, at least for a
while. In the mornings he skipped the household's breakfast and
went to the truck transport garage, maybe picking up something to
eat on the way. He put in for overnight runs, which by nature were
potentially dangerous, having to negotiate so much open counties
land. And on free-days both he and Auntie Virginia rarely came
down the stairs, and if they did, they scooted out as if they were late
for a shift. Where did they go? Maybe to a back booth in a tea parlor,
or to a big park, where they could walk about anonymously.

One day our cousins said our uncle and auntie didn't come down to breakfast or even pass by, and when they were sent upstairs to make sure everything was all right, they found their door unlocked, their night table lamp left on. The tiny, low-ceilinged room was as tidy as always, the corners of the laced bedspread on their double bed tucked in smooth and tight. The only thing different was that their stand-up wardrobe was empty, the shelf cleared of toiletries and other personal items. At the garage they told us that Uncle Kellen had appeared at work that morning with his wife along, a practice that isn't unheard of on especially long hauls, if not recommended for reasons of safety. But after their first stop they didn't check in and there were no further pings from their locator. They were gone.

Each day for the next couple of weeks we awaited their return, we children deciding on our own to post a lookout at the end of the block even if we could only do so after school or on free-days (as if they would reappear only when we were ready). While we sat about at the corner benches gaming and watching vids, we traded opinions on why Uncle and Auntie had decided to leave. Sure, at a free-day gathering some members of the clan who drank too much beer maybe uttered some unkind words after Auntie Virginia was listed in that second call-up; maybe she was asked to excuse herself from a cousin's wedding, not because of her presence per se but the needless commotion it might cause within the other clan; maybe there was something amiss at the mall, where no new policies were instituted but some shops displayed the list of names, bannering it below their daily promotions.

The truth, however, is that when you saw something like the listing, you began to look for it elsewhere, too. And after a while, when you didn't see it, instead of not noticing or being relieved you might feel oddly unsettled, like something was off in your own belly, a pang of nausea that made you realize you were, in fact, a lot hungrier than you knew, which is why you were impatient with your spouse or friend, which is why you snapped at your child.

Was all this intended, somehow engineered? Again, there were no newly instituted B-Mor rules, restrictions, covenants. Not even the Recommendations of Practice that are periodically general-messaged, such as parking one's scooter at a forty-five-degree angle to the curb (which are never, in fact, *recommendations*). Nobody was unduly demoted or fired. No one was dispatched. And a similar listing was never again posted.

It was only a relative handful of B-Mors who decided to leave, including Uncle Kellen and Auntie Virginia. After a few more weeks passed and we didn't hear from them and knew we never would, one of our older cousins packed up his and his wife's things and, without asking permission, moved upstairs to the vacant attic room. That was all it took. One phase had given way to another, the realm shifting without the least tremor. The new occupants stayed there until they had too many children to live in the tiny room, by which time Uncle Kellen and Auntie Virginia were just another faded memory.

These days we accept the various legacies of our corpus, from the time of the natives and originals right up to now, and live together in harmony as long as we don't linger too much on those legacies, which we have all agreed to do. We don't want trouble. Though looking back on it now, there were more tussles and even outright fights at school, when before there had been hardly any; or how certain cliques one had not really noticed in the lunchrooms and playgrounds and food courts seemed suddenly and sharply manifest; or how over the years as we grew up, certain, more mixed clans were more regularly pairing off, which is how someone like Reg can look like he does, the scantest fractions combining in that reversed, serendipitous math.

. . .

SO, DID THE SAME math deliver Reg to be C-free? They tell us every destiny is ordered and yet this one, concerning our Reg and our Fan, seems intent on exhibiting properties as apparent and ungrasp-able as the smoke from a mystic's joss stick. Where will the ribboning trail of this pair ultimately lead? How far and high can we rise?

This is the question girding all other questions.

Fan left B-Mor for love, but perhaps not for love alone. About the neighborhoods there is a steadily growing lore about their relation-ship, sundry anecdotes about the game parlors they frequented and the eateries they liked best and how, when the proprietor wasn't looking, Reg might puckishly reach over the glass partition at the gelateria and poke a spoon into one of the tubs to get Fan a free taste. There is also talk of their more intimate moments, how they sat on a blanket in the cloistered lovers' glade of the nearest park along with the other young couples sharing music through their earbuds and, of course, nuzzling and kissing. They were in the first blush of true romance and being sixteen and nineteen you would say it must be so that they were also sneaking off to the mini-inns. But they didn't, amazing to say, which the mini-inn records show; people who knew them corroborate this, insisting that Fan and Reg were happy to show each other their affections in the park, in the café, on the pe-riphery of busy clan gatherings. There was no way they could be alone together in their respective houses with so many relatives ever present, and thus by all accounts they were chaste.

It certainly seems they were content, and yet at some point the pair consummated their love. This must have been Fan's initiation, for Reg was a young man who blessedly could not view his present station as anything but highly satisfactory. He was not in essence desirous. It should have been our expectation that Fan was the opposite, if not obviously so. She was the one who arranged their free-day itineraries, she was the packer of the drinks and snacks, she the one directionally leading their scooters, with Reg winged behind her like a potted young palm. And we won't draw up some image of the two of them entwined the very night before he disappeared to illustrate the fact that Fan departed B-Mor in search of the father of her child.

ASIDE FROM THE UNFORTUNATE SOULS WHO CAME AND
went daily at Quig's compound there were forty or so people who
were settled there, children included. Most all of them, like Loreen,
had first come as patients or else had accompanied patients who died
and then, if they could perform some function or service the place
required, were allowed to stay on. The still luckier ones—chosen by
Quig and Quig alone—could reside in one of the rooms of the
winged main house, while the rest lived a few steps down the hill in
the complex of shanties that hugged the slope. Over the years these
cramped, head-high huts had been erected and added on to exterior
wall by exterior wall, and were connected via internal cutouts to
form a continuous warren of rooms. You could start from the top and
work your way downward through various people's lairs and end up
at the bottom and peer back to see the boxy assemblage of corru-
gated plastic and plywood and asphalt shingle and tarp, a miniature,
junked version of some ancient hillside town in Europe or South
America one can search in the archives.

You can imagine this is the sight Fan beheld after Sewey guided
her through the huts the first time. It was a couple of weeks since
leaving B-Mor and her leg was almost right, the injury in fact prob-

ably just a deep bone bruise and no doubt healing faster because of Fan's superior physical fitness. We sometimes forget that even compared with the most experienced tank divers in the prime of their careers she had a chance to be the finest diver B-Mor had ever known. Kilo for kilo she was stronger than anyone, squat-lifting a record factor of her mass, and as noted, she could hold her breath to that point when it seems certain every cell in your body is going to burst and then in a miracle push past it to the other side, to what must be an altered state of seamless quiet, as if you just broke past the speed of sound. It is a matter of singular will. The very will, we know, that Fan drew upon in the storeroom as she worked her legs in deep bends and stretches at night, often while Sewey jawed on, or when she forced herself to down an extra soy drink or braid of chicken jerky to build up her strength. Or most of all, not flinching and trembling whenever Quig unexpectedly appeared to examine her, his cool, rough fingertips testing her exposed thigh, knowing she was likely safest if he and everyone else in the compound considered her to be still a child, a situation that could not endure long.

It appears her plan was to wait until she was certain her leg was strong enough to set off again on her own. This seems amazing, given what we know, for we have to ask ourselves once more: what was she thinking, when she set out from B-Mor in the first place, and in so headlong a fashion? It is either outrageous fortune or destiny that Quig's car struck and injured her that first night and thus brought her to a place with shelter and food and that served as a crossroads of sorts in that part of the counties, where people naturally shared word of other settlements, villages, facilities. And although we can debate forever whether cruel fate or good fortune is Fan's predicating sign, it must be noted that when she left us there was no hope or consciousness of either in her mind, nothing but a furious purpose and the capacity to disregard the usual rational considerations of her own

well-being and the chances of reuniting with Reg, which were meager at best. Her endeavor was misguided and wrong and maybe plain
crazy, akin to someone waking up one day and deciding he's going
to scale Kilimanjaro because he can't stop imagining the view from
the top, the picture so arresting and beautiful that it too soon deliv-
ers him to a precarious ledge, where he can no longer turn back. And
while it's easy to say this is a situation to be avoided, isn't this what
we also fear and crave simultaneously, that some internal force which
defies understanding might remake us into the people we dream
we are?

When Fan was able, Sewey took her around the main house and
huts, as well as the land around the compound. It was mid-September,
still the heart of summer, the foliage of white oak and black cherry
and hemlock and countless other species of trees distressed and
washed out by the fierceness of the light. The trees were bristling in
the dry wind but they were full, crowding all around them, covering
the tops of the hills right down the steeply pitched slopes to the banks
of the slow-running rivers and streams. From the moment she hiked
down the hillside from the huts the first time she was startled by the
denseness of the trees, for the school units and evening programs at
B-Mor would have you think that the landscape of the open counties
was mostly stripped of vegetation and thus devoid of any wildlife save
for insects and ground-dwelling rodents, a stretch of dusty nothingness and grubby, wayside slums stitched by the network of major roadways that ran between large grow facilities and the Charter villages.
Fan was accustomed to the trees in the parks of B-Mor, every last one
of them strategically placed along paved walkways and the hawker-
thoroughfares to provide shade, or set in a bower for the sake of pri-
vacy, or dotting the banks of an engineered pond where pedi-boaters
could wade to shore and secure their crafts to the trunks. Along the
straight, lengthy avenues they were planted one for every two row

houses, selected for ease of care, the kind that did not throw off too many nuts or pods or sprays of pollen. These were maintained in equal measure by the bordering households and pruned to a specified height and girth.

Of course, there were plenty of sawed-down trunks dotting the hillside of Quig's compound. The cutting had been done spottily, however, so that the main house and huts were still continuously surrounded by woods, the perimeter of which was patrolled by a platoon of men known as the Boys. They were not boys at all, though a few of them were in their late teens, most being men who had experience or training in security or the military. Like everyone else, each man or a beloved had been treated (probably in a dire moment) by Quig, and by virtue of this and the bonds to their kin and friends who were similarly indebted, they were deeply loyal to him and the general welfare of the compound.

Sewey aspired to join their ranks and complained to Fan about having to do the boring job of passing out tickets rather than scouting the area and warding off bandits and hunting for squirrels and woodchucks while doing so, which he said was as good as he'd ever want, which is what he'd do for the rest of his life. And whenever they caught sight of a couple of the Boys with their rifles slung over their shoulders, he waved wildly at them, and if they waved not-so-wildly back, Sewey would bemoan his plight all over again, and Fan couldn't help but think how little where you were or the prospects of your circumstances mattered sometimes, for even out here in a place like this a boy's modest hopes could hold him in thrall.

Fan did her part at first by helping Sewey manage the waiting line of the sick and miserable. She watched how he gave out the numbered tickets and then took them back once they went in to be examined by Quig. Things got confusing with the bidding that often arose, people jumping places in the line and then jumping again, and Fan made it simpler by doing away with the tickets altogether and instituting a separate bidders' line alongside those taking places as they arrived. Soon enough there was a third line, for people with nothing, or at least nothing to give save themselves. Fan simply intended to help Sewey and wondered if she had done the right thing, for though it soon became clear that the new system was working, with fewer arguments and fights breaking out, the most surprising result was that people were offering more than before, perhaps because they could readily look across at the other lines and see the things others had come bearing. Loreen couldn't help but be pleased. Quig, whom they rarely saw, didn't seem to notice, or care if he did.

At the end of the day, Sewey and Fan would head down to the huts, where most of the children and teenagers lived. Sewey shared a bedroom with Loreen in the main house, but he spent as little time there as possible because he said he was too old now to be bunking-up with his mother. So whenever he could, he slept in some section of the huts where he had a friend, and now that Fan was moving around without much difficulty she tagged along with him, though she always hiked back up to the main house to sleep in her cot in the storeroom. She was lucky that it was Sewey who'd befriended her; he treated her like his baby sister, if one smarter than he, and being Loreen's son, he was humored by everyone with at least a wary kindness, and so Fan was as well.

The people of Quig's might not have been inclined to treat someone from B-Mor or another facility with any hospitality at all. The Charters were much more exalted settlements but they might as well be constructed up in the clouds; there was no way a counties person could even dream of residing there. But a place like B-Mor, with its safe, clean streets and full employment and the promise of a gentle end, was a theoretically attainable and thus resented possibility to them. One need not even mention its legacy of foreign settlers, which, of course, was expressed in Fan's face and name, and could only catalyze certain feelings of unfairness and displacement, whether they were justified or not.

Eli, Sewey's best friend in the huts, had no such feelings, being entranced by Fan from the moment he met her. Like Sewey, he was thirteen, though of more typical size and mental capacity for his age, a strawberry-blond-haired kid with a face so thoroughly mottled with freckles he looked like some aboriginal boy in an old-time nature vid, the skin around his eyes and nose and cheeks inked by the unmitigated open counties sun. No doubt if he lived in a Charter village, where on UV-alert days they project a special scrim into the skies and have public dispensing stations of specially formulated lotions, Eli might have been still unsullied and pink; but out here he went unprotected, and his mother couldn't always corral him inside on full-sun days or much scare him anymore with the story of what befell his father, from whom he got his coloring. Still, whenever Sewey and Fan appeared at his hut and there were no more tasks or chores to do, Eli pulled on his floppy bucket hat for their forays into the land surrounding the compound. The three of them hiked along the numerous streams and brooks coursing through the small valleys and followed them up to their sources, like one tiny but deep lake that was hidden behind a rise of rock that Sewey and Eli had named Cold Pond, which they said was icy even now. They spent afternoons sitting on an exposed mound of granite that pitched down right into the clear water where you could see tadpoles skittering over the brownish-greenish bottom, the boys throwing rocks at the fish rises or launching a raft of twigs Eli lashed together with weed stems and then throwing rocks at that. Eli sometimes made a separate one for

Fan and might festoon it with pretty leaves or wildflowers and nudge it in a different direction and tell Sewey not to aim for it, though soon enough Sewey would forget and do it anyway.

Fan liked that Eli never got mad at his friend, just sort of chuckled to himself as a much older person might when faced with so natural a way, and we can't help but think she was reminded of her sweet Reg, who never raised his voice in anything but song (he was a lovely karaoke singer, favoring pop ballads), who never complained about always being passed over for promotions, who never pressed her to do anything she was uncomfortable with, matters of love included. Sometimes during breaks they would sneak down to the sublevel nurseries of the grow facility where amid the endless trays of tender sprouts and shallow bins of fry fish and the drip-drip murmur of feed and nutrients they would kiss, Reg bending way down and his big hands cupping the small of her back through the neoprene suiting and staying there, even though nobody else was around, until Fan would tippy-toe or even give a little leap so he'd have to hold her by the bottom. The facility cameras caught such a glimpse of them, and if you viewed similar vids of other couples, you knew things would accelerate and there was nothing else to do but watch, but with Fan and Reg you couldn't help but keep wondering, for they only kept kissing, and you couldn't help but think about what it felt like to share a satisfaction so thorough that it compelled one not always to blinded fervor. For isn't this what any citizen of our difficult world would want if she had her choice, not to tilt ceaselessly or push-push for its own sake but to be quartered by her own best nature, the one most loving and restful and calm?

It was this she found fetching in Eli, though, unlike Reg, he seemed tinged through with what she could only describe as a somberness, his eyes peering out over the water as if waiting for something that would never come, or else had long come and gone. One bright afternoon while sitting on the slab of rock, Eli announced that he was burning up and was going to go in.

What? Sewey said, certain he'd not heard him right. Are you crazy! It's poison!

Eli replied that it was probably the very water they all drank (if after being boiled), and that the fish and frogs didn't seem to mind.

But it's too deep, Eli!

I won't go far in.

Don't!

But Eli had already kicked off his flip-flops and pulled his T-shirt over his unruly hair and the glare from his bony shoulders and back momentarily made Fan squint. She was going to warn him, too, as the fall-off was especially steep where he was entering, but he was in before she could say a word, his cargo shorts soaked nearly to the waist with his very first step. He was steadying himself to take another when he lost his footing and in an instant he plunged into the dark but clear water, going in right up past his head, his flowing hair beneath the surface looking like a sea frond inflamed, his arms and hands now stretched stiffly outward as if he were already dead. Sewey slid on his rear to the water's edge, extending his foot to try to let his friend grab it, but Eli, oddly unbuoyant, was only slipping down farther into the remarkably deep water, and so Fan jumped in after him.

The water was cold; the shock of it nearly forced her mouth open, her heart sprinting, the chill flowing past her feet as though it were being fed by an underground river spewing forth from just beneath the slab of the rock. Of course, she hadn't been in any water since leaving B-Mor, and without her suit or mask, a spark of panic momentarily froze her, and when she opened her eyes, all she could see was Sewey's block of a foot thrashing uselessly just beneath the surface and then, at what seemed too far below her to believe, the waxen glowing of Eli's hair. She hauled herself up for a full breath and snapped herself downward and right away she was with him. His eyes were closed and his lips were shut tight and she thought he must be caught on something, not to rise. But his arms and feet were free, and he was not yet at the bottom, and when she hooked him by his torso and kicked, it was not as easy as she expected, given his frame, which was slightly larger than her own. But now he was suddenly grabbing her around the neck, clawing at her ears, her hair; he was desperate to breathe. She fought him off and tugged at him and kicked upward with all her might when she felt a heaviness in his buttoned pockets. They were full of stones, which he must have collected during the hike. And although he'd gone limp, Fan had to undo the buttons and strip out the stones before she could swim him up to the surface, where Sewey easily lifted him out in one swift pull.

Eli lay shell-pale on the rock, the band of freckles on his face all the darker for having the color wholly washed out of him. From emergencies at the tanks, Fan knew what to do; she began pumping on his chest and blowing into his mouth, while Sewey craned wide-eyed above her. She worked back and forth pumping and blowing, and she was not willing to give up maybe ever when he finally bucked and coughed, then coughed again, water spilling from his mouth. Then he leaned over and vomited. After he gathered himself, he wiped his eyes and pulled on his T-shirt and his sun hat, and the three of them sat beside the still-again water, drying off, each wondering in silence what exactly had happened.

They never mentioned this to anyone. It seemed to them all nobody's business. Although Fan did wonder. It seemed to her Eli's family's circumstance appeared no worse or better than anyone else's in the compound; the hut he shared with his mother and younger brother and sister was like the rest of them, drafty and damp and rickety, a narrow door the only barrier to the elements, the lone window a hinged piece of cut plywood, the beds jammed tightly in one corner so that they all slept together, as was typical in the huts. In the other corner was set a small woodstove welded together out of sundry metal panels with an aluminum duct running up through the roof. Because it was summer, it was used now only for cooking the evening meal, which meant sometimes frying up eggs, or game if someone shot or trapped any, but mostly it was heating stuff right in the cans. Each hut had a stove and now they took turns starting the fires with those in the adjoining huts, and so people would drift in and out to warm up their dinners and often enough everyone would share what they had, a potluck of diced carrots and mackerel and kidney beans, and if someone was feeling extra-generous, maybe a tin of beef chili or chicken stew would get opened. Sewey was welcomed because he always brought something special from the house such as dried fruit rolls or energy bars, a share of which he gave to Fan to offer. You had to contribute something, even if it was totally unpalatable, like the can of teriyaki-flavored beetle grubs someone had slipped onto the stove the last time and didn't own up to until people tried it and actually didn't mind the flavor, which was sort of shrimpy and sweet. That evening it was Fan and Sewey and Eli's family along with two others, both made up of a mother and her children. Of the residents of the huts a majority seemed to be fatherless, or manless, a fact that seemed natural enough to Fan; though the households of B-Mor had plenty of men, there were always more females by head count because of the nature of the facilities work, not just in the tanks but in the nurseries, where smaller, nimbler hands could plant seedlings and prune and weed more efficiently. Reg had originally started in the jobs mostly held by men, whose tasks were physically demanding, having to handle large soil bags and drums of nutrients, but he wasn't very strong for his size and he'd shown a genuine interest in gardening, not to mention having the advantage of his wide wingspan.

Fan took meager portions from the cans, waiting for the others to coax her to take more. They were sitting on folding chairs outside Eli's hut in the still, pine-fragrant air of the late-dying evening light with their plastic picnic bowls and spoons, and ate while sharing stories of the day and of the various comings and goings of the compound residents and patients but mostly laughing and joking in a manner that Fan realized she didn't much see any longer back in B-Mor. These people didn't have the same ingrained knowledge of one another as did those in her household or, of course, that insoluble bond of blood, but what they did seem to share, despite or maybe because of the prevailing trial of their circumstance, was a kind of sharp appreciation of one another, their talk never quite easy or clement, and sometimes bordering on being cruel; after eating, they would usually play word games because there was little else to do once it got dark and the kids and moms would go round with something they called Roadkill, a memory word game that started at A and went through the alphabet, with the first person saying something you might find at the side of a counties road, such as *antelope* or *auto*, with the next repeating that and then offering his or her own word, *bones*, the following person restating both the previous and then offering *crow*, and so on, until someone either couldn't remember the string of words or come up with a new one, when the kids and even moms would lob abuse at the loser, especially if his word was particularly silly or desperate, like *igloo*, which would prompt a game within a game: a rushing litany of *idiot*, *inane*, *ignoramus*, et cetera. But they were always kind to Sewey, whispering suggestive clues or letting Eli recall a series of words for him when he faltered, exempting him from the mocking if he couldn't think of anything at the end.

Fan didn't play because she was new, and because of that, they weren't sure how she should be treated, but the truth was that she wasn't accustomed to such activities nor did she have much of a vocabulary, despite the fact that she went through the full seven years of formal B-Mor schooling while they had merely their mothers and one another to learn from; there was no signal out here (or if there was, it was too costly to buy a code), and thus they didn't have any games or shows or vids or messaging, and the only thing they could do was read the few dozen old books that were loaded on a couple of antique handscreens the kids passed around. Fan followed the game and played along inside her head, trying to generate her own word every turn, though she had some trouble; she was plenty smart but there was little occasion for her mind to be challenged at the facility or at home, where her aunts and uncles and parents and cousins would sit cheek by jowl for the meal but never really talk or if they did, they would just comment on whatever was transpiring on the programs they were all plugged in to, lamenting and bellowing about the show characters as if they were the friends and family and lovers in greatest question.

And maybe they were; for whatever was in question when the originals landed long ago is by now for us a set of curiosities, like the crank on an ancient automobile, or the virtual keys on a computer screen, the inconvenient or tiresome having been steadily engineered away. We labor hard for certain but the work is rote and our tomorrows are mostly settled and the way we love one another is cast by the form of our excellent contiguity, a rigorous closeness that only rarely oversteps its bounds.

Fan could see that these women and children she now sat amid were the lucky ones. Like Loreen, both of the women had come to

Quig's in dire need, Eli's mother originally arriving with a man who died, and immediately she found herself in a circumstance that presented numerous reasons to try to stay on—a regular supply of food, decent shelter, protection from marauders and opportunistic counties authorities—and only a single one to leave. All the reasons, of course, had their ultimate basis in Quig himself—this was his domain, indeed perhaps as far as the eye could see—and Eli's mother and Loreen and every other person who made his or her way here had to decide how much they were willing to cede in return for such succor. The men would work in policing/security, or procurement and trading of supplies, or in the maintenance of the compound, and the women were responsible for everything else, the daily pilgrimage of patients and the organization of inventories, the "cooking" and the cleaning, the raising of the kids, and if they were manless, and sometimes even if they were not, making a periodic nighttime visit to Quig.

This last fact sounds most unsavory, as well it should; there is nothing laudable about it. And yet it must be noted that no decree came from Quig. He was not the sort of man, it turned out, to force himself on anyone, which he could have easily done. Nor was there any punishment for not making a visitation. The practice arose on its own, and from the women themselves, a schedule drawn up each month by Loreen. It is not certain that he even liked the practice, for often enough one of the women would go up to the main house on her appointed night and come right back again. According to Sewey, Loreen had not been with him that way for many years, though she would still sometimes harangue him to take her into his suite, if only to remind him of her willingness. If there was anyone who was allowed to stay whenever she went up to the main house, it was Eli's mother, Penelope, who was tall and slender, bone pale like her son though not as freckled, and then quite young. She didn't look like a counties person, her prettiness not yet worn away. But it seemed it was her whole person that he favored, for she always had to take along one of the hand-screens with her, apparently so they could discuss whatever book in its memory they were reading together, and then it wasn't every time that she would spend the night.

On those that she did, Sewey and Fan stayed over with Eli and his siblings. The three boys would sleep in one bed, with Fan in Penelope's bed with the little girl, though all of them were pretty much jumbled together. We can only imagine how it must have been for our Fan, to be in such close quarters with children who could bathe only infrequently, if ever, their innate creaturely sweetness masked by layers of dried sweat and grime, nibs of soured grease clinging to the corners of their mouths. She must have become quickly accustomed to that sharp stink, and nestled down as she did without concern for the rampant bedbugs and lice to lie together like dogs in a den, with air just enough to breathe. The little girl, Star, clung fast to her all night, a slick of her drool settling in the well of Fan's throat, but Fan didn't mind or even move; in fact, she went half limp, inviting the girl to embrace her even more. And surprisingly, Fan was not thinking of the child growing inside her, for though she well knew that it existed, it was still purely a figment for her, a vague promise of something that made her think of Reg instead of some specklike being, an image of her lover rendered with a blunted glow, like a portrait done in memorial mode. Fan was not sentimental, we can say that now for certain, her blood running the same temperature as the cool waters of the tanks, and yet here she was encased in the humid nest of these shallow-breathing children with their limbs and hair splayed messily about her, and wishing simply that Reg was with them, his endless arms bundling them all tight. She did not, in fact, miss the people of her household, even though they were her beloved, this including her mother and father, who were perfectly fine parents but no more nor less dear to her than her aunts and uncles, her nieces and nephews and in-laws, for in essence everybody was like a cousin, which is the way we wish it, and so cast it, which is how we are certain B-Mor functions best.

She realized that if she did miss anything it was the household itself, the narrow, high-ceilinged rooms whose air was layered with the aromas of stale cooking oil and the earthy gas of the trooped footwear lined up inside the front door, the tall windows onto the opposing row houses more like mirrors than clear panes, the treads of the steep stairwells worn down in the middle by generations of bare and slippered feet. There were people moving about at all hours, snacking or showering or watching programs, and from the rooms of the younger couples, one could sometimes hear the murmurings and cries of passion, reports of B-Mor maybe everlasting, and it was this unitary vitality that was the girding of her feeling, its tireless, self-tuning motor.

Yet here at Quig's, she was finding herself becoming strangely and particularly attached, of course, to Sewey but also, for example, to little Star, who was slightly walleyed and talked in a stiff, robotic voice but who was magical with figures (she could correctly figure non-whole square roots almost instantly), and to Eli, who in his sleep scolded himself in the voice (presumably) of his deceased father, chiding himself for not being, oddly, more fleet of foot (*Damnit, son, just run!*), and to the other children who stopped by, their grubby mouths of chipped and misdirected teeth grinning madly for nothing other than the arrival of a just-bartered, unopened plastic sleeve of tennis balls, peering at them wide-eyed like they were gigantic furry candies. She was even warming to Loreen, who had accepted the idea that Fan was here to stay, at least as long as Quig was concerned, and had stopped being harsh to her for some consecutive days now, even allowing her to manage the patients' line by herself when Sewey was laid up for two days with an especially bad fever. And Fan found herself slipping out and trailing Penelope whenever she gathered her things to go up and spend her appointed night in the main house, watching her as she entered Quig's wing and appeared inside with the handscreen glowing and ready, his long shadow flicking across her face. Was her expression one of well-masked dread? Of hard-feigned interest? Or was it, in fact, a reflection of Fan's own feeling, this unlikely welling of what she couldn't help but admit was gratitude, surely measured, but tinged warm all the same?

A FEW WEEKS AFTER FAN LEFT B-MOR, WHILE SHE WAS making a place for herself in Quig's compound, the number of us here who were bringing up discomfiting questions had grown to the extent that the directorate even issued a reminder notice about the undesirable nature of nonofficial public gatherings.

A particular incident that occurred in one of the parks may have prompted the general notice. Various sundry B-Mors were enjoying their free-day. There was nothing out of the ordinary, no strange weather blown in, no special anniversary from our history, or anything having to do directly with Fan and Reg.

Apparently, it began with a set of parents and their young boy, who, suddenly tired of the crème-filled wafer cracker he was eating, chucked it into one of the ponds in the park. Ponds grace all of our parks and they are all stocked with fish, not the fast-maturing and easy-eating varieties that are grown for commerce, but rather the more colorful types of grouper and carp that can become immense over time, and are duly admired and prized. They are believed to be wise. These fish are primarily meant to be ornamental but are also inspirational objects, as their majestic way of arcing and gliding through the fastidiously maintained water, accented with picturesque lily pads and stone outcroppings and aeration fountains that are lighted at night, expresses the ideal shape of our exertions.

Every other year there's a select culling of these fish, with an associated celebration and feast, when all of B-Mor streams out to the various parks and scores of temporary food stalls are set up for deep-frying the flesh and making a special soup from the head and bones that supposedly boosts the blood's capacity to store oxygen, and which is known as milk broth, though, of course, there is no milk or cream in it. You see everyone walking about with a paper cone of golden-brown fish morsels and a cup of broth, and with the string lights and music coming over the speakers, the festival is one of the most cherished events on our calendar. It goes without saying that we appreciate the symbolism of the ponds and understand the importance of keeping the fishes' pelletized diet, formulated for optimal health and color, strictly dosed and unadulterated, which means monitoring by us and us alone, a concerted, communal vigilance being always more effective than any round-the-clock workers.

So when the little boy threw his half-eaten cracker into the pond, his parents should have immediately waded in and picked it out, or better yet, made the boy himself go get it. But for whatever reason they did neither, simply allowing the cracker to bob and float in the crystal-clear water until it was naturally snatched from below, the commotion of the big fish's rise enough to attract the attention of the other people at their pond-side leisure. That should have been the end of it, something like this happening probably more than we'd like to believe. But then someone else threw a shrimp chip into the water, provoking another thrashing at the surface, which in turn elicited more offerings around the pond. There is a brief vid someone took and uploaded that captures how quickly the few tossed tidbits here and there turned into a full-scale onslaught of snacks and sandwiches and poured-out sodas and then, shockingly, inedibles like straws and napkins and drink boxes. A frenzy of littering is what it was, with one older fellow in the background so frustrated that he didn't have anything with which to join the fray he pulled off his baseball cap and flung that in, though from his stricken expression it seemed he immediately regretted it. The whole episode lasted for no more than a few minutes, and when the park staff rolled in on their scooters and carts, you could see the young and old and parents and strollers scattering in every direction like just-disrupted ants, and then disappearing on the paths through the many shady copses and glades.

The pond was easily cleared of whatever the fish didn't instantly consume. They seemed to linger for a while near the shoreline, surely awaiting another rain of exotic treats. *Allow me another grilled chicken gizzard! How I would love a pineapple ice pop!* Those particular fish did not get a second chance but at most of the other parks in B-Mor they got a taste, a rash of pond "feedings" occurring soon thereafter. These, too, arose spontaneously, bloomed with startling speed and fury, and subsided just as quickly. Word was spreading but it must be said that there was no real talk of the incidents, no online discussions or gossip or even much commentary around the tables and row-house stoops, as if we each had a solitary desire that should not be named but whose expression, once sparked, was so instantly enacted that it felt as pure and instinctive as fleeing from a house fire. For how can it be denied that these incidents were in some tangled way inspired by Fan's actions? Moment to moment we act freely, we make decisions and form opinions and there is very little to throttle us. We think each of us has a map marked with private routings and preferred habitual destinations, and go by a legend of our own. Yet it turns out you can overlay them and see a most amazing correspondence; what you believed were very personal contours aligning not exactly but enough that while our via points may diverge, our endings do not.

And the funny thing, it occurs to us, is whether what Fan committed, as well as the fact that she left us, was aberrant at all.

We have not gone over what happened in the tanks that day because it is already recorded in the official B-Mor ledger, and maybe someday, when this era's troubles are not so much startling to us as simply fascinating, even quaint and benign, there will be a small interpretive installation at the historical museum that lights up with the account. Which will likely offer this: here was a young woman possessed of superior diving ability but with the burdens of an infirm mind, most clearly proved by her cruel, callous actions of leaving two tanks of dead fish, numbering in the thousands. Add to this the fact that she simply walked out of the gates, with no provisions and no hope whatsoever of finding Reg, and the portrait of her pathology should be complete.

But certain little-known details suggest that more need be said. A seasoned tank diver in Fan's facility, Selena Chiu, who had to retire unexpectedly because of a diagnosis of terminal illness, told some of her household that it was not just the fish in Fan's tanks that perished. There were *other* tanks of dead fish that had to be emptied and sanitized, their filtration systems and pipes and tubing dismantled and replaced as well. These blights occurred in a different facility altogether, one that Fan had never been to; Selena herself had been transferred there for several days, though just after Fan had departed B-Mor, to help train some rookie divers. Apparently, Selena noticed an empty tank being cleaned and assumed it was just a regular maintenance rotation, but one of the divers-in-training said that they were, in fact, cleaning out several tanks after a sudden die-off. Of hatchlings? Selena said, for the fry can be especially sensitive to water conditions and will sometimes get sick and die. No, no, the young diver said. A tank of mature fish. Practically ready for harvest.

When she asked another longtime diver at the facility about this, she was met with a faraway stare and a mumble of ignorance and an instant switch of topic to the latest doings on a popular evening program, which Selena, as most all of us would, seamlessly obliged. But after that, she couldn't help wondering how such a thing could happen, when over the years every factor of temperature and water composition and nutrients et cetera has been engineered and tested and monitored, the formulations optimized to the extent that there are code manuals for every stage of development, each stage broken down into smaller intervals, such that the tank operators can recalibrate almost hourly, say, by adding a certain mineral tincture or upping the temperature of the inflows a half degree. Even the daily cleaning of a diver's suit is done the same way each time, exactly, so as to minimize the introduction of contaminants.

Trace Levels Show Haste Levels! the facilities motto goes.

And while no word of other die-offs arose after that, it was clear from the incidents in the parks that people were conscious of the possibility, if expressing it in a surprising way. But perhaps it's not so unusual. Might an exhausted new mother force-feed a colicky infant to punish it and herself? Or might you mar your brand-new scooter if a part of you felt oppressed by its shiny perfection? For sometimes you can't help but crave some ruin in what you love.

And you could begin to think: so what if Fan poisoned her fish? What does all this mean for the rest of us in B-Mor, we who have made our way through steady work and, if not grown fantastically prosperous like Charters, have for generations endured with aplomb and dignity. If she did cause their deaths, what did she get out of it? What was she desiring? It's too easy to say it was some temporary insanity, or some raging, dark grief over Reg, especially when she never once exhibited such capacities. Her household is, of course, gone now and resettled out west, so there's nobody to query directly, but we know from pix and vids that she was a happy infant and schoolgirl and even adolescent, most often captured with her siblings and cousins, using her smallness and speed to swoop around as mirthfully as a swallow on the first day of spring. She was tiny at every age, but at every age she was well proportioned, her skinny legs sized just right so that she appears a person exquisitely turned and finished, only the fleeting presence of others in the frame betraying her stature. And if this is a roundabout way of suggesting Fan was incapable of perpetrating the flagrant or extreme—unless, of course, she was compelled—then let us move forward to the idea that she did so for a reason, perhaps the best and only one: to save us and B-Mor.

Back around the time that Fan left, there were rumors arising of a shift in demand for our goods in the Charter villages. Of a change in sentiment, in fact, about our products. For decades now there has been a very simple relationship between B-Mor and the Charters it supplies. We provide pristine, beautiful fish and vegetables, and in return we enjoy estimable housing and schooling, technical training and health care, and a salary (if prudently managed) that makes possible modest levels of entrepreneurship, and even some exotic travels. Last month another big group of the retired and the terminal flew their once-in-a-lifetime global to Amsterdam, one of the few cities that is still like it was in olden times, inhabited by permanent residents but also completely open to any who wish to visit and tour and buy souvenirs and snacks. The group crossed the city on bicycles and rode canal boats and brought back posters and placemats from the Van Gogh Museum, the overwhelming favorite painting being his *Almond Blossom*, which you see in every other kitchen and parlor of B-Mor, the celadon background and the dulled white of the petals and the twisting, mossy branches a tableau that somehow captures the exact hue of our lives, this bright-tinged gloaming. If only he had painted fish!

In any case, we have been fortunate in how solid the producer-consumer relationship has been for both communities, the sole inter-ruption being more than twenty years ago, when for several weeks every fish tank had to be emptied and scrubbed after an outbreak. The scales of the fish fell off in patches, which led to infections and suppurations and eventually death. As a precaution, the trays of plants suspended over the tanks were also completely cleared, and until the new fish and plants could become mature, our Charter customers had to source their food from unfamiliar facilities, which you can imagine made them very nervous. Charters are famously nervous, for despite their wealth and security and self-satisfied de-meanors, they are obsessed with minimizing hazards of any kind, and are perhaps racked most of all by the finally unknowable dangers of what they ingest. It's the only thing that they have not mastered.

As for B-Mor, it was a particularly difficult period, to say the least. With our routines disrupted and with no work to do, an unwelcome enervation set in, people quickly becoming irritable, and soon enough irrational; with so many folks milling about the streets and stoops, there were more scooter and bicycle accidents, plus incidents of fisti-cuffs and vandalism in the malls, with the few verified homicides in B-Mor history also taking place during that time, the usual lovers' quarrels and bad business dealings disastrously inflamed. A fourth cousin of ours, in fact, was poisoned by his wife, who found out he was going to leave her for a tea-shop girl the same age as their daugh-ter, and laced a sweet red-bean bun (that he himself had brought home from the tea shop) with rat poison, causing him a most pro-tracted death.

Charter biologists and engineers revised our feed and tank for-mulas, and instituted new facilities practices, and an outbreak of that scale has not happened since. Every level and composition—from the feed, to the water, to the air, to the grow media, to the spectrum of the lighting—is constantly monitored and reviewed, though the truth is that over the years the calibrations have grown so fine that new equipment was necessarily developed, given how decimal places kept being added, the measuring process itself evolving into a kind of test of our mettle, to see how far we could go in realizing an ultimate standard.

Which is why, when you think about it, there should be no sense in the notion that our Charter customers have lost a taste for B-Mor goods; they are *their* goods, after all, of wholly their conception, from genesis onward. We have simply made their wishes real. For what could be more important? Other settlements near and far-flung provide their clothing and gadgets and furnishings and so on, but we sustain them fundamentally, we enable their children to thrive, while all along offering them full confidence that there are no compromising or exogenous elements, nothing but the fortifications exactly specified by them and them alone.

And yet now there was noise of a new movement in the Charter villages, what the proponents were calling Back to Soil; it's said that select teams of Charter experts had identified certain experimental plots in the open counties, and even planted them, presumably to see what the qualities of what they raised and grew in a totally "natural" way might be. The fact that "natural" is no longer a dirty word is amazing, seeing how the Charters had pretty much given up on everything outside their gates and ours, leaving it to the livestock and agro-companies whose artificially boosted yields are purchased by the ever-numerous counties masses, both here and abroad. Most every canton of the world ecology, in their view, had been contaminated beyond remediation, at least for the foreseeable future, which is why a place like B-Mor was developed at all, and then replicated many times over after our successes.

Ensure the input to ensure the output!

Back to Soil, we have to explain to our young ones, is a reprise of an old philosophy about the unequaled purity of naturally growing things, that a particular and endemic matrix of earth and water and air and sun will result in the ideal expression of whatever one is growing, in color, structure, taste, and, of course, the most critical quality of all, which can only be healthfulness. The definition of healthfulness, of course, is different for Charters from what it is for us, and quite different still for counties folk, who can't hope for anything beyond the basic functions and have to trade away too much when needing attention (if they're lucky) from someone like Quig. We B-Mors are looked after pretty well, but once a potentially terminal episode is diagnosed and treated, it will not be treated again, unlike for Charters, who have enough wealth to visit their specialists as often as they wish, theoretically ad infinitum, or at least until their bodies eventually succumb to the accrued effect of the interventions. Nobody goes C-free—nobody—an axiom that we B-Mors and counties people have surely accepted but that Charters probably never will, given the obscuring veil their essentially inexhaustible resources can throw over reality.

Which brings us back to our most humble Reg.

Reg, whose gangly, sapling-like figure seemed ill suited to most every occasion and task, whose brightest sparks were borne of heart rather than mind, whose place in the annals of B-Mor before his disappearance was like any of ours, which is to say genealogical, and no more. For each of us has a perch on the tree. After we are gone, that perch is marked by a notch, permanent, yes, but with its edges muting over time, assuming the tree is ever growing. Years from now someone can see that you were here, or there, and although you had little conception or care for the wider branching, in the next life there might be a sigh of wonder at how quietly flourishing it all was, if never majestic.

But by now Reg—or more specifically, the idea of Reg being

C-free—had overtaken B-Mor. The place reposed anew. Was there more birdsong in the air? Did the streets show a heightened gleam? With the directorate gone silent, all that remained was our imagination, which had been ours alone but somehow felt completely unfettered now, like an old swaybacked mare whose pasture fence has been dismantled; she runs no faster but there's a lift to the breeze, a ready vault to the ground, and with the high motoring in her chest, she is almost certain that she will sprout wings and fly.

So we must picture Reg in a Charter laboratory, sampling from a buffet of typical B-Mor dishes prepared solely for him. Through a straw he sips a tall salt *lassi* in between nibbles. He hasn't gained any weight for his naturally speedy metabolism and his homesickness and most of all his lovesickness for Fan, even as he can't help but eat ingenuously and with enthusiasm. A troupe of physicians monitors him from behind a glassed booth, debating the interplay of his genetic panel, his blood and hormone levels, even his posture and demeanor, trying to unlock the secret of his constitution. Is it his minuscule inflammation factor, several deviations below the mean? Is it his particular fusion of original and native blood? The fact that he eschews alcohol? Spicy foods? Or is it the discovery, when the caterers took in the dishes, that the young man did not touch the fish.

Come again?

The caterers are instructed to provide fish again in several different preparations. It's verified. Again he does not eat any of it, not a morsel of sweet cheek, not a flake of the tail. The fish is ours, of course, fillet of #1 B-Mor primes, and when they ask Reg how long it has been since he's consumed any fish, he tells them he never has, as he's put off by the smell, which to him has the odor of a pair of old slippers left out in the rain. Indeed, he cannot be too close to Fan if she hasn't shampooed her hair after working in the tanks, though he doesn't mention this to the experts, saying only that perhaps he'd been fed fish as an infant, though he cannot remember for certain.

For the researchers, this is startling information. They can't quite believe it; for who in B-Mor would decline their single most prized product, drastically discounted for them and which not even every Charter could afford to have daily? Not to mention that it was a primary source of pure, low-fat protein in B-Mor, where red meats and fowl are served only for special holidays and celebrations.

Almost immediately public health surveys were ordered in the Charters and in B-Mor and its sister facilities to track the correlation between levels of fish consumption and every form of the disease, and though they would uncover nothing substantive, near countless other mandatory surveys were developed and distributed, testing hypotheses about various vegetables, grains, sweeteners, salts, et cetera, until there was almost nothing left to be examined and they returned to the inquiry into fish, which set off a mini-panic in the Charter villages and a precipitous decline in sales. Suddenly nobody had much of a taste for our fish. Within weeks, the Charter distributors halved their B-Mor orders. Tanks went unharvested, the volume of water per head steadily decreasing, and our pampered, exquisite #1 primes began to jostle for room, they started to nip at one another. Soon they couldn't help but bite, and when the first of them was gravely injured, the others didn't hang back as they might have before but pounced in a frenzy of flashing fins and teeth.

For a period, they sold the overgrown fish at B-Mor stalls, three for the price of two, then two for one, which was cause for great rejoicing and a rash of household gatherings and block parties until certain murmurs about what was happening in the tanks bubbled up and we, too, began to question why the fish were so plentiful and cheap. At the dinner tables the younger children were soon complaining about eating too much fish, for there was fish salad and fish fritters and countless tureens of fish soup, the air swam with the dead-sea aroma of salted fillets drying in the breeze like pennants, until in our dreams there were no more fish left and we turned to one another and wondered how we could feel so full yet so forlorn.

Was it Reg we were yearning for? Was it Fan? Yes. Let it be heard. We can speak it now. There are many who say there's no point, that these sentiments will eventually drift away like so much smoke, and they are most likely right. But if we resolve not to quell ourselves, to keep up the talk, to preserve the good picture of the pair in our minds no matter how contrary to the designs of the directorate it might be, this practice alone invigorates us, raises us up, even if there is nowhere else we wish to go.

And perhaps in the end this is the best reason to keep thinking about Fan and her trials, to exercise mental discipline in the face of what must be the most serious challenge to B-Mor since the originals first landed. An existential threat. For what would we do to support ourselves if the Charters, chasing the dream of being C-free, finally deemed our products to be unacceptable? For decades they've had drugs and treatments to address every expression of the dreaded C but still there is no blanket prevention, no inoculation, no ultimate cure. Is this a defect of their science and medicine, or of a philosophy that holds that nothing is beyond their reach? Either way, it left us like this: We could perhaps feed ourselves but what of our housing, our power and water, our schools and training centers and most especially our clinics? How could we assure our communal well-being?

The truth is that we could not. As conceived, as constituted, we may in fact be of a design unsustainable. Which is why we needed Fan, in both idea and person. For within her was the one promise that could deliver us, the seed of all our futures, Charters' and B-Mors' and even of the shunned souls out in the counties, at the moment Quig's foremost.

ONE MORNING IN THE PREDAWN LOREEN ROUSED FAN
from her spot next to a sweaty-headed slumbering Star and ordered
her to pack a bag. They were going to go with Quig on a trip for a couple of nights. Loreen didn't have to explain what was happening—
she'd outlined the possibility several days before—but the reason for
her presence was a mystery. Fan had no choice, so she didn't ask any
questions and simply readied her few things. Within the hour the
three of them were in a newer SUV kicking up a storm of dust on the
road that led down to the bottom of the hill. The weather had been
hot and dry for a long time but now it seemed a genuine drought had
descended upon the Smokes. The rains came infrequently, and when
they did come, they were brief. The streams had all but disappeared
and the level of the two wells of the compound had dropped below a
meter and the men were arguing about where they ought to dig a
third. Cold Pond, where Fan swam with Sewey and Eli, was plagued
with spongy islands of bright green algae, and even after the water
drawn from it was boiled, the essence of something reptilian or freshly
born from the mud stuck to the tongue in an undying rime.

They were heading for a Charter village far north, somewhere
near what used to be a city called Syracuse. Apparently, the residents

of this Charter were not as rich as those closer to the coasts, though, of course, by open counties or B-Mor standards they were still untouchably wealthy. Last year one of these residents had been treated by Quig; the man was driving through the area on an old bypass road and in swerving to avoid a thigh-deep pothole crashed his car into a tree. Quig saved his leg from amputation, and once recovered, the fellow invited Quig to work and live in his Charter village. Quig had no interest in returning to Charter life, but now fresh water was a problem and he required a heavier drilling rig than could be hired nearby to plumb the solid fields of granite beneath their land, and so had contacted the former patient, who was the owner of a major mining corporation.

There was no talk in the car except for the murmuring conversation Loreen was having under her breath as she knitted Sewey a sweater for the winter. Along with the painkillers she was regularly popping for a bad tooth, the knitting acted like some kind of mood drug on her, as she conversed with uncharacteristic levity and patience with a voice she was hearing in her head. Her companion was none other than a younger, sweeter version of herself, and with this still joyous but innocent girl Loreen was maternal and generous. It was difficult to make out every mewling word but she gave boiled-down advice on how to deal with overzealous boys (Keep your knees together) and techniques of basic cooking (Prewarm the pan) and what to do in the event you disturb a nest of hornets (Hold your breath and run like the wind), and it was only after she joined the next ball of yarn that she stopped talking, having fallen asleep, her ratty hair pressed flat against the window, the tips of her needles slowly uncrossing. In the backseat Fan watched the countryside drift by—the counties road was typically cruddy and hazardous—while Quig stared straight ahead with his rakelike hand propped on the wheel, earbuds lodged, listening to what sounded like old-time fiddle music, twangy and swinging. Eli had loaned her a handscreen for the trip but because of the unsteady speed of the car she couldn't read very long without feeling sick. Of course, there was the bigger thing, too, that was roiling her gut, as she wanted to ask more questions about why she was accompanying him, but she was both afraid of him and of the reason, the most chilling possibility being that he was intending to sell or barter her.

For Quig had just traded some people away, two young men who were around Fan's age (she was still successfully pretending to be much younger). They had come to the compound the previous week with a relation in need of emergency attention, who'd obviously decided to hand them over to Quig. They were undoubtedly brothers, sharing the same frontward stoop to their bony shoulders and a thick dark brush of monobrow. They were kept strictly inside the main house until Quig exchanged them for a fairly new vehicle equipped with four-wheel drive (which is what the three of them were traveling in now), the brothers carted off in what looked to her like a Charter medical van. They were led from the main house by a few of Quig's men, and though they weren't handcuffed, the expression on their faces as they stepped up into the rear compartment was the slack-eyed wonder of the damned. Fan's heart panged with the image of Reg probably having to bend down so as not to strike his head on the door frame, and how confused and scared he must have been, not understanding why they were taking him away. Of course, she didn't yet understand, either, what exactly was going on, but she'd overheard Loreen trying to explain to a pushy new arrival that people under a certain age were not automatically taken in trade here at Quig's, despite the rumors that the compound was an intake facility for some purported "Charter call" for youths. And while Loreen appeared genuinely irritated and put out, hadn't she eventually led the three teenagers being offered by the stubborn, shrill woman to the examination rooms, where Quig surely saw them? And although they soon departed with the woman and nothing else came of it, were not other healthy young people in the days since brought straight to the head of the line?

Fan didn't remember Quig administering any blood tests on her, but in those first woozy hours she would not have noticed. He certainly hadn't said or done anything to indicate he had discovered something special about her, like she was C-free forever, which, of course, she wasn't. Like everyone else in B-Mor, she had been periodically tested, the last time being a year before, which was when she and Reg were just starting to talk about their future together, about marriage and children and with which of their households they might reside. By custom they would normally stay with Reg's people, but their double row house was already at overcapacity and so was Fan's, and they were musing about starting from scratch in a less established neighborhood of B-Mor, though realizing they would be at its head.

This was somewhat comical to them, as neither was the type to take up such a mantle, but the more they thought about it the more they felt that they should try, as they had solid jobs in the facility and could afford the loan and, most important, finally came to understand that they would be better off on their own. They were probably right to think this. We won't say it or admit that we know, but we can all appreciate how people with some part of Reg's native line can be very subtly or unwittingly lodged in the lee of prime conditions. Everyone knows that certain spots in the tray don't quite receive the same flows of water and air, where perhaps the nutrients are either diluted or oddly concentrated, and the green shoots there might on first glance look fine but are, in fact, just that bit leggier, more prone to blight. We have raised this notion previously and bring it up again because it seems obvious now that Fan was not only searching out

Reg because he was the father of her child and likely future husband but also that she was testing herself, seeing whether she could truly follow through on her intention of leaving B-Mor behind forever. One could argue that only if you defy from within are your demonstrations valid, but perhaps her plan was for us to have to focus on ourselves, what we and we alone would have to shoulder.

It's not that we're too fearful or comfortable, too cautious or reluctant, but that, as we have never experienced life outside these bounds (save for what's glimpsed in the evening programs or, if we're lucky, on our once-in-a-lifetime global-flight tour), the reach of our thoughts has a near ceiling. Imagination might not be limitless. It's still tethered to the universe of what we know, and as wild as our dreams might be, we can't help but read them with the same grounded circumspection that guided our forebears when they mapped out our walls. Fan, though, made a leap, which was a startling thing in itself.

Something she couldn't explain, then, made her say to Quig from the backseat of the car: Whatever you're looking for, I'll help you find.

He didn't answer right away, tapping at the wheel with his long fingers. Loreen was dozing, her jaw sunk, her tarnished lower teeth jammed together like kernels on a stunted ear of corn.

You're going to help me find a well drill?

No, she said. The other thing.

The other thing, he repeated, his tone raised.

Yes, she said. This was, in fact, only the second conversation they'd had.

How do you imagine helping, little girl, if you don't even know what I'm looking for?

You'll have to tell me.

And if I did tell you, what would you do first?

I'd ask you to teach me how to drive.

He chuckled, the first time she'd heard him do that. He sounded exactly like one of her uncles who always had a pocketful of honey-sesame candies to give out.

And why would I do that?

So you can keep your eye out for what you're looking for.

In the rearview mirror she saw he almost smiled. They drove in silence for another half hour when he pulled over and got out to pee. Loreen awoke and teetered out, too, half asleep, and drifted off into the bushes. Fan waited until they were both out of sight to find a spot to relieve herself, noting that her belly was as flat as ever, despite having missed her period. She was not even five weeks on. When she was done, she stepped out to the clearing while buttoning up her shorts, only to find Quig standing there, waiting.

Thought maybe you ran off.

I didn't.

I guess that's right, he said, his face deeply shadowed beneath the bill of his faded blue baseball cap, the cloudless sky glaring above them.

Fan stood dead still.

But he looked at her somberly and said, Let's go.

When they got to the car, Loreen was leaning against the passenger door, her fleshy arms crossed, and before she could say anything, Quig told her Fan would be sitting up front for a while. Loreen made the sound in her throat that Fan heard whenever she was annoyed at someone in the line, but she just grabbed her knitting from the seat and climbed in the back, where she set up her pillow against the inside of the door so she could stretch out her legs. As Quig pulled onto the road, Loreen went right back to her knitting, her murmurs resuming at a slightly lower pitch as though she were growing impatient with her charge, if still doting. She certainly hadn't been the same brambly Loreen of late, and it was obvious why;

Sewey had been very sick again, the second time now in the last few weeks, and though nobody in the compound was saying anything, it was pretty much accepted that what was wrong with him was his blood (as it usually was with the younger ones), a form that was certainly treatable but so fantastically expensive to do so that the drug might as well be a global, it was so far out of reach. Plus, she had been under the weather herself, having been up many nights looking after him. Sewey's most recent fever broke a few days before and Loreen was on this trip in part to see if she could somehow get her hands on the particular geno-chemo at this Charter, though not, of course, by paying for it. Naturally, her expectations were very low, as they are with all counties people (as is with us B-Mors, too) when it comes to the sentence of this C-fated life, and although she would try her best, the resignation, as for all of us, would come swiftly and finally once she was thwarted. There is no point otherwise.

Quig did not comment on Sewey as he drove, nor upon anything having to do with the compound or where they were heading. All he seemed interested in was describing the various parts and functions of the car to Fan. Of course, she had been in passenger vehicles before but they were B-Mor minibuses and taxis and she'd never actually sat in the front of one until now, everyone going around on scooters and bikes. When Quig heard this, his solemn, roughened face appeared to light up, and without her asking, he explained how everything worked, from the gearbox to the pedals to the dashboard to the steering wheel, then went over all the gauges and knobs and buttons, even the power seat-controls, which Fan worked on her own side, moving back and forth and up and down. He had her move her seat up as far as it could go and extend her right leg and he handed her a plastic container of dried fruit Loreen had packed for the trip to use as a steering wheel so she could practice matching the turns. It was silly at first but Quig was serious and reminded her to keep her eye not on him but on the road and the more she focused the more it seemed her actions began to have a magical bearing on the car; on the sharper curves she slowed down and she pressed her foot against the firewall when they had a clean straightaway and she wound gingerly through a bunkering of potholes on the ruined main street of an abandoned town. They drove through that town and another in the rolling countryside wilted and bleached out from the lack of rains, the saw of Loreen's reprised sleep-breathing sounding just as husky and dry. Fan's arms began to ache from holding up the container but she was beginning to enjoy herself, too, feeling an unlikely liberty and exhilaration, which if you think about it, can be seen as a good approximation of this life, where control is more believed than actual.

Which is, of course, what Fan took for granted when she happened to glance over at Quig, who to her shock was not facing the road but focusing on her instead, his hands mirroring hers. The sight caused her to jerk involuntarily to the side, which Quig couldn't help but follow, and the high-riding car swerved, tires in full wail, until he fought the nasty, scary snaking and steadied it, and they were once again rolling calmly down the road. It was a good thing there was no other traffic. Loreen had been roused awake, crying out when one of the knitting needles poked her in the chin, drawing a trickle of blood.

What the hell happened?

Big rock in the road, Quig mumbled, like it was any fact of nature.

And you didn't see it? she complained, dabbing at the blood with her shirtsleeve.

Nope.

Fan saw Loreen looking back over her shoulder, dubiousness crimping the corner of her mouth, and although Quig didn't meet Fan's gaze and was driving again, she was sure he winked at her. She wondered about him, the person he might have been when his wife and daughter were alive. Fan had heard more about them from Penelope, who mentioned once after a meal that Quig's daughter had been, in fact, very pretty, beautiful in that way girls can sometimes be when bearing certain of their father's features (even if, like Quig, he was nothing special to look at), this from when she'd caught sight of some pix in his albums while he scrolled through his handscreen. He didn't try to hide it from her, but otherwise he never talked about his daughter, and if a visitor asked innocently after his family or children, he would simply stop whatever he was doing and leave, even in the midst of cutting into someone or stitching them up. The compound knew better and Fan did, too, but she pressed Penelope for more about his past Charter life, details that between her and Loreen and a few others who'd been at the compound from early on could be gathered into an unofficial history of what had happened, and how he came to make a life in the Smokes.

QUIG, WE NOW KNOW, HAD ENJOYED THE LIFE OF MOST any other Charter citizen. He was born and raised in a Charter village down south and was educated in the customary fashion, attending school for many more years than a B-Mor ever would and then enrolling in a Charter university for a specialized degree in veterinary medicine. His wife was a trained veterinarian as well, and after their internships, they opened a practice in a village where they would live for nearly twenty years, before having to leave. After the first few years, his wife quit working to have their child and Quig combined with two other vets to run a busy, successful practice, the largest in the area. People from other Charters were soon bringing their pets to the practice, and so he and his partners came up with the idea of servicing the area in call-vans, charging high fees to treat and groom the many pets and animals a typical Charter family owned.

Given the exorbitant costs of living and schooling and health care, Charters usually had one or at most two children, as well as because of the frankly limited opportunities for having a full-on Charter life. There was fierce competition for whatever one might do, at every level, whether it was playing the trombone or being on the swim team and, of course, succeeding in the classroom, where every-one was routinely tested and ranked in all subjects. In fact, there were rankings as well on the teams and orchestras and even in the special-interest clubs, where if it was difficult to gauge talent, then enthusi-asm and leadership were appraised. It went on from there through university and professional school, and then careers, the weekly Power List of who was at the head spurring ever-accelerating achieve-ment but also in certain cases a kind of malaise that B-Mors and counties people never really suffered, that empty-lunged feeling that can come from being measured, unceasingly, from the moment of birth.

Pets were simpler to raise, in every way, plus they couldn't disap-point the family or themselves and naturally offered and received affection unconditionally, which in this world is rare, all of which accounted for why the Charters loved them dearly, and insisted on menageries of them, outfitting the expansive-by-design balconies of their condos or their backyards with romper equipment and ken-neling for their squads of cats and dogs but also the toy swine and hens and even goats a growing number of enthusiasts raised for healthful meat and eggs and milk. Quig and his partners did very well for themselves, and while they weren't as rich as the people-doctors or business executives, they were as secure as any of their Charter neigh-bors in what they expected from their lives, content with the kind of condo they inhabited, the vehicles they drove, how many helpers (just one, for Quig's family) they employed, where and how fre-quently they dined out, all the vital metrics, as Charters would say, duly aligned. Quig and his wife and daughter were in this sense happily unexceptional. Trish was talkative and bubbly and a tad plumpish, with loose chestnut brown curls just like her mother's, and she was a brainy girl, too, always high in the rankings from preschool onward, her parents probably thinking that she had a good chance to be an engineer or executive or maybe even a C-specialist. They also entered her in the Charter Association beauty pageants, and though Trish was not the most fit-looking entrant in the preteen category, her gifted viola playing and her astounding retention of arcane historical facts in the knowledge rounds made up for somewhat lower scores in the yoga demonstration and evening-gown promenade. She could also look stunning; her last competition gown, Penelope said, was made from a brilliant copper silk taffeta that stunningly set off her tresses. Plus, she had that electric smile you saw in nearly every page of Quig's albums, the wide, free grin that to the judges seemed to express the most genuine, deep-seated glee, and reflected not just the glowing inner girl but the wider Charter clime that shone just as bright. She was twice a regional finalist and was preparing for a third attempt at the nationals, practicing her yoga positions and musical pieces for many hours each week when the first animal plagues struck out west.

No one, Quig included, could have predicted how quickly things would change. Initially the cats got sick, and then the dogs, followed by the hobby livestock, but then a small percentage of the human population became infected, which wouldn't have been so catastrophic had not nearly all of those unfortunate people died. The affected villages were immediately locked down, Charter epidemiologists flown in from around the world to determine what was causing the sickness (expressed in a catastrophic hemorrhagic fever) and how it had crossed multiple species barriers; while they were working, all pets and animals in the affected villages were ordered destroyed, whether sick or not, including, as has been noted, the fish in home aquariums. Families who tried to hide and save their pets were made examples of and banished to the open counties; soon enough every last animal was tendered. Naturally, panic spread around the Association (we B-Mors heard nothing about it until much later) and it wasn't long before every Charter village in the country and many abroad decreed the same, banning all animals indefinitely.

Which then became forever.

So what happens to someone when his livelihood disappears literally overnight? It's not the same as losing one's job and having trouble finding another like it. The entire reason is gone, like the old-time writers who at some point found that very few people, if any, actually practiced reading anymore. But at least those writers had time, the change happening over many decades, until readers became rare enough that they were believed to be nearly extinct, like some twitchy, sensitive creatures who lingered in the twilight brush. But for Quig, it was as swift as awaking one morning to see that every appointment for a procedure or examination to come was gone, the entire calendar voided. He and his wife had some savings, plus partial equity in their condo, but his veterinary group had borrowed heavily to finance recent expansions of their staff and the call-van fleet and major office renovations. With no income and huge debts, Quig's family had to sell their condo and move into the rental dorms normally reserved for service people, the nannies and landscapers and teachers and security/emergency workers et cetera who could never afford to own Charter real estate but wanted for obvious reasons to live inside the village. The idea was for Quig and his wife to take on whatever work could sustain them until he could figure out another sufficiently profitable line of business, and so they did, she cleaning office suites at night and he in charge of linens and towels at a health club. They borrowed money from friends for Trish's school and music lesson fees. He applied to all of the industrial livestock corporations but got nowhere, as there was a taint upon not only veterinarians but also breeders and pet store owners, as if they had somehow allowed or even caused the outbreak.

Pix of Quig before and after the animal ban show a profound

change in his appearance. Look at the man he was, reading poolside or picnicking with his wife and daughter in a park, sporting a tidy beard and moustache, the prosperous fullness to his neck and jowls like that of any respectable midlife Charter professional who knows he's belted in and secure, and then at his drawn, clean-shaven twin (the facial hair removed along with anything else that might appear remotely sinister, down to the kitten silhouette stickers on their car), whose newly yielding posture (lowered shoulders, a forward pitch of the chin) also contained an ever-tightening coil of disillusion, this reserve of bitterness and anger that might never spring outward but was steadily grinding its way into his psyche, forever hollowing out shadowy pockets in him that he himself was unaware of. Look at his attractive but weary-faced wife, Glynnis, who could no longer afford to have her hair colored or her crow's-feet smoothed, time catching up and passing her by right before your eyes. And yet there she is at the boutique with their gleaming, unsullied Trish being fitted with a new carmine gown and matching shoes for the coming pageant, her thumbs-up salute to the camera betraying nothing of the bellowing wonder of how any of it would be paid for. Look, at last, at the former call-van Quig converted himself, stripping the Mobile Vet lettering from the sides and refitting it as a delivery truck for a new linens business he was about to start, the blooming of his hope reflected in the shine of the freshly dressed tires, Trish and Glynnis crammed at the wheel behind him and mugging for the camera, this family for whom he would do anything, no matter how humble or retrograde, accepting whatever destiny his needed to be.

But the descent is the harshest journey, and for Charters especially.

The linens service was doing all right, but a former veterinary client who was a restaurateur was the source of most of the billings, and Quig couldn't yet afford to go less than part-time at the health club. Glynnis took a position there, too, in the women's locker room, and it was here that she reconnected with some members she knew from before the ban, girlfriends who commiserated with her plight. Glynnis would never accept charity and in fact none was offered, but they wondered if her husband had leftover stocks of the anesthetics they used on the pets. He did, in abundance, as there was no market anymore for them, and to her surprise her friends offered to buy the drugs at an extraordinary price.

There are illegal drugs in the Charters, of course, but they are extremely difficult to get, given the security measures, and it dawned on users that after the animal ban that certain tranquilizers might be more readily available. So it went for Glynnis, one tiny vial at a time tucked inside a rolled hand towel and placed where the cash had been left for her in the locker. Word spread and soon she was selling a dozen vials a week, and as the supply dwindled, she charged double and triple, which didn't deter the Charter women from telling their friends. Glynnis didn't tell her husband about what she was doing until one day he found stacks of money in the storage locker where they kept the veterinary supplies. He was furious at her—the huge risks she was taking, given the penalties for drug dealing!—but she was just as angry with him; the linens business clearly wasn't growing and meanwhile their standard of living was steadily falling. They couldn't see their friends much anymore, because seeing them required spending a surprising amount of money on drinks and meals and activities, something neither of them had ever paid attention to before. They had traded in their sleek silent-running sedan for a clattery old electric wagon that partly ran on diesel, a kind that mostly counties people drove. And of course, they lived in a small two-bedroom flat instead of the airy, light-filled duplex with two balconies overlooking the village reservoir. How did he think they were still eating out once a month at places like the Tomato Grove? How was Trish able to go on the weeklong school trip to Paris with her French class, and take cooking and oil painting classes? Where did he imagine the money was coming from? It surely wasn't put on credit, as theirs had been cut off by the banks, they would find out, the day *before* the ban. Glynnis wasn't ever a spoiled Charter wife, but once things changed, it seemed she just gripped tighter to whatever semblances of their former life they could manage. Up to that time, Quig was perhaps the dreamiest in the family, the one who passionately but unassumingly went about his work with animals while Glynnis and Trish were in perpetual motion with the packed agenda of a full Charter life, his former partners the ones who arranged the marketing and expansion of the veterinary business and liked to be taken out for golfing and wine-themed dinners by their suppliers. Quig always chose to stay home with his family, and if he traveled, it was in one of the call-vans for work, when he never bothered to explore the shops and facilities of other Charter villages but instead called home to say he would be back in time to go out for dinner.

Glynnis convinced him to allow her to continue selling the vials, which she did, and once their former stocks were exhausted, she got him to contact his old partners and other colleagues to replenish their supplies. It wasn't long before the linens service turned into a special-delivery scheme, Quig himself at the wheel of the van with Glynnis and a former veterinary assistant named Ricky bringing the "linens" to many of the most exclusive residential lanes of their village. For Charters, we all know, relish their wine and spirits, frankly in many cases to the point of dependence, and it followed that the prevailing thin trade in illicit pills and powders and herbs had much room for expansion. They're so busy, so focused as a lot, seeing everything they tackle in work or leisure as an opportunity for personal "leveraging," that their tightly compacted psyches require regular and deep unwinding. The vial business boomed, the level akin to when an enterprising fellow in B-Mor marketed a scientifically for-mulated "synaptic-booster" cookie for our school kids to eat before the annual Exams (which turned out to be simply full of caffeine), the money piling up so fast, in fact, that they were planning to repur-chase their old condo, though they couldn't quite figure out how to pay for it aside from using hard cash, which is all they had.

If this brief period was not exactly a golden time for their fam-ily, it was certainly a heady stretch, when Glynnis and Quig (and even Trish, who didn't know really anything of what was going on, save that her parents and especially her mother seemed much hap-pier) could imagine themselves to be making the climb back into their life, reinstating their tennis club membership, renting a proper non-service-people's condo, and traveling for the regional finals of the beauty pageant to a major Charter village on Lake Erie, where they stayed in a double suite at the best hotel with views of the water and a king-sized bed for Trish as well as for them, their splurging a way to spend the hard cash for sure but also to suppress the gaining feeling of impermanence that must have been marking their days, each sweet moment tinged dire.

It happened this way: Glynnis was making up Trish's face and hair, and Quig was on a call with Ricky back home going over the heavy weekend orders when the line seemed to buzz. The suite door burst open, an angry platoon of midnight-blue-clad Charter security rushing in with their powered batons. Quig instinctively resisted and they shocked him nearly senseless, and they jolted Glynnis, too, when she tried to pull them off him. All the while Trish was scream-ing in horror and confusion in her lustrous dress that would get badly torn in the melee. They were flown back to their village and on Ricky's testimony, Quig and Glynnis were tried and convicted.

Within a week, the family was forever banished from the Charter, allowed only what they could fit into their wagon (less the confiscated cash) as their worldly estate.

Here was the point at which Fan's knowledge of his past life ended, Penelope having gone no further in her postmeal tellings, and as they drove on, she found herself filling in possible details and events that had followed, glancing at Quig's faraway glare and imagining what he must have been compelled to see, and possibly do, to arrive at this place in time. Had he witnessed the last moments of his wife and daughter? Had he killed a person, or two? Fan, being raised in our fashion, was not given to probing into others' lives, at least not face-to-face, and so it was startling that she asked him right there, straight out, whether he could let her see a picture of his family on his handscreen.

He didn't acknowledge her, or maybe he did; all the color had rushed out of his face. The muscles of his jaw were clenching, and now he worked the slow turns of a curvy descent with two hands instead of one. Of course, he knew people at the compound speculated about his past but gave no quarter.

If you don't want to it's okay, Fan said.

What's it to you? he asked her, his voice, to her surprise, full of echo and ache.

I was just wondering, she said, which we must believe was the case. He must have, too, and not just because like everyone else he thought she was younger than she was. Fan was not one to say things for her advantage, even out there in the counties. Often she remained silent, but when she did speak, it seemed only forthright and sincere, which is why people responded to her in the way they did.

There was a long silence when only Loreen's faint snoring could be heard.

But then he said: Yesterday was her birthday.

Your daughter's?

He nodded.

How old would she be?

He gave a sighing half chuckle, like he wasn't quite accepting the turn of this conversation, or maybe that it was happening at all.

And yet he offered: Twenty-five. Maybe just about to be married.

From the side of his sunglasses Fan could see his eyes, searching the empty road, blinking steadily.

Penelope told us she was a very pretty girl. With many talents, too.

That's right, he said, the idea of this seeming to crumple him inside, the points of his shoulders collapsing just that bit. That's right. After a while, he touched his handscreen in the compartment of the middle console and some classical music came on. It was a viola concerto by Bach, he told her, a piece his daughter was beginning to play quite well.

Was she going to perform it for the pageant?

He asked if Penelope had told her about all that and she nodded.

She was, he said. She wasn't a prodigy like some of the girls but she was very good. She had a fine ear. And she played with real enthusiasm, like she was enjoying it. The judges always appreciated that.

There are no pageants in B-Mor.

I suppose not, he said. Can you do anything special?

I can swim.

That's what I hear. You were a tank diver.

Yes. I can hold my breath for a long time.

Really?

Yes.

How long?

A while.

Show me.

She took a round of slow, deep breaths to prime her lungs and then she took a last one in and closed her mouth. She pinched her nose so he could see she wasn't cheating. At first he kept his eye on the road like he wasn't paying attention but soon enough he had unconsciously slowed down, waiting for the moment she would crack. But she just sat there, totally composed, the coloring in her face unchanging; in fact, it looked like she was about to fall asleep. He ordered her to stop. She couldn't quite hear him, or at least immediately react, as she had entered that state whenever she was in the tanks a long time and aligned with the underwater rhythms, that quelled, half-alive feeling that was neither frightening nor fraught but rather strangely liberating, for the wanting of nothing, not even air.

Stop it now, she heard him say from an outer orbit, that's enough, yet she was fine, not even close to done, and she was notching herself down another rung when he slapped her face.

I said that's enough, he barked. Loreen momentarily roused but nothing else was spoken and she fell back to her dreams. He was pushing the car faster now. He was breathing fast himself, like he was running and running. Fan touched her cheekbone, more startled than scared. He hadn't hit her hard but he had scraped her eye slightly and it was tearing and she dabbed it with her T-shirt sleeve.

You all right? he said after a pause, though not looking at her.

Yes, I'm fine.

You're a good girl, he said, if sorrowfully.

Thank you.

Listen, do you want to drive again?

That's okay.

I mean for real. We have a long flat stretch here and I think you can do it.

Okay.

He pulled over and they quickly switched, Fan moving the seat all the way up so she could reach the pedals. She put it into gear and started too slowly and then jerked them forward, but once they were under way, her driving was smooth and assured. Quig picked up his handscreen and restarted the viola piece, the music filling the vehicle.

This is a nice song, she said.

Yes, it is.

After a while, he tapped at his handscreen a few times and he held out a picture for her to see: it was Trish, standing with her mother post recital, the gleaming viola at her side.

You want to know about them? he said. I'll tell you what happened. Do you want to hear it?

She wasn't certain anymore if she did. But he was going to tell her anyway. And so she said yes.

AND SO FAN, DRIVING, LISTENED TO THE TALE OF THOSE first days for Quig and his family. Despite the awful details, his telling must have helped her relax at the wheel, the way music can allow our instincts to take over the countless mechanical operations that you couldn't possibly orchestrate if you had to think through each one. Perhaps it's the same for a storyteller, the sound of one's own voice caretaking this turn and the next, and allowing the full flow.

Like everybody, Quig told her, they had read about banishments and would not hear again about those people, and so the day they drove away from their village, Glynnis was terrified, feeling certain that it was their death sentence. She couldn't stop weeping, these squalls welling up from her chest. Quig was scared, too, though he tried his best not to show it. What helped was that he was preoccupied, though of all the things he should have been worrying about or focusing on, such as where they would spend that first night, or how they would defend themselves if confronted (like all Charters, they couldn't legally own any weapons), he simply couldn't settle on whether he should be driving slow or fast, which speed would attract less attention and thus be safest. So he kept alternating, slowing down and then accelerating for arbitrary stretches, until Glynnis finally begged him to stop driving that way. This broke the looped chain of his thoughts, and soon enough he realized that it was probably best to proceed smoothly and purposefully, as if they were heading someplace specific. But when you consider it, one comes to understand how the question might have gripped him. For what do you do when you truly have no idea where you're heading? At least a pet could revert to its instinct to hide and forage and defend itself and even kill, but what of a former Charter family with meager funds and mostly useless trading possessions (a toaster oven, a cocktail dress) and just a tankful of fuel? Of course, there was no possibility of being accepted into a production settlement like B-Mor (which is always restricted) or trying to gain residency at another Charter, as their banishment was in force system wide. Imagine yourself at the helm of a ship slingshot beyond the Earth's pull, one course into the spectral chasm as likely as any other, all coordinates open but potentially full of peril, each completely unknown.

He couldn't help but think, too, that in her own way Trish was tilting with the same dreadful notions. She was totally quiet, which wasn't like her, not making a sound from the backseat and barely grunting when he asked if she was hungry or had to go; aside from his own fear, his heart was breaking with the inescapable fact that her future was null and that her parents were the sole cause. He had considered suicide but he was sick with the idea of where that would leave his family, which in turn made him think of simply driving off the road at the next drop-off or ravine, delivering them together to a swift, merciful end. But that would be the coward's path, and he was already angry at himself for the too easy slide he and Glynnis made into their illicit trade, when he should have been putting all his energies into retooling himself, and recalibrating his aspirations, even if it meant descending into the Charter's service class and perhaps not rising for years, if ever. He should have allowed the linens business more time to grow; he should have been harsher with Glynnis when he first discovered the selling and demanded she cease, but he didn't blame her, for he knew it was squarely his fault; he should have had more faith in himself rather than give in to his weaker qualities, in particular his overeagerness to please and aversion to conflict and a lifelong infatuation with hope, which had him dreaming more than doing. While his vet partners and Glynnis had been the entrepreneurial ones, he would have been content to welcome the pets and animals into his single office one by one, administering medications and performing surgeries and even brushing their teeth and clipping their nails if needed.

But now here he was, at the wheel of his family car, trekking into the open counties. There were some motels up ahead where you could also get a meal, but they were known at best to be grubby, dingy establishments, and very expensive, being relatively secure, certainly not affordable for more than a few days for any non-Charter. Naturally Charters would never stay there; they traveled by private copter or plane, or on upper-atmosphere globals if they went overseas, and would rarely take a car ride of more than a couple of hours.

Quig passed on the first two motels, one being full and the other so decrepit that it appeared it might imminently collapse, but there was nothing on the nav for a half day's drive past the third one and he was compelled to stop. The large sign at the place read Who Falls Inn, as it was set beside a stream that ran, if meagerly, over a poured concrete dam, which was what made up the "falls." What purpose the dam served, either past or present, was not apparent. There were a good number of other cars parked in the fenced-in lot and the two-level building was an aqua blue with roiling cascades of white water painted on the roof and on the walls under the eaves, well rendered in a certain way, if looking more like surf than gushing water. The place was tidy and well cared for, the plantings of flowers and shrubs around the building healthy and attractive, the footpath through the grass that unnecessarily snaked toward the front entrance lined with clean white stones and trimmed out with lengths of red garden hose, such that all in all the impression was of an establishment one might encounter in a folk tale, this colorful, friendly-looking hostelry in the middle of a nether land, which surely could not be as inviting as it seemed.

Which was why Quig and Glynnis had to warn Trish that they might not be staying there, their immediate shared thought being this was too good to be true. They waved to the vid cam and got buzzed in through the rolling section of fence gating. Quig composed himself by taking a series of long, deep breaths—he was not the man he'd soon have to become—and walked to the office window. He tapped on the three-fingers-thick plexiglass and a shade went up, revealing a bespectacled fellow, youngish but already bald, his Afro tightly sheared on the sides and meeting his neatly groomed beard and moustache. He wore a crisply pressed white dress shirt with a diamond-shaped monogram (LWA) stitched into the breast pocket of the shirt. When he saw Quig, who back then was wide-eyed and pale-skinned and looking very newly out of his element, the fellow's expression hardened, no doubt anticipating the lengthy, pathetic sob story he'd endure and have to ignore once again. But Quig simply asked if there was a vacancy and if his car would be safe overnight, and the fellow—his name, they would soon learn, was Landon Wiggins Anderson—grumpily gestured that he should go retrieve his wife and daughter, and then he had them step through the metal detector.

Landon co-owned the inn with his partner, Dale, a short, tubby, florid-faced older white man who ushered them inside with a butterfly fluttering of hands and comments on how darling Trish looked in her polka-dot sundress and white patent-leather shoes and purse, an ensemble Glynnis had bought on their last day as Charter residents. It was something they could ill afford but Quig was actually happy she had splurged this one last time. Trish hadn't said much at all about her new outfit but she was now showing off her new clutch to Dale, who disappeared and then returned with a box of costume jewelry pieces guests had left behind, and he said she could choose from and take as many items as she liked. Trish was a good girl so only chose a ring and a necklace, and it was only after Dale goaded her that she selected a ruby-crusted hairpin and a cowrie-shell bracelet.

Then he showed them their suite, one and a half rooms decorated in an English-hunt-country style (at least that's how Dale described it), the walls painted to look like they were paneled with burled wood and the overstuffed furniture upholstered in faux leather and suede; framed prints of riders on horseback and foxhounds hung in sets of six along with the mounted heads of a horned gazelle and what looked to be a bobcat. There was a baronial carved-post bed in the inner room and the sofa outside was a sleeper and the bathroom, though not large, was beautifully tiled and set with an antique basin and claw-foot tub fitted with nickel-plated fixtures. There were only eight suites total (refitted from twenty rooms when they bought the property) because they never had more than a half-dozen guests and wanted each room done in a distinctive style, Vienna 1900 and Old Plantation and Balinese Treehouse, the work of finding and restoring pieces gradually accomplished over the years. They finally got everything done this spring, and though Dale was clearly pleased and proud to show off the inn, he admitted that without an ongoing project it was much too quiet, though Landon preferred it that way.

That evening at supper they met the other lodgers, two couples who owned their own businesses and a salesman for one of the huge agri-food concerns and a family of four from Denmark, who were touring America and were intentionally spending some time in the open counties. The Danes were exceptionally tall and attractive, and spoke a perfect, grammatical English, which was a stark contrast to the couples and the salesman, who were counties people of clearly decent means but were coarse in their manner and expressions and what they were willing to talk about at the table with strangers. One of the men kept going on about the side-by-side basins in his bathroom (the Aix-en-Provence suite) and how he made the mistake of doing his business in the wrong one and having to transfer it by hand to the other, which his wife and the other couple and the salesman wildly hooted at but that made Glynnis blanch with revulsion and misery. The Danish family was neither delighted nor disgusted, but rather fascinated, taking detailed mental notes about the social character and practices of these endemic creatures.

It was a good thing that Dale and Landon were in the kitchen at the time, as Landon in particular would have been appalled and perhaps demanded the rude guest leave the table and maybe the inn; you could see he was a fastidious and somewhat severe young man who held himself to an impossibly high standard and was being ground down inside by the burr of constant compromise and disappointment. But this made him, among other things, a needlessly excellent cook; the platters of pasta and salad and grilled wild pig that Dale brought out (it was Tuscan night) were as deftly executed and maybe tastier than most Charter restaurant fare, and he served to the adults *tout compris* a small glass of red wine—something you never saw outside of Charter villages because of its ludicrous price—simply because it was the perfect accompaniment to the meal.

The deep flavors and genuine warmth filling his belly made Quig think that perhaps life in the counties wouldn't be as horrible as they assumed. Of course, they were spending a near tenth of their money stash for this single night and couldn't justify staying for any longer, but the rational calculations that he would normally make didn't seem relevant, not when he saw how the good food and softly lighted dining room was definitely calming Glynnis and had already lifted Trish out of her silence, as she was now gabbing with the Danish girl about their favorite pop singers and boy bands. They asked to be excused and went off to the chintz-heavy "reading room" to exchange songs and vids. Meanwhile, the adults discussed the issues of the day, at least as far as the open counties were concerned, the Danes and their teenage son listening intently and nodding and periodically asking for clarification of a certain term or reference.

The primary focus of their talk was an enduring counties topic, at least as Quig and Glynnis understood it when they were Charters, which was the idea of confederating the many hundreds of counties communities in this part of the country, much like the Charters were organized. One of the problems was the sheer number of them, some constituted and run like any old-time town or small city, with a fairly dependable infrastructure and public services, the much greater number being impromptu settlements that had grown over the years and were known only by somebody's name, such as Tinkersville or the Vromans. Those who believed in confederation were always trying to enlist the contiguous or neighboring settlements to pool security and emergency resources, and increase their negotiating power for services, but it never got very far, the leaderships of the entities ultimately unable to agree on who would subordinate themselves, despite the fact that joining together would likely benefit their people. The settlements originally developed because the old-time towns and small cities were dying off because of crushing debts, as they couldn't afford to run the schools and repave streets and fix the sewers, the last intact services usually being the police. There were many opportunistic gangs and sundry marauders. But it didn't take long for the inevitable turn, which is that the police forces took over the towns, the chiefs and their officers deposing (often violently) the mayors and other administrators; in fact, many of the settlements are now led by the descendants of those first strongmen, who generation after generation have exercised a martial level of control over their residents, and have profited commensurately through the direct or shadow ownership of food stores and the flow of utilities. Naturally, the generally dismal quality of life from time to time fomented brutal coups, the latest instance of which usually pushed another round of chatter about confederation and its promise of stability and security, which is what was happening now.

The whole idea is to follow a Charter model, one of the women said. Her name was Ursula. It's better for all. Why should Bennett and I keep trying to expand our clothing business when we know somebody from the counties council is going to come up and threaten to shoot us in the face and sell our kids to slavers if we don't give them a quarter of our receipts?

We oughta live in a more civilized way, the fellow who brought up his bidet replied. But then we're not as smart as Charters!

Or as good-looking! Bennett hooted. They toasted one another, not with the precious wine, which they'd instantly slurped down, but with a big bottle of moonshine one of them had BYOB'd.

I think it's about the councils just stringing us along, the salesman said. They know what they're doing. Keep us talking and arguing about this detail and that, keep us off balance. Keep us wondering. But they're not going to give up anything of real value, let me tell you. Your grandkids will be having this same conversation when they're our age. That's why I'll never have a family. No offense, but what's the point?

So why the hell bother? Ursula asked him. What are you even hoping for?

The salesman extended his own emptied wineglass and Bennett poured him a shot of the clear spirits. Who knows? he said, drinking it down, wincing but satisfied. His voice was whispery from the burn. I'm just passing time, like everybody else. I try to earn enough to always have a full belly and a warm, dry place to sleep and to cover my handscreen fees.

And hootch and cootch with whatever's left over! the bidet fellow cried.

They drank again to that, as did Ursula, who in the end didn't seem to mind very much, if at all. In the counties you better have it while you have it, is what Quig and Glynnis were realizing, and they gamely tried some of the homemade booze, too, though neither of them liked it, as it tasted like turpentine. When the others asked what they did and where they were heading, Glynnis simply blurted, We're visiting a supplier back east, a reply that was sufficiently non-sensical and blunting that no one inquired any further. The striking gray-eyed Danes, who had been observing the proceedings with a scholarly detachment, were now drinking and joking with great en-thusiasm, their English not spoken as cleanly as before but rather lustily and with a more pronounced foreign accent, the father ani-mated enough that the odd Danish word elided into his phrases and his rectangular-framed glasses kept steaming up and needed blotting. For dessert Dale brought out a platter of individual mini-cheesecakes topped with wild blackberries, and when the coffee was served, Landon emerged from the kitchen in a clean white apron and mod-estly acknowledged the compliments from the table, before retiring for the night. Dale then told them how Landon's parents were well-respected Charter chefs who were killed by carbon monoxide poisoning from a faulty gas-powered refrigerator in their restaurant while Landon was away at summer camp. He lived with foster fami-lies until he was of age, when he left the Charter for good. They had met at a counties LGBT roadhouse where Landon was cooking short-order, Dale commenting to the bartender how the cheeseburger was the best he'd ever had, though he couldn't exactly say why, which is when there was a murmur from the pass-through that it was the cat-sup, which was made from scratch, along with the mayonnaise and pickle relish. Dale peeked back and there was Landon, a skinny, pre-maturely balding kid working alone in a tiny but spotless kitchen, the pans and utensils organized by size and kind. It was love at an instant, at least for Dale—Landon was not one to be swept away emotionally—and here they were all these years later, growing older together, if somewhat now in a rut.

The other woman said they were obviously doing a good business, judging from the quality of the rooms and furnishings, and Dale admitted that it wasn't terribly profitable, though could be if they didn't always spend so much on doing everything "right," which was a point of contention between them. With a different emphasis, someone else could make a good living, and they were considering selling and moving on to something new, a possibility that Quig and Glynnis ruminated that night in their huge plush bed, imagining how they might settle right here, where everything was already set up, learning the hospitality business while homeschooling Trish. Glynnis was not the cook Landon was, but she was definitely good enough to make simple, satisfying fare for their guests. Dealing with strangers all the time, they'd rarely be alone, which seemed a vulner-able situation but was likely safer than homesteading or living in some anarchic, lawless settlement.

The problem was the money; there was no way they could pur-chase the inn, not with their pathetic store of cash, not with their car, which wasn't as good as the one Dale and Landon already owned, not even, they coldly calculated, with their lives, i.e., giving one of themselves over to be done with as the innkeepers wished. Glynnis was obviously not of interest to them but neither was Quig, for Dale and Landon would probably never countenance such a thing, which was not unheard of out here in the counties but clearly not truck for decent fellows like them. The only scenario they could come up with was that Dale and Landon mortgage the business to them and that Quig and Glynnis agree to pay all the profits until a certain sum was satisfied. For as long as they could feed and clothe themselves and maintain the property to an acceptable level, what more could they hope for?

They slept late and while the others were having the breakfast buffet (freshly baked scones, soft-boiled eggs and toast, good strong coffee), Quig and Glynnis and Trish sat down with Dale and Landon in the office and made their pitch. Surprisingly, it was Dale who was sour on the idea, his face screwing up as they outlined their proposal. Landon asked what they were thinking in terms of a price, but Dale immediately pointed out that they had zero experience and stood up, saying he had to go clear the dining room. Glynnis started to cry and Quig, realizing that within a mere hour they'd be out on the road again, clueless and wandering, said they had no idea and that he should just name one, that they'd agree to anything that was doable. They would work for free while getting tutored in the operation to show that they could do it, clean the rooms and wash the linens and do whatever else was needed around the property.

Landon asked them to wait outside while he and Dale discussed it. This is going to be history's shortest conversation, they heard Dale say, as Landon shut the armored security door. They could only hear faint murmurings through the fortified panel but the murmurings went on, taking a higher pitch before they went silent for what seemed a telling amount of time. Almost but not. Quig regarded his wife's desiccated expression and thought he could see in her widened eyes the darkened wells of their future. But it was also clarifying; immediately he felt that they should quickly gather their things and leave behind forever this lovely but false dream. This was not their station because such a station was not to be bestowed or bought or discovered. It was up to them to fashion one, this was the only way. They would either forge a living according with their character and capability, or soon suffer.

The office door opened and the two men emerged, Dale going straight for Glynnis and embracing her.

It's all yours if you wish, he said, holding her by the shoulders, and seeing her face light up, he embraced her again.

We will have to discuss terms, Landon said to Quig, who was speechless. Quig needed to pry Glynnis from Dale but she was shuddering with tears of exultant relief and his present resolve was now dissipating in his own eyes that were welling with gratitude and love for his fragile wife. In fact, he was about to collapse fully inside and take her up in his arms when they heard a blast, like a backfire, and then a sharp, yawing scream coming from the other end of the building: it was the voice of the Danish girl, Caroline, whose name Trish now muttered.

Trish instinctively rose to go toward the ruckus, but her mother cuffed her. Trish begged for someone to go see what was wrong and Quig said he would, Landon already retrieving an old pistol from the office desk and ordering Dale to lock himself inside, along with Glynnis and Trish. Glynnis didn't want Quig to go but they both knew that he probably should, given what they'd bargained for.

Landon and Quig stopped and crouched in the corridor before reaching the dining area. Through its wide opening they could see the salesman, or what was left of him, shot in the neck and lower face and slumped backward in his chair. Caroline sat beside him, her face and shirt brightly flecked with blood and bits of flesh, as a lean, bearded young man pushed the nose of a shotgun barrel into her temple, manically threatening to shoot her and everyone else if she didn't shut up, while his accomplice, similarly scraggly and youthful, picked through the jewelry and handbags and wallets that had been tossed into the center of the table, a pistol tucked into the back of his jeans.

But Caroline couldn't stop spastically huffing and crying, and her father, Jørgen, was going on in what came across like a clipped, haughty tone (it was his accent plus high breeding plus extreme duress expressing themselves in this unfortunate way), arguing that the gunman think about what he was doing, that there was no reason for further violence, that they were all "in compliance," but the young man was clearly drugged up and getting unhinged by the girl's crying, and perhaps even more so by her father.

Yo! Didn't I just shoot that guy's face in half when he got mouthy? You want to see this girl look like that, too?

Jørgen said of course he would not, and might have continued had Ursula not told him to quit talking right now or she'd kill him herself, adding that he was already to blame for letting these boys into the building. How insanely stupid could he be! The gunman hollered at her and she insisted she was on his side, and he said, Shut up now! and she said, But really I am! and he said, No, you're not! and shot her point-blank in the chest, instantly killing her.

His partner in crime, who was serenely inspecting the loot right next to her, hardly seemed to notice. Everybody else then went perfectly silent, if you didn't count the crying. And from the corridor Quig and Landon kept quiet, too; Quig, who we must note again was then much younger, and Charter-raised, realized he had lost feeling in his hands and legs, crippling fear as he had never known it. Landon pulled him back into the corridor and motioned that they should retreat to the office, which Quig was all for, given his palsy and Landon's frozen visage and the fact that Landon was gripping the pistol so tightly it felt as if he might accidentally pull the trigger.

They got on their feet ready to sprint back to the safety of the office, but Quig stubbed his half-numb foot on the edge of the carpet runner and toppled like a headstone. The thud brought out the quiet accomplice, who walked straight up to Landon with his gun drawn and told him to put his down, which Landon did.

I think you two own this place, he said, neither Landon nor Quig able to speak.

It was soon thereafter that everything went to hell. Surely we can imagine how horrible it was, how utterly debased and hideous, the senseless waste and loss that is an ever-present counties possibility and that in one swift, complete act remade Quig. Which was this: the whole dining room was shot dead. Then Landon and Quig, after being badly pistol-whipped, were pushed to the office by the youthful robbers.

They're gonna get it if you don't open up, the hyper one bellowed at the armored door. He had already attempted to shoot out the lock, but it was a custom-made blast door that magically absorbed the pellets.

Don't open no matter what, Landon shouted. They'll kill us anyway, like they did everyone else.

That may be true, the quiet one muttered. But it won't be quick. He then took hold of Landon's hand and shot it, blowing off parts of some fingers. Landon screamed as he fell to his knees and you could hear Dale's muted cries of his partner's name. This only prompted the young man to tap the door with the butt of the pistol and say, Listen, and then he shot Landon again in the hand, ruining what was left; the poor fellow wailed again but much more weakly, overcome by shock as Quig braced him.

Dale was now frantic and pounding on his side of the door. Quig hollered for him not to open it, his fear now replaced by fury, at the marauders but also himself, for literally falling down in every way. He had committed a crime, yes, but it was never one of malice and so what greater transgression had he done to bring such profound misfortune upon his beloved? He had only done fine veterinary work, with caring and integrity. What was otherwise so wrong with his character and life? These were his instant, infinite-sided thoughts while entreating Dale at the top of his lungs, but all at once he was prone, bludgeoned with the butt of the shotgun. He was losing consciousness, the world going milky. The door then swung in, revealing Dale lamely holding a knife, Trish and Glynnis barely shielded behind him. And before he could say a last good word to them, the one with the shotgun stepped over the threshold and began blasting away.

For us B-Mors it's difficult to accept such a transformation, being as willingly cloistered as we are, even our entertainments and tours designed to take us the middle distances, the thrums never so intense as to invite anything more than the standard extrapolations. What's the point? In essence, people don't want to go too far, at least not for long. It's too much for the mind. Charters are equally sheltered, but whether they wish to recognize it or not, the native fuel of their society is risk, and when they fall, they fall from heights that very few can survive.

Fan, gentle-hearted girl that she was, couldn't bear to ask what the scene was like when Quig came to. She thought she could see it anyway, flashes in the cold screen of his eyes, burned in. For Quig didn't quite survive, Fan knew that. The robbers left after a futile search of the office for cash, leaving him and Landon alive, he later realized, only because they'd run out of ammunition. So instead they set fire to the inn, Quig roused out of his unconsciousness by the heat and choking smoke. The office, with its tragic hold, was already

ON SUCH A FULL SEA

aflame. He managed to drag Landon a safe distance from the building but realized once in the clear that he had lost too much blood and was dead. Quig lay down again, spent by vertigo, and for the rest of the night felt the heat of everything torching. In the morning it was a stand of char. But his sense of balance was back, and he walked to his car, the keys in his pocket and the contents of the vehicle the only possessions he had left.

FAN DROVE FOR ANOTHER STRETCH, HAVING NO TROUBLE. But Loreen woke up to see her at the wheel and cried out in terror for Quig, which caused Fan to cross the roadway and head straight at a car that happened to be coming in the opposite direction. Had Quig not grabbed the wheel to make a split-second correction the collision would have been surely head-on. Instead, their front bumper glanced the back end of the other car at an angle that had little effect on them but sent the other vehicle into a wild spin, kicking up a huge cloud of dust before it suddenly straightened and ran off the embanked road, disappearing. Fan slowed down and stopped and looked at Quig, and after a pause, he had her turn around. Loreen was woozy but livid and saying how she was going to throw up any second. They let her out and then drove back to the spot where the tire tracks left the road, and when they looked down, they saw the car, a wagon, on its side in some high weeds. It sat, ticking. Then passengers calmly climbed out of the windows. They kept coming out and coming out, and before they knew it, a near-dozen of them had exited the car, among them a middle-aged couple and an elderly man wearing a tattered straw cowboy hat and an assortment of children of various heights and ages. Save for the couple, who were fleshy and plump though not quite as big as Loreen, they were lithe and muscular, and every one of them wore a clingy burnt-orange-colored overall, some with T-shirts underneath and others with no tops at all, a few of the younger girls included.

With a nod, the man of the couple acknowledged them for having come back, and as they stepped down the brief slope, Fan noticed that Quig had a small hunting knife tucked in the back of his trousers; out here it was always best to be prepared, especially in a chance circumstance. The couple shook hands with Quig, who apologized for the accident and suggested they set the car back upright to see what kind of damage there was. The man agreed and he whistled at some of the larger children, who immediately took their places about the vehicle and with him and Quig rocked the wagon and gently eased it back down on its tires. There were long fresh scratches on the side of the car but no serious damage otherwise, as it had tipped over and slid a couple of lengths in the weedy vegetation. The man didn't seem concerned about the scratches—the car was ancient and rusted about the wheel wells—and hopped in to start it. But as much as he tried, it wouldn't turn over. It was agreed maybe the engine was flooded and they ought to wait for a while, during which time the couple talked with Quig and now Loreen, who had walked back from where she had gotten sick.

The couple was relaxed and cheerful, not at all as if they had just been in an accident in which they might have been badly hurt. This seemed to unsettle Loreen, who couldn't quite suppress a slightly scowling expression, as though the faintest funny smell hung about them. Quig mostly listened to the chatty couple and spoke calmly and evenly in reply to their queries. Their surname was Nickelman. Meanwhile the children plus the very old man crowded around Fan;

they appeared related enough, their features mostly elfin and bird-like, golden haired to the last except for the old man, whose long bristly hair poking out from beneath his hat was silvery white.

Because of her looks, they wondered if Fan was from one of the facilities, and when they found out she was, they asked her all about what it was like there, though by custom not inquiring about how she had come to be in the counties with Quig and Loreen, as that was nobody's business and, besides, wholly moot. The old man said he remembered visiting a B-Mor–like settlement as a child on a school field trip, their group touring the production facility where they made specialty sweet baked goods, things like egg custards and tea cakes meant to be shipped back to New China, and how they got to put on gloves and hairnets and were even allowed to take a fresh warm almond cookie as it came off the line.

You told us that story like a billion times already, Pappy! one of the little girls cried. Now just let her talk!

The others chimed in the same. Fan patiently answered every one of their questions about her work and her household and her favorite things to eat and do with friends, leaving out, of course, certain details about Reg or anything else that might reveal her true age. They were genuinely excited to hear about whatever she described, their eyes ready and bright, and their mouths of typically awful open counties teeth all yellowed and crooked or plain missing now agape with the yearning wonder of children. They would have queried her for hours had not the adults begun trying to start the car again. But it wouldn't turn over, and after some discussion, it was decided that they would tow the car back up onto the road and then to where the Nickelmans lived, which was apparently about five kilometers away. The Nickelmans invited them to stay the night, if they wished, which you would think was not something offered casually out in the counties but which was, in fact, pretty much customary, an odd instance of expected etiquette. Of course, you could always decline, but the offer had to come, maybe because in the complete darkness of the nighttime roads (no streetlights or working streetlights), it was easy to blow out a tire in a deep pothole or, worse, run into a large fallen rock or downed tree, which would leave you vulnerable to opportunistic parties. It was different at the Smokes because that was a business operation and there was no expectation of any quarter. Quig said thanks but no, thanks, that they had camping gear for the night and anyway should drive some more.

They hitched the Nickelmans' wagon to theirs with a length of thick nylon rope and all the Nickelmans quickly crammed back inside except for the very old man and one of the boys, who rode with Quig to show the way. They hadn't seen any houses back in that direction as they'd passed and they didn't see any now, just the dense, weedy brush and knotty vines that were a pox upon the beleaguered trees with the ever-lengthening season of high heat. At an otherwise nondescript bend in the road the old man told Quig to stop and stepped out. He removed some large fern fronds and pine branches from the weeds, revealing the start of some rutted tracks through the undergrowth. He motioned for them to take them, which they did, and once the Nickelmans' wagon trailed past the entrance, he replaced the camouflage and then ran up in front to guide them in, going maybe another fifty meters through the vegetation until the tracks opened onto a very large clearing, where there was an extensive vegetable garden and a mini-grove of fruit trees and a wire pen containing several goats and a chicken coop with chickens loitering inside and out. A stout black and brown rottweiler wandered out to greet them, wagging its tail. The dog followed closely alongside Mr. Nickelman, and Fan noticed the man had a very small brass whistle on a lanyard around his neck. In the clearing there was a pickup truck set on concrete blocks and a washing machine and what looked to be the head of a working water well, all of it looking rustic but still quite orderly and neat. There was also a tiny guard post–like outhouse at the far end of the clearing, from which, when the breeze was right, issued an odor so vigorous it seemed alive. But there was no house.

The Nickelmans streamed out of their wagon, and without instruction, the old man and the teenage boys unhitched the vehicles and rolled theirs beside the pickup truck. They propped the hood to start working on it, while Mr. Nickelman ushered Quig and Loreen and Fan to one of the picnic tables to have a drink and snack before going on their way. Soon enough the engine was running again and everyone cheered. He nodded to his wife, and she and a few of the older girls walked to the edge of the clearing and then disappeared through an arched passage in the dense, weedy bower of the forest. Loreen asked Mr. Nickelman where they went and he said to prepare a small supper, which didn't quite answer the question. Loreen then asked what they did for trade and he said they were entertainers; in fact, they were returning from an overnight gig up near Niagara Falls where they put on shows at a big regional fair. They—now really just the kids, each of whom they had trained from the time they were walking—were acrobats, doing a cheer routine with synchronized dance moves and power lifts, throws, and flips. They ended their performances with a medley of old-fashioned country songs. Counties people all over loved their show, and they were paid well, considering, though in the winter there were hardly any fairs and festivals, and they made just enough to get them by until spring, when the bookings started coming in again. They were flush now, he said, not with pride but a wistful relief, the disclosure itself a clear endorsement of the trustworthy character of his guests.

Fan wouldn't have understood this, of course, but she did notice that Quig and particularly Loreen visibly relaxed, and when Mrs.

Nickelman and one of her older daughters brought out trays of drinks and food, they all partook with gusto, the old man and children sitting in the grass with their plates. For it was wonderful food, maybe miraculous, for being served out here, the sort of vibrant, wholesome fare you only saw on the evening programs when Charter characters dined and argued with one another amid a fully laden table. None of it was anything elaborate but that was its simple, delectable beauty: thick chunks of ripened tomato with little knobs of homemade goat cheese curds; scrambled eggs and summer squash sprinkled with herbs; fried corncakes; sliced fresh peaches in cream; and a cool sarsaparilla and mint tea to wash it all down. Of course, at the Smokes they ate food mostly out of cans and pouches, or dried items such as instant noodles and meat jerkies, everything to be warmed up and rarely ever fresh, as that's what people can easily bring in trade. The Nickelmans were cooks, and also vegetarians, which seemed a crazy way to live when you couldn't depend on regular supplies of anything. They were disciplined, one of the children proudly told Fan, for even when they were down to just a few mouthfuls of beans each this past winter, they still never thought about touching their goats or chickens, which would go against their beliefs.

Fan didn't ask what those beliefs were, as she would have no real idea what the cost of transgressing any specific doctrine would be, religious or philosophical, as we in B-Mor pretty much practice none; other than an undying habit of pragmatic attention and action, there is no overarching system we subscribe to anymore, no devotion to a deity or origin story, no antique Eastern or Western assertions of goodness and badness to guide us. We abide by directorate regulations, yes, but are mostly ruled by one another as to what is optimal, which is debatable but in fact no more so in B-Mor than anywhere else, even as amoral as we may be considered by others. At least we are not wholly ruled by the pursuit of wealth like Charters, or by the specter of ill chance like open counties people, which endows us, we will say, with a certain equable stance that does not tip us either too far forward or back.

Which is how the Nickelmans seemed to Fan, and as well to Loreen and Quig, who marveled not just at the tasty food but at the oddly prosperous calm of the family, their easy generosity that was at once so thorough and modestly offered. Now was now and it was plenty. Toward the end of the meal the children huddled and pronounced that they wished to give a mini-performance of their show, and as Quig and Mr. Nickelman shared puffs from a water pipe and his wife and Loreen sipped some moonshine, the kids ran through a couple of their gymnastic cheer routines, the smaller ones climbing on their bigger siblings and leaping off into the arms of others; they even got Fan to get up on their shoulders and stand with her hands held high and then freely fall backward until she was caught and then rolled deftly onto her feet. They taught her a few steps that she picked up quickly, and within a few run-throughs, she was in sync with their slides and hops and twirls. Aside from her bloodlines, she could have been one of them, her control over her body total and natural, such that some of the Nickelmans, including the parents, couldn't help but wide-eye one another. For you could easily imagine her integration into the group, an unlikely addition that would give their show a most memorable punctuation of shape and color: the Bounding Nickelmans, now featuring Fan the Fearless!

After the demonstration, the plates and cups were cleared (they used real ones rather than throwaways), and Quig commented on their need to be moving on, which drew a chorus of moans and pleas from the children. But he didn't sound terribly adamant, and then Loreen, despite the liquor, was suffering from her toothache again, and Mrs. Nickelman offered to make a poultice that she could lodge against her gum and tooth, which Quig had offered many times to pull but that Loreen had resisted, as she didn't want to relinquish any more of the front ones that were left. This was when they received a tour of the Nickelmans' living quarters, which the visitors assumed was set secretly on the far side of the passage leading through the dense mountain of kudzu and other vining weeds that had overtaken the entire region.

But once they stepped beneath the bower, the passageway veered sharply left, and right, and then slightly downward for a short stretch, the light diminishing and the temperature dropping with each turn such that it felt they were venturing into a cave. But they were not going below ground. The footing of the path was shored up by plank-ing but it was hard to see much and Loreen was starting to make the whistly noise from high in her throat that came out whenever she got a little twitchy. Fan herself was wondering where this would lead but she kept her focus on Quig, who didn't seem at all worried or per-turbed, just grunting assents as the nerdy, enthused Mr. Nickelman recounted how he, too, had been raised in a Charter village, though his family had been forced to leave when he was still a boy; his father had died unexpectedly of a heart attack, but because of an accidental lapse in his paying life insurance premiums, his mother couldn't sup-port the family at the necessary levels with her own job. They had come out to the counties and been taken in by a community that had a famous theatrical acrobatic troupe among its members, who saw his potential and trained him, and here he was all these years later, with a successful show composed of his own children and a wife (born of that famed troupe) he respected and loved, living in a home they'd constructed themselves, or more like cultivated, for it was evident now that the Nickelmans lived beneath a single tree.

And what a tree! was the thought their visitors had as they entered the large circular space beneath its immense canopy, the sunlight filtered by the vines so that there was a cool glow of jade upon everything, like the color of newly sprouted leaves. The scent of the air was richly herbal and of clean, slightly dampened earth. Loreen asked what kind of tree it was and Mrs. Nickelman said a live oak. It was of extraordinary scale; the trunk was massive, indicating a specimen of a couple centuries' age, and when Quig questioned how it stayed alive with the normally choking vines, Mr. Nickelman explained that the vining wasn't as invasive as it looked, as they were constantly pruning it back to allow the tree's own leaves enough air and light, the intertwining complete but not stifling. The vines offered them extra cover, however, from the weather and bad people, and whenever it did storm, the Nickelmans unfurled circular tenting—like a circus top, in fact—from the middle of the tree to both shed and catch the rainwater. Whenever it got too cold in the winter, they let the tenting out, too, and kept warm under that, using electric space heaters running off a diesel generator outside; though, of course, it rarely got too frigid anymore, and then never for very long. The space under the canopy was partitioned by waist-high walls of plyboard into sleeping and living areas, the kitchen just a simple worktable and unplumbed laundry sink and an electric cooktop with two burners. There were a few axes and machetes and pruning clippers for clearing brush. There wasn't much in the way of possessions, a few plastic storage tubs for pantry items and for their clothes and shoes, and then a big screen for watching the vids Mr. Nickelman took of every performance, which is what the children were doing now, the older ones stopping and starting the vid to analyze their moves and transitions between routines.

Fan was enjoying the vid as well as their serious and thorough discussion, but she had to use the outhouse and one of the girls practically leaped to her feet to accompany her, crying out that she had to go, too. Her name was Hilton and she was maybe nine years old with corkscrew curls and dark brown eyes and reminded Fan of little

Star, back in the Smokes. It was obvious she already had a crush on Fan, who was very different from anyone she'd ever seen, plus oddly grown up in the way she held herself but still closer to Hilton's size than anyone else. She took Fan's hand and led her back out to the clearing, and when they were halfway to the outhouse, the breeze turned and carried its stink to them. Fan, who was feeling funny, had to halt and bend over and throw up on the ground, her body feeling as though it were turning itself inside out. It was the whole wonderful supper, now wasted, and she thought it was probably because of the fresh vegetables, which she wasn't used to in such abundance. But she felt instantly better. Hilton said *Gosh* and that she still had to go and so they went to the outhouse, Fan waiting while Hilton relieved herself, which seemed to take a long time but was filled with the girl airing her wishes about Fan staying the night and maybe living with them for a while or from now on and, of course, performing, too. This was when Fan learned that some of the children were adopted, including Hilton, who was only a baby when she came to them.

While Hilton was prattling on, Fan noticed the dog, which was now in a pack of five or six other large, muscular dogs, all of them pushing and growling and madly lapping about the spot where she'd gotten sick. It was a repulsive sight and she turned away, drifting toward a flagless metal pole with beaten-down grass all around it. This part of the clearing was much messier than the rest, marked by loose piles of surplus junk like PVC piping and chicken wire, large rusted bolts and fence spikes. And a smell that was faint but squarely awful now rose, very different from the outhouse stink, like something rotting and drying up rather than foaming and fetid. It was then she was drawn to something bright in the weeds. It was a bone, long and pitted and bleached white from the sun, scarred and gouged down its length by chew marks. She figured it was the dog's plaything and picked it up, surprised at how heavy it was, when she realized that she was standing in a veritable field of bones, most of them tiny and broken, like bits of branch or stone, with only some of them as large as the one she held.

Hilton stepped from the outhouse with a wide skewed smile, which was not for Fan but the rest of her family, who were now out in the clearing and heading toward them in a pointed mass, Mr. Nickelman at the front, the brass whistle in his mouth. The biggest boys carried machetes. He blew the whistle and the dogs magically aligned onto the family's formation, trailing them. Shuffling in their midst were Quig and Loreen, who appeared to be clasping hands but were, in fact, secured by their inside wrists and ankles with locking plastic ties. They walked most unsteadily from whatever they'd been given, their eyes glassy but lightless against their pale faces, and before Fan could run, Hilton embraced her from behind with startling strength, a furious but loving hug that would surely never let her go.

I won't let it happen! Hilton shouted. I just won't!

Don't worry your sweet head, Hilly, Mr. Nickelman said, cupping her chin as well as Fan's. His hand was dry and cold. She's going to be one of us from now on. She's just right.

You promise?

I promise. You want to be part of our family, my dear? Why not, right? You'll have lots of fun.

The entire family was expectantly nodding as though she were simply deciding on whether or not to go on a trip to the mall. And although we can't be sure exactly what was crossing her mind at that moment, we do know about Fan's character, which never wavered through her many trials. Was she an especially moral person? That's difficult to say. She was consistent, is how we will put it, ever the same and same and same, which we suppose can be seen as a kind of integrity that is all too rare these days.

Okay, she said. But why not all three of us?

There was a communal groan and Mr. Nickelman scratched his head, saying, That's really not in our plans.

That's right, the old man concurred.

We're a bit crowded here, Mr. Nickelman said. You'd fit in easily enough but not two more full-sized people. The missus and I are getting full-sized enough, to be honest.

Oh, Philip!

I'm just trying to explain things to Fan. She's a very capable girl, I can tell. A special girl. We figured out a long time ago what the best way for us was. Others will go about their living differently—he glanced at Quig and Loreen—and that's neither here nor there. But we choose to live as simply as we can, as sustainably as we can. It's a wonderful feeling when things are in balance. We feel liberated but we're not afraid because of our liberty, as most people out here are compelled to be. And we are as free as anyone in a Charter or where you used to live. Maybe more. Sometimes we have to buy or trade things, of course, but we've become pretty good at gardening and cheese making and raising our beloved animals, and I'm sure you could help us in that regard. The main thing is, we strive to be completely independent. Certain times that's impossible, especially in the winter. But each year we always get by and we gain that much more know-how, and we hope some wisdom, too.

And if I don't want to stay? Fan asked.

But we know you do! Hilton cried, who was now holding her hand, if just as tightly.

That's right, Mr. Nickelman said, though not quite sounding so nerdy anymore. He blankly regarded Quig, who was clearly not of his own mind and trying to hold back the mud-black tide surging behind his eyes. But he was failing, failing, and maybe finally giving up.

We know you do, Fan, Mr. Nickelman said. You like our show, don't you?

Yes.

You want to be in it.

Yes.

You like our family?

She nodded.

And we like you! We do, don't we?

Yes, yes! their chorus implored.

You see, there's not much else to say. Not much at all. So why don't you go in now with the ladies. Hilly and the girls will set you up with bedding. Boys, you know the drill.

The younger boys led Quig and Loreen to the pole, securing their free hands and feet to it with more plastic ties.

Oh god! Loreen cried miserably. We're going to be their meat!

We don't eat meat, Loreen, Mrs. Nickelman gently corrected her. We never have and we never will.

But the dogs were silently poised, their maws slick and drooling, the muscles of their shoulders and hindquarters pulsing with anticipation.

I want to say good-bye, Fan said.

That's so good of you, Mr. Nickelman said. So very good. Please, go right ahead.

Fan, with Hilton still in tow, approached Quig and Loreen, who had slumped down to a half crouch, propped by only the pole and each other. Their eyes were open but not fixing on her, and when she hugged and even kissed each of them, the only thing Loreen could muster was a whisper of *little New China bitch*. Quig said nothing. Fan and Hilton then stepped aside into the weeds and Mr. Nickelman told her it was time now to go inside. This was something she should not see, at least until the next time. But Fan shook her head, which surprised but deeply delighted them all, the blood rising in their necks. The machete-armed boys trooped forward, their blades gray and iridescent.

But then Hilton screamed, holding the side of her face. When she examined her hand it was smeared with blood from a cut running down her cheek. Fan had slashed her with the point of a fence spike. When the armed boys moved toward her, she garroted the girl with the crook of her arm and pressed the point of the spike against her throat.

My Hilly! What are you doing to my baby? Mrs. Nickelman cried. Let her go! Philip!

But Mr. Nickelman couldn't do a thing. He didn't dare try to use his whistle. The boys stood down. Fan ordered that Loreen and Quig be cut from the pole and slowly walked to their car and placed in the backseat. She took Hilton in the front seat and started the car, turning it around and rolling slowly back to the main road. The Nickelmans all ran their hands on the car, bleating crazily. Once the entrance cover was cleared by the old man, Fan let Hilton out and then pressed as far down on the pedal as she could, slinging them north in the dusk.

WE HAVE PREVIOUSLY INDICATED THAT FAN HAD LARGER aims in leaving B-Mor, but perhaps this is not necessarily true. It may be more a matter of our own shifting perspective on that brief period, what we have come to overlay upon her journeys as we revisit them over time than anything she herself was conceiving, planning, implementing. It would appear that she was completely rash in her actions, even reckless, as she set out from our gates and went forth in search of Reg, armed with nothing more than the force of her feeling. We won't say "convictions," because it is not in the least clear that she was marching for some cause or platform. And though it seems impossible to think this now, she may not have had any of us in mind, at any juncture. Indeed, she may have had a purely singular concern, which she followed one step at a time, via one person at a time, trusting (perhaps blindly, certainly stubbornly) that each succeeding moment would obtain enough security and succor and an incremental measure of knowledge, which can only lead to greater wisdom.

If she possessed a genius—and a growing number of us think she did—it was a capacity for understanding and trusting the improvisational nature of her will. This might seem a contradictory state, and for most of us it would be. We have hopes and make plans, and if they are dashed or waylaid, we naturally rationalize and redraw the map to locate ourselves anew. Or else we brood and too firmly root. Very few can step forward again and again in what amounts to veritable leaps into the void, where there are no ready holds, where little is familiar, where you get constantly stuck in the thickets of your uncertainties and fears. Fan was different. As we have come to realize, she was not one to hold herself back. Or to be fettered. In this way she startles us, inspires us. She was someone who pursued her project as a genuine artist might, following with focus and intensity as well as an enduring innocence a goal she could not quite yet understand or see but wholly believed.

On the other hand, she may have had more particulars in mind than anyone knows. It's perhaps the only way to explain how she decided to try to make contact with her eldest sibling, Liwei, the one who also left B-Mor, though many years prior and under very different circumstances. Again, we can't be sure what Fan thought or planned from the beginning or decided along the way, except, of course, for the goal of reuniting with Reg, but she must have known all along that her brother was out there, beyond the walls, and most likely in a Charter village.

Liwei, as we all know, was among the rare few from B-Mor who are promoted each year to join a Charter village, and if they succeed with their foster families and in school and, of course, engage a sustaining career, they can live there as fully fledged citizens. The determination is made solely by the results of the Exams, which the Charters take a grade-specific version of each year but that those B-Mor (and like settlements') children interested in promotion take only at the age of twelve. It's primarily a test of mathematical problem solving and logical reasoning, with multiple sections of number and word and spatial puzzles, all of it extremely difficult and not material that is fully covered in our schools. We have made light of Reg's not even bothering with the test, but the fact is Fan did quite poorly on it, as did most everyone else who takes it. We're all in a range, as they say. It's best this way.

For the Charters, it's much more fraught a process, at least in their last year (when they're eighteen), with the lowest-scoring decile put on a probationary list and given the chance to take the test once more, when they must score better than half their flagged peers or be slated for service jobs such as retail or teaching or firefighting, unless, of course, they inherit enough money to make a sizable contribution to the directorate as well as permanently sustain a Charter life. There's always a path. Still, with the stakes so high, Charter parents will spend whatever they must to prepare for this, hiring developmental therapists and tutors when their children are as young as six months of age. For B-Mors, of course, it's no big deal, for as previously noted, one of ours must score in the top 2 percent of Charter results to be eligible for promotion, this without any enrichment training or tutoring at all.

No surprise that those who do attain that mark number in the handful each year, across all facilities; sometimes there are just two or three; and about a third of the time there is no one at all. This is not to say that there isn't great excitement when someone does make the grade, as Liwei and a girl from West B-Mor did a few years before Fan was born. Their names along with the others are etched in a stone monument that graces one of our parks, this roster of the exceptional, and departed. Before they leave, their clan will typically host a massive block party that is something like a public festival and an important wedding combined, with long banquet tables of food and drink and loud popular music and booths where they run games of chance, the profits going to defray the costs of traveling to whatever Charter the gifted child has been accepted into, whether here or, very rarely, to a Charter abroad, as there's a Charter association in pretty much every country, even if there is only one village, as in places such as Iceland and Laos.

The party that Fan's clan threw for Liwei was especially memorable, as they hired musical performers and had a dunking station with water stocked with some of our very own fish, swimming around clueless as the clan patriarch—a famously grumpy man who has since passed—sat on the plank in his pajamas, kids and adults alike taking their turn hurling a ball at the target beside him. Even he was giddy that day, making the funniest faces for the littlest ones, all the while gamely goading and taunting the long line of throwers. He got plenty wet but climbed back up each time with a smile, knowing that someone in his line would be attaining the heights.

Fan was, of course, not yet present, but with all the stories she must have heard over the years, she must have felt she had been there herself, chanting her sibling's name with the rest of the crowd at party's end as he raised his fists over his head, which was donned with a customary crown of herbs and flowers grown in our facility. With tears in his eyes, he waved and bowed good-bye to us, and we shouted: Liwei is our champion! Fare thee well, Liwei!

The understanding, of course, is that we'll never see this person again, that he or she will not return, even for a visit. For what good would that do? What lasting joy would it bring, to us or to them? Isn't it better that we send them off once and for all beneath the glow of carnival lights, with the taste of treats on our tongues, rather than invite the acrid tang of doubt, and undue longing, and the heart-stab of a freshly sundered bond? Isn't it kinder to simply let them exit the gates, and for us to turn away, too, and let our thoughts instead draft up on their triumphs to come?

Because it's known which Charter they're headed for, it's easy enough to picture, given the scads of material you can browse, spying the streets and fields and commercial areas of the village, its layout rarely rectilinear like ours, perhaps to heighten the sense of insularity, perhaps so that you don't have to see the disheartening terminus of any path or lane. We don't as a community much concern ourselves with Charter life except in this one regard, but ultimately our annual interest remains an abstraction, seeing the promoted child the same way we might imagine a friend on a foreign tour, say, climbing the steps of some postcard ruin or sampling a local delicacy, giving ourselves just enough detail for shape and color but not for any lingering anxieties, such as how he'll be welcomed by his new family or accepted at school, which career he'll pursue, or who will be his mate. You just see that he's traveled to a kind of heaven, if that's in your belief system, a place that is presumably better in every way than it is here, and surely never worse.

Fan certainly could look up where Liwei had been accepted, a village named Seneca Hamlet. It's a simple matter of record. And although Charters are indeed mobile, and can buy a seat on a global and pop in on other Charter villages around the world, and even have the right to live there if they can afford it, very few choose to leave their home village permanently, even for one within the region. Like everybody, they rely on their families and friends and associates for not just the practicalities but for moral support as well. So chances were good enough that Liwei was still in the same village. And probably she couldn't help but wonder, too, as we would, whether he had successfully assimilated into the life of his adoptive family and community, and taken up a sustaining career, and, most of all, enjoyed the rarefied prosperity that his exceptional performance had surely promised him.

That it might be the very Charter that she and Quig and Loreen were now again speeding toward after the encounter with the Nickelmans would be too coincidental. And yet, even before she was struck that very first night by Quig's car, she must have had a north-ward heading in mind, and in this light her initially compelled and then willing residence at the Smokes can be seen as an instance of her singular patience, and faith. Again, we don't speak of faith much in B-Mor, as there's really no religious or spiritual practice to speak of, no worship of any kind either in public or within the households. It's not clear what our people think of the existence of God, or the afterlife, or why we are here. What Fan's position was on these ques-tions will never be known. She simply had a faith—an amazing, pro-found faith—that like some great waterfall would not stint or diminish. Where it came from or how she nurtured it is a mystery, and what we can see is that she drew upon it in every episode of her quest, for fortitude and strength. It is thus partly faith, and solid rea-soning, at least from Fan's perspective, that her never-met sibling might be helpful in her aim of reuniting with Reg. Liwei was a Char-ter, after all, and by definition would have the necessary means or connections or maybe even some power.

After narrowly escaping the lair of the Nickelmans and camping well off the road to pass the night, it took them another full day on the poor roads to reach their destination. Fan drove the entire way, whatever substance Loreen and Quig had been given still affecting their systems. Fan had to stop several times for each of them to vomit on the side of the road, Quig especially pale and sweaty and hardly able to support himself. Fan had to come around the car and help him, using all the strength in her legs to buttress and lift him up from his sickly crouch and push him into the rear seat, where Loreen lay back against her window. At the few service stations along the way, Fan had to buy criminally expensive water to slake their extreme thirst, and if they tried to eat anything, they soon felt sick again. At one point Loreen soiled herself and Fan helped clean her and get fresh clothes from her backpack, after which Loreen mumbled that she was sorry for what she had said, after which Fan simply nodded. She'd hardly registered the slur, given the extremity of the moment, though while driving she did note the epithet. She'd known only B-Mor and so had all the preceding generations of her clan, New China a most distant notion that was hardly ever mentioned, and if so, somewhat disparagingly, say, to point out someone's haughty airs, such as That's some N-C style! Yet in bloodlines it was where she came from, it was what she looked like, and when she mused about it now, she wondered whether the legacy should mean more to her, especially as she was carrying a child. It was a talisman that was hers but which she kept solely on a shelf, an object that might indeed be powerful but only if she brought it down and pressed it to her brow and asked something significant of it. But what was that? And how would she ever come to know? .

Before they got onto the stretch of well-kept toll road that would take them to the Charter village, Quig took the wheel. They didn't want to be turned away as diseased so he tried to clean himself up but he still looked ghoulish, his eyes weary and bloodshot, his hair greasy-looking and matted in a lopsided fashion. Loreen appeared no better, crystals of sweat and dried spit clinging to the corners of her mouth. But when he pulled up to the guardhouse of the Charter village, he gave their names and the guard checked them against his screen and scanned their eyes, not bothering with Fan at all, assuming she was either theirs or on offer.

The village sign read Seneca, simply Seneca, and it was the first Charter village Fan had ever visited in person. Was it the same? It was not exactly the name she had looked up, but it was familiar. The village didn't look totally strange to her, perhaps for the viewing she'd done of other villages, many of which were similarly laid out by one of the two major construction firms. From a satellite view, everything looks crisp and tailored, the curves of the streets and sidewalks arcing out in equal increments from a central open space, like ripples in a lake. Whenever she browsed, and it was not often, she liked to peer in close with the ultrazoom, inspecting the waxed finishes on the cars and ruler-straight joints of the sidewalks (never any renegade cracks) and the tiles of the roofs, which were not plastic or asphalt shingles like those of our free-standing houses but made, incredibly, from a piece of natural stone, each one with a distinct pattern and hand and its own earthy or flinty shade.

But this Charter was even better. In fact, it was hard to believe. It was the last gasp of the afternoon as they slowly drove, the sunlight angling through the voluminous hardwood trees, their broad leaves tittering and waving with a coolish breeze, the stately houses and sleek, jazzy condos set well back from the road rather than built right on top of it like our airless, chockablock row houses. There were tall-ish, attractive people of various races and ethnicities going about (no pets, of course), some striding quickly in fancy exercise clothing, arms a-rowing, some smartly dressed for office work, others carrying little shopping bags full of goodies one couldn't see. There were nannies, generally darker skinned and squatter, either pushing prams or leading a pack of colorfully jumpsuited toddlers, but they, too, seemed somehow light of heart and tender and happy enough in their mobile sphere of cry and babble. Where the shops were more concentrated it was busier but no less tidy, the windows of the businesses sparkling enough that you had to look twice to see the exquisite displays of women's bags and dresses or elaborately iced cakes or the mock-up of a luxurious bathroom festooned with speckled soaps looking good enough to eat and towels so fluffed and white they made you want to bathe. It was still too early for dinner but the all-black-clad waiters of the restaurants were setting the outdoor tables with splendid burnished cutlery and massive wine goblets and tastefully spare bouquets of tiny wildflowers, the plush-lined bars within already mirthful with the cocktail hour. She saw the same around every curve, this unbroken continuum of soft, prosperous light and richly textural detail and the unerring sensation that this would be a moment lovely and eternal.

In a word, it was beautiful. A bit unusual, yes, with the living and shopping so fully integrated, but beautiful nonetheless. She hadn't been hoping for it to be any particular way but she hadn't been expecting this. It almost made her feel nauseous, but it wasn't illness so much as an upending awe, neither exactly good nor bad, a state of being she realized she had never experienced back in B-Mor, where routine is the method, and the reason, and the reward.

If Quig and Loreen did not appear to be impressed—they'd seen plenty of Charters before—their lackadaisical attitude was likely due more to their still miserable condition; Quig was driving tentatively enough that he was attracting attention, people on the sidewalk staring at the dusty old-model car with a mismatched wheel that squeaked at low speed, one of them, Fan was certain, now making a dour-faced call to village security. Quig soon turned off the main street and drove through a clearly special neighborhood of single-family homes, all very large but in differing styles (if perhaps designed in the same way behind the façades, with prominent center halls and matching wings for bedrooms and vehicles) and with front lawns completely cleared of trees to afford the fullest view of the homes from the street. There were no fences or walls or gates, everything wide open save for the side yards between the properties, which were left densely wooded.

They found the right house number on the mailbox and went up the driveway, Quig parking before the triple garage doors. It was a Mediterranean-style villa, beige-stuccoed and topped not by stone but terra-cotta tiles, and as they stood before the front door, they realized music was being faintly broadcast from speakers hidden in the eaves—a famous aria from an ancient Italian opera, Quig noted.

When the door opened, a petite middle-aged woman in a light gray service uniform greeted them. She was clearly expecting them and led them to a suite of bedrooms on the second floor. Quig and Loreen took one room and Fan, to her surprise, was given the other, equally large, which was furnished with a king-sized bed and an overstuffed reading chair and antique writing desk and a bathroom with two washbasins and both a shower and a tub. The soaps and shampoos were arrayed just like in the shop displays, along with cotton balls and swabs and a packaged toothbrush on the vanity, and the thick towels on the tub surround were stacked three high, a child-sized robe splayed out beside them. The helper, named Mala, invited them to wash up and rest before having dinner with Mister Leo and Miss Cathy at eight o'clock.

Fan ran the tub right away, pouring some of the bubble soap into the water, as she'd never tried that before. She stripped off her dirty clothes and looked at herself in the mirror, especially her belly, to see if there was a change. Was there the tiniest bulge? The light was different from when she'd peed on the road, and in the mirror it was evident. She sucked in her stomach and it didn't go away. Still, she looked mostly like she always did, nothing too out of the ordinary. She was going to brush her teeth—it had been before the Nickelmans when she last did—but a funny feeling crept over her and she quickly slipped into the bubbly water, despite how hot it was. She scanned the ceiling, the seams in the molding, even the artwork on the walls, to see if there was an eye of a vid cam, but she couldn't find one. When she was done scrubbing and washing her hair under the cover of the bubbles, she plucked the robe while sitting in the water and quickly stood up and put it on.

After cleaning her teeth and brushing her hair, she tried the bed. She was shocked how pillowy-soft it was, so unlike her firm cotton-batting mattress back in B-Mor and about five times as large. She lay

down in various orientations and parts of the bed until she got back
to the appropriate position, and she was going to shut her eyes for just
a minute when suddenly she was slowly floating down a river, past a
burning Who Falls Inn, before going over the lip of an artificial ledge
into a deep pool, where Trish and Glynnis were swimming. They
were splashing and gay, and it was all fine and easy with Fan showing
Trish how to stay vertical underwater while keeping her feet above
the surface. Quig was not present but for some reason Loreen was,
complaining as usual about something from the water's edge. But the
three of them were ignoring her and Fan was on to showing Trish
another trick, this one for twirling underwater, when the girl began
to sink deeper and deeper. Fan couldn't understand what was happening but she was sinking herself, or more like being drawn toward
the bottom with greater and greater force, just like what happened to
Joseph. Fan was a strong swimmer and could just escape the flow, but
Trish couldn't resist and dropped away into the depths. Fan let herself get drawn down right after her, and when she neared the bottom,
she saw Glynnis pressed against a very wide metal grate, already
drowned. Trish was stuck against the grate, too, fiercely struggling,
and Fan kept trying to pull her from the main drag of the flow but it
was no use. The poor girl couldn't hold her breath any longer and
opened her mouth, her body instantly rebelling against the water
filling her lungs. She relented; then she was gone. Fan let herself get
drawn in, too, and though she knew she could hold her breath a
while longer, she was thinking maybe she should just give up, let the
water cool the burning inside her lungs, when the flow suddenly
ceased and she floated upward to the surface, Loreen's voice coming
clearer.

It's quarter to eight, Loreen was saying, looming above Fan as she
lay in bed. It's time for dinner. Loreen said to get dressed right away.

She looked mostly recovered, her face no longer so terribly pale like soap, and having washed and combed her hair and put on a beaded necklace, she looked almost glamorous, even with the shapeless, smocklike dress she was wearing. As Fan changed in the immense walk-in closet (into clothes Penelope had given her for the trip, a simple blouse and long skirt borrowed from another family), Loreen reminded her how important this meeting was, for Mister Leo was going to give them the geno-chemo Sewey needed, as well as the drilling equipment for the compound. When Fan stepped out, Loreen had her sit beside her on the bed, so she could brush Fan's hair. Loreen took her time, running the brush gently through her short locks and pinning up one side and the other and then both, finally pulling all the pins and brushing her hair out again.

You know now why you're here, right? Loreen finally said. I know you do. You're not a dumb girl.

Fan nodded and said she did.

You're going to be that woman's helper. She'll show you how to take care of the house. You'll train under her and then someday take over when she retires. And you can live here the whole time, probably right in this room. But I will tell you this. These people don't have their own children. It's just the two of them. So who knows, if they really take to you, maybe someday all this will be yours. Can you imagine that?

Fan said she couldn't, but that she understood. She knew she wasn't going to live at the Smokes forever, so this was the best way, helping get the equipment for the new well, and especially Sewey his medicine. The one sad thing was that she would never see him or Eli or the others again.

Loreen pressed her hand between hers and, with what Fan could sense was genuine gratitude, said she would let them all know how she felt. That was when Quig knocked on the door and poked his head in to say they should go downstairs. Like Loreen, he looked chipper after washing up, like his usual self again, if much more nicely groomed, the one difference now being that he wasn't really looking at her, seemingly unable to meet her eyes.

like he was an old childhood friend, taking both his hands for a hearty shake and addressing him by his full surname, Quigley. Quig reintroduced him to Loreen, whom he smiled at but clearly didn't remember, and then to Fan. Mister Leo bent down with his hands extended and said, What a darling girl.

Loreen nudged her and she went to Mister Leo, who was perhaps ten or fifteen years older than Quig, though he looked just as young if not younger, being well fed but still impressively fit. Fan, like any of us B-Mors, would not have ever encountered such a person; the directorate people we might come across in the facilities or observing us in the malls were Charters, yes, but they were often technical types, engineers and accountants who seemed always tightly wound and focused, unlike this Mister Leo, who exuded a pure easeful sense of confidence and command and ever rightful ownership. He was very handsome as well and could have been spliced right into a spot for a supercar or luxury clothier, with his strong chin and full head of salt-and-pepper hair and startling cobalt eyes that matched the face of his bulbous platinum-cased diver's watch. He was dressed in a silken black mock turtleneck and pressed black jeans with an alligator belt and he wore sleek tasseled black loafers made of a leather whose texture even from a distance looked to be extra-buttery and soft, which it was. He clasped Fan's cheek and she braced at the surprisingly rough nubs of his fingertips on her jaw, exerting the subtlest pressure. Then he let her go. Mala brought out a tray of glasses of Champagne, and one with mango juice for Fan, and they followed Mister Leo as he showed them the artworks around the room, an abundant collection of sculptures and paintings and objets d'art. He walked with a limp—the leg Quig had saved—but not in the least pathetically, his gait more like it was lingering intentionally than it was skipping a measure. The art was pleasing enough to Fan, who didn't know the first thing about what she was seeing; obviously Loreen didn't much care. Quig, however, was quietly amazed, his eyes widening at certain pieces, as if he'd seen them before only in museum catalogs. Mister Leo was talking about a painting of the Italian countryside circa 1890s, highlighting its use of heavier brushstrokes and purer colors, when Fan glimpsed Mala walking off with the empty tray down the other end of a hall. She slipped away when they had moved on to a tabletop sculpture of a very skinny, very elongated figure and found Mala in the kitchen, working at one of two stainless-steel-topped islands.

The woman was alone in the immense, brightly lighted space, which felt to Fan more like a testing laboratory than a place to prepare anything edible. A steady draw on the air made it cool and dry and odorless. When Mala saw her, she smiled and motioned for Fan to come forward. Why don't you help me? she suggested. She was making various canapés and gave Fan the cookie press to cut out the last few rounds of cheese and smoked meats and toasts. They assembled the components on the toasts as well as on slices of cucumber, and once they filled the appetizer tray, Mala asked Fan to bring it out to the others.

Mister Leo was delighted at the sight, giving her an approving clap-clap, and saying that if she would rather keep Mala company than look at boring art she should. Fan nodded. When she returned to the kitchen, Mala was on to getting one of the dinner courses ready, a salad of tomatoes and fennel and fresh mint. Fan must have paused, for the produce surely originated from a place just like B-Mor, if not B-Mor itself, and if she wasn't recalling how Reg would test the ripeness of the fruits with his long, skinny fingers and in his joking drawl announce Yup or Nope or Maybe, how could she not think about the members of her household and their tireless labors in the facilities? She missed them and had even cried once early on at the Smokes after spooning out dinner from yet another blackened can, her heart heavy for the clinging odor of fry oil in their cramped row-house kitchen, but the truth was that she missed her own work of diving in the tanks just as much, if not more; it was in the work that she came closest to finding herself, by which we don't mean gaining "self-knowledge" or understanding one's "true nature" but rather how at some point you can see most plainly that this is what you do, this is how you fit in the wider ecology; in the water she felt fine-tuned, most thoroughly alive, for she could gauge the hardness and pH and trace salinity simply by how it played between her fingers, how it tingled her cheek; she could tell by how the fish were schooling whether they were hungry or stressed or content. And if all of us thought of our work more like this, wouldn't we be better off? Although certain wider questions can needle if you let them: How did this ecology come to be? Is it the one we wish to endure?

Mala was surprisingly talkative as she readied the other dishes for dinner, going over unprompted how she had prepared each one with careful attention to healthfulness. It was all very fresh and vibrant and delectable looking, but afterward Fan had to say that none of it was half as tasty as she expected it to be, though she couldn't exactly say why. It was seasoned enough and not unusually bitter or sweet, but there was something fundamentally sterile about it, as if the food had not been touched by human hands. Mala, of course, was touching it, and now so was Fan, having been enlisted to chop some herbs to sprinkle on the pasta, and ladle a dollop of sauce on the chicken pieces. Mala seemed to know that she was originally from a facility and didn't ask about it or why she was with Quig and Loreen, only inquiring whether it was still the case that facility couples were encouraged to have at least four children and received special bonuses for having more, which Fan informed her was no longer so, given the gradually declining need for workers since the worldwide recession began, now quite a number of years ago. In fact, new couples were taxed on the third child and thereafter to offset the costs of health care and schooling and training. This seemed to intrigue Mala, and Fan wondered if she had been born in a production settlement, too. She was an Asian of some kind but her skin was quite dark and her hair wiry and thick and she didn't look like she was of New Chinese blood. There were some facilities that had experimented with bringing in groups from places like Vietnam and Indonesia and the Philippines but that didn't continue, often because there was trouble integrating them with our clans, both in the neighborhoods and on the facilities floors. They were eventually forced out, and there was a period of much strife and even violence and some bloodshed, worse than what happened between the natives and originals way back when, but soon enough it was done. Yet Fan still couldn't help but feel an affinity for this woman, maybe it was the one-piece uniform so much like what Reg and his workmates wore; or her simple, unassuming expression; or that she chewed on a strip of dried ginger, just like Fan's grandaunt used to do, her breath always spiced and aromatic. Mala also had these wonderfully petite hands like Fan's, much smaller than it seemed they ought to be given her otherwise normal size, though looking very sturdy as well, like they could manage whatever task or operation that might be necessary.

While they arranged the food on separate platters—this was an informal dinner and so would be served as a buffet—Fan asked if she lived in the house all the time. It was an odd question to pose, but something about Mala seemed hidden to Fan, and she couldn't help but ask. Mala told her that she lived here at the house twenty days in a row and on the twenty-first she spent the day and night away. The next morning she returned for another twenty before going away for a full day again. That was the schedule for the last seventeen years.

Where do you go?

Outside.

To the open counties?

Mala nodded. She was carefully layering the fruit and berries on the cheesecake and did not stop until she was finished.

You're going to ask where I stay.

Yes, Fan said.

I will tell you. It's nothing not to tell. I stay with my family. With my husband and my children.

They must miss you.

We're accustomed to the schedule.

And apparently, Mala went on to describe, to the money, too. She had no need of any funds when she was working, and what she was paid went very far in the counties, enough that her daughters and her son could attend a tutoring center four days a week and her husband could have a dependable car to drive them there. Naturally, he didn't have his own job, as he had to take care of and safeguard the children and the house. He was a good man. There was a rough period of adjustment but they made it through. Only once was the house not cleaned and vacuumed and the meals prepared for her day at home, when he was already drunk when she arrived in the morning and asked what happened, and he shouted, You're not the king! She did not argue with him and went about picking up the toys on the floor and gathering the laundry and washing the dishes when he knelt before her at the kitchen sink and with tears in his eyes begged her for forgiveness. He was so lonely it made him crazy. She told him he was a man and should act that way, and that as long as he was faithful in his heart nothing else mattered. After that he was fine. And her children were fine, too, although she worried that they spent too much time on the handscreens she'd bought them last Lunar New Year, rather than studying. But the truth was where would that studying lead them, especially her son? Because of her work, her daughters, now sixteen and thirteen, would at least have sizable dowries they could offer to suitor families. But her son was eleven years old and disliked his tutors and shirked his studies, and she had little hope he'd do well enough on any tests to have a chance at one of the few corporation jobs. What would he have to do? Could he sell enough of something to make a living in the counties or else with mixed fortune marry someone like her?

They made up a fresh tray of drinks and brought it to the gallery, and Mala then gave Fan a quick tour of the rest of the house. They started from the kitchen and went upstairs to where Fan and Quig and Loreen were staying and then to the other guest bedrooms, which were also richly decorated and outfitted, but they didn't venture inside the rooms at the other end of the house, as they were the master suites, one for Mister Leo and another for Miss Cathy. On the main level there was a vid room and gym room full of exercise machines and there was Mister Leo's huge office full of screens that connected him to his mining operations all over the world, plus the commodity exchanges where the metals and rare earths were traded. There was a glass sunroom where Mister Leo and sometimes Miss Cathy had breakfast, which looked out onto the swimming pool and gardens and the rest of the spacious if not immense property. In the finished basement there was a wine room and a massage and sauna room and a very small pool that was meant for swimming when it was too cold outside, a continuous current flowing from one end. Perhaps Mister Leo would even let her use it. They toured the three-car garage, which seemed just as scrubbed as the kitchen and did not smell of fuel or oil, the vehicles sparkling under the bright lighting.

Finally Mala showed Fan her own suite next to the kitchen and laundry room, which, in fact, was quite nice, if downright spartan in decoration and furnishings when compared with the rest of the house, a bedroom and sitting area with a desk and a full bathroom, all finished in standard white paint and tile. There was nothing on the walls in the way of decoration except a few printed photographs of Mala's family above her bed. Her husband was Caucasian and her children were exceptionally attractive in the way mixed offspring often are, enough so that it was hard to see how they were derived from their very ordinary-looking parents. There was a viewer on her desk and Fan checked with Mala before tapping the screen. It lighted up with more pictures of her kids, separately and together, and then of her husband standing in front of their house, a tidy-looking cottage painted yellow with white shutters and a dark asphalt roof. His expression was cheerful enough but not quite fixed of feeling, his gaze tentative and faraway. There were many other shots, most of them, Fan could see, obviously taken on her free-day, everyone dutifully assembling in various family combinations at whatever locale they'd decided to visit, a mini-golf or bowling center or an outdoor eatery at a lakeside beach, with Mala pressed in close among her loved ones but maybe with too much hopeful lean. Or maybe not.

There was a thumbnail of an unfamiliar girl, and when Mala excused herself to use the toilet, Fan tried to bring it up. But a passcode was required and Fan was not going to bother but then idly keyed in

2-0-2-0, the days Mala worked. Nothing. Then she tried 2-1-2-1, and amazingly, this brought it up.

It was a girl, Asian, too, around eleven or twelve years of age. But the difference now was that the pictures were taken here at the house, out back in the gardens, or in the kitchen, or downstairs by the little pool. None had Mala in them, just the girl. There were albums of other girls, too, seven in all, again in and about the house and property, each captured solo. They were smiling and not, engaging the camera and not, the backgrounds showing every season and various times of day, nothing common about the portraits except that the girls were all around the same age and of some kind of Asian blood. She noticed something funny about one picture, not the girl so much as the shrubs behind her, which were tiny. She could hear a toilet flush and the faucet running, and she touched one last image and it was of the same girl and Mala, the picture clearly snapped by Mala herself as she extended her hand. They were happy, even giddy, like a joyous mother and daughter, but what Fan was startled by most was how young Mala was, the image clearly many years old.

When she came out, there was an unmistakable tension in the air and Mala looked straight at the viewer, which Fan had just shut down. Mala asked if she liked the pictures. Fan said she did. If she liked, she could look at them again after dinner, but it was time to get back to the kitchen and clear a few things before the meal. Of course, she could rejoin the others. Fan said she would keep helping, which she did, taking the platters out to the buffet table so that Mala could clean up the island. Fan then loaded the dishwasher with the cooking utensils and heavy mixing bowls, Mala commenting on how capable she was for such a little girl.

And very strong. How old are you?

Fan had the strange urge to tell her the truth but in the last moment caught herself and said, What do you think? and that she should guess. Mala took Fan's hands in hers and gazed into her face, squeezing her palms with enough increasing force that Fan began to wish she'd just said some age to the woman. She was going to shout out. But then Mala let go, for the lady of the house, Miss Cathy, appeared in the kitchen. Immediately Mala retrieved a carafe of water from the refrigerator and poured out a small glass for her, which Miss Cathy drank down with some pills she had in her hand. Her eyes were sleepy and bloodshot. She had not yet seemed to have noticed Fan. She was wearing a striped-print caftan and was tall and full figured, and you could see that she was once probably a very beautiful and commanding woman, with her fine cheekbones and regal, straight nose; but she was definitely only half a figure now, and sickly looking, her reddish hair going uncolored for some time, as the roots were prominently gray; her forehead was broken out in the center with a rash of tiny pimples, the skin of her hands and forearms papery-dry and flaking.

Are those people of Leo's here yet?

Yes, ma'am, Mala said. They've been here for a few hours. This is Fan, who came with them. Fan, this is Miss Cathy.

Miss Cathy turned to Fan and looked at her as blankly as she might a statuette in the gallery, one that had been there a very long time.

Does she speak English?

Yes, ma'am, Mala told her.

That's good. She looked glumly at Fan and said, Do you think you'll like it here?

I don't know yet, Fan simply answered.

Her matter-of-fact tone piqued the woman's attention, as she was obviously expecting a different reply.

Where are you from?

The counties.

She's from the Smokes, ma'am, Mala said.

Where's that?

I don't know, ma'am.

You must know, Miss Cathy asked Fan.

She shook her head because she didn't know, not really, and whatever else she could add did not seem worthwhile.

Miss Cathy was now staring at her, examining, it seemed, every hair on her head, the shape and color of her eyes, the texture of her skin.

She touched Fan's face. And then she turned away. She said to Mala, Should I go back up or are you serving now?

I think Mister Leo will be ready for dinner soon, ma'am.

Well, then, let's do so.

In the dining room they served themselves except for Miss Cathy, whose plate Mala filled with small samples of the dishes. She sat at one end of the table, Mister Leo at the other, with Quig and Loreen to either side of him and Fan closest to Miss Cathy. Mala went back into the kitchen. Everyone ate quite heartily, save for Miss Cathy, who took an exploratory bite of each dish and then no more. She just drank her wine, though not with any gusto. She didn't say much, either, even when her husband tried to bring her into the conversation by saying how she had selected much of the art to buy at auction, as she was a talented painter herself. He didn't seem to mind when she showed no interest in engaging with him, and he simply went on to other topics, among which were the misguided new policies of the directorate, who were stifling free enterprise with a host of new taxes, and the worrisome trend of Charter youth, who despite all their advantages and test prep were scoring lower and lower, in raw terms, on the yearly Exams.

No one seems to care because the results come out in percentiles! he said. But I've looked back at the historical numbers and performance is declining at every grade level. I will assure you the tests are not getting harder. In fact they're getting easier, is what I am told. So we must conclude that Charter children are not as bright as they used to be. Or else they are feeling less pressure to do well, being disincentivized by the wealth of their parents. Either way, it's an ominous sign. We're losing what makes a Charter a Charter, which is the tireless drive for excellence. The compulsion to build and to own. Meanwhile, the number of outsiders testing into our ranks is ever rising. *They* aren't in decline. This alarms some people, but I'm not so against it, actually, if it means we're getting top-notch young minds.

You believe in new blood, Miss Cathy mumbled.

Yes I do, he replied, not acknowledging her weary tone. No truly intelligent person can be a bigot. We welcome all as long as they have drive and a capacity for hard work. He briefly glanced at Fan and then took Quig by the shoulder. Of course, talent and skill count for a lot. I never told you the whole story, Cathy, but were it not for this good man I'd be a cripple, if not a corpse rotting on the side of a counties road. We need people like him. I keep trying to tell him we could arrange for a review of his case, a reinstatement hearing, but he wants no part of it. Do you, my good man?

Quig said he did not.

No, you don't. It's my one criticism. You are stubborn. I hope not fatally. But nonetheless we're going to help you out. The drill has been scheduled to be trucked down to you. And about the geno-chemo for Loreen's son. I'm happy to tell you it was just sent over this morning by a friend I have on the pharmacorp board. It's right in my office.

Loreen thanked him profusely, reaching out to clasp his hand, though her touch seemed to disagree with him and he leaned back in his chair, interlocking his fingers behind his head.

And what do we receive in return? The joy and satisfaction of knowing we've done some good. And I have my leg! My dear wife has me! And Mala, Mala, please come out here, Mala gets a new young helper to train and to be her companion. I'm afraid we're not the best company, are we my dear?

Oh, Mister Leo, Mala said, that's not true.

Tell the truth! Mister Leo teased her.

I am, Mala insisted.

No, you're not, Miss Cathy pronounced, to which Mala didn't respond. She stood there awkwardly for a moment before asking if she might clear people's dishes. Fan rose to help and Miss Cathy told her to sit, that she was a guest tonight and Mala would take care of it. Isn't that right, Mala?

Yes, ma'am, of course. She is a guest.

She wants to help, Mister Leo said.

A guest is a guest, Miss Cathy said, with an unusual amount of feeling. Then she winced, pressing a hand to her chest. Whatever struck seemed to pass but she took a blue pill anyway from a tiny silver case, set atop one of her rings.

Are you all right, my love?

Did you hear what I said?

Yes, we did, my love.

No one spoke for a while. Loreen was staring at her as if she was crazy while both Quig and Fan had just begun to fathom the steep troughs of this woman's sadness.

Mister Leo finally said: I think you're tired, my dear.

I just woke up, she replied. But you're right, Leo, I am tired. And so tiring, too, for your guests. Excuse me. I am going to bed.

And with that, she left.

Mister Leo did not appear in the least perturbed, asking Mala to serve dessert. While she did, he went over the usage of the special drilling equipment with Quig; it would be a two-day loan, but if it went a third because of difficult ground conditions, there would be a cost, as it was being taken off a big job up in Ontario. Quig said he wished to pay for the first two days as well but Mister Leo wouldn't hear of it, just wanting to set out the deal, though it was obviously not a matter of money to him. Rather he was the owner, he was the builder, and the price of his engagement in any agreement or sphere was the primacy of his executive privilege. Quig did not protest, and whether it was more to save the charges or his rapidly expanding dislike of this man whose life he saved was not clear. All we know is that he was still avoiding eye contact with Fan, who surely must have been making some calculations herself. She had come to value and maybe even adore her entrenchment in the dank but cozy Smokes but it was never a solution and now with circumstance conveying her here she had to determine whether to try this strange household or somehow split off again on her own.

And so in her forthright fashion, Fan said to Mister Leo: Do you know of someone in this village named Bo Liwei?

Who? Mister Leo said, between sips of his coffee.

Bo Liwei. He is now thirty-two years old. He is the second son of Bo Qianfan and Xi Shihong. He tested out of B-Mor Facility 2A twenty years ago. He is my brother.

Show me his picture.

Fan didn't have one; in fact, her household never had one, following the B-Mor practice of consigning everything about the promoted to the status of lore. In fact, there were no uploaded pictures of him, either, only that sharp etch of his name with the others on the big monument in the park.

He was accepted at Seneca?

Fan said, Seneca Hamlet.

Seneca Hamlet? I haven't heard that in a while. I think it was one of the villages that was dissolved, or maybe absorbed, at least fifteen years ago now. There used to be five or six very small villages in the vicinity of the lake but not all of them could make it work. They combined with us, we were the most established, and Seneca became Seneca as it is today. But a lot of those villagers went elsewhere.

So have you heard of him?

No, he said, with a surety that suggested he could not possibly know of such a person, despite his earlier comments. You've not heard of him, have you, Mala?

Mala said she hadn't and began somewhat hastily clearing the dessert dishes. She dropped one and it shattered and this time Fan helped her. Mala's thumb was bleeding quite badly and Fan said she should see to her wound. Mala excused herself and Quig and Loreen and even Mister Leo started helping Fan pick up the shards from the floor and then bring the rest of the dishware into the kitchen. By the time Mala returned, everything had been brought in and Loreen was washing and Quig drying, Fan loading the dishwasher. Mister Leo was trying to put away some of the glasses and bowls but in fact didn't know where they went. He handed the stemware to Mala and asked Fan if she would come with him for a moment.

As they walked to the other end of the house, he cupped her shoulder and then the back of her neck, and she tensed at the weight of his cool, strong grip. He was the same height as Quig but he seemed to loom much higher as he opened the door to his darkened office, only the dance of the numerous screensavers murkily lighting the room, which now looked like the waters of her awful dream. He touched a wall panel as they passed and the lighting turned on to a gentle level of brightness. He had her sit in his large leather chair while he retrieved some items from the credenza behind the desk; the first thing was a glass-encased set of small vials, the geno-chemo for Sewey.

I thought you could give this to Loreen, he said, kneeling so that he was at her height. She said you and her son were good friends.

Fan said they were.

Is he your boyfriend?

She shook her head.

It's not as though you'll never see these people again. Someday, if you still wanted, you might have the means. But you'll decide then.

Fan nodded.

And this is for you.

It was a pretty little box of red lacquered wood, its lid inlaid in faux pearl with the figure of a delicate, reposing crane.

Go ahead, open it.

She suddenly didn't want to, but he insisted. It was a silver locket on a silver chain. He had her open the locket and inside there was a diamond, small but dazzling and cut in a perfectly faceted oval.

It's a real one, he said. Antique, not manufactured as most all diamonds are these days. It's worth quite a sum. Probably more than you can imagine. It's all yours, Fan. But don't put it on now. Let this be our secret, yes? Why don't you wear it only at night, when you go to bed. All right? How nice that would be. Will you be a good, sweet girl and do that?

Our Fan, we can well imagine, could not sleep that night. After returning with Mister Leo from the office and giving the therapy to Loreen, she went right up to her room. The necklace was in her pocket and she dropped it on the night table, not wanting it touching her. The others had been wondering where she and Mister Leo had gone, but once she presented the vials Loreen was overjoyed, hugging her and Quig and even Mister Leo, despite his visibly stiffening at her embrace. Quig was squarely looking at her now but Fan wouldn't acknowledge him, afraid she might betray her dread. She must get away but not before Loreen and Quig were back at the

Smokes and Sewey's medicine was secured and after the well-drilling was done. She would have to endure for that long at least. But there was no lock on her bedroom door or on the door of her bathroom, and she wondered whether Mala would let her stay in her room after tomorrow, when Quig and Loreen departed. Although when she pictured the girls on Mala's viewer, a streak of panic flashed through her; was she imagining it, or had some of them been adorned with an inordinately fancy piece of jewelry, a stud earring or gold ring or pearl necklace? And through all these years, with all those girls, had Mala been a knowing bystander, or abettor, or worse?

She kept the bed lamps on and read from Penelope's handscreen. She was going to stay up all night, fighting it. Yet at some point in the scant moments before dawn she must have fallen dead asleep. For the lamps around her were turned off, the veil of the night drawn down over her. And we can barely recount what was about to happen next, for how awful it could have been, for when she gasped from the touch on the cap of her knee, and the horrid murmuring blandishments, she half cried out. There was the stricture of Mister Leo's hand. She did have time to deeply breathe. She was passing out. He was fully heavy on her and now she wished to be gone, but before anything else could happen, he was sliding away. And the voice she heard was not his but Miss Cathy's, telling her husband to get off the bed.

WHY, IN THE LIFE OF A COMMUNITY, DOES A CERTAIN HAP-
pening or person become the stuff of lore? You would probably say
great accomplishment is the reason, such as when one of our B-Mor
children triumphed in an event for the first time ever in the biannual
regional track meet (in the four-thousand-meter event), this against
a field of intensively coached, superprimed Charters. We will note
the historical significance of the achievement, basking in the reflected glory, for naturally we would like to think how it is emblem-
atic of the best qualities of our kind, even if we ourselves can hardly
summon the effort to jog half a block in pursuit of a candy wrapper
skittering away on a sudden gust of wind.

It's our common character on display, which is why we invest so
much of ourselves—often totally beyond reason—in particular figures and performers, both fictive and of flesh. And when that display
is unsettling or notorious, we can collectively wring our hands and
wail and then try to assuage the disquiet in our hearts by more coolly
interrogating its antecedents, the conditions and causes of its expression, and debate about how we might curb a future recurrence, none
of this cynically posed but subtly servicing the final hopeful notion
that This Is Not We.

Yet sometimes, as in the instance of our dear Fan, the talk lingers. Perhaps it's because we don't have much actual footage of her, unlike that of the long-distance runner, or even of Joseph niftily curling a shot into the goal. There's no more to see on our handscreens after that first surveillance vid of her exit, nothing at all, and so the secondary rumor and conjecture continues to root and grow. We reshape the story even when we believe we are simply repeating it. Our telling becomes an irrepressible vine whose hold becomes stronger than the originating stock and sometimes even topples it, replacing it altogether.

And while we shall resume our trailing of what happened to Fan et al. after Miss Cathy's intervention, we feel the need to return at least briefly to B-Mor, where rumors had spread about imminent cutbacks in the production facilities because of the oversupply of fish and now produce and then even some outlandish scenarios about the eventual shutdown and closure of B-Mor itself. For after the price of fish dropped precipitously, so, too, did the prices on our succulent vegetables, the markets of our neighborhoods for a time selling produce by the crate, the obvious explanation being that Charter suspicion of our products had widened, branding even those perfectly sheened and plump tomatoes that Reg and his coworkers would pick to be somehow perilous to their health.

As with what occurred with the falling price of fish, our first impulse was to buy as much as we could of normally very expensive Charter-bound fresh peas and cucumbers and sweet corn, most everyone freezing and salting and canning whatever their households couldn't consume, so much so that the price of pickling jars tripled and then quadrupled before the containers of new jars finally got trucked in. By that time, the supply of ripened, ready produce had more or less equilibrated, our facilities adjusting accordingly to the lowered Charter demand, and the unfortunate B-Mor fellow who remortgaged his clan's row house to bring in the jars was ruined, as the price suddenly dropped below what they used to cost.

In fact, we just heard of his body being discovered blocking one of the intakes of a pond in West B-Mor; he'd come up from the bottom, having drowned himself by tying dozens of jars filled with gravel to his wrists and ankles. Apparently the pond fish had pecked enough at his body to release him from the twine, and not just where he was anchored, which precluded any traditional viewing of the body at his funeral. There were whispers that his clan had done him in, in retribution for being saddled with a now enormous, multigenerational debt. There was also a spate of ironic, off-color comments on the boards and in the neighborhoods, about how the fish were developing their own taste for "B-Mor prime," for the truth of the matter is that there has been a noticeable rise in the number of people choosing to do away with themselves, and then selecting the park ponds for the site of their demise. Firearms are banned in B-Mor, and the only widely available lethal weapon is a kitchen knife, which is no easy instrument when contemplating suicide. Most people have neither CO-producing vehicles nor garages, there are few accessible, assuredly high-enough places from which to jump, pills are strictly regulated and meagerly dispensed, and so the waters beckon the hopeless and desperate (plus the fact that very few of us can swim). In the commentary there were jests about the tenderness of the cheeks of Jar Man versus those of Popped Rice Cake Lady (who rashly sold her successful kiosk and invested in opening a fancy health-smoothie shop), or the likely gamey flavor of another fellow who was known to spend whole mornings eating slices of blood sausage dipped in pepper salt while he wagered on New China cockfights streaming live on his handscreen.

We know of others who, perhaps shaken by the soured spirit of our community, have also chosen the nether path. There are no official directorate numbers—never would such things be published—but it seems that everybody has heard of someone from the block or the neighboring clan who has chosen to depart. Maybe they would have done so anyway, maybe their own demons were inevitably going to consume them, but we have to wonder why there have been so many in such a relatively brief period, and what this might suggest about the relationship between the public realm and private lives in our settlement.

Some have proposed that we need to do more in encouraging individual interests and pursuits, even if they don't appear terribly useful or practical, to bolster and deepen those inner reserves that "make" a person into who she is, and how, by extension, she identifies and values herself. Other, more conservative, voices balk at this, countering that we need, in fact, to strengthen the bonds of the commune, so that to end one's own life would be tantamount to a grievous assault on us all. Still others have begun to take a nihilistic approach, posting their skeptical thoughts and going on about the futility of doing much of anything in the face of what they clearly view as a pointless way of life. All these and other opinions smack of some truth, and if they ultimately fail to convince, it's probably because they can never quite acknowledge the other aspects and sides. But if we calm ourselves and open our eyes and step back far enough, we have to admit that our society, if not fundamentally unwell, has been profoundly wounded.

You need look no further than when you're at the underground mall, as a glance across the main food hall will confirm. For you can't help but notice the awful marks on some of the faces, the bruises and scratches and sometimes outright swellings and suppurations, most often on women and children and even on a few of the men.

Just the other day we saw a young woman working at a dumpling counter who, we are sure, could not see through one of her eyes, for how badly swollen it was. It looked like a mashed jelly doughnut. If she'd not had to work, no doubt she would have stayed in her house that day or the whole week, but there she was, in her smart pink and gray uniform and white gloves, and her otherwise wholesome, pretty face, and then there was this monstrous marring that made you want to cry and get furious at once, and somehow, even more monstrously, also direct your feelings at her. Why was she just standing there, why was she still folding the dainty pockets of filling and dusting them with flour as she set them aside, when what we really wanted to see her do was smash each one flat?

The odd thing, the funny thing, is that there has been very little chatter about any of this, when, of course, if there was the simplest outbreak of lice going around, there'd be a wild cry of concern from our citizenry, along with a round of alerts and recommendations from the authorities. And while the posts go on and on about the fluctuating food prices, or the latest schedule of mandatory furloughs for certain facility workers, or (as ever) how the evening programs are once again cycling repeats, will there be—disregarding some very crude adolescent jokes about people needing to use more makeup—a single serious voice on the matter? Will there be one honest, substantive remark about what is happening?

Which we find not just in the vicinity of the food hall, or way down the block, or in a slightly down-in-the-mouth section of West B-Mor, but perhaps close enough to be right here in our household.

For during the past month, have we not periodically seen some dark purple markings and blotches on the skinny arms of one of our elders, Cousin Gordon? Did he not come to breakfast with a fat lip a couple of weeks ago? Or gingerly drink from his mug of tea the other day with two crooked, swollen fingers? These days he doesn't say more than a few words at once, but back when he was still strong and spry, Gordon was a bit of a trickster, never too serious, a bright, talkative fellow who liked to tell tall stories to anyone who would listen but especially to us younger ones, though always purely for entertainment. We remember how he had pretty much convinced us that we were descended from Old China royals because of the rounded shape of our earlobes, or how the harbor waters of B-Mor were once as clean and fresh as our facility fish tanks and bristling with millions of sweet-fleshed blue crab.

The adults all seemed to like Gordon, too, and one never heard anything negative about his presence or contributions at work, and his wife and children seemed to adore him, though it has come to be that in our large and intimately integrated households the significance of who is whose has diminished over time, such that we're all a kind of cousin, even across generations, direct blood having no deeper feeling for one another than for the rest of us.

This is all to say that Gordon was pretty much like anyone else in the household, simply going about his days from the morning meal to the facility to lounging around with the rest during the evening programs, the rhythms kind and unsurprising. And even when he began to decline a couple of years ago—he was not extremely old, not yet sixty—nothing much changed in the way people treated him. Sure, he seemed to age very quickly, all his hair thinning out and going white and the flesh on his face and neck drawing off. And at first it was amusing how he began to mix up people's names and confuse opposites like stop and go, cold and hot, but he'd quickly correct himself and make a joke, and you could put it down to his being a bit tired after his shift. Or maybe it was somewhat enervating to have to walk with him around the underground mall, as his normal stride shortened and he began to take these mincing little steps, as if he were checking the firmness of the ground, clearly being afraid of losing his balance. Or when later on he would not speak until spoken to, and then when engaged, offer no more than a standard response or truncated phrase, it was a bit disheartening, and perhaps a few times his son or wife or one of us might mildly chide his silence and passivity, our frustration borne clearly from our simple wish for him to get back to his usual ways.

There were no brain scans or tests ordered for Gordon at the clinic, for in B-Mor aging is aging and there's nothing to be done about it, even when people are stricken well before their time. That's fine, we know the score. And we know, too, that because of the composition and character of our households those in need will be clothed and fed, washed and groomed, and generally upheld as deserving of our ministrations. Yes, times have changed and demonstrations of filial attention have no doubt diminished in frequency and quality, but it's still practiced, still genuinely unconditional, being ingrained into our basic strands. But after Charter demand for our goods suddenly dropped, and the entire community fell into a state of anxiety, we seemed to see less of Gordon around the household, and then when we did, we began to notice the first of those telltale signs.

We recall getting up to fetch a drink in the middle of the night and hearing the water running in the far hall bathroom. No matter how often we remind them, the younger children will often neglect to jiggle the flush handle and turn off the light, and when we went to fix it, we saw instead through the ajar door that Gordon was at the basin, the faucet running, pulling on one of his front teeth with his fingers. His expression was not one of distress or pain but instead a kind of dulled regard, his eyes staring at the fellow in the mirror as though his were a familiar but meaningless face, a random person he'd seen before at the park. There was an ugly color to his lip and some bloody spittle trickling down his fingers, and with an off-key grunt, he tugged and the tooth came free, root and all. We would have said something then, asked him if he was all right, but he saw he was being watched and shut the door.

At the morning meal he was there as usual beside his wife eating a cob of leftover corn and although it was glaring that one of his canines was missing and his lip was bulged, no one mentioned it. He worked slowly through the cob, if favoring one side of his mouth, and when everyone was done and idly chatting and picking at their gums with toothpicks, Gordon did the same but remained ensnared in the silence that was steadily webbing his mind.

About a week later, in the late afternoon, we found him in the backyard of the row house. He was sitting on his rear in the grass; apparently he'd fallen. He was lightly bucking himself forward, then waiting, then bucking again, as if that might somehow help him up, and the thought occurred that he had momentarily forgotten how to go about getting back on his feet. He wasn't in the least frantic or distressed. And for a few long seconds we let him keep trying, despite the fact that he would obviously not succeed, and not because we thought he would eventually figure out a better way. He was stuck in a rut of wrong thinking, or no thinking, whatever you wish to call it, and was never going to break out.

We lifted him up—he was as light as a child—and brushed the dirt off his cotton trousers, which hung loosely about his hips. With a stammer, he thanked us, patting us on the cheek like we were children, when we noticed that the back of his hand showed a pattern of perfectly round burns, as if a lit cigarette had been pressed against it. The wounds were smooth and reddish and just now beginning to heal.

What happened here, venerable cousin? we said, clutching his narrow wrist.

What? he mumbled, suddenly very confused. He thought we were asking about his having been on the ground.

We nodded to his hand.

He pulled it back. For a second his eyes flashed. And then they were distant, his mouth pinching up, his face flushed with bitter shame. He huffed and bit his lower lip, suppressing a cry. He didn't say anything else and he seemed stuck in place so we pointed him toward the house, watching as he shuffled inside in his poky, inching way.

Who could do this? Could it be his seemingly too-contented wife, or the son who was always too quiet, or another cousin, whom we saw coming up with Gordon from the basement the other day for no apparent reason? And for goodness sakes, why? Good Cousin Gordon had never been mean or cruel to any of us. He did not owe money. He had not crossed or let anyone down. By every measure, he was harmless, a complete innocent, a fellow who should rightly live out his waning days free of untoward attention or circumstance; and yet here he was, ill equipped to defend himself or even to understand what was going on, his mind likely growing ever more bewildered by the assaults, retracting into its muddied depths. And what disturbs one most is the idea that in a densely inhabited household, one in which he had resided nearly all his life with a sense of sanctuary and succor, he now felt utterly alone.

Perhaps the rest of us, too, are experiencing a similar feeling. Do we not pause the slightest bit as we pass one another in the hall or on the stairs, checking each other's eyes? Do we not scuttle a bit more quickly into our beds at night? Do we not brace ourselves and listen, when the house is silent, for the squelched bleat of an old man's cry? We wait and wait but somehow it never comes.

Then tomorrow, or some other day, in a moment that catches us by surprise, the poor fellow will limp down the front stoop in his shower slippers, his big toe gnarly and black from being smashed. And a startling thing happens, on having to see this kind of thing once again. We get a quickening in the gut, a vestigial node glows hot behind the eyes. And though we betray nothing, we're suddenly enraged, our fury hurtling and bounding but no longer for the person or persons responsible, or even for ourselves, but finally, at the pitiable fellow himself. We can understand better now: how when your hand on his neck means to comfort, when it hopes to assure, its grip only kind, can another impetus breathlessly arise, a strangely related volition that craves witness of the most wretched of sights, the just-crushed spirit.

WE ARE THE SINISTER AND THE VIRTUOUS AND MOST everything in between, and we know too well that in their visitations the fates appear to pay us scant attention. One might ask our good Cousin Gordon how he thinks of his current affairs. Or in a certain frame of mind, perhaps Quig would offer some thoughts on the wayward procession of his life. Or if we were put on the spot to take a philosophical stand, we might well decide to no longer demur and full-throatedly say, We do welcome our turn.

That it may never come only prepares us more.

And things can change. We don't fret so much, despite what is occurring. Instead of anxiety we have discovered, in the face of alarm, a burgeoning hope. Hope that if our livelihood dwindles we will learn to do something else. That we can remake another place. That we have one another and always will. And in certain rare moments, we think, we feel as free as Fan.

This may sound strange, given where we last left her, barely delivered from the most vile of clutches. But she was free, wasn't she, and maybe well before she left us? For we must now realize how even in the confines of the tanks, Fan had begun to understand the true measure of her world.

Of her control, however, there is a different story. That night in Mister Leo's house she was terrified, as anyone would be, and we shudder to consider not just what would have happened right then but on subsequent nights, and for a lengthy, miserable epoch. We would like to think that we or our loved ones or especially Fan would have somehow repelled the assault and immediately ended any further terror; but then certain cruelties have a way of engendering compliance, which only feeds the hideousness, the sequence cycling on. Poor Gordon knows this, as no doubt did the girls on Mala's viewer, and the reality is that Fan might have had to know it, too, for the rest of her days.

Instead it was Mister Leo who was trapped in a dark equation, slackly sitting in the sunroom most all of the day as Mala brought him food and drink and, when necessary, called over Tico, the new home nursing aide. Tico was there to lift him up from his wheelchair and onto the toilet basin, or to hold him up so that Mala could change his pajama bottoms. At supper Tico rolled him into the dining room, where Miss Cathy was already eating. She was still fragile but the incident sparked something in her now, a new savor or hunger piqued each time she looked across the table at her husband slumped before his bowl of blended food, waiting with a blank face for Mala to come and spoon it in. Sometimes Miss Cathy rose and helped him herself, took the spoon and gently nudged it in between his resistant lips, patiently waiting for his tongue to remind him what to do, her hand prickly with the memory of how she struck him, just once, at the base of his skull, with the head end of a stone statuette, the bulbous nude on display in the hall. It must have left no mark. After they followed the ambulance to the Charter health center and waited around, the doctor woefully informed her that Mister Leo had suffered a massive stroke, which they'd treated just in time to save his life. He woke up like this in the health center bed, wholly palsied and mute. He could no longer write or read or do his minerals trading, but of course, they had enough money to live several lifetimes, even Charter ones. Now, Miss Cathy missed him and also didn't. When he gagged on the spoon, she awoke from her uneasy reverie, but try as she might she didn't relieve him right away, keeping it there and maybe pushing it in just until he made a funny sound she never heard before he was stricken, this wan, alto squeak.

Fan would be a witness to these dispositions, but not Quig and Loreen; they left soon after coming back from taking Mister Leo to the hospital, Loreen anxious to bring Sewey his treatment. Quig and Loreen bid Fan good-bye, and she bid them well, and they drove off in the old car after a quick embrace. No one seemed to be much bothered by what had befallen Mister Leo, or even to wish to comment on it. Miss Cathy honored the deal her husband had with them, promising to send the drill, as well as giving Loreen a second, equally necessary set of vials her husband had been holding back (in case they'd balked at leaving Fan). She handed them a wad of money, too, for the purchase of another geno-chemo round, if they so needed.

But all this was in trade: she wanted Fan to stay. She wouldn't say why and Loreen said fine but Quig told them, with a finality that seemed to shock Loreen for what he was willing to give up, that it should be up to Fan. He hadn't said a word since the commotion on the other side of the wall roused him and drew him to Fan's bedroom, where Miss Cathy was standing over a seizure-gripped Mister Leo, whose fit was causing him to bite his tongue. It looked as if he was eating a slick piece of ham. Fan had pressed herself back against the headboard, wrapped up in the bedsheet. She had a superficial scratch on her cheek but otherwise she was unsullied. Mister Leo was bleeding all over himself and the carpeting, and the blood had begun to choke him, as he was lying on his back. Quig simply stared down at him, seething with weariness and disgust at the scene but perhaps as much at himself as for the foaming mess of a man at his feet. For was this not yet another instance of his wrong-pathed life? Was it not a variant of the same ill-made picture? He had not much countenanced this girl but it turned out from the first moment on the road she had somehow latched on. Or the other way around. But Miss Cathy was panicking and imploring him to do something. Quig finally turned him on his side, and when the man momentarily rested between fits, Quig stuffed the corner of a pillow between his teeth, if too forcefully jamming the material back between the molars. Mister Leo reflexively bit down and caught him, but rather than automatically try to escape, Quig let himself get gnashed for a long breath, the sharp pain from the man's teeth digging into his finger bones so searingly pure it was nearly self-erasing.

And what of our Fan? The more we follow the turns of her journey, the more we realize that she is not quite the champion we would normally sing; she is not the heroine who wields the great sword; she is not the bearer of wisdom and light; she does not head the growing column, leading a new march. She is one of the ranks, this perfectly ordinary, exquisitely tiny person in whom we will reside, via both living and dreaming.

We know, of course, that Fan decided to stay. There was no talk of how long, but after a week, it soon became apparent to Fan that Miss Cathy was not conceiving of an end.

In fact, it was quite pleasant at first, just as one might expect life to be if you were the only child of a Charter family. Miss Cathy decided that it would be best if Fan stayed at home to be schooled rather than take the huge leap into the hyperdriven Charter system, but instead of junky handscreens loaded with ancient storybooks to wade through, Fan was visited by private tutors in math and writing code and finance and design and everything else that was useful to know. Brought in as well were athletic coaches, who looked immediately crestfallen on seeing her size but were soon impressed by how strong she was, and swift, and nimble with her feet and hands. Though when a swimming coach arrived, she decided it was best not to show what she could do and Fan said she was afraid of the water. She was seven weeks on and didn't yet look pregnant, just perhaps like she was gaining some weight with the regular, wholesome Charter meals. She was certainly hungry, feeling this new volume steadily opening up below her, this canyon she could eternally fill. So she ate as she pleased. Miss Cathy was tickled at this, as if her perceptions of this deprived lone waif were being duly confirmed.

Each afternoon they went out to town, where they would have lunch at one of the many sushi bars or brick-oven pizza places, then visit the galleries and confectionaries and shops filled with trinkets for the home and garden, and then end up at Miss Cathy's regular salon and spa, where they took skin treatments and exotic massages of the feet and hands and face and neck. Miss Cathy was having her hair regularly colored again and had her stylist give Fan a cut in the current popular Charter style, a messier, slightly teased version of her bob. Although Fan didn't mind it, on certain nights she'd brush it out and straighten it, and Miss Cathy would bemoan the job the stylist did and have them go right back again. But perhaps Miss Cathy's favorite activity was to go to the children's clothing boutiques, where the thrilled salespeople would crowd around Fan and dress her in a dozen outfits or more, shoes included, little party dresses and pantsuits and loungewear just like Miss Cathy's and then take half of them home to model in front of Mister Leo in his wheelchair, his eyes straining with some dire message or emotion no one could begin to decipher.

When they returned home, Miss Cathy always rested and this was the time Fan spent with Mala, often helping her in the kitchen during the late afternoon while she ironed linens or polished silverware and prepared a small supper for Miss Cathy and Fan. It was Mister Leo who had wanted big, elaborate meals, and now that they also no longer entertained, Mala hardly needed to cook, usually just throwing together a salad and some buttered pasta and never any dessert, which is how Miss Cathy preferred it. Mister Leo would get a blending of mushy rice and some canned meat. Often enough Mala would make an extra, tasty dish like chicken adobo for herself and Tico to eat, which Fan always had as well, as it was by far the best food she made, and the three of them would eat while Miss Cathy watched her programs in her husband's office, different shows going on the multiple screens, with her muting whenever there were commercials. Tico was a huge young man who didn't talk much and always ate as though it were the last meal of his life, which in this case meant very, very slowly, the fork looking like a baby's utensil in his fat mitt of a hand as he placed the morsel in his mouth and closed his eyes and very gently nodded. Fan and Mala always finished in half the time and, while cleaning their dishes, would sometimes make each other giggle by mimicking him, which Tico didn't mind in the least, and which, in fact, made him giggle as well, the shelves of his wide, womanly breasts shaking in alternate time with his jowls. Once done, Tico would go give Mister Leo his nightly sponge bath and medicate him and lift him into the bed in a former mud/storage room adjacent to the garage that Miss Cathy had Mala set up for him with a screen, as it was the only spare space on the main floor that was wheelchair accessible and had a toilet room nearby. There were no windows but it did have a utility sink, which was handy for Tico for the sponge bathing and whenever the pathetic man soiled himself.

Meanwhile, as they dried and put away the clean dishes, Mala would ask Fan how each of her lessons went, or what Miss Cathy had gotten her that day, and Fan would describe everything in great detail whether it made any sense to Mala or not, and then invite her up to her room to see whatever fancy new blouse or dress or shoes they'd brought home. It was a pity that Mala's daughters were too big for any of it, as Fan didn't really care about the clothes, which had never been of interest to her back in B-Mor. It was simply stuff to wear to town, acquired in order to buy more outfits to tour town again the next day, and so on, and mostly, of course, for satisfying Miss Cathy's whims, the dormant blooms of which had seemingly burst open with the permanent diminution of her husband. Miss Cathy no longer seemed depressed; in fact, if anything, she had swung too hard to the other end, seeming now restless and overboosted and collecting all that buzzing for Fan, adoring her bedecked in the outfits and adorned with new jewelry (the silver locket had long been tossed into the compost heap of the garden) and sitting with her among the other ladies in the handsome eateries of the village.

Fan enjoyed these excursions enough and didn't want to displease Miss Cathy, but the secret reason she dressed up each afternoon without hesitation was the slim chance that she'd come upon Liwei, whom she hoped might appear in a shop or on the street and be immediately recognizable to her. She imagined he looked something like her, though perhaps with the steely expression of a brilliant student, but with each day he did not appear, her belief that he had remained in the new Seneca after the villages combined steadily eroded. Still, she asked if they could explore other sections of the village, even the service people's neighborhood, which Miss Cathy dutifully took her to like any good mother enriching the life experience of her naturally curious, bright child.

There were plenty of shops and eateries there, too, though they were clearly not as elegantly designed and appointed as in the sections Miss Cathy frequented, being more like the mall stores and restaurants of B-Mor, which you surely didn't patronize in order to lounge about, but simply because the prices and dishes were good. It was all very respectable, the idea being to offer these people a true sense of participation in Charter life, even as the sidewalks weren't quite as hygienically scrubbed, the window displays of merchandise not as thoroughly dusted and polished, maybe the spackling of the wallboard featured a rougher finish, the coats of trim paint not as numerously or thickly applied; and the same could be said of the "dorms," which was where Tico was born and raised and was living with his parents before being hired through an agency, these thirty-story-high brick-faced towers of modestly sized apartments with glassed-in balconies festooned with air-drying clothes, surrounded by grounds planted with sturdy shrubs and large sections of lawn but that lacked the ornament of artfully chosen annuals and topiaries and blooming fruit trees that graced the best avenues of Seneca. Indeed, by any measure it was a very decent place to live, a setting we B-Mors would be more than content with, though the lingering feeling was that here was a place that, once settled, was not easily decamped. Of course, you could say the very same about B-Mor, but with us, we know from the start this is the case, we understand it in our bones, and because we're mostly among brethren and share a storied past and can take a daily pride in our productive, orchestrated labors, we feel fortunate to remain, rooting in as deeply as we can.

But the truth of the dorms, as Tico would tell Fan after she first saw it, was that life happened behind the doors, the people rarely coming out and communing. Unlike us, they were from everywhere and were derived from all strains, universally diverse but perhaps too much so for their ideal collective good. And then there was the more significant matter of their work, as with Tico's and his parents' before him, which was mostly off- or long-shift service jobs, one-to-one or solo tasks such as home nursing or tutoring, waitressing or village security. Of course, the children got together in the neighborhood academies, but there were limited slots on the few sports teams and

choral or theater troupes, and most had to go back to the towers right
after the last bell anyway and look after their younger siblings, as
every able-bodied parent was working to cover the ever-rising costs of
rent, and food, and schooling. Though some moved up and out, most
dormies were stuck, as Tico's parents had been since they were young
people, never quite making enough to make an entrepreneurial stab
at opening a main-street business or to save for a down payment on
a real Charter condo.

Miss Cathy had never actually driven into a service
neighborhood—why would she?—and after a few moments parked
in one of the lots beside a tower, she put the car into reverse to
leave. But Fan spied an empty playground behind the building and
asked if they could try the seesaw and swings. Miss Cathy looked
repelled by the idea, but she agreed when she saw how much Fan
wanted to, deciding the poor girl had probably never seen a playground before. So they rode the creaky seesaw, Miss Cathy having to
sit toward the middle for balance, and then took turns on the swings,
with Miss Cathy in fact going first, as Fan insisted on pushing her.
Which she did, with all her strength, digging in and bursting forward
like a sled driver while timing her push on the woman's soft rump
and ducking beneath her to send her soaring. Miss Cathy gave a
whoop at the height, and when she began swinging her legs on her
own, Fan quickly ran into the lobby of the building, from where she
could see Miss Cathy happily propelling herself. She touched the
screen and scrolled down the names to see if she could find any Bo
and/or Liwei in the resident list. But there was nothing. A woman
and her son came out of the elevator and Fan asked her if she could
bring up a master listing of the residents of all the village's towers.
The woman asked why and Fan told her the reason and she said she
wasn't sure it was possible but would try, but then an urgent knocking on the glass window of the lobby stopped her. It was Miss Cathy.

Her face had gone pale, her expression one of acute hurt and bafflement, her jaw now threaded through with cords of rage.

I didn't know where you were! she shouted, making herself clearly heard through the glass. She entered the lobby and grabbed Fan's hand from the screen and said, Don't touch that, and dragged her to the car.

When they got home, they had to wash. They had done something like this before but now Miss Cathy knew exactly how she wanted it done, her brow tensing with expectation. Mala was ordered to get fresh towels and the bar of green laundry soap flecked with grit while Miss Cathy ran the water in the vegetable sink in the kitchen until it was hot. First she took Fan's hands in hers and moistened all four of them in the water. She then used a tile scrubber to brush the skin of their palms and backs of the hands, spreading out their fingers to get in between. She used a different brush to clean under their fingernails, just as a surgeon might, working between the fingers and again on the palms and up the forearms, right to the elbows. And when the soap arrived, she rubbed the bar all over the prepped, reddened skin, softer now and pliant, which harshly stung, though not as much as when she redeployed the first brush, working the soap into a lather before spraying it off with the steaming water. Only then did she let Mala blot their hands and forearms with the towels, and after Mala took them away to be laundered, Fan thought she could catch mixed up with the pine oil and lye the babylike scent of raw new flesh.

After that, though they never went back to the towers, when they returned from their afternoons out, they went through this ritual. Miss Cathy never mentioned venturing into the service neighborhood, or the fact that anything was at all different, and that they had visited only her customary shops and lunch places was of no consequence; for once the shopping bags were set down, they had to roll up their sleeves and run the hot tap, Miss Cathy retrieving the brushes from under the sink while Mala fetched the soap and towels. It was as if after that brief moment in the lobby a dormant circuit had been restored, an accidental rewiring that changed nothing apparent in the woman's revitalized mood or other routines but which set in motion this one, unerring operation. Fan complied without a word, scrubbing her skin as vigorously as Miss Cathy did her own, though the action seemed more to awaken the woman than punish her, her eyes never as lighted and alive. To Fan it was painful but the pain was made worse by the iron schedule of it, the thought of the hard scrape of the bristles to come, and once she set her mind to blocking the anticipation, the sensation itself could be endured. In fact, if she cast it right, she could believe that she was being honed instead of abraded, ever sharpened in her resolve to find Liwei, despite having no signs of him whatsoever and no other way to search for him. She was certain all she needed was time, and time—Mister Leo now comprehending this best—was plentiful in this house. Indeed, of the three of them, it was Mala who appeared to be most distressed, for she had to attend to their washing and simply stand by, wondering when Miss Cathy would reprise what she had done with every other girl before.

One evening after dinner, when Fan was sitting with Mala and Tico having a snack and tea, Miss Cathy appeared in the kitchen. She had appeared so before at night, always viewing her programs in the office. She was holding a remote, and when Mala saw this, she immediately apologized for removing the recharging deck from the office, as it was not working anymore. She said a new one would be delivered in the morning, but if Miss Cathy wanted, she could call and perhaps have it delivered tonight, but now Miss Cathy was completely unconcerned with this fact. Instead she was glaring at Fan sitting before the plate of *mochi* at the kitchen table as though she had committed a terrible crime.

Have you been here since we ate dinner?

Yes, Fan said. I often help clean up.

I thought you went to your room to study or watch. That's always where I find you.

Fan told her she did, usually right around now. At this point Tico excused himself to give Mister Leo his bath.

I thought you were in your room, Miss Cathy said, with a sharpness that officially ended the conversation. She dropped the remote on the island and left.

When Fan went up to her bedroom, Miss Cathy was already there, waiting for her. Usually Miss Cathy came in and sat down on the bed, and they briefly talked about what Fan was doing, either in her studies or the program she was watching, though never for very long. She was not terribly interested in the details Fan offered, as Mala always was; it was simply about their convening before each retired for the night, checking in, as a mother would, to make sure her child was comfortable and happy and ready for sleep. But of course, Miss Cathy would take the many extra steps of inspecting Fan's hands and nails and teeth and hair, the soles of her feet and toes, to make sure she was as clean as could be, though still rarely touching her. In fact, she almost never did, except for that first time they did their scrubbing, nor did she ever caress or embrace her.

But that night she did, gesturing Fan forward and hugging her; she even kissed Fan on the forehead, her lips dry and cool. She pressed Fan to her chest for what seemed a very long time. And then the woman took a step back and beheld her, with what to Fan could only be described as a great welling of satisfaction and pride.

We're finally getting to know each other, aren't we? Miss Cathy said.

Yes, answered Fan.

We want to be happy, don't we?

Fan nodded.

As happy as we can be?

Again she nodded.

And do you know, Fan, how we can make that happen?

No, Fan said, taking a step back now, from the wildness in the woman's eyes.

It's how it always happens. You're young, but I think you know. It's this way: We make our special place. Our very own little spot. Our little world. Where we'll live with one mind and heart. Do you understand me?

Fan said she did, though this time just with her eyes.

Oh, Fan, you've done so well here!

Miss Cathy leaped forward and embraced her tightly enough that Fan nearly became faint, her face jammed between the woman's plush breasts, which smelled of nervous dampness, a fast souring.

I'm so proud of you. Everything's changed since you've come!

Fan figured she was referring to Mister Leo, and that she had somehow spurred Miss Cathy to do something finally, though seeing the woman's heightened, almost disordered, expression, it wasn't clear this was what she meant at all.

Miss Cathy asked her if she wanted to take one of her "friends" with her, namely one of the many dolls and stuffed animals she bought for Fan on their sprees.

Where are we going? Fan asked.

To my place, Miss Cathy said. You've not been there yet but I know you'll like it. We have a special spot for you.

Fan shook her head but Miss Cathy did not notice, or did not want to, and simply cupped Fan's shoulder and walked her down the length of the house, to the far end, where she and Mister Leo had had their separate suites. There were double doors to each, and when Miss Cathy touched the knob, there was a click and they entered through the doors on the right, which automatically locked behind them. The suite was an immense multichambered room, the first part of which was furnished with a loveseat and armchairs and coffee table. Next was the bedroom, where Miss Cathy's king-sized bed was made up with fancy linens and abundant throws and shams. Beyond the bed was another entire section of the suite behind curtained glass French doors, which Fan assumed was where the dressing room and bathroom were. Miss Cathy led her around the bed. On the far side was a young child's mattress on a low steel platform, short enough in length that Fan's own feet might hang over its edge. It was made up very plainly, with just a white sheet and a thin gray-brown flannel blanket, which made it seem almost penal, particularly in contrast to the opulence and great size of the bed beside it.

Miss Cathy was almost teary-eyed, she was so pleased with the sight.

This is where you'll stay, she beamed. Right next to me. No one else but you for the next three days. It'll be so nice.

I prefer to stay in my own room, Fan told her. Or else downstairs with Mala.

That's no longer possible, Miss Cathy said. This is your place now. We'd like to keep you.

You and Mala?

Mala? Miss Cathy said, her voice gone totally cold. Mala has nothing to do with anything.

That's when a giggling could be heard coming from behind the curtained French doors. There was a tiny knock. Miss Cathy said,

Yes, dear, and the door opened. It was one of the girls from Mala's viewer, though a few years aged. She wore a simple white cotton nightshirt with an embroidered collar, rustic and old-fashioned. A second girl came out, wearing the same, though she was much taller and older. And then another followed, and another, until it was all seven of the girls Fan had seen in the album. Some were grown women, twice as broad as the youngest. But something was different about all of them, and not just that they had grown older. All of their eyes were huge and shaped in the same way, half-moons set on the straight side, like band shells but darkened, their pupils being brown. They were all giggling now, shoulders scrunched, their high pitch cutesy and saccharine. They crowded about Fan, bright of teeth. They smelled laundered and dryer-fresh. And now one of them was gently touching her face, others her hair, the rest clasping her arms, her hands, already vining themselves through her, snatching Fan up.

WHENEVER WE TELL THE STORY OF FAN, DETAILS ARE APT to change. You don't mean to alter anything; in fact, your intention is the very opposite, you want nothing more than to be an echo of the previous speaker, who, you decide, did a perfectly super job. And try as you might to match the very tone of the telling, the bellow of certain episodes and the half-breathed whisper of others, isn't it the truth that, despite your fealty to the story, a moment will arise that compels a freelancing, perhaps even rebellious, urge?

Of course, those moments will vary depending on who you are. Like everyone else, we have a sensitivity to particular incidents, which can strike a nerve. For example, when we hear about Miss Cathy's girls surrounding Fan, we're as startled as anyone else, the same hard knot instantly twisting in our chests as in yours; and yet we can't help but add a little of our own special imprint, a tiny re-marking here, a slight miscoloration there, and sometimes even more than that if the feeling is intense enough.

For what comes to us when we picture Fan's last circumstance is not solely worry or fright or repulsion but also a fascination with this unlikely gathering, which, we are quite sure now, did not alarm Fan as much as one might assume. And why not? The Girls were only nice to her. She was certainly in shock when they appeared and quickly conveyed her back into their room behind the curtain, helping her change out of her regular clothing into a nightshirt exactly matching theirs, even squeezing toothpaste onto a new toothbrush and placing it in her hand. They brushed her hair and washed her feet and lightly misted her with a fruity, candy-sweet perfume. She would sleep in the bed next to Miss Cathy's bed for several nights before moving in with them, after which they would resume their nightly schedule of taking a turn to sleep in the bed outside.

Apparently Miss Cathy could not sleep if sleeping alone in her room, and when she didn't rest well enough, the following day was often very difficult because of the pall of her mood, which perhaps prompted the Girls to bring Fan right back out to Miss Cathy, who was already in her own bed, eyeshade on. Fan realized how chilly it was in the room—the AC constantly pushed icy air down from the vents—and she turned off the lamp and slipped beneath the tightly tucked sheet and blanket of the tiny bed. She found she had to lie on her side and bring up her knees a little to keep her feet from over-hanging the edge, which she would have done anyway to keep from shivering, as the cotton nightshirt was thin and the sheeting was starchy and cold. Miss Cathy had a fluffy duvet covering her and Fan wondered if she was supposed to freeze and thus be compelled to climb up into the big bed. In fact, for nearly all of the night the woman did not stir, which Fan knew because she could not fall asleep herself, given the frigid temperature and the high beam of her own vigilance. What perverse episode lay ahead for her now? How might she have to defend herself? And how would she ever manage to escape, which she needed to do soon? She was at last thinking about Mala as she finally did relent and lose consciousness, wondering if the woman had been wholly false in her kindness and feeling, acting out yet another round of temporary friendship that would reside as a set of glimmers in her bedside viewer, to be accessed when it appealed.

Miss Cathy did, however, wake Fan up in the night. A light tug on her shoulder roused her and she instinctively curled up at the sight of the woman above; the bedroom was faintly lit by moonlight and the expression on Miss Cathy's face was of a ghoul, lifeless but hungering, her eyes half lidded, her mouth slackly ajar. But all the woman did was nudge Fan off, and the moment she cleared the bed and stood up, Miss Cathy took her place. The woman even expropriated Fan's meager blanket and wrapped herself in it as she curled into a tight ball, which was the only way she could fit, this sonorous mound of a whorl. Fan did not quite know what to do. After a while, she climbed up into the huge, high bed and got under the heavy duvet, which was still warm and dampish from Miss Cathy, the downy pillow laced with the powdery, floral scent of her facial cream; and she must have fallen asleep within a minute, for the next time she stirred it was morning and Miss Cathy was gone from the little bed and the Girls were enveloping her with their excited warbles and trills and their many petting hands, conveying her straight back into their lair.

They sat with her on a circular sofa in the middle of the very large, airy room and introduced themselves by number, One through Seven. Fan could keep them straight for it was the order of both their coming to the house and their ages, One being the eldest and so on down the line, although their identically altered eyes made it harder at first. Fan had heard of girls and boys doing this long, long ago to make themselves look like their favorite anime characters but had never seen it done. Apparently early on One and Two had asked Miss Cathy if they could have their eyes done and then each successive girl wanted it as well soon after her arrival. Their bizarrely large eyes made them look deeply attentive, like some puppy or doe who craves only your company and succor. But there was also a welling of wistfulness in those big brown discs, as if they were all quietly longing for someone or something, that they would always be searching.

As for their names, they'd had their original ones before, but once there were three of them, it seemed best to shrug off the markers of the near and distant past, and start anew, this world of a room peopled only by themselves and, of course, anchored by Miss Cathy, who rarely came inside but always received one of them nightly. And what happened with Fan, said Five, was exactly how it went each night, Miss Cathy arising at some point to switch places, something about the temperature and smell of a girl's just-vacated bed helping Miss Cathy to go back to sleep after she awoke from her nightly bad dream.

The Girls didn't seem to know what had happened to Mister Leo, and Fan did not say anything, perhaps concerned that such news would be too disruptive, or simply because of her characteristic reticence. What is clear is that she joined their grouping without resistance, the only worry being that they would assume she'd want to have her own eyes done, too. But none mentioned it. They seemed simply pleased to have a new addition, a brand-new sister, and Fan let herself be appended on their line when they asked if she would be their most propitious number Eight.

Of course, there was an eighth bed already made up for her, the last along the wall. All the beds were made up exactly like the one next to Miss Cathy's, with a white sheet and thin flannel blanket, and they were the same shrunken size. At the foot of each was a small white plastic set of drawers on black plastic wheels, just enough storage for perhaps underclothes and socks, some toiletries, maybe a few pieces of jewelry, and an extra nightshirt. It could have been like a barracks but the huge square room was bright and fresh smelling, despite having no windows or even a skylight. This now explained the massing above the garages, which was covered in ivy and looked like the broad tower of a granary and which Fan had assumed housed a personal gymnasium or some such thing. The space was well lighted by numerous can fixtures set in the double-height vaulted ceiling, as well as by the lamps on the night tables beside each bed. The carpeting was wall-to-wall and white, though more like the white of an animal, vaguely richer in tone, and in fact, Fan would learn that it was made of many sheep hides all stitched together, practically a small herd. She'd never seen a live sheep, so she didn't know that they could look like this. The carpet was wonderfully plush on the feet, which was good, as they only went barefoot. The four expansive walls were white, too, except that approximately one and a half of the panels had been painted from ceiling to floor.

It was this Fan kept glancing at, for there was something strange about it, and the Girls tittered with glee as they vied to show it to her. It was their work, Three said—she was broad shouldered and had sparkling teeth and was obviously the most strident of them—and this was how they spent most of their waking hours. From the center of the room you couldn't make out any particular images or shapes; in fact, the walls appeared to Fan as a murk of brown-blue, with random crosshatchings and blotches of brighter tones, which seemed the oddest and slowest way to paint a wall, if it truly took up most of their day. There were several stepladders at the edge of the painted section and Fan drifted toward those, but Three insisted that she should start at the "beginning," at one of the corners near the curtained French doors.

The nature of their work became apparent as Fan drew closer. It was miraculous, in a way. We have mentioned the "guerrilla" images of Fan and Reg that have popped up on the walls of B-Mor in the last couple of months, billboard-sized portraits of the pair that are mostly simple and crudely executed, and then another kind you see more and more of late, abstracted or surreal images of such things as a pair of weeping lovers' hands, or the widened maw of a pond carp, or a floral burst that in a certain light looks like an immense suppurating sore, all of which, we have begun to feel, are now an expected feature of a B-Mor stroll. They are eventually whitewashed or papered over, and if the individual expressions won't permanently linger in our minds, the ready regeneration of them does, this irrepressible urge.

But an urge was trebled in the handiwork of the Girls. The work covered every square centimeter of the nearly four-meter-high wall. It was not paint that they used but colored magic markers, of which Miss Cathy had provided thousands, in every possible hue and a half-dozen widths, and that filled three rolling towers organized by gradations in the spectrum. Fan had to get up fairly close to make out what was depicted, which was basically the story of their lives, separately and together. The mural was begun when there were two of them, and so naturally the initial images, drawn in the style of anime, showed One and Two in their much younger days, the very first scene being a pair of nightshirted girls crouched down in the corner of a room with markers in hand, dabbing at the wall, the skin of the bottoms of their feet crinkled as they knelt, the picture they were working on being the very picture of their kneeling selves but in the appropriate minuscule dimension. The size of this and the rest of the scenes was small, no wider than the span between a young girl's shoulders, and half as high, though in comparison with the great panels of wall, it was tiny, a mere footprint in a field, as if they understood before they started that this would be their enduring task.

How they did it was this: One and Two (and now Six as well) would sketch out in faint pencil specific moments from their lives, for example, how they were separated from or lost their original families, how they came to Seneca to work in this house, how with each new arrival, the girl who worked with Mala was then sent up to Miss

Cathy's suite to live with the rest, the scenes rendered from bottom to top in a narrow column and then shifting to run down before they went up again and so on. The scenes were not separated by borders or other framing but rather magically melded into one another, via all sides, a detail of background or figuration of one threading into the fabric of the next so that the whole appeared to be roiling in a continuous, visceral flow.

The quality of rendering was impressive, as polished as in any of the anime movies regularly playing in the B-Mor mall, the figures and objects and backgrounds not simply in the right proportion and perspective but rich of presence and sentiment. The scenes with Mister Leo were moodier, of course, but no less finely executed. The noteworthy detail about his panels was that he never appeared whole but rather as an insinuation or part; in one scene, for example, of one of the girls ironing napkins in the kitchen, a line of wine goblets on the shelf behind her kept watch, their bellies twinkling with his eyes. Or another, showing Three vacuuming the seat of a stuffed chair whose arms looked just like his, right down to the stout pink fingers. Or just Mister Leo's mouth, five-o'clock-shadowed, saying HERE through his heavy, almost womanly lips. And the few that showed his face were in the motif of a group portrait, their number growing with each arrival, nightshirted and barefoot and so skillfully captured you could distinguish them from one another simply by their posture, except that each girl possessed not her own face but Mister Leo's impassive, once handsome visage, now repeated in a line.

They had her pose for the newest version. The latest columns were still marked out in pencil, and while the others, laddered high and low, colored in the scenes behind her, Six sketched Fan into their group. The girl, perhaps seventeen or eighteen, wore thick spectacles and had a faint shading of dark hair on her upper lip, but there was no concealing how pretty she was, her especially dark, glistening eyes and high, sharp cheeks, and how talented she was, her hand moving over the blank white space with speed and assurance, like a tiny champion skater, the other girls almost instantly appearing in their present sizes and shapes. Fan, after being appraised by a brief but locked-in glance, swiftly came into being with the exact splayed angle of her feet and her petite hands and the curt bob of her hair. For the moment Six left their faces blank, working instead on the background, the detail as ornate and filigreed as the sheeting of the Girls' nightshirts was plain, and as it came to life, Fan could see that it was an underwater garden, wildly overgrown, of entwined sea plants and fabulous creatures such as tusked fish and many-headed eels and fat man-o'-wars whose insides contained miniature worlds of the same, though the sheer density of the images made the scene appear more like a design than a place.

After a while, Fan asked Six why she had decided on this to draw.

I'm not sure, Six said, her tone unlike the others', not nearly as high-pitched or girly. I looked at you and just thought of the sea.

Have you ever seen it?

Only on programs, she said. Have you?

No.

The others had, of course, been listening and began to pipe in about how they had been or not been to the sea, whether they liked to swim or were afraid of the water, or what kind of fish they would be if they had to live as fish, all of them instantly agreeing they would be manta rays, winging their way through the water in a silent squadron. Six assented but didn't say anything, continuing her drawing while the others went on about what they had discussed earlier or the day before, all while coloring, which Fan had now joined them in. She was handed just one marker, and whenever her color was needed, she filled in a space or the hatch of a shading, the chatter around her echoing in the large room like in the aviary of the one zoo in B-Mor, which had no large creatures but lots of birds and reptiles, the sound oddly both distant and cacophonous, so that Fan later realized how her ears ached with the ringing.

And she realized that they had not left this room since their respective arrivals in this suite, not even once, the glow of their skin just that of an eggshell, but on its inside, a limpid, silken white. It was why Mala would sometimes receive an extra order of foodstuffs from the delivery van and put it away herself in one of the pantries of the house kitchen. The groceries were sent up to the Girls via a dumb-waiter that opened up into their small but functional galley kitchen near the bathroom, where they prepared their own simple meals. The bathroom was outfitted with two basins and two toilets and two shower stalls, plus a closet with a washer and dryer, though all that needed to be laundered were the bed linens and towels and night-shirts. For exercise they practiced a special mix of tai chi and yoga that Miss Cathy had read about in a magazine and instituted into their day, though they all suffered to varying degrees from sore joints and fragile bones and periodic bouts of an intense dragging weari-ness that Fan would later learn were all caused by lack of sunlight. In fact, they were definitely stooped in their posture, slope-shouldered and none very tall, which made them look even more like blood sisters than they already did. Fan herself felt fine, maybe extra-fine because of the pregnancy, her joints seemingly more flexible as she led the exercises. Her skin was certainly more supple, her hair more luminous, her chest seeming to have become fuller, though in a way only she could notice and feel. And she was beginning to yearn for the water again, to stretch her arms, motor forth with her powerful kick, but not in the confines of a tank.

Fan would have expected that one or two of the Girls would have long rebelled at spending a life in a room, would have begged, say, the dentist, to help them steal away, but the funny thing about this existence is that once firmly settled we occupy it with less guard than we know. We watch ourselves routinely brushing our teeth, or coloring the wall, or blowing off the burn from a steaming yarn of soup noodles, and for every moment there is a companion moment that elides onto it, a secret span that deepens the original's stamp. We feel ever obliged by everyday charges and tasks. They conscript us more and more. We find world enough in a frame. Until at last we take our places at the wheel, or wall, or line, having somewhere forgotten that we can look up.

At first Fan went right along with the rub of the days. A week passed, then two. The Girls had been especially pleased that she asked Miss Cathy if she could move to their room a full day early, spending only two nights out in the main bedroom. She responded to being called Eight right away, but the truth was that each Girl had already begun calling her Fan. Three and Four always seemed to be sitting next to her at meals. Seven followed her around. Six loved the shape of her eyes, saying they were like the daintiest pea pods, and even drew a special panel of them alone, floating above a field of waving girls' hands. And aside from her own wall coloring, with which she was very careful and slow, knowing herself not to be naturally skilled, Fan helped out as much as she could with the few chores they allowed her, such as the sweeping and dusting, and then in assisting Four, who led the daily period of exercise.

Fan was strong and limber, practically in world-class condition compared with their chronically achy and weak array, instantly able to do what they considered to be the most difficult poses, and soon enough Four asked Fan if she would lead the session. Fan got them to try simpler, if more strenuous, exercises like push-ups and sit-ups and deep knee bends, and although it was tough at first (especially for the older ones) and a couple of them even half fainted, they grew accustomed to the burn in their arms and thighs, and to the dew of sweat dampening their brows and the cloth between their shoulder blades, and soon they were counting out the increasing number of reps they could do in an urging, tweeting chorus. They grew stronger for certain but the greatest change was in their level of energy, they seemed to be quicker in rising from bed, or stepping in and out of the shower, or even while taking their meals with their newly piqued appetites, when the play of their chopsticks over the platters seemed more vigorous and pitched.

Soon work on the mural was moving faster, too, Six having to draw several new scenes a day instead of just one, the girls behind her more focused and engaged, sometimes even nudging one another because of their tighter assembly. In fact, there was a genuine flare-up between Four and Five, who bickered about whose shade of blue marker was most like the color of the blank screens of Mister Leo's office, this for a scene portraying Fan's first solo encounter with him. This was the way of the mural; it reflected whatever was happening at the moment, and by reading it from the beginning, Fan could trace the looping arcs of their time and how each girl had come but also whatever was of interest or concern, becoming a more intricate map of their consciousness as it was emended and evolved.

For example, the scenes before Three appeared were generally straightforward and even childlike in their depiction of their lives before they came to the house and then after they began working with Mala, the renderings of chores and games and girlish pastimes shown simply and often sentimentally, happy girls ironing or painting their nails or brushing each other's hair. Mister Leo was not yet shown as an ominous presence, but once Three appeared on the wall, those "parts" of him showed up, too; the broader mood of the renderings seemed to shift as well, the emotions of the Girls becoming more patent, raw, the backgrounds sharpened by bolder colors and menacing geometrical shapes, and then new images of long-suffering Miss

Cathy as their beacon, their savior, respectively delivering them from the prison of Mister Leo's downstairs world.

Indeed, they didn't seem to blame Miss Cathy for standing by while her husband took a turn with each of them, and though at first this bothered Fan, she soon understood why: to them Miss Cathy was their wounded and vulnerable big sister, if one distant, stuck in an ugly misery herself, and from some of the mural scenes, it was evident she had been compromised, too, in her youth, by a gaunt-faced man in a business suit, who may have been her father or stepfather. He showed up here and there along the wall, stiffly eating at the dinner table, a murky silhouette in a nighttime doorway.

The primary problem, of course, was that they were locked in. Only Miss Cathy (and Mala), by a mere touch of her fingertips, specifically right index and thumb, could unlock the suite doors. And now her schedule had changed; after awaking in late morning and going through her ablutions, she went downstairs in her housedress and then didn't return until evening. With Mister Leo incapacitated, you would think that her days would fully extend, open up to catch the best air and light, but the funny thing about a life is how eventually it will adhere to certain routines of mind, those tracks or grooves laid down in special pressure and heat.

She had already lost interest in shopping with Fan, and lunching out, and getting together with her few acquaintances, realizing now that what was most important was that her husband have her company. It was no matter if that company was gentle or sharp, if she spoon-fed him or let Tico do the job, if she shaved his chin with utter care while humming the melody of a favorite song or if she badly nicked him, if she alerted Tico that he had to empty his bowels or simply stood by as his face contorted with the strain while he was slumped in his wheelchair, letting him brew in the stink. She felt the compulsion to be there, to let him always see her face. But she was growing nervous again, too, tight and jumpy for stretches and then rooting for a period beneath an almost discernible cloud, through which you could tell she needed him, too, for no matter how homely or grotesque the bond was unassailable, having been once pure.

The other matter was indeed how fully the others took to Fan, this Lucky One the latest but also the Last, the role of which instantly elevated her along with the quality we all can't help but recognize and admire: that effortless anchoring of being, that nascent stillness that typically occurs only in nature. They tended to gather around her, slyly jockeying about the marker tower so they could take the one that would have them coloring right beside her, or be at hand with the ladle to add more broth to her bowl. Though they did not change the position of her bed, they took turns sleeping in the bed of Seven (who was the youngest and quite liked moving about each night) to whisper numerous queries about her life and views, and re-count their more curious dreams and then gently rouse her in the morning with an especially wide-eyed smile and their customary greeting, a sweetly harmonized croon: "New-day, new-day." And then one day someone noticed that the group portrait of the eight of them featured not Mister Leo's face but each of their own. When they asked Six why this was so, she simply told them she was tired of drawing his face. But of course, they all knew that Fan was the dif-ference.

Another sort of person might have thoughtlessly disrupted their corpus, but Fan was careful not to bestow or withhold any special attention. In part, she accomplished this by regularly moving about the room, breaking from the mural work to take a cup of tea or use the toilet, and then linger alongside whoever was busy in the kitchen or bathroom before returning to the wall. There was no stratagem to this, no intention of gaining favor or influence or trying to engineer her own escape by employing them as cover or diversion. Indeed, Fan was growing fearful for what she might leave behind in these hardly grown-up girls, who seemed too fragile as individuals to endure any change or trauma like a sundering of their group. They had been practically orphans to begin with, toss-offs from the counties who were damaged by Mister Leo and then quartered in a literally hobbling protective custody.

Yet it was not simply the limits of the room but also their own order that had formed them, the expressions of which Fan could see played out on the wall. For there was now nothing that *could* happen to them, no new experiences whatsoever save their routine, and aside from the more plain, commemorative images that appeared whenever a new girl entered their realm, the scenes portrayed in certain detail the fantastical alternative lives of each: picture tales of the broods of children One and Two bore (and even those they sadly had to bury, a pair from a sleeping sickness and one, of all things, by a fall from a tree), or of the dazzling acting career of Four, who starred in an imagined long-running program about women cattle ranchers in Argentina, or the unsung missions of Three, who brought much needed basic dentistry to counties children by opening a string of spotlessly clean free clinics. And if the trajectories of these seven interlacing mangas were variously modest, heroic, unlikely, they were also thoroughly voluble and peculiar and dense enough in their particulars that after hours of study Fan herself began to feel that it all must have transpired. And she supposed that in a manner it had, and with enough vigor that their yearnings were sated.

Naturally, they began pushing for Fan to reveal what "happens" to her. Six was excited to begin drawing it out, the coloring of Fan's arrival and attendant documentation already completed. They kept clamoring: *We want to know where you go!* Finally, Fan said she had some ideas but that they were not yet fully formed. This was half true; the distant future indeed was blank, but Fan's sighting of the near was as concrete as anyone's, we B-Mors and now others know this well, she was as clear-eyed as the fortune-card readers in our malls purport to be. A self-visualizer, as they say, one who engenders the path on which she'll tread by dint of her pure focus, her unwavering belief. And so she would have had to describe how she led them out of this room, out of this house, perhaps even through the secured gates of the village altogether; but of course she did not. Who could know how they might react? Who could anticipate the shape of their fascination, its hot gleam or trembling?

She didn't want to incite anything like a rebellion. She figured any direct push against Miss Cathy would be futile, given their utter acclimation to their lot and devotion to her. Miss Cathy was not their antagonist. There was no antagonist per se, not even Mister Leo, who for them was the most distant star in the most distant galaxy, undying yet irradiant. She had still not revealed that he was a bare fraction of his former self, again afraid of the psychic consequences. Instead, she began to tell them about Reg, of her love for him—hiding her true age, at least from them, seemed no longer necessary—and that he had disappeared, and how she was still, in fact, on her journey to find him.

The information unsettled them, with One almost unable to comprehend the idea that he was not a story boy; she kept asking what happened to him next. Fan responded by asking Six to sketch him out.

You mean right now? Six said.

Only if you want to.

Sure! Six said. She got right to work, starting with a panel of Fan on the road with a ghostly beanpole of a boy floating out on the horizon. The Girls were instantly enamored of his cheery face, his puffy, imperfect Afro.

He's as cute as a play doll! one of the girls cried.

He is a play doll, but tall!

He looks so kind and sweet!

He *is* kind and sweet, Fan said, with enough pause in her voice that the Girls magnetically clustered about her, their warm breath slightly tangy from the dried fruits they constantly snacked on.

Tell us more!

Fan did, saying how Reg did not enjoy being alone, and how he would hold her hand through an entire evening program, whether it was scary or not. How he never hesitated to walk right through the middle of a puddle.

He's perfect! Two said, to which One responded by saying she thought him perfect, too.

What have you learned of his whereabouts? Three asked. Anything?

She shook her head.

No! Nothing?

She shook her head again, causing a pall to shade the Girls' faces. And with one voice they groaned, keyed in purest sorrow.

Please don't worry, sisters, Fan said. I will find him.

But how?

Fan said: Bo Liwei.

Who?

She told them more, and they were doubly astounded. A brother? And one who lived in this Charter or one nearby? Three said that if he was a true Charter he might be powerful or have powerful friends, and so could at least learn something of Reg.

It's what I must hope, Fan said.

Right away Six quickly drew the scenes of Fan approaching Liwei, his face like hers but squarer-jawed, leaner, heartbreak in his eyes. How agonizing! How wistful and ironic! It was almost unbearable to see, even in the faint pencil, Six able to render the moments with so much saturated longing that Fan herself felt something like a shallows in her chest. It was then that the Girls realized what they must do: help Fan. And to help her, they agreed, meant that she must leave them. Four and Five wanted her to be away for just a short while, but then return. One and Two unhelpfully suggested she wait a few months, as they had gotten into their heads that it was already winter. Seven, with surprising astuteness, asked if Fan still had a pair of her own outdoor shoes. Six was mum as usual, already back at the wall, doodling. Finally, Three made a decree: Fan must depart as soon as possible, as there was no more time to waste.

THE FUNNY THING ABOUT THE TALE OF FAN IS THAT MUCH of what happened to her happened to her. She showed plenty of her own volition, really more than any of us could ever dream up, and yet at the same time her tale demonstrates how those who met her often took it upon themselves to help her, without really any hesitation. Without always a ready self-interest. Every once in a while there are figures who draw such attention, even when they aren't especially charismatic, or visionary, or subtly, cleverly aggressive in insinuating an agenda into the larger imagination. For some reason, we want to see them succeed. We want them to flourish, even if that flourishing is something we'll never personally witness. They draw our energies so steadily and thoroughly that only toward the finish of events can we recognize the extent of our exertions, and how those exertions in sum might have taken the form of a movement.

We have noted the sundry demonstrations such as the chattering commentary on the web boards, snide and earnest and critical, if rarely outraged; the strange acting out at the ponds as well as other, more disquieting, expressions, as seen in the plight of sorry Cousin Gordon; or the most recent sign, which is that a notable number of people are shaving their heads, men and women alike, some old and even a few children.

That's right. Bald heads are popping up here and there at the mall and in the facilities and maybe even at your own morning meal, when daylight enters at such an angle that the reflection off the clean-shorn pate momentarily casts upon the usually dimmed, cheerless room an illumination that seems generated from within, this lustrous fire. You pause at every sighting, that paleness bobbing across the street, or leaned over the rail of the catwalk above the grow beds, and if you're close enough, you can't help but take an extra-long look at the particular scalp and try to read the sheen and textures of that most vulnerable-looking skin, for a clue to why this person has done this to himself. Do they have something in common? Are they nubbier than normal or creased in a similar but distinctive way? Do they appear just that bit transparent so that you're almost believing you can see the workings of their recusant thoughts? And does it seem that the faces of these people are more unyielding than what the rest of us offer to one another, which is not exactly warmth but rather what you expect in the wordless company of an old friend or cousin, that easy nonchalance?

But something is different; they might be sharing a snack with a companion or browsing a rack of dresses and yet what comes through is a hardness, a blocking, this clear sense that they can no longer share. They are suddenly apart from us, as well as from one another, for there appears to be no secret society bonding them. They are lone agents in a nonexistent organization. They are playing a solo. Perhaps because of this, they appear all the more anchored, all the more unitary. But do not automatically think they have become "individualistic" or, in fact, aim to be. It's not that. Of course, someday soon they'll grow their hair again, and we'll have forgotten that it was ever gone. And, in time, so will they.

For now we wait and wonder. We wonder when it will be that we slip away one ordinary evening when everyone else is busy with their programs or games, and find ourselves before the bathroom mirror, turning this way and that, regarding everything and nothing with our minds strangely blank, and work the powered razor or blade. The first pass is horrid, as you would expect, though not for how awful it looks, but for how it feels, the sensation of an animal slowly prying itself from its shell. You shrink with the exposure, the chill of the air. You're not ready for this. But as you clean up the rest, make it even and smooth, you begin to understand. You understand that the time has come for you to go downstairs in the morning and sit in your customary spot by the far corner of the table and eat without any self-fanfare, and just as you had earlier, let everyone take in the alteration, let yourself become one more notation. For at some point each of us will be asked to embody what we feel and know.

Is this what the Girls realized when they deemed that Fan must be allowed to go on her destined way? As with everything, they decided this together, although it was surely catalyzed by Six. One morning Six rose many hours before the rest of them and by the mere glow of the nightlights drew and fully colored the picture that she said was "crowding" her mind. Some of them gasped on seeing it, if simply for how large it was; the scene was nearly three times the width and length of the abutting images, the great stamp of it jutting out into the rest of the wall's blankness like a continent suddenly born from the depths. The run of the panels was forever altered. But immediately they agreed it was her most beautiful work. Its scale had allowed her a freer hand, and although you could not make out any pencil lines, one could almost imagine Six's movements, the wider arcs and glides of her arm, with the enlarged fields of the figures and shapes not uniformly markered (for that would have looked blotted and primitive) but rather painstakingly flecked with numerous proximal shades of a color, for richness and depth of hue. The scene itself was an underwater realm bristling not with creatures or fish but with a dense forest of marine plants, wispy tendriled corals and bushy anemones and in the center of the panel, broad ribbons of electric aqua-green seaweed flowing wildly upward, seven of the thick shoots transforming into seven faceless girls, with Fan, of normal body, being pushed by their number to the surface and reaching for another pair of hands, which at this point were only loosely sketched.

I wanted to wait for you before finishing Reg's, Six said to Fan. I wanted to get them right.

Once Fan described them, Six did get them right, all the way down to Reg's spindly wrists, and the stubby nails of his long fingers, and the tender-fleshed pads at the base of his thumbs, so much so that Fan could almost feel a lifting to go along with the pangs. She was thankful that Six hadn't rendered the rest of him, the sensitive, gifted girl perhaps understanding that it would be too much for Fan if he loomed there fully on the wall. Indeed, Fan had left her album card with his images back at the Smokes (it had died anyway, with no way to recharge it), though in truth she had probably done so to deny herself too easy a means of viewing him, which would only amplify her longing, something she had plenty of from the beginning. And too intense a longing, everyone knows, can lead to poor decisions, rash actions, hopes that become outsized and in turn deform reality.

First, they made a formal request of Miss Cathy. This was much more complicated than it might seem, for they had never done such a thing before. Aside from leaving a brief weekly listing of foodstuffs on her night table, and a monthly one for basic toiletries and some nail supplies, they'd never asked her directly for anything, everything else such as paper goods and cleaning supplies being sent up in the dumbwaiter (presumably by Mala). They took their turn out in the little bed and really there was nothing else to ask of Miss Cathy, who was "keeping" them, as this uncommon but growing Charter practice was called. The Girls were lodged in the same way beloved pets were once kept by their owners, who, of course, did not query them as to what they might desire. And while the Girls professed undying devotion to Miss Cathy, none of them relished the idea of having to ask her for so drastic a thing as Fan's release, which might as well have been like petitioning the Sun not to set this day.

Still, it was decided that Three should do it, as she was the most outspoken of them, and because it was her turn to sleep out in Miss Cathy's suite anyway. But when she slipped back inside their room the next morning, she was as upset and shaken as any of them had ever seen her, telling them how instantly cross Miss Cathy had become, and then deeply hurt by the idea that the Girls were even considering that she had anything but their best welfare in mind. Fan was a part of them now forever. In fact, Miss Cathy decided that no one would stay out with her for an entire week, effectively barring all of them. This caused an immediate panic in the group, for she had never done such a thing before, and poor old Two, who was perhaps the most fragile of them, became so anxious that she had to be given nighttime ibuprofen dissolved in some ginger tea to stop her obsessive throat-clearing, which is how her nervousness expressed itself. Miss Cathy had, of course, taken off a week or two when she and Mister Leo went on a rare vacation, but she had never been home without having one of them sleep out.

While they were all comforting Two as she sipped her tea on the circular sofa, Fan told them that they should not concern themselves with her plight and that she would somehow find a way to reunite with Reg. They protested, bemoaning her lot, though finally assented with kindly murmurs and exhortations, hugging her in turn. Of course, their aim of liberating Fan was not in the least diminished. And after years of intimate domiciling, a shared glance among them was enough to cement the understanding that only they would constitute the solution.

The first attempt was mostly exploratory. Six and Seven, perhaps wanting to be daring, intentionally ate some moldy Korean rice cakes they had unearthed in the back of the pantry closet, in the hopes that they'd become ill enough for Miss Cathy to call the medical center for help. An ambulance had come a couple of years before, when Three suffered an attack of appendicitis, with the EMTs waiting outside Miss Cathy's suite; the doors were briefly unlocked for them then, several girls carrying Three to the gurney in the corridor. But now Six and Seven only got ill enough from the *dduk* to throw up and suffer a half day's bout of diarrhea, after which they felt fine. Miss Cathy could not even be alerted.

The second try was more serious. Four and Five, who most often prepared the meals, were making a cold bean salad for a lunch. But when Four opened one of the cans of kidney beans—it was slightly bulged on the bottom, so that it wobbled as she clipped the can opener onto it—a horrific, apocalyptic smell filled the small kitchen. They had to turn on the hood fan, though it did little good; the smell was practically vicious, similar to the awful odor last summer when an animal died in the venting for their room, but ten times as potent, sickly sharp and alive. We can imagine them holding their noses, and looking at each other to see if one of them might be willing to eat it. But it was far too foul. Finally, Four was about to zip up the can in a plastic baggie to throw out when Five suggested that they make a spicy curry out of it for themselves. They got to work, adding a good can of beans to the fry, trebling the dry spices and chilis, until the dish became in fact somewhat edible, being at least intense and fiery.

Indeed Five kept saying how they ought to make it this way always, even ladling a second helping on her slice of bread.

The two waited. But nothing happened. Nothing happened during the afternoon or when they were cleaning up the dishes or while they played their nightly game of hearts. They'd served everyone else instant ramen. After the cards, everyone got ready for bed, each taking a turn at the toilet and then the basins to floss and brush her teeth and wash and lotion her face and hands and brush each other's hair. It went exactly as it did every night, an orderly march through the stations. Nothing went wrong through the night.

Instead, the trouble began the next morning, when Five suddenly lost her balance and had to prop herself on the counter of the vanity. She kept insisting she was fine, she just felt light-headed, taking a drink from the faucet with her cupped palm, when Four leaned over the very same basin and retched so forcefully that the spew splashed up and flecked the mirror. They told the rest what they'd done. Five had to lie down, but Four felt better and the rest of them decided they would get on with the day and their work at the wall. But within an hour both girls had to get up and run to the bathroom to vomit, each looking heavy-lidded and talking in a funny way, like they had a little square of cloth stuck on their tongues. Five was unable to keep her eyes open, even though she wasn't sleepy at all. Her shoulders felt stiff and tingly. She was very thirsty but had no fever. And while she seemed sound of mind, she said she was seeing two of everything. Or maybe three.

Two of the girls went to the suite door and urgently knocked for Miss Cathy. When the door finally opened, it was not Miss Cathy but Mala, which surprised and pleased them, as they saw her only every other month, when she was allowed to come up and visit for a while. At the moment Miss Cathy was out in the garden with Mister Leo, and the frantic raps on the door had compelled Mala to open up, despite how angry Miss Cathy would surely be were she to find out. Mala asked what was happening and they told her, saying Four and Five needed a doctor.

When she came inside, she gave Fan and the others a quick embrace. Then she examined the stricken ones, checking them, Fan thought, with the same care she would her very own daughters. She tested each girl's forehead with her lips, took a sniff of their breath, then gently pinched their arms to see how dehydrated they were. Four clung to her, moaning her name pitiably as if from underwater; Five was too weak to do anything. Mala gently assured them that they would be all right. To the rest of them, however, Mala did not say anything afterward, simply telling them to wait. It was not quite an hour later that she returned. This time it was with a man, a lean, fit, tall young doctor from the medical center.

The fellow—stitched into the breast pocket of his scrubs was V. UPENDRA, M.D.—seemed put out at first for having to make this outcall, and then by who the patients turned out to be, his chin stiffening at the strangeness of the large, open bunk room. But once he began examining Five, who could now hardly raise her chest to inhale, he camped beside her on both knees, his eyes narrowing as he took her pulse and temperature and listened to her heart. He asked what exactly they'd ingested and when. He processed the information with full attention and gravity. Then he asked Mala to have the owner of the house come up right away, and she went down to fetch Miss Cathy.

While they waited, he looked about the room, Fan getting some water for the sickened girls. The five other girls—two of whom were older than he was—had retreated to one arc of the circular sofa, bunching together. They had not encountered any outsiders since Three's appendicitis, and perhaps no one else for years before that, and so they were thoroughly unsettled by the presence of this man, who was unshaven and looking like he was at the end of a double shift in his wrinkled scrubs, though still certainly handsome. In fact, they could hardly look at him, keeping their gazes lowered, all except for Six, who snuck long looks at him.

Fan couldn't help but think he was similar to Reg, at least in frame, bony-shouldered and bony-elbowed, though, of course, he had commanded the room when he had first come in, merely by the ease and authority of his posture, something Reg—or most any other B-Mor—couldn't do if he tried. Or perhaps it was simply a Charter thing.

What's that? he asked Fan. He was looking at the wall.

Fan told him it was what the others were doing, not sure now how else to describe it.

Not you?

Fan said she was only helping a little. He walked to the wall and surveyed it, instinctively beginning at the corner and following its progression around to the second wall. The Girls nervously tittered as he viewed it, for they suddenly realized that a stranger was perusing their innermost thoughts and dreams. Two covered her face entirely and then all the others did the same. The young doctor was not paying any attention to them, however, despite the fact that he could have easily matched a scene to a girl. He was clearly fascinated by the wall, its many shapes and colors, and when he reached the panels in which Fan first appeared, he seemed to pause, checking back for her in the previous images. He stood for a while before the largest scene of her being pushed upward.

What's your name? he asked Fan, and she told him.

You're not one of them, are you?

Our Fan offered neither expression nor word.

I figured, he said, regarding her intently. Did she feel a thrum in her chest when confronted so? Was it his light brown skin? His blue eyes, almost like Reg's, as deep as a sparkling island sky? His lips full but defined, the head of densely dark wavy hair? Yet there was something about him, not at all superficial, that spoke to her of Reg. Perhaps it was a core of sanguine innocence beneath all the Charter self-assurance, a node of vulnerability that had not been trained away, dissolved.

You don't move like the others, he said, glancing over at the Girls. They were peeking now at him again. They go around like they're following something. Little heeding steps. You're not a Charter, though. That's obvious. But then you're no counties person, either. You're from a facility, aren't you? Which one?

But before she could answer, or not answer, Mala and Miss Cathy appeared. The Girls instantly rose and schooled about Miss Cathy, and for some reason they began to cry, shaken perhaps by the sudden and unprecedented fullness of the gathering. Miss Cathy, who didn't appear put out or perturbed at all, spanned them with her arms, her manner that of an all-loving school headmistress, patting each girl on the head to try to calm her. Once done, she broke from their ranks and in her willowy dressing gown fluttered to the beds of Four and Five, practically ignoring the young doctor until the moment she spoke to him.

So why can't you help my girls? she said.

They can't be treated here, he replied, clearly annoyed by her tone. But this didn't deter him from explaining the situation to her fully; their lack of fever was a clue, and that while only lab tests at the medical center could confirm it, he suspected it was botulism, which was something that occurred rarely, and then only out in the counties. They were breathing poorly as well, and if it was indeed botulism, they might eventually require a ventilator.

A ventilator? Miss Cathy said.

Yes, the doctor told her. They could lose the ability to breathe. They could die.

Miss Cathy nodded. Then she asked him to arrange to have ventilators delivered, and have the testing done here, as she didn't want the Girls to be separated. But he said that was not possible.

Then please ask your superior.

I'm the superior, he told her. Apparently he was the ER chief, and had only come because the outcalls resident had suddenly taken ill. It was a simple choice; she could have them transported, or they would remain here.

Miss Cathy said, It's my decision, yes?

Assuming you're their keeper.

I'm their keeper, she answered.

We know, of course, that Miss Cathy deemed the two would remain in place, to which the rest of the girls, shaken as they'd never been before with real confusion and fright, could only assent. It was happier for all of them, especially Miss Cathy, to believe that the sickness would pass. Even Four and Five tried to agree, waving from their beds. It had been most difficult, Miss Cathy now recalled for them, when Three developed an infection from the burst appendix and had to stay at the medical center for a week. With one of them missing, they couldn't sleep. They couldn't eat. Even the wall work went badly. Nothing was right.

Mala asked Miss Cathy to reconsider, but the woman literally blocked her ears, no doubt startled to hear such questioning from her helper. It may have been the very first such instance. Mala pleaded some more and Miss Cathy finally shouted, Enough! Mala shrank. Miss Cathy now mentioned to the Girls that she had been planning to bathe and wondered if they wished to be with her afterward, to do their hair and nails. They cooed in happy panic; it was a rare treat to be invited for a beauty session in her suite. Before leaving, they all kissed the sickened girls, Miss Cathy telling Fan to stay and watch over them and call the doctor if necessary.

Upendra, who had been gathering his things, reiterated that it would only be an ambulance returning to transport them to the medical center, as there was nothing more here for any doctor to do. Miss Cathy didn't respond, though her tight huddling with the Girls reminded one and all that they were in one another's care, just as they always had been, just as they always would be. They disappeared into her suite. Mala had to go downstairs, so she would let Upendra out. But before he left the Girls' room, the young doctor took Fan aside, handling her by the elbow, kindly but with grip enough that she could distinctly feel each pad of his fingers pressing on the joint and bone.

You don't have to stay here if you aren't hers to keep. You know that, right?

She nodded.

He waited for her say something, perhaps to ask him for help, but she remained silent.

Okay, then, he said, seemingly unsettled by the moment. He was going to say something else but then he simply left. The Girls' room door was locked shut. Fan must have known, if anyone would, that she wasn't Miss Cathy's to "keep." She wasn't anyone's to keep, perhaps not even Reg's, which is in part why we admired her so. Yet there are times when one must simply endure, as was the case now, with Fan alone watching the two sick dear girls, their color already going to slate.

THERE IS AN OLD B-MOR SAYING THAT ONE HEARS A LOT
these days. Or so it would seem. It came over with the originals,
surely, and like many of their sayings, notions, traditions, it has remained in currency. It goes like this:

Behold a fire from the opposite shore.

For the originals, it was advice to be taken literally, for back
where they came from there were indeed real fires raging (whether by
accident or design or negligence), plus constant plumes of lethal
smoke from the primitive industrial processes, not to mention the
attendant spews of fouled waters, and countless megakilos of buried
waste products that eventually poisoned the entire subdistrict. You
had best stay back, suggested the sage. Or flee.

Proverbially, of course, it means to indicate that one can rightly
look after one's own, that you are not obligated to address the plight
of others. This may strike us as inconsistent with what we think of
as the primary ethos of our community, namely, that it is a community, right down to our slippers, in which we shall labor and prosper
together, or else tread at our lonely peril.

Sayings are employed for a purpose, reflecting what we want of
them and the larger world, as well as the very time of that wanting.

Everyone knows a truth can be a falsehood (or vice versa) depending on the context. So, too, with the recent frequency of this "fire." Are we afraid of what seems to be happening, and so are justifying a retreat into ourselves? Or is it being spread by people secretly working for the directorate, for the same reason? Either way, we have begun to feel the rends in our finely spun society with each outbreak of vandalism and impromptu public protest and then the rash of the newest graffiti, spray- or hand-painted with what must be a widely distributed stencil.

FREE REG

No matter if we agree. And we do agree, as does everyone else we know. Is even the directorate in opposition? But it's the fact that the sentiment is being duplicated, in most every hue, with both the faint smudge of haste and the meticulous intricacy of design, which unnerves. It's gone wide. One example that we saw the other day clearly looked as if a small child was barely able to hold up the stencil before messily overspraying it, the part outline of his or her stout little hand floating faintly above the drippy letters. It was practically heartbreaking—and disturbing—to think of that innocent young person wholly caught up in this broad surge of feeling.

But it is a genuine surge, and like all surges that rise up and tide and maybe threaten the bulwarks, it will eventually recede. What it shows of us when it does is difficult to say. We are not accustomed to thinking too far ahead, no doubt because of our longtime security and prosperity. We are engaged in the regular business of our living, as always passing the hours mostly hived in our households, though these days, despite the cooler weather, you see more and more of us outside, just as we would be on especially hot summer nights.

Though now, instead of the children playing their games of tag and hide-and-seek, and the adults arrayed on the stoops fanning themselves and drinking iced tea and smoking, we are milling about on the sidewalk or in the street. The children are actually aware of us, awaiting our next move. Most everyone is standing. Maybe there's a food hawker, maybe there's a reader of palms or cards, but even these are behaving with politeness and reserve, just as though they had set up outside a row house holding a viewing, to serve any craving mourners. They're acting this way because we are murmuring to one another, and not of garish happenings on the evening programs, or of the unusually pronounced bitterness of the bitter melons at market. We are sharing a different kind of report: of ongoing shift reductions at the facilities; of ever-increasing class sizes at the schools; of a spate of postponed overseas retiree tours, with no further word of rescheduling. And along with these and other observations and gripes, which have all been made before (if privately), what's arising are the exhortations people are giving to one another to bring about change. And whether or not that change is possible does not seem paramount, at least not yet. It's the very practice of our talk that warms enough, how we face each other and speak.

Maybe Reg could hear us, too, wherever he was. Maybe he peered out the window of a building or vehicle and caught sight of some of the tags, repeated in their sundry, modest fashion, and felt the buoy of our call. Such that he thought about us as we had been compelled by events to think about him, as our being just one, as beset with joy and pain as any single person. Maybe that inspired him to keep on, to endure.

And in the unknowably connected way of things, this somehow bolstered, too, our dauntless Fan. For within an hour of when we left her last, she realized that poor Five could now no longer make a sound and in fact was barely sustaining herself with her breaths; the rises of her chest stalled halfway and then could not get shallow

enough. Four appeared to be approaching the same condition. Fan
had already banged on the door to Miss Cathy's suite but there was
no answer. She even swung a night table at it to smash the panes but
they were thumb-thick unbreakable plastic and the flimsy piece of
furniture instantly broke apart at its leg joint. In the small kitchen
she searched for something she could use as a lever but all the knives
were short, thin-bladed parers. She was wielding one anyway and
ready to try when the half-opened hatch of the dumbwaiter caught
her eye. No, even our Fan was too big to fit inside. But she had an
instant vision: she tore up a cereal box and piled the pieces in a soup
bowl, nesting some toilet paper on top for good measure. She found
matches—the Girls loved scented candles—and when the flames
leaped up, she sent it down, knowing that when it reached bottom it
would sound a bell in the main kitchen. She pressed her ear to the
metal door and heard the faint ping.

But nothing. Just smoke, sharper now, and noxious enough that
she had to lean back.

Then a shouting from the other end of the well: Mala frantically
calling for Tico. Was the woman on fire? Fan hollered down the well.
But less than a minute later the door of the room opened and it was
Mala, wholly fine. Once she saw the girls, however, her expression
grew stern, now resolved in what she needed to do. She asked Fan to
prepare a bag of things for the girls; she herself would go downstairs
and call for an ambulance. She wasn't going to ask Miss Cathy's permission.

This is your chance, too, little one, she said. Pack a bag as well.
This is not the place for you. I'm so sorry. So sorry for everything.

Fan said, You don't need to apologize to me.

Yes, I do! Mala held her by the shoulders. You most of all! I could
see you were different, but what did I do?

It doesn't matter anymore.

Yes, you're right, Mala said. You should just go, right away. Take any bus heading out the gate! Here's my fare card. There's enough on it to take you quite far. So go as far as you can!

Fan could easily see this was her best chance, too. It was a matter of simply walking out, though of course there were awful possibilities that she would be leaving behind. And yet there was not a mote of her that could have abandoned these girls now. If she didn't love them as Mala did, or even Miss Cathy, whose feeling for them, if unnaturally skewed, was arguably the most intense of all, Fan at least loved them as if they were of her household, these dear cousins whom she ought to always nurture and safeguard.

I can't leave yet, Fan said.

No one would blame you! Not even the Girls!

That's exactly why I can't, Fan said. Mala clasped her cheek and then ambled away, though not before propping the Girls' door ajar with the broken night table leg, and Miss Cathy's suite door with a chair—in case, Mala said, Fan changed her mind.

Of which there was very little possibility now, as Fan made her way to Miss Cathy's immense, many-chambered bathroom. She did not know what she would do or say to the woman, holding out zero hope of convincing her of anything. But she must have been caught up by a fury, for we can see how there was a new propulsion to Fan's step, not a speeding up but rather a feeling that she could pass right through a solid if she wanted, that she would not be halted. And that's one of the funny things about Fan, as we think about her now, which is that when it mattered most she was an essentially *physical* being, rather than some ornate bundle of notions, wishes, dreams. Perhaps that other sort is more often seen to be heroic these days but we B-Mors—and maybe now you, too—respond more deeply than the rest to someone's determined gaze, or the way they move across a room, or simply stand there, as Fan did that day at young Joseph's wake, with such solidity that you might think the world and every-thing in it was, for a flash, turning around them.

Though naturally not everyone can appreciate this. Miss Cathy, for instance, was surely thinking of the impudence of our Fan as she appeared in the doorway of the bathroom, rather than of her re-markable presence.

What are you doing here? Miss Cathy said, no doubt startled by the fact that Fan had somehow gotten out of the other room. The Girls were attending to one another with various implements and tonics and polishes, with Miss Cathy herself, hair turbaned in a towel, in the midst of curling Seven's hair. It could have been a scene from one of the ancient oil paintings in Mister Leo's gallery, an array of fleshy, radiant maidens in an opulent marbled bath, though of course in this tableau the maidens were petite and angular and variously aged and orbiting about this much larger, paler, older fig-ure, this cold sun of a woman who seemed to pull every mote of warmth and color from the stone-tiled room.

I want to join, too, Fan said. May I?

Miss Cathy hardly seemed to have heard her words, gazing ab-sently at the brush in her hand and then rolling the brush under to give the girl's hair an inward lilt. But she said, Come in then. The others lightly murmured. They were beaming kind smiles but they were clearly uncertain as to why Fan would now leave their sis-ters, who were stricken in the other room. They must be doing bet-ter, was what they silently concurred with one another, though none of them dared ask her for confirmation.

Had they been different souls, Fan might have tried to rally them with some sign, had them ring their keeper and bind her up with the belts of their terry robes, ensuring that whatever Mala could arrange would go unimpeded. Perhaps someday they would thus act, but for now Fan could see that there was no chance for such an uprising. And so she did what she must have thought was best, which was to sit herself down among them and select a bottle of polish from one of the baskets and ask Two if she liked the color she'd chosen, a milky, opalescent silver, to which Two nodded, giddily flapping her extended feet.

Fan remained patient, despite the fact that with each breath of her own she surely felt the straining of Five's chest in the other room. Yet what was she intending? What was she waiting for? If her aim was to ensure that Four and Five could be transported back to the medical center, she might have tried somehow to trap Miss Cathy inside, maybe dammed the bathroom threshold with the massive bed or stuffed armchairs while the others spirited them away. But no, she did this instead, placing herself into the heart of the group, the strong solvents sweetening the air enough to lodge them all in a heady register.

After Fan painted Two's toes, Two naturally wanted to paint Fan's. But to everyone's surprise, Miss Cathy said she would do it, handing the hairbrush to Two. She would often brush hair and sometimes paint fingernails, but it was very rare that she would do one of the girls' toes. In fact, it had been many years since she had. Yet now Miss Cathy had Fan soak her feet in a small tub of hot foamed water. Then she filed away the softened skin of her soles, afterward buffing the toes and the spaces in between with a soft brush and wiping the nails and cuticles clean with rubbing alcohol. She dabbed each one with a cotton puff like they were tender little wildflowers. All the while Fan was surely wondering why Mala had not yet returned with help; yet there was little else for her to do. Another sort of heroine might have summoned the darkest parts of herself, resolving, by either bestial fury or righteous mantle, to wield the scissors sparkling right there in the open drawer of the vanity, or else raise her wooden footstool high above this woman's bent head, and transgress all.

Of course, she did not. We have to view Fan as recognizing, at that moment, not just Miss Cathy's mania but how much the Girls meant to the woman. This might seem exactly wrong, given how apparently willing she was to leave poor Four and Five to the full run of their fates. For it was ultimately not a particular girl or girls who were most important but their totality, the way they could web her and cocoon her and settle her down each night and day so that there was no untoward pinch or ache or wrinkle, the temperature of their corpus always regulating and kind. It was all about her, yes, it was solely her storm or fine clime they were subject to, and in this regard the greatest potential disturbance was not their complement being diminished but the specter of sudden change. What the woman needed now was to put a scrim up against the sky.

And soon enough, the feeling was right; it seemed Fan had found the necessary position. They all chattered back and forth about how they would color a panel of their wall with this activity, about what they might eat. Seven kept talking about craving *oden*, Miss Cathy finally asking what that was. It was as if nothing were awry, which was obviously what Miss Cathy and by extension the Girls wanted most, especially in this uncertain moment, and surely in every other moment, too, the primary dream of keeping being the dream of consolation, of feeling at last solved and right, for kept and keeper both. And doesn't that dream, in truth, endure for the rest of us, too? Perhaps in this regard we B-Mors—and perhaps your people, too—are merely the Girls writ large, our leagues, clustered for best use and sanctuary, at last achieving a modest state of grace that for too long has been our lone, secret pride.

After Miss Cathy had painted the last of Fan's toes, she rose and sat before the basins and the mirrored wall in the swiveling salon-style chair, one of the girls automatically ready to brush her hair. The rest of the girls as well as Fan gathered about her, and the picture of them grouped thus was something one might imagine in a catalog for the strangest kind of institution, this most bizarre and intramural of schools. But their number did seem off. Something flashed then in Miss Cathy's face, as though she had just finally reached an ancient mountaintop ruin that she had half feared was a fantasy, the shadows breaking over its tumbled ramparts, darkening all. She now asked the girls to go check on Four and Five, which was cause for gleeful sighs all around, everyone immediately curtailing whatever she was doing and stowing the mani-pedi paraphernalia. It was as if the whole time they had been awaiting such word, whereas Fan was just beginning to think how mistaken her strategy had been, that she should have taken harder, more extreme measures right from the start. But as they made their way back out, Miss Cathy asked Fan to stay. She had Fan sit in the salon chair, standing behind her and regarding her as a stylist might, even weighing the ends of her hair in her palms. She took up a brush and worked it through the straight, thick tresses. The tines sometimes grazed Fan's neck and she tensed for the strokes to become harder, harsher, but they stayed steady and full, the sound like heavy threshing.

Finally Miss Cathy said: When I was a girl, my mother brushed my hair every night. Yours must have, too.

Fan shook her head; sometimes she and a cousin might sit up with each other, but more for play than in some familial bonding.

But it's wonderful to brush hair like yours, Miss Cathy said to the mirror. My mother would have admired it. She would have said yours was a pony's mane, sturdy but still tender and lustrous. She would complain that my hair was too fine and broke and tangled too easily, which is why I had to go to her each night before bed. I think she

CHANG-RAE LEE

hoped to train it to grow thicker and straighter, but naturally it never did.

Fan said it must have been a good feeling, to have such a ritual.

Miss Cathy smiled weakly. She unfurled the towel from her head, her hair damply clumped in fraying ropes. Fan moved to hop down from the chair but Miss Cathy placed her hand on both of her shoulders, bending so that their faces were side by side.

I know you can't see it, so you don't have to agree, the woman said, her eyes wide and focused. But I see a lot of me in you. Not me now. You're so fresh and alive, and I have nothing more of those things. But when I was younger, even younger than you, you would be surprised by the girl I was. I used to walk to the edge of the village and wait for the gatehouse guard to take a bite of his lunch and then slip out between the bars. I was that skinny! And you know what I did?

Fan shook her head.

I would run.

Fan said, Where to.

Away! Miss Cathy cried, her face, in fact, suddenly alive. I would just run, at first as fast as I could so the guard wouldn't see me, but when the road started getting rough, I would slow down and try to stay out of sight. I'd keep going the whole day. Sometimes I saw cars and people but then I hid. It's amazing that I didn't get hurt or lost.

Fan asked if her parents got frightened or angry.

They never knew, Miss Cathy said. My father only came home after supper, and my mother was busy all day with her projects in the garden and with her friends. Our helper was terrified for me, but I made her promise not to tell.

You must have traveled far.

I don't know exactly. You should tell me. How far can a little girl really go? Miss Cathy paused at this notion. One time I was caught

248

in a thunderstorm and I wasn't sure anymore where I was. I had to hope the sun would break through so the rainbow from the village's sky screen might reappear, which it must have. Otherwise I might not be here now. I'd be someplace else.

Fan, no doubt sensing the woman's yearning, said: Where do you think?

Not a Charter, probably. Though I'm not sure I would have lasted out in the counties.

I think you would have, Fan replied, saying it as if surely believing it.

Miss Cathy seemed to gleam with this notion. She then said: Sometimes I wish I could see myself like I was then, but from above. Out there.

But you can, Fan told her. You can see it.

How?

You can see whatever you want.

And it was then that Fan did a funny thing. Without asking, she clasped Miss Cathy's hands, which were still resting on her shoulders. Miss Cathy instinctively pulled back—she might touch you, but it was never the other way around—but Fan held them firmly, Miss Cathy looking alarmed in the mirror. And before the woman could say or do anything else, Fan closed her eyes. She asked Miss Cathy to do the same. She could feel her pulling, but Fan could be very strong physically when she needed to be. Miss Cathy shouted for her to let go. But she wouldn't. Then Miss Cathy was thrashing against her, their hands locked together while they boxed at Fan's ears, her temple, her jaw. The blows, dense and mean, fell heavily on her, and though she wanted to cry out or groan, she kept as still as she could, as if she were not made of flesh but the oldest stone. And just at the moment that it seemed Fan might yield, when tears began to wet her cheeks, when she felt her clutch finally giving way, the woman relented. She could hear Miss Cathy breathing miserably behind her. And it was then Fan described the scene she wanted Miss Cathy to picture: a counties landscape, mottled sage with dense growth, and run through by gravelly roads, and pocked with the rusted shanty-tops of cottages with the smoke from cooking fires spiraling forth, and there, in the shadows of the underbrush, a wispy, pale-shouldered child with fine strawberry-hay hair stepping sprightly through the thickets, almost dancing, skipping free.

When Fan peered again in the mirror, Miss Cathy's eyes were still shut, though barely, her face slightly uptilted, as if she were taking in a rare gentle spring sun. She might have stayed that way, and Fan no doubt would have let her, had a commotion outside the bathroom not dispelled the reverie. When they stepped out, the Girls' door was flung open, as were the double doors of Miss Cathy's suite. Had all fled?

But inside the room everyone was assembled, the large space suddenly feeling much smaller for all the new and different people; it was not just the other girls who were there but also Mala, and then Tico, who stood alongside a pair of EMTs almost as hulking as he; and to Fan's particular surprise, and what must have been a small burst of happiness in her, there was also young Dr. Upendra, too. He had come back. He had not abandoned them. He caught her eye but just as instantly went back to Five. She was in distress. No one was making a sound, not even Miss Cathy, because it was clear there was not enough time to take her back to the medical center. And as we regard the moment and all and sundry gathered, we suppose that they must have figured the doctor would certainly save her, that this whole situation, if deeply fraught and shocking, was one in which a state of normalcy would prevail, or would at least be reverted to. That however stunted and peculiar these girls' lives were, their days would inexorably string along, if only adding up to a thickening in the torso and the flowing colors of their intricate mural work that no one but they and a few others would ever see.

Five stirred in her bed, her feet finally moving, if in shivers. Then she hiccuped, or spasmed, pivoting onto her side, pushing out a sound that her dear sisters would later hear as something like *I can* or *My Fan*. Spent, she rolled onto her back. Tears trickled down her tensed-up cheeks. She was smiling widely and the tears seemed to be only those of joy. But Miss Cathy gasped, hands over her mouth. Upendra dropped onto his knees and listened to her chest. Then he used an air bag, next his own mouth, as well as compressions on her chest. Her pupils stretched wide, space black, the whole of her looking as if every drop of her blood were turning to plainest paint.

THERE IS ALWAYS SOMETHING ENTRANCING ABOUT AN image on a wall. Perhaps it's because it's frameless, threatening to break wider, maybe free. From the youngest to the oldest we know its purpose, which is to inspire and incite and celebrate, maybe question and even criticize, and then, of course, simply to record a version of what has happened, or should have happened, were our world a more genial place. And seeing those splashes of color along with others (or the thought of onlooking others) is totally different from seeing the same images alone, the former sensation, when it is right, akin to sharing a long-harbored secret.

What we have perhaps not considered enough is the maker and why she's done what she's done, whether it was some unexplainable artistic urge or else an impetus of conscience, and then, most important, what the making made her think and feel, whether back in an alleyway of B-Mor or deep inside a Charter villa. For did it allow her to feel larger, more connected? Did it settle a self-quarrel? Did it offer her liberty from some private boundary that heretofore she had not understood or even noticed?

Because when we look at the final great work of Six, as well as the broader field-coloring efforts of the others, that ended up completely covering not just the white space of the partly finished wall but the entire blank run of the remaining others, we can conclude whatever it signifies is no more important than that they did it without pause, hardly eating or sleeping or much concurring with one another, caught up as they were in the virulent bloom of a fever. Yes, poor Five had nearly succumbed before their eyes. Yes, both she and Four would be hospitalized for more than a week. Yes, Miss Cathy had fainted from the shock, striking her head on the corner of a night table, her blood blotted all over Mala, who insisted on cradling her while Dr. Upendra stitched up the scary but luckily superficial wound. And yes, Fan had exited the house and climbed into the medical center van with Four and Five and Dr. Upendra, all in full view of Miss Cathy, who didn't protest or say another word. These moments might have been rendered as always in the flow of connecting panels, with attendant realistic detail and texture, and maybe even in the larger scale of the underwater image of their pushing up Fan to the surface. Or they could have been depicted expressionistically, as was sometimes done before, some exuberant spray of spectral colors or surely, given the mood, a panel microscopically crosshatched in a dread hue.

What Six conceived instead was literally the biggest thing she'd ever done. In fact, it wasn't a panel at all, but a panorama, the work beginning where she'd left off and stretching not just to the corner but onto the next wall and the next, wrapping the whole way around to where One and Two had begun the mural many years before. In a single immense stroke the project was complete.

And what was this last image? It was at first difficult to tell. Six started penciling the whole thing soon after the medical center van departed, working steadily and purposefully all night. The others even watched her, no one talking under the pall of what had occurred, though each wondering what it was they were seeing. Six was clearly energized by the work, rapidly mounting and dismounting her stepladder and shifting it by herself as she went along the walls; she refused any help. Her motions were unfamiliar to them, as they were accustomed to painstaking rendering, the scribing out of one tiny section at a time. Her hand now swept across the wall in wide arcs, slashes, the furious action of her arm looking like she meant to deface the surface rather than decorate it, the scrape of the pencil raspy and sharp. She labeled the colors to be done as she went, though in fact it was mostly just black, and some grays, and then a few skeins and patches of brighter colors here and there. These were filled in with the especially thick poster markers they already had on the racks but rarely used, the four others coloring while Six directed them from her perch atop the stepladder in the middle of the room. Then she'd come down and join in. By the end, they had gone through a half-dozen additional sets of the markers, their hands and fingers inked, their cheeks smeared by stray smudges and flecks, their lungs so numbed by the sweet vapors of the markers that they felt they were hollowed out, floating with the lightness.

What they made was a portrait. Or a portrait of sorts. Seven said she wished Fan could see it, no doubt assuming it was of her. And maybe it was. It did look like her or, at least, like the curtaining sway of her hair; there was great movement in the work. For what you saw was merely a swath of a much larger image, running the height and length of two and a half walls, a banded glimpse of a girl's head angled up in quarter profile, such that only the ends of her black hair (flashed by electric glints of violet), a line of cheek, a nub of chin, could be seen. The full portrait, were it apparent, would have been billboard-sized, as tall as the villa itself. And while it surely could have been Fan—Six just shrugged when asked—when you stepped to one corner of the room or another and took it all in, you could also think to see Five's fullish lips, or the most solid set of

Three's cheek, or some distinctive notation of each of the Girls, and maybe Mala, too. Naturally, Miss Cathy was a presence, if only in the watery rays of sunlight that the girl was craning up to and catching, the blurred streams of them the exact color of her auburn-dyed hair, a shimmering penumbra of the gray-green of her eyes illuminating the field.

That Fan did not see any of this is not so ironic, for all along her journey we've observed more of her than she'll ever know. She moves on, she pushes forward, this her guileless calling, and we have to remind ourselves that it's perhaps more laudable simply to keep heading out into the world than always tilting to leave one's mark on it.

And surely this is how it was that she ended up leaving the villa that day with Dr. Upendra, who had noted to himself, with great surprise, that he had returned to Miss Cathy's not strictly for her, but at least to close the loop of his piqued regard. For we know he had gone back to the medical center after that first visit to pick up his things—it was long past the end of his shift—but instead of heading home to his condo, he chose to chat and joke with some of the nurses and even began reviewing the past month's charts, a chore that had to be done but rarely until the last possible moment, and then lingered in the staff lounge over a vending-machine coffee and pastry, something he would normally never do, given his dining standards. As he bit into the gelid, ungiving muffin, there was a certain notion about Fan that kept circling back to him; not that she was *fresh* or *virginal*—he had no such coiling for her that way—but rather the sense that he had come upon an arbitrary plant or small tree in a section of counties bush, the specimen mostly ordinary, except that it was in its own unassuming way superbly formed, despite surely not having had much room to be.

It was not exactly that Upendra yearned for such spaciousness, as Fan would soon discover. The issue of his state of being was not stunted or malformed. If anything, he was as highly evolved as any successful young Charter could be, the elements of his existence rigorously tuned, as were those of all his peers, with "best practices" in mind, those ever-optimizing metrics that we in B-Mor know as well as anybody, though ours are, of course, designed ultimately to smooth our unitary workings. Charters, on the contrary, are always striving to be exquisite microcosms, testing and honing and curating every texture and thread of their lives, from what they eat and watch and wear to whom they befriend and make love to, being lifelong and thus expert Connoisseurs of Me.

As the youngest chief of emergency medicine the Charter medical center had ever appointed, Vikram Upendra seemed to have already attained an enviably advanced status. He lived in a smartly outfitted two-bedroom apartment in a top condo development in the village. He spent liberally on hi-tech athletic clothes and specialized kitchenware and the globals he took for long weekend vacations with his girlfriend, Ludmilla, a crack management consultant who literally never stopped working and whom he practically only saw on late-night calls from her hotel in some far-flung locale, the padded headboard behind her ever different but enough the same, too, for him to feel comfortable if they felt like getting intimate.

The last time they were physically together for more than a few hours was in the private sleep suite they got upgraded to on the global back from Angkor Wat, this a full two months before. And although they agreed and understood that they were committed to not being serious, quite recently she had recommended that if they were to get married it should be in the near to mid term, if only, as most other young professionals did (he was thirty-two, she twenty-seven), to pair up and pool resources early in order to borrow enough for a starter villa and begin accumulating wealth for the countless expenses a typical Charter family must incur. Charter property and income taxes are curiously negligible but everything else, from refuse pickup to primary school tuition to the neat bundles of kale and rainbow chard, carries a dear price. He didn't disagree with her assessment but both were too busy to pursue the issue, tabling it for their next holiday.

It was the fact that Ludmilla was never actually around that allowed Vik to even consider Fan's startling request, which she made after the tumult of Four's and Five's admission and initial treatment at the medical center. The two of them had watched the girls get rolled through the doors of the intensive care ward, and Vik, now ready to go home, casually offered to give Fan a ride back to Miss Cathy's or wherever else she wished—he'd noticed how the woman had literally looked the other way when Fan left the villa with him and the EMTs. Once they were in his coupe, he waited for her to speak and in the awkward pause he must have been unconsciously hoping for some nearby direction because when she said, May I stay with you today? he didn't even flinch, clicking the car into gear and pulling away.

At his condo he showed her the full bath and the linen closet by the front door and how the loveseat in the study/second bedroom pulled out into a bed, and even though it was still daytime, he then simply retired to his bedroom for a nap; he had been up for two days. Fan sat in the living room, taking in the rest of the place, which looked to her just like the Charter homes in the evening programs, lined by burnished wooden and metallic and stone surfaces with hardly anything else in the way of decoration or objects. She heard the shower in his en suite bathroom start and cease and then a murmur of his quick conversation with someone and finally his snoring, which was wheezy but low and chesty.

She then washed her own face and hands and feet, pausing to examine herself in the mirror before pulling on the nightshirt one of the Girls had packed for her. Her belly looked fuller, but the rest of her had filled out ever so slightly, too, which made it seem less prominent. She certainly felt a thickening, as if she were lined inside with dense icing, and as oddly healthful and happy as this made her feel, she was also struck by how suddenly drained she could get for no reason at all. Her body now had its own aims, flipping on and off new switches. She quickly made up the loveseat bed. She wasn't planning to sleep, but lulled by the steady saw of the young doctor's snoring, she drifted off—she had not gotten much sleep herself—without any dreaming, at least until she was sure she was back at her row house in B-Mor with the scent of cooking from down in the kitchen funneling straight up to her room via the air shaft of the stairs.

When she awoke, she was drooling. It was now dark outside, the only light coming from beneath the study door. When she opened it, Upendra was at the prep space of the open kitchen, where he was now preparing some food. She came out and sat on one of the stools set before the counter cooktop. She could see he was making mapo tofu, something he no doubt figured a B-Mor would like. He had also steamed some jasmine rice and had a small pot of chicken broth on simmer.

Are you as hungry as I am?

Fan nodded.

He ladled broth into a coffee mug for her. It was rich and chickeny, gingery and salty, too, and although it was hot, she couldn't help but take full sips of it, not caring that the soup was half scalding her tongue. She wasn't scared that he might have laced it, either, for of course she was the one who had asked to be here. But it wasn't simply that. She had seen how forceful he had been at the medical center in commanding the staff, who at first were confused and perhaps even reluctant about what to do with such keeperless patients. He had them care for the girls like they were any deserving Charters, glaring at one of the doctors who seemed to balk, ordering batteries of tests for Four, then hooking Five up to a breathing machine himself.

He'd even assured the sour-faced medical director that he would cover the costs, which at that moment was still a possibility, for Miss Cathy had merely deferred in having them transported, never specifically agreeing to anything, and of course had not accompanied them. The medical director said she would hold him responsible, and it impressed Fan how unstinting Vik was, how duly fixed—an appreciable tilting of his head, an upcurl of his bottom lip. Aside from his studious, painstaking manner, he was otherwise, from what she had witnessed, squarely decent and kind. He did not seem devious or sneaky or lecherous, signs of which she was by now extra-vigilant for, given all she had endured.

When the dishes were ready, he set two places side by side at the counter. She finished two full plates and half of a third, every motherly cell of her leaping, yawing wide like a starved mouth. For dessert he peeled and sliced a pear, and after they finished that, she must have looked unsatisfied, because he offered her some ice cream. He spooned her two large scoops. When she was finally done, she took a deep breath and realized he had been closely watching her the whole time, as one might do when feeding a stray cat.

I will leave in the morning, she told him, mistaking his silent regard for disdain.

Whatever you like, he said. Nobody is your keeper. Do you know where you'll go?

She wondered if her brother's house was similar to this one. But she still didn't know where it was. Where he was. Or Reg. She touched her hand to her middle.

You're pretty far from B-Mor, he said. But you don't want to go back there, do you?

She shook her head.

Well, you can do what you want. There's the extra room and I'm hardly here. But I don't mind either way.

Okay, she told him.

Okay, he answered. During the meal, he had asked various questions about her life, though unlike Sewey or Mala or Miss Cathy, Vik was clearly familiar with the basics of settlements such as B-Mor; he focused mostly on the particulars of her work in the tanks, being more curious about the details of the fishery, its engineering and operational processes, than her personal experiences or feelings about the job. It was the same with his probing of her household, his queries having to do with the number of floors and rooms in the house, and how its members were situated, depending on age and family relation. Unlike everyone else she'd met the last few weeks, he seemed to know how old she really was. He did not ask why she had left, or where else she had been before finding herself imprisoned on the other side of the village at Miss Cathy's.

He rose from his stool to clear the plates, and suddenly it was obvious to Fan that despite the nap he was still very tired, his eyes sagged and bloodshot. She offered to clean up and he let her. While she washed the dishes and wok, and wiped down the counters, he sat in the living area, taking out a small metal box from the undershelf of the coffee table. The box had a lid with a mini-window and clear tubing attached, and he plugged it into an outlet. From a special tin he plucked a tiny, sticky brown cube from rows of cubes and placed it inside the box, turning a dial. When a ping sounded, he took the tube in his mouth and inhaled. He did this a few more times and Fan could smell it, a syrupy botanical funk, the scent very similar to what one of her oldest aunties would smoke nightly out behind their row house. She was always the happiest auntie, never irritable or gossipy and forever fixed with a wan smile.

When Fan was done, Vik asked her if she wanted to watch a vid

with him. Apparently, he'd just found and ordered an original file of
one of his favorite movies, an old-time full-length anime about a girl
counter-cyberterrorism agent. Fan had never heard of it but was
immediately engrossed in the story and the way it was animated in
an antique handmade style, much like, she thought, the Girls' wall
was (at least until the final gargantuan image), though this heroine
was endowed with the body of an impossibly slender if still volup-
tuous woman and looked nothing like anyone Six would have ever
conceived. It was a lengthy movie and in the middle Vik paused it
and zapped a bag of popcorn, which they steadily drew down as it
was lodged between them, he nodding and snorting and sighing in
boyish delight at the familiar action and images, Fan following along
as well as she could, perhaps intrigued most by the idea of the cyborg
heroine, whose powers were superior and who showed great resilience
of spirit but was also made vulnerable by her consciousness of the
hybrid nature of her being. Fan wasn't sure if she had been affected
by the residual vapors from Vik's contraption, but the muted colors
of the anime seemed somehow especially rich and haunting, and the
sequences of violence and protogenesis so strangely beautiful, that by
the end, after the heroine is physically destroyed but rises again,
whole in form but entirely changed, Fan felt a sudden hollowing in
her chest, a flash cavern of longing that she had not yet known.

And what was that longing? It was certainly not for Vik, although
she must have already been comfortable with him, sitting as closely
as they were in the murky light of the vid. It wasn't, surprisingly,
about the tiny thing growing within her, which by now was perhaps
just endowed with a real human shape, if not so in her consciousness.
And it wasn't even about Reg, as her feeling for him was all too constant, self-generating like some massive falls, which would not diminish even over the millennia.

Vik's hand grazed hers and she pulled away. But in fact, he just had fallen asleep, his mouth barely ajar, a dusting of popcorn salt clinging to the corner of his lips. She powered off the screen and in the pitch black she made her way to her pullout bed in the study, turning on a light to find a blanket. When she came back out to cover him, Vik had slid down on his side, his bony knees already raised up toward his chest; this was probably what always happened on the first night off call. In the study Fan lay unsleeping, though with the door to the living room kept open. She listened to his breathing, light and fine at first and then deepening to snoring, which did not bother her at all, in the way it did not bother her in the thinly partitioned row house back in B-Mor, her uncles and aunties and cousins pitching their nightly calls in an unmelodious orchestration that heralded her blood.

But in fact, we suspect she did not miss them, or us. We were still in view but as heatless as any patch of distant stars. For the enigma of her longing, it might be said, was of no longing, not one born of selfishness or egoism, some belief that she was scaled (and now colored) larger or brighter than the rest, but that after two and a half months away, having trailed down those unmarked and twisted roads, and been subjected to the warped designs (and hopes) of sundry citizenries, when it must have seemed each time that all was lost again, the tethers were now released, the moorings finally dismantled, and she was floated out, alone. Which was strangely fine.

IT WAS ODD FOR FAN TO SHOP AGAIN ON THE MAIN THOR-
oughfare of the village. For one, it was much more pleasant now. Of
course, she was with Vik instead of Miss Cathy, and rather than
being the focus of the shopkeepers' overbearing attentions, she was
simply tagging along, observing Vik navigate the various stores on
his mental list and peruse their offerings with a seriousness and sense
of purpose that made their errand feel vitally important. It did not
matter that he was just buying a housewarming present, which in
B-Mor would have been something like a boxed set of five unblem-
ished persimmons, or a tin of *sencha*, somewhat dear items that were
of unquestionable value and practicality and, with any luck, might be
shared with the giver (it never being poor form in B-Mor to swing
soon back around).

Vik, on the other hand, was searching for the singular gift, something they might use often or not at all but that would complement
the distinctive needs or lifestyle of the receiver, which included the
very fact that he or she might possess such a thing. So they went in
and out of food shops and gadget shops and home furnishings shops,
too. Then shops for drinks, and bathwares, and kitchen supplies
and equipment, these last of which there seemed to be the most of,

seemingly every fourth store lined with unending inventories of luxury glassware, pans, ladles, and spatulas, such that Fan had to think that every dish that Charters made (or was made for them) had to be served or prepared with a dedicated series of implements, vessels. And by extension, that every movement or act of Charter life, however trivial, required specialty objects and mechanisms for the best chance at an ideal outcome.

Take, for example, items Vik briefly considered, a device for spearing and pulling out accidentally pushed-in wine corks, or a pillow that inflated/deflated and heated/cooled via customizable programs. For nearly two hours they went up and down Seneca Avenue, not pausing to eat or drink, until he finally found the thing he thought they would like, in a former pet store, of all places, which now sold all kinds of stuffed animals, both plush and realistic, as well as accessories for them, such as clothing and toys and "food." He picked it out while Fan was in the toilet, and when she returned, they had already boxed and gift-wrapped the present, which was very large and heavy enough that the proprietor said he would deliver it directly to the housewarming party tomorrow afternoon. Fan asked Vik what it was and he was going to tell her but then thought it should be a surprise for everyone.

It was a rare off-weekend for Vik and besides the morning's gift shopping and the next day's party he was completely free, which Fan assumed would mean he'd be off someplace or out to restaurant meals. Although he messaged his girlfriend dozens of times, and browsed various pictures of her, some, she noticed, quite racy, and did actually speak to her once (Nothing really, how about you?), he didn't make any plans with her or seem bothered or disappointed by that. He was content to remain in and around the condo. He did bring Fan along to the extensive fitness center in the condo development that was skylit by huge panes of glass, like the nicest production facility one

could imagine. The gleaming, spotless hardwood floors were set
with all sorts of first-class cardio and weight machines, and in the
back were lots of VACs, virtual activity chambers for exotic sports
such as skeet shooting and snowmobiling, though most all of the
residents Fan saw there just jogged on the treadmills while they
watched their programs, or else swam slo-mo laps in the twenty-five-
meter pool. They looked fit enough and not one of them could be
termed fat, but it seemed to Fan they were maintaining themselves in
a stressful way, such as not quite eating enough, their dogged faces a
bit too drawn, even slightly desiccated.

Vik was lean but strong. He was a swimmer, too, but of a very
different order: he had emerged from the locker room sheathed in a
full-body racing suit, loosening and stretching on the deck for a long
time before donning a cap and warming up with a few smooth laps.
When he was ready, he had a fitness center employee sound a horn
for timed fifty- and one-hundred-meter sprints, three times each;
later he told Fan how he had been an Association champion when
he was younger, being unusually long limbed. He could have continued the intensive training to try to make the Charter Globals but
had decided to pursue medicine instead; one had to medal (and win
gold) to parlay all those hours in the pool into a substantial windfall
or successful business career, otherwise the most one could expect for
all that effort was becoming an elite-level coach or athletic administrator. And although he had been one, he never much enjoyed the
company of jocks. He was heavy-footed and lanky as he walked on
the deck, but in the water he motored himself forward with a remarkable ease and gracefulness, particularly given how fast he cut
through it. When he had glanced at his watch timer, he seemed satisfied, and reminded Fan while catching his breath that she was welcomed to swim, if she liked. She did like, for the water looked so
perfect and clear, just like it did when the tanks were newly filled for

the generation of new fry, this pristine little ocean, but she had to decline. The modest swelling in her lower belly could still be over-looked, or mistaken for incipient plumpness, but she couldn't take the chance, especially in the presence of a Charter doctor, even one she thought she could trust.

After Vik completed his warm-down laps, and showered and changed, they spent an impromptu half hour trailblazing an Alpine glade on snowboards in one of the VACs, which Fan mentioned hav-ing once seen on an evening program. Neither of them was any good at it, Vik crashing into at least a dozen trees, Fan able to crouch down low and shoot under the snow-laden pine branches but twice flying over an outcropping and tumbling head over heels down a steep slope. When she looked back up the second time, Vik was waving her out. He wasn't in a rush and they even stopped to have smoothies at the fitness juice bar but once at his place he changed into a pressed shirt, slacks, and pointy leather shoes, and said he had to go out; he added she would have to be by herself the rest of the afternoon. Fan, of course, had been alone in the condo for many straight hours while he was at the medical center, not even consider-ing venturing out, but the funny shift in his manner gave her pause. Had he found out something about her? Discovered why she'd left B-Mor? Again he hadn't been the least interested in such things, but as he left her in the apartment, he offered to order her a delivery of sushi or a burrito if it turned out he would be late. She said the left-overs in the fridge were fine. He said sure, if that suited her, shutting the door, and Fan couldn't help but think that the next time it opened, a squad of Charter security would rush in and take her away, though perhaps that would be her best true chance of getting closer to Reg.

She went to the window and watched Vik angle himself into his two-seater and drive off. All in all it seemed Vik simply liked her company, even if she was mostly silent (or maybe because she was). She had the sense that he admired the way she was, not discretely so much as a new element in his life, her pale skin and inky black hair complementing the uncluttered and calm spaces of his private life. Still, when she tried the door, it surprised her that it opened freely. She was glad for it but was conflicted. Shouldn't she go right now anyway? Certainly it was getting to be time, and the longer she stayed the more potential trouble it would be for Vik. She could walk out to the road ringing the development and catch one of the guest and resident worker buses that routed through this part of town and then went out of the village. From there, Mala had once told her, the buses went to a central depot thirty minutes away, which was the closest hub with numerous route spokes, though most of those went south and west. Mala's home was on a spoke after the second hub, near a major facility out there known as Y's-Town, or Wise-Town. Beyond those were other hubs, each with spokes, and so on, repeating all the way across the land. It was awfully slow but you could mostly get there, wherever there was. Of course, this was only if you had to go by bus.

Fan had spoken to Mala yesterday, reaching her at Miss Cathy's while Vik was at work, to see how the Girls were doing with Four and Five still not at home. Mala said they were fine, though clearly anxious about not having to live upstairs anymore. They and Miss Cathy had decided they would spread out into the rest of the house, using their former room however they might like, or not all, as now Miss Cathy was saying she wanted the house filled, all the time, and forever. She'd even moved herself downstairs to live with Mister Leo, Tico moving their beds into the former study. There's a full bathroom in there, Mala said, so it works.

Fan could not believe the Girls could live in separate rooms.

They're not yet, Mala said. They were excited at first. They came downstairs to try it but the younger ones were scared by all the rooms and hallways. The sunlight was too bright for the older ones. So they all went right back up. Plus, they didn't like being near Mister Leo, even with how he is. But they'll try it again soon. And you know what else?

Fan asked what.

I told Miss Cathy I needed my own family. To live with them. And she agreed! Now they're coming next week, my husband and children. They're going to live here in the villa, maybe upstairs if the Girls are able to move out. If they do well enough, my kids will be full Charters. Not me and Francisco, it's too late for us, but that's okay. We don't have to be Charters. We can take care of them.

Yes, said Fan. They need your care.

Mala asked where Fan was going next and, of course, Fan couldn't answer.

Well, you will make it the right place, she said. Some people are like that. You are one of those, I think. It does not matter who is there or what is there. You will make it right, and not just for yourself. And you know, now there's going to be an empty house far out in the counties! Both of them laughed, though Mala mentioned the name of the settlement, if no more than that because out there were very few, if any, named streets.

You will know it when you see it, she added. It is the nicest house.

Fan said it sounded very nice, after which there was nothing much else to say and so they bid each other good-bye, something we B-Mors do not customarily do (unless, frankly, someone is about to die), for the obvious reason of our living in a cloistered, intimate society, but perhaps, too, because to do so is to acknowledge that almost no one ever leaves.

Fan had gathered her few things and was looking in a cabinet for some dried and canned food to take along when the apartment door opened. It was Vik. It looked like he'd forgotten something, a certain crimp to his expression, no more than a quarter hour having passed since he'd left, but he walked in and just stood at the kitchen bar counter in his impressive, stiff-looking clothes. He noticed the open cupboard and asked if she was hungry, a question, she realized, that didn't occur to her anymore, as it seemed of late that she was always willing to eat, even immediately after she'd eaten. But he didn't wait for an answer and suggested they take a ride and get a snack.

Where? she said, being wary as she should be, but also thinking that she should tell him she would soon depart.

A fun weekend place, he said. Let's go.

It was a short drive, but out past one of the village gates. After heading about five kilometers on the secured, fenced tollway, Vik took an exit ramp and got onto a free road. He drove faster now, despite the poor condition of the road surface, for technically they were in the counties and should not dawdle. The coupe was powerful and nimble, and had a tracker that could steer him through the most damaging bumps and potholes but he wasn't using it. He seemed to know the road, disregarding the all but faded center line as he swerved back and forth, racing in the clearer stretches and then braking hard at the rashes of ruts. Fan had begun to feel sick when he finally slowed and turned into a former rest area, paying what seemed to Fan a great deal of money as an entrance fee. Armed men gestured with their weapons as to where they should park. Vik didn't seem in the least concerned. There were at least twenty other vehicles, most all Charter-level, though there was room for twice as many. Once they parked, they walked up a path through a brief stand of scrub. The path opened onto a grassy field dotted with two concentric circles of tents, or what looked like tents, but which were, in fact, semipermanent structures made of steel poling and covered with plastic tarps, blue and brown and orange, wisps of steam and smoke filtering out from the flaps. And then Fan could smell it: the cooking.

It was the weekly Saturday market, Vik told her, unofficially known as Seneca Circus. Of course, there was no actual circus of animals and acrobats, just these many tents set in the round, where one could buy food and trinkets from late morning to well past dusk, when they turned on the floodlights. It was midafternoon now, so the trade was a bit slower, but there were still all kinds of Charters and a few better-to-do counties people milling about after their meals, mostly younger couples and families, poking into the merchandise tents, where counties people sold handmade crafts of a typically high level, nothing like the junk the counties peddlers would hawk back in B-Mor, items such as paper fans and placemats mass-produced in a rustic style, which soon proved cheap and flimsy. Here, however, there were finely turned wooden bowls and handblown wineglasses, and custom jewelry, not all of it equally attractive but clearly produced painstakingly, and with pride. Of course, most Charters would not deign to leave the comfort and safety of the village for such peculiar stuff, the notion of handmade to them suggesting a thing slightly fouled, probably dirty, and in comparison with the time-honed, market-engineered perfection of their beloved brands, as special as the doodlings of an idiot. Vik was evidently not that kind of Charter, at least as far as this place was concerned, Fan recognizing the style and shape of a vase like one back at his apartment, as well as a set of inlaid cutting boards. There were wall hangings and wind chimes and soapstone sculptures for the garden; handwoven slippers and embroidered belts and vests; all kinds of old-fashioned table games for children, often involving the guiding of a small steel ball; and every variety of handcrafted natural lotions and soap, which one would assume no Charter would ever buy but did by the kilo, if more for ornamental rather than actual use.

As much as there was to purchase and take home, the primary draw was the food, especially for Vik. Each food tent was pretty much the same, the space approximately a four-by-five-meter rectangle with a cooking station centered against one long side and a counter and seats running along on the other three, the backs of the patrons sometimes brushed by a flap of the tarp. Again here was something one would never expect Charters (or even us B-Mors) to tolerate, food made and served practically outside, without the usual hygienic safeguards and standards. But this is precisely what drew this venturing lot, the chance to eat dishes prepared by an authentically ordinary person, one standing directly before you, dressed in unremarkable clothing, whose bare hands touched everything, from the raw ingredients to the plate. Whom you could speak to if you pleased. For a certain person, this was thrilling dining, an experience further heightened by the fact that the food itself was old-fashioned and indifferent to the Charter prerequisite of having to be healthful; you could get Belgian street frites, or a Hiroshima-style *okonomiyaki*, or a gravy-sopped plate of chicken and dumplings. They went to Vik's favorite, the Chinese-Korean tent, where he ordered them bowls of chive *jajang* noodles and a small platter of braised sea cucumber, which Fan could not stop eating. Vik asked the proprietor where she had sourced the sea cucumber, as it was especially firm and sweet.

Where you think, the busy woman murmured, and not in the most friendly way. She was thick of waist, with a sturdy neck, and had prominent uplifted dark eyebrows that made one feel that she was already dubious. Ocean.

Pacific or Atlantic?

Which you want?

I don't have a preference.

Okay. All of them.

Vik grinned, and the proprietor appeared to grin for a millisecond, too, before she went back to dipping strips of beef in batter and then into a pot of fry oil for the two men around the corner. The other four stools were unoccupied.

You like *hae-sam*, huh?

Fan nodded, assuming she was referring to the sea cucumber. She had just taken the last bite of it.

I like her, she said to Vik. Good appetite.

Vik smiled and asked Fan if she wanted to try the deep-fried beef with sweet-and-sour sauce. It's excellent here. Fan said she did but that she was too full.

Better than other one, the proprietor said, which Fan took to mean the beef. But Vik didn't respond, instead absently rooting with his chopsticks at the remaining noodles in his bowl. The woman made a deal of wiping her fingers of the batter before stepping over to the pair of men to refill their beer glasses, lingering to banter with them.

Vik took a sip of his tea. Fan now pictured what might have happened; he had left the apartment to pick up his girlfriend, who must have been back in town, and maybe come right here, but something had clearly gone wrong, a sharp disagreement or even a fight. That he had hidden his chagrin this well was something she found both sad and endearing. He was not at all like Reg, who if anything was too quick to express himself, leaping up with exuberance when a performance review went well or tugging at his hair in frustration when he couldn't get the scooter started, though the acting out seemed to temper him, too, serve to settle him back more easily into his naturally clement rhythms. Vik, on the other hand, appeared in constant control, and when he shouldn't be, such as right now, he invisibly exerted himself even more to master the chaos.

Do you like pies? There's an old man here who makes ones with wild berries.

Fan was not particularly enamored of such pies but said she did, clear that Vik was restless. He paid the bill and the proprietor thanked him, murmuring, See you again. Vik crisply told her, Sure, giving a thumbs-up as they pushed the tarp out of the way to exit. Where the pies were sold it was busier, people always ready to have dessert, and they had to wait on a line that trailed outside the tent, people holding their shade umbrellas. There were no seats free inside so Vik bought two blackberry-pie slices to go plus a whole apple pie (just now in season) and they sat at one of the picnic tables, which were completely empty, despite the ideally temperate and dry day. Beyond the footprint of the villages and their scrim of projected sky domes, Charters stayed out of the sun whenever possible. Vik had had them apply sunscreen in the car but otherwise seemed unconcerned; in fact, he was craning up his face, his dark sunglasses sparkling with the uncut plash of the sun. The pie was indeed excellent, as Vik said they were, much more tart and not half as sweet as the gloopy B-Mor versions Fan had tasted, the berries mostly whole and still with their seeds, the crust crumbly and light. Vik said it was made with lard. Fan observed to him that unlike most other Charters he didn't appear worried about toxins in his food or, for that matter, the effects of the sun, even though he was a doctor.

Perhaps it's because I am one, he said.

Because you'd get treated first?

He told her that used to be the case, but no longer. Now, like a lot of things that were once available to certain people, treatment was sold at hourly auctions. And doctors were far from able to be the highest bidders. But it didn't matter to him. He wasn't even sure he believed in the idea of C-free, at least not anymore.

Fan took in the notion but did not reply. Rather, she now took another forkful of her pie, deciding it was indeed excellent, as untroubled and pleased by it as any B-Mor would be, whether with child or not. But the big piece was still too much for her and Vik had to finish her slice. He ate without worry as well, seeming more contented now, and this, to her surprise, pleased her equally.

THE HOUSEWARMING PARTY, IT TURNED OUT, WAS GOING to be a retirement party as well. They had messaged everyone the news yesterday, after Vik and Fan had returned from the Circus. Apparently, Vik's colleague, who was also in his early thirties, a blood C-specialist at the medical center, had been developing an antirejection drug for the last eight years, starting from when he was still a medical student. Although just 60 percent efficacious in year-long trials, the drug had been deemed promising enough that all three major pharmacorps joined in a frenzied auction for his patent. The winning bid was certified by the respective attorneys yesterday afternoon, and was a sum of cash and unrestricted stock that Vik's colleague and his wife and their three young children could live on for the rest of their lives, and in the finest Charter style. This was why Vik was only half joking when he said that they would be tearing down the new custom-built villa they now pulled up to. The driveway was nearly full with catering vans and the immediate street spots were all taken, so Vik just parked right behind the vans. The neighborhood was an elite one but not as elite as Miss Cathy's, certainly a rung below, with smaller, narrower lots, the houses appearing surprisingly modest from the front but extending far back from the façade, and in some cases right to the rear property line, such that there was hardly any remaining yard.

Oliver and Betty's house had a span like this, and to Fan's eye was not nearly as attractive as her own clan's row house, which though meager in comparison and attached on either side gave one a feeling of ever-abiding welcome, with its fetching stoop and the timeworn textures of the brightly painted brick. Even Miss Cathy's villa, grandly imposing as it was, seemed more friendly than this one, which looked like a leaden two-and-a-half-story coffin, clad in graphite-colored brushed metallic panels, the nearly flat and barely visible hip of the roof spined with sharp-edged beams, all the windows of irregular sizes and shapes in the most haphazard placement, as if a child had chosen and affixed each by pure whim with no regard for the final pattern. There was a short line of other guests at the front entrance waiting to be greeted, and Fan could overhear some of the comments about the new house, which were mostly positive, except one fellow who wasn't taking to the landscaping and wondering why there weren't a lot more flowers and shrubs. His wife shushed him, saying they'd only moved in last week and that Betty's magical hand would have the place all together in no time.

Vik didn't betray any feeling or opinions about the property, his general demeanor on the drive over and now even-keeled, if not one of great eagerness. Yesterday when they returned to the apartment, he was in improved spirits and they'd watched a different old anime film (after he inhaled some vapors) and afterward had gone for a bubble tea in town, as he was craving one. As they drove back with their drinks, the message came in about his colleague's good fortune, and he had actually laughed on viewing it, rapping at the steering wheel as if at once pleased and befuddled, as well as perhaps panged by the rueful envy one can suffer on learning of a peer's success.

Maybe it was this jealousy, or simply the sugary tea and tapioca balls, suddenly fueling him, but Vik started to talk about how out of curiosity he'd graphed unpublished Charter C-death rates against those from 125 years ago and how, though it appeared there was vast improvement after controlling for nascent-stage diagnoses, which is how Charter survival rates were measured, Charters didn't actually live more than a few years longer than they did back then. People now just knew much earlier that they were diseased, literally sometimes mere days into the condition. And while they were being "cured" with all the therapies available now, it could be argued that they were never actually "well," given the constant stress of regimens and associated side effects.

But all this masked a more serious and underreported issue: the fact that a growing number of patients, after near lifelong serial therapies (some from when they were in preschool), had stopped responding to the treatments altogether. This was antithetical to the stance of the all-powerful C-therapy industry, which held that there was always a cure and had, in fact, always come up with one, no matter how a C-illness might express itself or evolve. But now—though, of course, Vik did not know this—it was like what we ourselves faced in our grow houses early on in the originals' history, when it was found that a certain blight had developed that could not be eradicated or prevented with any known chemicals or change in practices. They examined the grow media, the water, the grow-house air, the particular mélange of engineered nutrients, testing each and then all the possible matrices, and in the end it was decided to dismantle the grow houses and literally incinerate every last thing inside them, right to the concrete flooring, and start over again, which indeed solved the problem. But of course, this was not an option with what was now facing Charters.

This was why Vik's colleague's new therapy was so valuable, as it could address a profound threat to the entire C-industry, its companies grown massively rich over the last one hundred years, certainly the most profitable on the planet. Fan, if not comprehending every particular of what he said, gathered enough to ask him why he chose to work as an emergency room doctor, rather than be a C-specialist. This seemed to short-circuit Vik; he took a long sip from his bubble tea straw and told her that people got sick, they always did and always would, and in the end no one would ever figure out why. But he found addressing their immediate ills gave him satisfaction. So, yes.

The moment passed and he made no more of it. Vik now carried the boxed apple pie stiffly before him like a ritual offering, and when they reached the door where Betty and a helper were greeting everyone, he gently deposited it into her hands and quickly whispered something—*Vous êtes ma tarte aux pommes*—which was audible only to her and Fan and perhaps the helper. Of course, Fan didn't understand the breezy, lispy words, but assumed from Betty's stricken expression that he had said something confusing or maybe even rude, and certainly not amusing to her in any way. But Vik was almost sweetly smiling and the helper behind Betty was smiling back at him, if only reflexively, and Betty could do nothing but hand back the pie box to the helper and air-kiss Vik quickly and, with an effortful smile, ask who his young friend was.

Meet Fan. She's the niece of a friend. I'm keeping her company today.

Hello, Fan. I'm Betty Cheung. Welcome.

Fan thanked her and shook her warm, dry hand. Betty was quite petite, not too much taller or broader than Fan, in fact, and very beautiful in a needlessly perfected way, as if a higher power had taken a woman who was similar to Betty and plenty pretty, and decided to bestow the most shapely cuteness to her nose, and fund a sappy darkness into her brown eyes, and draw rounder and fuller her smallish lovely mouth, and envelop it all in a slip of clean pure skin that could never possibly pale or blush or sweat. Having somehow unconsciously grasped that this had happened, Betty dressed herself just as exquisitely, no matter the occasion, and whether it was a dress or jeans or apron, the faithful cut of her clothing never allowed the impression of her smallness to supersede the faultless lines and proportions of her figure, surely fit but never too drawn or lean-looking.

Betty had to greet the next guests and the helper ushered Vik and Fan into the rest of the house, pointing them forward to where the party was before she peeled off to the kitchen with the pie. Vik had not brought up with Fan beforehand how he would explain her presence and they did not discuss it now, this being his style. But he had also grasped what everyone who met Fan clearly sensed about her, that among her numerous capacities there was her ready ability to acclimate to any temperature. She certainly wasn't the kind to query him about the particulars of his relationship with Betty, despite how curious she was and what she was beginning to think. Of course, none of that mattered to Fan. It was Vik's life to do with as he pleased, to follow as he pleased. She had come along to enjoy one final day's outing with him, and she wondered when he left for the hospital tomorrow morning whether she would leave a good-bye note and resume her path, too.

The interior of the house was an open plan, dominated by a long central living room with an exceedingly high ceiling and an exposed, intricately engineered steel catwalk offering access to the five bedrooms, two on each side and the master at the far head. The main level felt like a chapel that had been cleared of its pews and filled with multiple conversational sets of furniture, though all the sofas and armchairs were empty now with everyone gathered in the rear under an immense full-height conservatory with operable glass panels that were darkened when needed. The conservatory was essentially the backyard but a backyard screened and lighted and plumbed and under complete climate control, the size, it seemed to Fan, of one of the natural-light B-Mor grow nurseries where they didn't also raise fish.

Some people caught sight of Vik and waved him over, drinks in their hands. They were a group of younger doctors like Vik, both women and men, perhaps a bit more ruffled and unkempt in the hair and clothes than the other guests, who were mostly in their thirties and forties, and children, seemingly scores of very young ones, each being held or closely trailed by a nanny wearing sweatpants and a T-shirt. Vik's colleagues hardly acknowledged the niece-of-a-friend Fan, partly for her presumed age, but mostly because of how focused they were on the subject of the Cheungs' windfall, reportedly worth not only cash and stock but also offered a contract for Oliver to continue directing the development of his therapy for the next five years at twice his current salary at the medical center. He hadn't decided what to do yet, naturally torn between wanting to guide the research on his brainchild and doing absolutely nothing, at least as far as working was concerned.

I know what I'd do, one of the women said, swirling her glass of white wine. She was gangly and sallow with frizzy dirty-blond hair, her dark brown roots grown out too long. I would have gone in and quit this morning and then chartered my own global for a six-month tour of vineyards. Vineyards in every continent. But I wouldn't care if it was just one. I haven't been anywhere!

None of us has! the other woman responded. How could we? We've all been in school forever and then went right to work!

And will do so forever! an unshaven man piped in. He wore a funny little brimmed hat that seemed too small for his big swarthy head.

I took a global to Fiji in the spring, another of the men offered.

I think I remember that, the second woman said. Wasn't that just for a long weekend?

A regular weekend, actually. But it was really great.

What'd you do?

Swam some. Mostly slept.

Solid.

The first woman said, Do they have vineyards in Fiji?

The Fiji fellow said he thought not but couldn't be sure.

Would you go on your trip all by yourself? the funny-hatted man asked the woman with the wineglass. She thought about it.

I'd bring a man with me, maybe even several men, for the company but also so I would be sure to get pregnant.

You could get pregnant now.

But I don't have the time. I don't yet have the money. And when I finally have both, I'll be too old even to take drastic measures.

You can keep.

Don't be icky.

I think we'll all change our minds about that.

Not me.

I'd go on your global, the Fiji man said. I like those flights. But you can't get something for nothing. You'd have to buy my loving.

Maybe I would.

They all laughed nervously, though maybe not Vik. Being nudged by their huddle, Fan had drifted a few steps away and now stood among some children who were picking at the many rectangular platters of delicious-looking food on the catering tables, though to Fan it all tasted invisibly misted with the same half-stale sauce.

And what about you, Vik, would you ride my global? I'd pay lots for you. I'd pay twice your salary.

I wouldn't let you, Vik told her, accepting a beer from a roving waiter. Love should be free.

You're terribly wise, Vik, the funny-hatted man said.

It's because I'm much older than all of you.

What, by four or five years? You're the same age as Oliver, aren't you?

From eleventh year on, we were in the same form and section.

Wow, the man said. Must have been a drag to have all that brilliance with you the whole way through. I'd have gone blind.

We all did, Vik said, subscribing to the mood. But Oliver is too charming to despise.

And Oliver knows it, someone said brightly from behind Vik.

It was Oliver.

Hail Caesar! the group quickly roared.

Ditch the rotgut, he told them. With him were three waiters, one of them cradling an inordinately large bottle of Champagne—a double magnum—by its bottom and neck, the other two ready with flutes. Oliver gave hugs to the two women and chest-and-shoulder bumps to the men, with maybe an extra-heavy bump for Vik. Oliver was the shortest person among them and a bit stocky, though, as with his wife, there was something highly crafted about him, plus in his case also unmistakably, irrefutably, clean, as though he had showered twice, a third time, then gone back and fine-scrubbed himself again. He scanned Fan as Vik repeated what he'd already said about her, though to Fan it was clear that Oliver wasn't in the least believing him. But he didn't say anything, simply shaking her hand, or rather giving her his to shake, not exerting the slightest bit of pressure.

This just got delivered and I want you guys to have the first taste.

He took the bottle and propped it on his thigh, thumbing at the cork. It shot out and hit a panel of the glass ceiling hard enough that they all winced, though it didn't appear to have cracked it. But now wine was fountaining over Oliver's hand onto the tiled floor, and he pivoted to the waiters so they could catch as much as they could in the glasses they extended.

My God, Oliver, the second woman gasped. Is that real Champagne? You could have bought a car instead!

Maybe a used one! he said, pouring out the glasses, the foam overflowing the rims. But I don't care. I love you guys. I want to share everything I've got. The other guests were looking over jealously at them, but what made Oliver the master of such potentially awkward situations was how obliviously enthused he was (though he could never be oblivious) with those he engaged, so that one couldn't help but be awed by his attentions, even when they were directed at someone else. It was like watching the turn of the Earth from a global, the continents getting lit by the Sun. You could not feel too bereft.

The Fiji man began making an odd, lame toast to used cars, which was snuffing the moment until Vik saved it by proposing they drink to the stunning new house, the design and construction of which Betty had so skillfully overseen. They hear-heared to that, though the Fiji man joked as to what the proper waiting period was for redoing the place altogether.

What? I wouldn't pry a nail, Oliver said, sounding put out. But he grinned. This house is so perfect I'm going to build another one exactly like it on that lot over there, then connect the two with bridges.

Don't I see a big house on that lot?

Not for long, Oliver said, his innate keenness showing, the long saber of his confidence. They'll have to sell, for what I'll offer them. Then I'll buy the two adjoining lots in the back, so we can have a real play yard for the kids. Then my work will be done.

What about the new company job? the second woman asked. What about Asimil? Don't you want to see it through?

Oliver said of course he did, but that from everyone he'd talked to as they prepared for the sale he understood it would never be how it was, he'd never again have full control of the direction of the lab. He and his researchers would be employees in the end. After a few months, he would find it maddening; in a year, impossible. He would then quit in frustration, leaving the lab and project rudderless.

So better not to waste a whole year. They already have a plan for Asimil anyway. And I decided I don't want to treat patients anymore, either.

But they love you!

Thank you. I will now entrust them to all of you. Day by day I was a medical doctor but all these years I've also been an entrepreneur. I was building a business. That business has significant value now. It exists. So I'm going to begin doing that again.

Another kind of therapy?

Probably, but not necessarily. Something in medicine for certain. Maybe devices. But not directly, not bench work. I'm going to be an angel investor, right here from the house. I can leverage an expertise very few people have. So I'm having an office set up. This way I can watch the kids grow. Betty and I can have lunch.

It sounds wonderful, the vineyard woman said, everyone tinkling their glasses again. Another rush of guests had stepped into the conservatory, including a few of his lab assistants and Betty's parents, and so Oliver went to meet them, handing the massive bottle to the catering waiters to go around and pour glasses for the other guests. It seemed everyone's eyes and murmurs were following him, this generous and gracious and even filial genius who'd made good on the promise of his powerful intellect and leveraged it, as he'd said, to this now magnificent scale. Vik told Fan he was going to the bathroom and she nodded, though she noticed that he, too, stopped by and greeted Betty's parents, who warmly greeted him. She was fine to stay here alone but she wasn't alone now, as a pudgy young girl with black bangs had latched on to her by the banquet table, saying, You want to play? Her thoroughly exhausted-looking nanny entreated

Fan with a desperate smile and Fan naturally said she didn't mind. The girl was four or five years old and her name was Josey. Josey was very bright and talkative and decided to make up a plate of food for a play dinner party and did so with startling care and maturity, choosing a healthful mix of fresh veggies, plus a second plate teetering with cake slices and cookies.

They settled at one of the many small bistro tables that had been set up for the party. The nanny sat on a folding chair on the periphery, finally having a chance to eat something herself. Josey demonstrated how to dip the crudités in the whipped dressing she'd dolloped on the plate. She bit half of a carrot stick and gave the rest to Fan, but when Fan only pretended to eat it, Josey scowled and took Fan's hand that was still holding the jagged rest and pushed it up toward her mouth. Fan could have resisted, easily reclaimed her hand, yet there was something about the fierce set of the girl's chin and the pinch of her tiny dampish grip, a focus and determination that was so pure and elemental (and that undoubtedly had not yet been thwarted in her life) that Fan thought it best the moment be played all the way through.

Once they had eaten enough veggies, Josey pronounced they could have dessert, and it was now that the young girl seemed to forget they were sharing, as well as maybe forgetting everything else around her, clutching the big chocolate chip cookie in one hand while forking pieces of carrot cake into her mouth with the other, and then even dipping the crisp cookie into the creamy icing and having it that way, the combination pleasing her immensely. In fact, she was eating a bit too avidly, in Fan's view, when the girl stood up and tried to cough. She shivered and dropped her fork, and without a thought, Fan rapped her squarely on the back once, quite hard, which caused the girl to yelp and shook the piece of cookie forward onto her tongue. She kept chewing it even as she wailed from the surprise blow and the frightened faces of Oliver and Betty's parents, who had already rushed over.

Daddy! she sobbed, Oliver taking her into his arms. He thanked Fan for her confident action, as he'd noticed them together just before Josey got in trouble. One would think Josey's grandparents would be busy offering her comfort and assurance, too, but instead the wispy, lamb-faced, stylishly dressed pair had turned a radish hue and were flaying the terrified nanny, who had bounded over still holding, the misfortunate thing, her piled-high buffet plate. She tried to explain but they weren't hearing any of it, calling her lazy and incompetent and stupid for not sticking by Josey at all times, until Fan finally said she was to blame for asking to spend time with their granddaughter.

I should not have let her eat so fast, she said, which to her mind was certainly true.

Who in the world are you? said the grandmother.

She's Fan! Josey cried, unlatching herself from Oliver and taking Fan's hand. And it's not her fault!

It's not anyone's fault, honey, Oliver said to her, though the flash of his icy regard for the nanny seemed to wither the woman instantly. He told her that she could go home for the day. Dr. Oliver, please, I will stay, the helper meekly said, patting Josey on the back, but before anyone could say another word, the grandparents had already summoned a brace of other helpers to lead the helper away, all of them whoop-cooing the shunned one like she was a strange, just-alighted bird.

I'm going to play with Fan! announced Josey. Oliver, craning about the crowded party and the various guests signaling him with their wineglasses, asked Fan if she would stay with her for a while. Josey immediately led her upstairs to her bedroom, a pink-and-white paradise of frilly-gowned dolls and sleepy polar bears and herds of unicorns, her canopied and skirted bed made to look like an icing-dotted pink princess cake, wall-to-wall fluffy sheepskins carpeting the floor. They played some vid games and next with the dolls and animals and then a pretend, with Josey as the nanny and Fan as Josey, in which nothing unusual happened, just Josey combing Fan's hair and rattling away idly in remarkable detail about the troubles of her adult son, Raymundo, who evidently drank and gambled away most of his meager counties earnings, as did all of his friends. No worlds made for us, little girl. At one point Josey stopped brushing and tapped Fan on the shoulder and whispered: I have to do a stinky. Fan took this to mean what it did, Josey leading her through a short hallway of closets to the connected bathroom and having her stand sentinel while she sat on the toilet. This always takes *forever*, Josey said theatrically, rolling her eyes, and then picked up one of the handscreens from a bin of toys beside her to start a game.

Fan heard some muted voices—the bathroom was Jack-n-Jill, shared on the other side by an as yet unoccupied child's bedroom—and as Josey became engrossed in her game, Fan drifted toward the sounds, realizing she was hearing Betty and Vik. They were trying to keep their voices down but they were arguing. They were arguing about messages, and no longer sending messages, about the sweet gone past and the harsh press of the present, about the time being wrong and then never wrong, which even Vik, clearly the more wounded and angry party, didn't sound convinced of. But he kept on beseeching Betty. She was now rich beyond imagining, yes, he could never offer her such heights, but at least they weren't blood-less and joyless together, and cast to conduct their lives ever the same, merely with nicer things, the same-same-same. You'll take a global every month but you'll never go for pie! He was not sounding very rational now. Then it was silent for a moment, like they were embracing, even kissing, and then all there was to be heard was some shuffling of feet and Vik's groan of Oh, come on, before the sounds of a door slowly opening, and closing.

When she and Josey finally returned downstairs, the determined girl at last successful in her business, people were gathered in the main hall around the collection of gifts they'd brought and deposited there, Betty and her helpers presiding.

There you are, sweetie! We're going to open the house presents now. Didn't you want to help?

Josey squealed and threw herself into the pile. She shred away the wrapping papers like a ravenous big cat, precariously showcasing each gift over her head—a custom-forged chef's knife, a crystal wine decanter—and then handing it to a helper, who would put it away safely and catalogue it for Betty. There were thirty or forty presents, all so luxuriously wrapped and fancifully ribboned, the strappings slowing Josey down enough that another helper was tasked to snip them unobtrusively so when she touched them, they fell away like loose straw. Still it was going to be a lengthy process, everyone fully indulging the giving and the delight of the child.

Fan looked for Vik but he wasn't there. Was he still up in the bedroom, slumped in a chair, disabled by heartbreak? Or was he alone in the conservatory, trying to stunt his grief with drink? Suddenly she felt herself lost. After Betty left him, Fan had tried to listen for his movements, she had nearly gone into the other room to console him. But like too many of us would, she determined he was better left undisturbed than be forced to commune with her. No matter, solace; the problem of sympathy is that it requires two. Despite having followed her many travails, whenever we put ourselves in Fan's place, we can't help but feel unsettled. It's not because of the many palpable dangers, or the strings of awful suffering she had to witness, the homeliest aspects of our citizenry. Instead the feeling can come from something as unpitched as this: standing among a roomful of strangers in a house far away.

After a few more unwrappings, Josey discovered there was a very big present that had been hidden by the stacks of others, covered in sparkly white paper with a huge sky-blue bow. It was nearly the size of an outdoor AC unit. Though it wasn't labeled, Fan knew it was Vik's gift. Josey brazenly shoved a few smaller presents aside and paused a moment before it, as if taking its measure. The helper unclipped the bow and then Josey clawed a corner and ripped at the paper, dragging it across the front. There was a cardboard hood over it and together Betty and the helper lifted it up and off.

It was an aquarium. Someone said plug it in, and someone did. Its lights flicked on and everyone clapped. It was a popular new kind, called the Full Sea, one that was already filled with water and completely sealed. There was a gravelly seafloor and a mass of gnarly coral and sea plants that looked like threaded sugar and ribbons of dark green silk, which swayed with an invisible, gentle current. There was a remote that came with it, and someone pressed it and out of the gaps in the coral came tropical fish. They looked so alive and real someone gasped—all household creatures having been banned—but these were artificial, if perfect, spotted catfish and striped angelfish and red discus fish and iridescent barbs, their fins fluttering, their mouths working, their bodies flashing away whenever someone tapped at the glass.

It was then Fan strode quickly from the main hall to the front door, coming out on the landing. When she got there, she saw Vik's coupe, already backed out and just now spinning away. She waved for him to stop. She didn't want to be left. She shouted, running down the steps and across the front grass. But he was gone.

And it was now that she saw Oliver had watched him drive away, too. He had been standing in the driveway on the other side of the catering vans. He approached her slowly, his face somehow somber and sated all at once.

And in a voice that shook her, he said, I know who you are, Fan.

She didn't answer, or couldn't, sure that she'd now come to the end of a line.

You're my sister.

OUR SISTER FAN.

Brother Reg.

Sisters Claire and Ji, brothers Darren, Sho, Tien; we will say it like that now, wherever we are, to those beyond our households, beyond our clans, unafraid of what might happen if the bosom address is spurned. Flag us if you must. What can they do? Detain us all? Have most of B-Mor disappear? It's a matter of numbers, yes, but there is an altered thrum in the air. Too many of us are together now. When we're at the theater, even for a wildly popular film, not a single seat free, the murmur before the lights dim is often word of the latest gatherings around the settlement, demonstrations that are no longer just spontaneous (like the littering of ponds), or stray (tags on walls), these keen if mostly isolated bursts of feeling. Talk has it there was a meeting at the big children's park in West B-Mor, openly planned and announced, and at the appointed hour, instead of the wary, measured trickle that might have come before, a few elders sent out with toddlers in tow to test the directorate's response; they say the grounds were filled nearly all at once, adults with infants strapped to their chests sitting on the swings, the abler-bodied climbing into the rope structure of the forts, the organizers standing on facilities palettes stacked three high so that everyone could see them, passing the bull-horn to one another to speak about the recent raising of the qualify-ing score of B-Mor children for promotion to a Charter, ours now having to test in their top 1.25 percent instead of the 2 percent be-fore, which seemed already unfair. This is not about the price of fish anymore. Regular people, including people who were even childless, asked to be helped up onto the palettes, to speak of our most talented children and our bittersweet willingness to part with them, and did so without attempting to mask their faces. In fact, someone with high access leaked a security vid of the rally, the face ID predictably focusing on the organizers first and their deputies next and then sys-tematically sectioning the crowd, but the drone's zoom-and-pan kept moving too slowly and then too fast, perhaps not programmed for such large and dense and shifting numbers, and in the end the vid was rendered unviewable, jittery and useless, until it zoomed out to capture the entire massing. It turns out we are one, if not ever how we expected.

And it cannot matter that outwardly nothing has yet changed. Maybe we don't even expect things to. Maybe we know that next year it will be deemed that 0.75 percent is the allowed fraction. We may not soon be heeded, but at least we can feel the long-held rum-bles, now open-throated, our lungs warmed and aching with this special use that we know may be poignant only to us. There was so little of this voicing before, and now that there is much more, we see it takes as many forms as there are people, though some don't easily align. There are instances of overexuberance, when someone is so stimulated by this unfettered exhibition that he loses all perspective and control. Take the case of one B-Mor fellow, who, after receiving what he felt was poor care at the health clinic, set up a camera in the staff restroom and took vids of the nurses and PAs, posting them for all, and going further by captioning each with the names and house addresses of these supposedly rotten individuals, who are of course our brethren. While we well know that our clinics are not the finest centers, and that the staffs can often seem indifferent to their charges, there is no excusing this fellow for trying to expose and humiliate them, something we have all darkly considered (not by using surreptitious vids, of course) but would never dream of enacting. And yet this B-Mor did, taking on the mantle of witness, prosecutor, judge, and jury, and executing in an instant the full bore of his malice that was unleashed, in great part, by this new and wide enthrallment.

The feeling he was free.

We will bear his blight, and others, trying to understand them as what naturally attends any plenitude, the rise of certain kinds of pests. But what gives us pause is what also may be happening to the rest of us, who have not gone to any extremes and never will and yet are differently engaged, not ultimately self-celebrating and self-aggrandizing like our health center muckraker but oriented in a way we haven't quite been before. Are our thoughts angling as much toward ourselves as to our household or clan? Have we become as primary as the collective rest? Such indication may be in what we have begun to hear and see of the concern for Reg. B-Mor remains focused and worried about his whereabouts and welfare; there are growing calls for official information; there was even a lie-in at one of the main intersections of the settlement, in which a thoroughly organized group of younger people spelled out his name on the asphalt with their bodies, causing a jam that took some hours to undo, an inconvenience for sure but one we abided.

There are other Reg notations that don't at first blush appear out of the ordinary. Newer tags, hand done, that only slightly revise what we've seen before, such as:

FREE ME, REG.
I MISS REG.

And amazingly, REG ♥ ME, which must have inspired the now popular eponymous song, whose lyrics, quirkily charming as they may be, are remarkable mostly in how much they reveal the fascination the singer has with herself. She goes on and on, and by song's end, we can't help but think only of her sitting at the mall café, her tea getting cold, waiting for a boy who might never come. We end up losing Reg all the more. Hey, that's the point, some say, though it doesn't feel in the least convincing on that score. And although the majority of us are still fixed on Reg's happy images about the walls and streets, on the shapely simplicity of his name, on the hope that he will return to us unchanged and whole, it seems some of us have already skipped a few beats forward with no wearing effects at all.

What stands besides is that there has been nothing of Reg. Nothing at all, if you don't count the wild rumors, which have him simultaneously manning a handscreen accessories kiosk in D-Troy, and gravely injured while attempting to escape from wherever the directorate was detaining him, and currently living among us after being cosmetically and mentally altered, which set off a brief period in which younger men of his build and height were regularly corralled by people absolutely sure it was he. Perhaps you find yourself trailing a gangly figure at the park, the kid jogging with a friend, a ball cap on his head, tufts of curly hair poking out the sides. You actually run alongside for fifty meters or so, eavesdropping on their breathy dialogue in the hope of gleaning some telltale remark or tendency that can't be surgically erased—the way the bridge of his nose lightly twitches as he laughs, how he makes a tiny throaty rumbling *urr* if you startle him when he's on his ladder—and while there is no definitive display, you can't help but see him locked away behind that boy's pale face and greenish yellow-flecked eyes, and reach for his pointy elbow. The boy sees this and swerves, sneering as though he's seen a diseased cur, and then he and his friend bolt down a diverging path, giddily cracking up as if they know they just barely got away.

Which makes us think all the more that if we stop looking he'll never emerge. It's in the tilting and thrashing that we wangle our luck. Otherwise, as a wise man once said, we'll be bound in shallows and in miseries. For the truth is that we can't help but envision what may well come; for what happens when there are no more songs and postings about Reg or Fan, when all there is remaining are weather-faded portraits and scribbles on the walls? Will we look upon these as our originals did when they tried to make out the ghostly hatch of the old-fashioned firm names and advertisements for things like tooth powder on the sides of the derelict buildings and idly marvel at what times those must have been? Will we have forgotten how impassioned we became, along with the details of the cause?

Or will this capacity be a part of us now, inform from this point forward how we view these long runway-straight streets, these heartening low-shouldered homes, and our modest and well-meaning brethren, who have worked assiduously all these years in the grow houses and tanks and treatment ponds, hardly ever looking up? "B-Mor being B-Mor" is how the saying goes, but whenever someone repeats that now, there's a rankling in the belly that makes you want to grab the person by the ears and bark, No more!

In fact, this became a refrain during the West B-Mor playground rally regarding the new promotion standard and led to a proposal of a general strike to protest it. Whether a work stoppage will really occur remains to be seen, as it would be a most serious turn, for it's something that's never happened in our history, not even when the directorate shut down two very busy health clinics for budgetary reasons or raised the minimum occupancy number for the older row houses after a second boomlet in our population.

You may wonder why the change in the qualifying percentile should be the inciting element when so very few of our children will ever attain it, the likely difference being one or two promotions a year, if any. Aren't we, as is oft noted, a most practical group? For a couple of generations there was no means of promotion at all, which our forebears didn't question, and once the chance was introduced by the directorate it was a double gift, for (1) being begun at all, and (2) rare enough that the character and constitution of B-Mor would not be eroded, say, by all of us constantly striving and angling as to how our children might leave. It is a lottery, aptitude based, of course, but a lottery nonetheless, and therefore functions primarily in the realm of imagination and dreams. We have already noted how the winners are feted, memorialized, and then duly consigned to a status like that of the heroic dead, shed of body, ethereal, mythically sublime.

But with this newly raised bar we can only ask: What else must we do? If someday not a single one of our very best can venture beyond the gates then the bargain is too skewed. Enough is enough. And it makes clearer now that the addition each year of those few hard-emblazoned names serves less to mark our progress or manifest our hopes than to parch the bitter seeds lurking beneath our endeavors, which is that where we are does not wholly comfort us. And perhaps never truly has.

BO LIWEI

Like the rest of us, Fan must have at some point gone by the monument and plumbed the etch of those letters with her fingertips, never thinking he was anything but a glimmer in the firmament. But here he was, as Oliver, though not in the least trying to hide himself from her. They were still standing on his lawn, the noise of the party briefly escaping whenever the front door was opened by someone going to their car or a child being trailed by his nanny. They would see her and Oliver, and wave, and he'd wave back, suggesting with his gestures that he was explaining something about the new house to Fan. But as he did, she thought he could not truly be Liwei, for she had been certain she would sense it the very moment she came upon him, that a certain feeling would overwhelm her, but there was no tightened roping in her chest now, no flitting chill across her skin. He didn't much look like her parents, either, or any mixing of them, though in truth she herself could hardly remember their faces or those of the rest of the household, which made her wonder if she'd looked at them much at all. But then we know arduous journeys can make a blur of heart, and home.

Seeing her skepticism, Oliver asked her if Old Yellow was still there, something he could have viewed but could not have known the name of; it was what all the children of the household called the ancient lion-head knocker on their front door, and always would, as long as it was there. But if he was Liwei, maybe she couldn't know, for she had never known him and had never seen his picture. And then it was generally acknowledged that those promoted changed profoundly after leaving (and rightly should), that they became thoroughly transformed, just as happens, say, if you let a pink farm pig out into the wild, they grow hairy and tusked and feral, though people will say perhaps the opposite holds here, any B-Mor coarseness and deference subsumed under the pressure of Charter stresses and expectation, which not only clarified one's character and views of self but recast your very posture, your color, the now ever-fronted way you held your chin.

You want to know why Vik left without you? Oliver said, the question clearly still evident on her face.

She nodded.

I told him to. I said, You should leave her here with me. She's my sister, after all. Plus, you'll probably only get in trouble.

There was no trouble, Fan said.

I didn't mean *that*, Oliver said. I know that. He told me you were from B-Mor. But it's funny, and totally Vik. How many people does one ever encounter from B-Mor? He didn't even know that people were talking about you back there. You and this "Reg."

Fan didn't reply.

But that's the thing about Vik. He's as smart as anyone I know. Probably the smartest. He could have done anything he wanted. But he can't do something as simple as say your name to a handscreen. Oliver showed Fan his, her name and household address and then countless links to discussion strings about their whereabouts, to all the theories and rumors about Reg and the directorate.

It would never occur to Vik. That's why he'll always be stuck in the ER. He gets on to something particular, and if he's satisfied, he won't bother to look up, he won't go beyond.

Fan said: Maybe he doesn't want to go beyond.

Oliver sort of chuckled, or suppressed a chuckle, as if to say where should he begin. There was a long-seeming moment in which they simply stood there, these putative siblings, the straight roofline of the brand-new house framing them, if Fan could see it, in a way that indeed suggested like blood, perhaps the shared squareness of their shoulders. But he was looking at her now as he did when Vik was driving away, a pain bubbling up.

You know about them, don't you? he said. He was about to say something else when his expression changed, and she turned to see Betty behind the glass storm door. Betty opened it enough to poke out her head, wave her hand.

Would you come in now, Ollie! We're nearly done with the presents and everyone is wondering where you are!

He called, All right, and Betty smiled, and gave them another
hurry-up wave. Then she disappeared back inside.

Oliver rubbed his chin. He said: I discovered it last month, just as
we were setting up for the sale. Her handscreen must have fallen out
of her bag in the kitchen and it was buzzing below the chair because
it was nearly out of power. I plugged it in and a message from Vik
came up. I know his number. Then I found all the rest, hundreds and
hundreds of them. Maybe a thousand. It was amazing. Do you know
how innocent most of them were?

Fan shook her head.

They were. They were almost all like that. Essentially just versions
of What are you doing, I'm fine, This is on my mind. Truly nothing.
You would think that would count. But of course, there were other
kinds.

He paused, letting out a trapped breath.

Well, it doesn't matter now. It's over between them. At least Vik
made that clear. Over for good. It's nothing that should be thought
about again, right?

He wasn't really asking, but nevertheless Fan did not know what
to say. And whether or not Oliver was truly her brother didn't seem
paramount at the moment, either, for how stricken he was, if almost
undetectably. He just kept slowly blinking, like his eyes were too dry,
the sole stirring in the impassive pane of his face. Did our Fan wish
to reach out? Did she want to comfort him with an embrace? Of
course, yes. So she did. It took him by surprise, but then he recipro-
cated with a firmness that surprised her.

When he let her go, he started heading toward the house, but Fan
simply stood there.

Oliver turned to her. What are you doing?

She said she thought she should go.

What do you mean, to Vik's?

She said yes, though in truth she didn't quite know. Hadn't she seen him drive off like he wouldn't ever be coming back? The curving street before her, which led somewhere deeper into the development, was densely quilted by kempt lawns and houses, by cars and tidy young trees. No one else was around.

Listen, Oliver said. You should at least spend the night with us. There's no place else to go right now. You can stay with us, with Josey and the twins. Josey would love it, I bet. I've been thinking about something since the sale. We can do whatever we want now. We can make everything happen. We can look after our family, our kin, all the time. I don't want only helpers around us, not anymore. Now you're here. Of course, it's up to you. But think about it. Whatever the reasons that you've come out from the walls. Who else would ever help you? Who else would ever care?

THAT NIGHT, WE KNOW, after the party, after everyone (the guests, the caterers, Betty's parents, all their helpers save the two who slept with the twins) had left, Betty and Fan made up her bed together in the companion bedroom to Josey's, the one in which Fan had overheard her and Vik. Oliver was on a conference call with the pharmacorp's scientists from their labs in Kuala Lumpur and Palo Alto. Josey had, of course, gone crazy when she learned that Fan would be staying with them, giddy with the assumption that Fan would be sharing her bedroom, but there was no other bed to bring in easily and Betty didn't want Josey up all night playing or talking, and it took both of them a long time to calm her down after her tantrum and refusal to brush her teeth and a bout of forced sobs and the books each had to read to her and her last-gasp entreaties before her little body finally relented and she fell dead asleep. It had been a long day and it was late and even Betty, Fan could see, looked exhausted as they stretched the sheet over the mattress, strands of hair loosely screening part of her face, the slightest crook to her back. Fan insisted she would do the rest and Betty thanked her but instead of leaving she plopped herself into the downy armchair beside the bed, taking up the very large glass of wine she'd brought up and placed on the night table. It was as big as a bell. She was absently slow-swirling the ruby liquid but not yet drinking it as she watched Fan spread the top sheet and pull on the pillowcases.

After so many years, Betty said. I know you never even knew each other but it's wonderful to see you together. Oliver seems so happy. This was going to be a happy day, for him especially, but not like this. I was afraid there would be a letdown after the sale because, frankly, what would we do with ourselves now; it's like winning the lottery, but I don't feel that way anymore. There's suddenly a new shape we can see. And we have you, in part, to thank for it.

Maybe Vik, too, Fan said.

Yes, for sure, Betty said, taking a drink of her wine. I'm sorry he had to leave so abruptly. I didn't even know.

That's okay, Fan said, thinking as fast as she could to make sure not to cause any undue trouble.

Did he say why? Betty asked, as if asking most casually.

Fan told her he had to go to the medical center. She said she would call him tomorrow.

Yes, please do, Betty told her. But I did wonder when you two arrived. Vik is always doing and saying the strangest things. I knew you weren't someone's "niece." I guess I thought he was just embarrassed to have hired a helper for himself.

He's too neat for a helper.

That's certainly our Vik, Betty said, her eyes a little tickled. You know, we've known each other since we were children. Our fathers were colleagues at an engineering firm, and our families and a couple of others liked to go to a lakeside park together, well outside our village, where most other Charter families wouldn't go. The mothers weren't as high on it as the dads. They wouldn't let us swim or even go near the water. But the dads played bocce and badminton, and bought and drank the counties beer, which they said tasted better than what they had in the village.

Fan said that Vik never mentioned his parents or displayed any pictures of them.

I'm not surprised, Betty said. They passed away while we were just starting university, his mother first, and then his father almost right after, though from different Cs. It was a terrible time for him, as you can imagine. He was totally lost. He wanted to quit school, maybe even leave the village and go overseas, but we convinced him not to. Mostly I did. It was around that time I met Oliver . . . I mean Li . . .

Liwei.

Liwei. I almost like that better. In fact, I do. It's certainly more dashing. Do you know if it means anything?

Fan did know, as from time to time someone in the household would brag to a visitor about how a member of their clan had once been Chartered.

She said: Profit and Greatness.

Of course, Betty said, almost sighing. It couldn't be any other way. Oliver was destined to succeed. Everyone who's ever met him has thought it. Especially back then. Vik introduced us at the gathering after his father's memorial service. Of course, Oliver wasn't trying to be charming, but he was all energy and funny and sweet, and before you knew it, there was a crowd around him, including Vik, who badly needed cheering up. When Oliver was younger, he couldn't as easily dial himself back, not like he can now. He was always on because he had to be, being where he was from. You can imagine. I almost felt sorry for Vik, but you could tell he was grateful not to be the focus of everyone's sadness and pity. He was even a little happy. That evening, as we left him to be with his relatives, he said, "Are there two more perfect people more perfect for each other?" and actually made us hold hands. And now look at us. Here we are.

Here we are, Fan said.

Betty took a last big sip and finished her wine. The bed was made up now and Betty believed she had a nightgown that was left behind by a houseguest that might fit Fan. She wobbled to her feet and said she was going to find it, and while she was gone, Fan simply waited, leaning against the foot of the bed. But after a while, it was clear Betty would not be returning tonight. Fan brushed her teeth quietly so as not to rouse Josey, then returned to the new bed and pulled back the covers. She wasn't sleepy yet. So she just sat, waiting for the long night to come, laden heavy, as she must have been, with the truck of these many strange souls whom she had come upon and who had fallen upon her, all their hopes, and wants, and sorrows, and wounded dreams filling up the room of her thoughts. Could she still see out? Could she still see Reg? Yes. She wasn't dreaming him anymore for she had him in her constant sight, and he was coming ever closer now.

The next day Oliver and Betty—Betty apologized for having gone right to sleep once she got near her bed—sat her down in the main hall living room to outline what they called the Next Stage. Josey was playing with the new aquarium while she waited to be picked up by the preschool shuttle, having already figured out she could point the remote and control this fish or that or even a group of them. Her twin baby siblings were set up on either side of her in bouncy seats so they could watch the action, and they bucked and flailed their chubby limbs whenever Josey had the fish retreat inside the nooks of the coral and then pop out all at once. The twins' helpers were there, too, plus the three or four others who took care of the house, who were now dusting and damp-ragging on the periphery, though in this huge airy room and its vaulted ceiling it felt to Fan as if they were sitting at the dead center of a soccer field, the stands empty around them, the yawing space a phantom, coolish draw at her back.

Oliver and Betty were clearly unaware of the feeling, and between slugs of their iced coffees, alternately described to Fan what they saw of their new life, a life they hoped would include her. Oliver had woken Betty up before dawn and they'd talked all morning; they had many of the same notions about how they envisioned their lives, what, in their words, it would "look like, act like, feel like," this wondrous creature of their new existence. To begin with, they were going to have another set of twins, fraternal, of course, and probably another set after that, though Betty wouldn't carry those. She would become an all-hands mother, which meant managing every last aspect of the helpers' and cooks' tasks and responsibilities, and overseeing the post-school tutors for the children, as well as the clothes shopping and interior design, plus of course arranging the doctors' visits and the vacations. Oliver would be involved as much as possible, for they decided he'd invest in companies only sparingly, focusing instead on running the charitable foundation they were going to start, maybe for the benefit of Charter helpers' or even counties children's health care, though of this they weren't yet sure. What they were certain of was that this was an unparalleled opportunity, one very few people of their relative youth would ever have, which was not just to hop a global whenever they pleased or drink genuine burgundy at lunch but to spend their precious time together forever, whenever they could, without stinting.

The way they would do this, Oliver explained, was not simply by "wanting to" and "promise keeping" but by making, literally, structural changes; the plan, still preliminary, of course, but at the same time something he had seriously thought through last night, was to reorient this brand-new house, changing everything so that the entrance and front were on the driveway side, which would be mirrored by a similar construction on the abutting lot that he was going to buy. He made a quick perspective drawing of the imagined site on one of Josey's big sketch pads, his breezy, flowing hand impressively rendering the brick and plaster façades of now more conventional doors and windows. The two new structures would face each other, with the current driveway widened past the lot line and curbed just like a street, though it would serve more as a gathering place than an avenue for cars, the sidewalk lined with healthy young trees, the asphalt marked by the chalk of a few children playing knockout, an older couple cheering them. It was homey and tidy, safe and happy, a prettified version, Fan could see now, of a B-Mor street, one that seemed like theirs, as he rendered what appeared to be a tiny lion head on one of the front doors.

He was going to build the old neighborhood, right here in the Charter.

It would be inhabited, in their vision, by their many children (and helpers, though this was understood), and her parents, and her siblings' families, and any other relatives who might want to live there, rent-free of course, as long as they understood and believed in their "familial project" of not simply spending a few prescribed if pleasant hours of the holidays and birthdays together but engaging in the "real business" of living, the modest quarters, the joys and frictions of the communal table, the intimacy naturally elaborated enough to encompass every moment of their days, which, frankly, none of them had been experiencing much, if at all, and would have gone on missing if this great fortune had not come.

This is why we're asking you to stay here with us, Betty said. You know what it's like to live in this way. I never knew, nor did my parents and siblings, and Liwei—she paused and he smiled gently at her—he's all but forgotten. You can be our guide, Fan, you can show us what to do when we're not sure or doing things all wrong.

Now Oliver said, And we'll do everything we can to find out what's happening with your friend. I have colleagues all over, likely some with connections to the board of the directorate for B-Mor, if not on the board themselves. I'll bet someone is. Regardless, we'll get the information. And if it's something we can file a formal petition on, we will. Obviously I'll have more standing now, and so I have to expect that whatever can happen will happen.

And once we find him, Betty added, he can come live here, too, and be a part of the family, part of, what do you call it, the household?

She winked. Though best for a while in his own room, right?

Fan nodded, to this and the rest of what they were saying, not exactly because it was all pleasant and good (even if it was) but because the manner in which they spoke, with such confidence and reason and the heat of just enough ardor, made it impossible to view them and their desires as anything but highly agreeable, this being a Charter trait in general but one that Oliver and Betty had refined to a spell of enchantment. Indeed, Fan couldn't help but picture her Reg clopping down the stairs in the morning, sleep still sanding his eyes, delighting in the arrangement of fresh fruits and baked goods (just like what was put out this morning, none of it repurposed from yesterday), or using his height to allow Josey to decorate the street trees for Lunar New Year, or just riding scooters together again, feeling free enough to fly away. For none of us can resist such hopeful flashes, which are, in the end, what lights our way through this ever-dimming world.

SOMETIMES OF LATE, WE GET SCARED. IT'S SURPRISING when it happens, because it's often at a moment when our feeling should be the opposite of fear or panicked worry, a moment, for example, such as the other afternoon, when many of us were having a free-day, plenty of folks enjoying the temperate weather and sitting beneath a peerless clear sky in our rear plots or on the stoops, the children engaging one another in their street games with sweaty-headed abandon, scooting and dashing between the various food-hawker carts that seemingly materialize in precise accordance with our as yet unregistered hankerings. And just when we have a treat in hand, this most humble savor that nevertheless speaks so aptly to our clement realm, we wonder why it is that we now pause and loll the morsel on our tongues until it's common mush, why there's a shivering in the belly, which should otherwise be ever ready, avid.

It's irrational, for sure, maybe even mad, but as our recent hopes for B-Mor have evolved, everything else has begun to seem precarious. Suddenly all the sturdy engineering and constructing, from the originals to now, feels as though it's been resting upon an insufficient base, the same way a thoroughly elaborate and convincing dream can hinge upon an entirely impossible premise, which, once examined, exposes the rest as a mirage. The pilings are dust, the slab a matrix of silken spiderwebbing, and the very place we reside, our narrow row houses that have stood stalwartly wall-to-wall through a checkered history of caring and neglect, are but cells in a chimera, some bloodless being in whose myth we have believed too deeply and too long.

What we have left is our assembly, and therein lies the unexpected trepidation. We have lashed ourselves together, we are cheek by jowl but now in an entirely different way, yet we can't help but murmur the question that is surfacing in all our eyes: so who are we now? Yes, we are figuring out our conduct—the demonstrations, the speeches, the murals, even the improvisational work slowdowns by the more daring teams—but none of that retrofits or instructs us on how to think about what we believe in and why. For what are we aiming for, in the end? To be more like Charters? To have built, each of us, some private fortress impenetrable to everyone save a few cousin achievers? We allow that it's simple instinct to wish to be secured against all manner of riot, whether natural or human, and to strive however long—and sometimes ruthlessly—to make that so. We're not the kind to decry such pursuits and the fruits that might come of them, even when they are so luscious and rarefied that they become the cardinal imperative, the first and last passion. We won't fret when someone perches upon his lofty black rock; he can look down without having to endure any harsh caws from us.

At the same time, however, it chills us to think that despite how much we care about one another, and trust that we always will, some fundamental shift is under way. The more we modify longstanding assumptions and practices of B-Mor, the more we can't help but worry that rather than evolving our corpus we're in fact undermining it, just as some unrelenting C-illness would rewrite the normal patterns with an adverse instruction set of its own. These days you can even hear the refrain of a certain wild sentiment, basically summarized to this: that someday we'll have out-Chartered the Charters, that they'll be bunched about in the cool shadows of our walls, queuing all around to get through our main gate. As much as we'd like to see it—can you imagine?—we pause with what it would mean for us, what price we would have exacted from one another, to become so special and dear.

Perhaps we have already seen a form of this inversion, in what Fan would next encounter with Oliver and Betty. For it was amazing to us, and to Fan, what two focused, otherwise unencumbered Charter people could make happen for themselves so quickly and well. Yes, they were smart, yes, they were talented, yes, they now had such means as to simply require leveling their gaze at a desired "outcome" and deeming it be so, but the thing about Oliver and Betty was how unceasing they were in their formulation and management of the new master plan, applying themselves as though putting on a full-court press, covering every angle and lane, though theirs was more like an offensive pressure, relentlessly pushing as if they were trying to overcome a huge deficit, despite how far they were already ahead.

From a command center in a fully outfitted and climate-controlled trailer they rented from a commercial construction firm and had parked in front of the house, they (along with several bright new assistants) directed the numerous projects and subprojects, each of which required permitting and zoning variances and the vetting and hiring of contractors and their constant coordination to make it run and develop without not just undue delay but really any delay at all, so successful they were (with both incentives and their charms) in getting the excavators and carpenters and plumbers and electricians to take full ownership over what they were doing, as if it were their very own massive twinned house where they would live long and with fulfillment until a gentle good death.

Within two days of Fan's residing there, the Cheungs had already purchased the property next door and had its house razed, the own-ers so thrilled with the price that they only bothered to take their clothes and most cherished personal items, leaving the furniture and rugs and plates and everything else to be demolished and scooped up into the dumpsters that were backed in and out through an entire day and night, the *deep-deep-deep* seeming to disturb the neighbors more than the crashing of the debris so that Oliver had the loaders dismantle their horns. Their own brand-new house was dismantled within the week as well, the shell left standing but almost nothing else, although their furnishings and artwork were moved to storage as Betty had spent the last year choosing them. They could have eas-ily waited and resided there while the other was being built, but it was decided that the houses should be constructed and renovated together for sake of consistency and efficiency and to satisfy Oliver and Betty's desire to begin the Next Stage as soon as possible.

So other trailers were trucked in and situated on the far side of the sister property to house the family and the helpers and Fan, quar-ters that Fan assumed the Cheungs would find barely acceptable but that turned out to be as luxuriously appointed as their home and, in fact, at an even higher standard (they'd built and furnished the house pre-deal, after all): the trailers, Betty told her, were meant for hous-ing evening-program stars when they were shooting in remote loca-tions, and were made by the same company who built the planes that flew the upper-atmosphere globals, the interiors of the double-wide trailers lined in natural marbles and leathers and rich silks and hard-woods. There was a kitchen trailer for the cooks so the family would be assured of having its meals and snacks and beverages prepared exactly as Betty wanted them sourced and prepared, plus an exercise and virtual-activity trailer where Fan and Josey always spent time right before dinner. Though the trailers were much smaller than the family was used to and the first few days were difficult (the twins seemingly crying nonstop, Josey crabby and nervous, Oliver and Betty suddenly so busy and stressed that they began to snap at each other and everyone else, though not at Fan), they soon began to appreciate these less exalted proportions, where there wasn't so much space around them; they felt like they were finally living inside, even safer and more secure, especially with the volumes of noise and dust and all the other probably C-accelerating chemicals and particulates stirred up by the construction. And maybe because the trailers were made just like the globals, they were upper-atmosphere quiet and pressurized with purified ionized air.

Fan tracked the progress of the project perhaps as closely as anyone, what with the children not really caring and the helpers out of sorts with the changes in routines and Betty and Oliver neck deep in every detail, watching the stages of the work from the foundation pours to the framing in what seemed to be a time-lapse vid, the new building going up literally overnight (there were so many tradesmen bolting and joining the metal alloy studs that they jostled one another for room), and then sheathed like the original house while the complex innards of both structures were fashioned and fed in, all the labors and change orders and supply drop-offs and debris pickups going on simultaneously like an orchestra tuning up, but under Oliver and Betty's guidance not making any of that daft, unhinged music, instead sounding out a somehow harmonic, not unbeautiful tone. It was almost magical to behold, and although Fan still harbored many-sided reservations about her brother and his wife, she was like any of us would be, which was awed not just by the inexorable progression of this Genesis-scale undertaking but by their unshakable belief that they were the very people who should bring it

off. In B-Mor such self-faith, such a singular audacity, would have
been dismissed or mocked, not only because we so value humility or
consensus but because most everything we want has already been
placed within our reach.

We must say that Fan was heartened by their striving, their devotion, and felt closer to them and their children and the helpers for it.
She was our good Fan after all, she wanted to believe in their ultimate
decency, to be a generous sister and auntie, and couldn't help but
also think that a small fraction of their efforts and concentrations
applied on her behalf would eventually lead to her reuniting with
Reg. This was actually being planned for by Betty, who already had
her architects draw in a new extension to the original house that
contained a full set of suites, with a dedicated entrance, and that was
labeled in the plans as BAY FAN/REG. There was much more space in
the extension than just for two, which was surely just Betty anticipating, rationally thinking things through; they did not know the
way Fan was, nor did she want them to know. She was wary as she
had always been that such a disclosure could only compromise her,
though with Betty and Oliver, who seemed so pleased and apprecia-
tive of her presence, she was beginning to imagine a disclosure of her
state, naturally wondering, too, if in telling them they would want to
help her even more.

With Oliver—whom she could not quite bring herself yet to
address as Liwei, as Betty did, as even he was now introducing
himself—she was spending more time than anyone, including Betty,
who was now camped at the center of the armies of salespeople who
came to the command trailer bearing samples of their lighting and
plumbing fixtures and bolts of fabrics and carpeting and wallpaper.
She had to figure out the countless combinations of such items and
the resulting design scenarios, altering course depending on what
was available and when and in what quantities, luckily cost not being

a factor. Meanwhile Oliver was overseeing the construction and the shuttling in of manpower and machinery, as well as donning a hard hat for part of each day and nailing or soldering something (though this, he admitted, was a noticeable drag on the schedule). He was exceedingly busy, but was also taking some time each day for himself, something Betty was encouraging him to do now that he wasn't going to work anymore. She proposed that he rekindle his past interests, which he took seriously and with enthusiasm, swimming and taking out his old violin—he played for the family on their first night in the trailers—but as he confessed to her during a break when he and Fan took a light jog around the neighborhood and down to the main square, he wasn't sure if those had been truly his interests at all.

He recounted to Fan that once assigned to a Charter foster family, a childless older couple (whom he had not been in contact with for a long time), he'd continued with the violin lessons and swim team he'd been doing in B-Mor, plus started a genetics club at the secondary school (where he met Vik, eventually convincing him to start swimming competitively because of his wingspan) and was involved with a social-service group that gave free math tutoring on the weekends to the children who lived in the service people's dorms.

I certainly found them engaging and enjoyable, Oliver told her. He took a sip from his iced coffee (which was all he drank besides a little wine in the evenings). But can I say that those were the things I really wanted to do? I started on the violin and swimming so early that that was never a question, and because I was good at both, there was no thought that they weren't the right activities. The other things I chose because there again I was very good at them and wouldn't waste my time or anyone else's, plus they fit in with my vita for medical studies. So does something you're excellent at and that people admire you for and that does some good for all make for an "interest"?

Fan said she didn't see why not.

It certainly can, he replied. But all that doesn't confirm that it really is. Maybe it should mean you can't love it, because what if loving something means you should mostly feel frustrated and thwarted, and then a little ruined, too, by the pursuit. But that you still come back for more. You're good at free diving, right? That must be why they put you in the tanks. But did you always like it, even before it was clear that that's what you should do? Was it something you loved? Or were there other things that you were doing that you might have enjoyed even more?

There weren't other pursuits for our Fan, of course, as it was only ever one boy or girl in any generation of a household who was allotted such opportunities, and only if they showed highest promise, a custom that Oliver had clearly forgotten or had never noticed. But Fan didn't tell him this, nor that when the first few times she dove as a little girl she nearly drowned. Nor did she tell him how much indeed she had loved it anyway, just as he was positing, even before she was able to describe the feeling to anyone in the household, and through force of will and mastery of her fears had made herself into a fine diver. Or that she sometimes trembled at the prospect of having been cut from the tank-diving track, despite all her efforts.

She told him there was nothing she found more enjoyable.

You're lucky, Fan. But what will you do now? There's no work like that here.

I'll find something else, she said. You can still play the violin so well.

I like that I can, he said, not in the least bragging. But if I never played it again, I wouldn't even think about it. I hadn't, for years, until the other night, when I was actually playing. Do you find that strange?

This indeed puzzled Fan, as he had played so very beautifully, making a kind of music she had not encountered on any evening program or even at the underground mall during the New Year celebrations, when B-Mor's best musicians would perform swingy, upbeat pieces, the instrument seeming to become creaturely the moment Oliver tucked it under his chin, it seemingly animated by its own wants and voice. She had never felt such pure, lovely, sad sound.

Each day they would jog together like this, and each day Oliver would ask something about B-Mor, what things were like in the facilities and at the mall, what people in the clan were up to, though not inquiring too deeply into any particular person. If there was a theme to his queries about an uncle or cousin or one of their parents, it was about how they had gotten on over the years, how they'd aged physically and which C-illnesses they'd suffered and how they managed the early mandatory retirement and what they did with their free-days. When Fan asked what he remembered of the older people doing around the row houses and stoops, he said smoking and drinking tea and gossiping and eating snacks and watching the programs and farting and belching, to which Fan said, Yes, that's what they still do, to which he shook his head and laughed, though with a quizzical expression that made Fan think he believed she was trying to tell him something else.

In fact, he responded to much of what she said in this way, with a half-incredulous grin that quickly compressed into a tiny pout of wonder, just as if a monk had uttered a particularly imponderable koan for him to unravel. But he continued to ask all about B-Mor, never anything serious or weighty like school or facilities issues or the directorate, but about what kinds of eateries there were in the mall these days, or the kinds of street games the children were playing, or facts he didn't get to know because he left too early to be interested in, for example, how the retirees going on a lifetime global were chosen, or what music and vids and games teenagers liked best, and where they went to meet for dates, and whether it still mattered which clan you were from, or which neighborhood, for someone to like you in that way. He was trying to get a feel again for what basic life in B-Mor was like, the day to day to day, which Fan thought he would certainly find dull and common but that he seemed to get more curious about as they spoke, wanting the most insignificant details that Fan herself could hardly recall (if she ever noticed them), like the colors of the sash and uniform of the salesgirls at the department store (crème and mocha), and the price of a *mochi* (hardly changed), and if the great aunties still used those long-bristled Stone Age hand brooms that the counties peddlers brought in to sell to sweep the walk in front of the houses (yes). In fact, their light jogs, which had eased to walks, became a shared act of cataloguing the many patterns and textures of B-Mor life, a modest cloth indeed, but one that Oliver kept wanting to examine and handle and measure against his newly aroused memories.

For in recent years, and as the promise of his research solidified, he had been thinking more and more of his time in B-Mor with a deepening glow of nostalgia, though one surely too warm and bright and that he was skeptical of, being trained as a scientist. He told Fan how after he was Chartered, as it was known here, he had truly not thought of B-Mor at all, not because he wanted to forget it, but because after all the celebrations and commemorations and absolute good-byes—there were no see-you-laters, no au revoirs—the feeling he had was that he was embarking on his own private global, out past any atmosphere, and leaving behind a world at which he could not gaze back, as it had already been erased. Everyone knows how hard it is for any Charter kid to do well, but he was a newcomer with surprisingly indifferent foster parents who were more interested in keeping than raising him, and so he realized that there was just himself, that he was the only person who would educate this unfledged boy.

In the first overwhelming and chaotic weeks of his new life at school and swim practice he'd come home and, after a mostly silent meal, retreat to his room and stand before the mirror in his dressing room full of new clothes and berate himself for the various mistakes and idiocies he'd committed and revealed that day. He hated the new name he'd been given and he channeled his fury at this pathetic Oliver, calling him out for his failings, starting with his vocabulary, which he'd prided himself on in B-Mor but was shockingly lacking here. He even misused the words he had, no teacher in B-Mor ever correcting him, confusing paramount with tantamount, egress and aegis, his teacher holding forth upon their etymologies for the class, to his utter humiliation. He was excellent at math but found he was a half year behind his new classmates, most of whom were not gifted at all, and he stayed up all night for a week to teach himself the units he was missing, soon enough leaping past them, though he never let on. And while in the pool he was nearly as fast as the others, he realized how much harder he was working because of his faulty technique and mechanics, his teammates languidly pulling themselves through the water with butter-smooth strokes while he brutally chopped at it, as his coach said, like a madman having a fit.

But he learned. He could not help but learn, as vigilant as he was for any sliver of instruction or advice. And this is what Oliver revealed to Fan he was best at, his truest gift: he was instantly able to determine who possessed expertise or useful knowledge, and then glean from them whatever he could, even if they were against him, which most everyone was at the beginning, his classmates and teammates and coaches and even his violin teacher, who had never worked with a Chartered student before. The only one who had been immediately welcoming to him was a very quiet but self-collected Vikram Upendra, who noted an error in a second-order partial differential equation Oliver had written out for the class, mentioning it to Oliver only afterward to make fun of their conceited instructor, who believed himself a rare genius who should have been designing propulsion systems or proprietary trading platforms.

Oliver admired Vik's mind, for sure, but mostly for how unruffled he was, how he let everything come to him and then made it fit into his own idiosyncratic measure. This could never be Oliver's way, but hanging out with Vik helped him understand the value of not always pushing and striving at full tilt, that there were situations best handled by patience or throttling back or maybe—and this had never occurred to him—by doing nothing at all. The funny thing was that there was a worrisome period in which his research seemed to have stalled, until one day he asked himself what Vik might do and proceeded to halve his large staff so they could concentrate their efforts on simpler approaches to the problem. Soon thereafter there was a breakthrough, and whether it was mere coincidence didn't matter, because in Oliver's own mind, Vik had a credit in his success.

It's why I could do nothing to him the day of the party, he confessed to Fan. They had stopped as usual at the coffee bar, Oliver having his iced Americano, Fan a tangerine juice.

I was going to punch him out. I was going to strangle him. But I couldn't. He said he was sorry, which I could see he genuinely was. That was it. That was my friend Vik. He could have tried to excuse himself, he could have easily pointed out how lonely Betty had been these last few years when I was working at the lab at night after seeing patients. Every weekend, too. It was why they began spending a lot of time together again, just as friends would, which they didn't try to hide and I was actually grateful for. Betty seemed much happier. And you know what? She was. I wasn't a very present or attentive husband and father then. Before that, too.

Fan said it seemed he was quite present and attentive now.

He nodded, though somewhat absently, as surely screening in his

mind was a set of pictures he would see from time to time, and forever, whether he wanted to or not.

After a pause, he said: Have you talked to Vik? Wait. You don't
have to tell me. I don't even know why I want to know.

She said, Maybe you wish to be friends again.

Oliver thought about it. He said, I guess I do. All these years, Vik
was my only real friend. But it's too late now. It's gone. And besides,
it would be too awkward around Betty, with us acting like nothing
was wrong. I appreciate it that you haven't said anything to her. You
may think this is odd. But I don't ever want her to have to apologize
to me.

It was then that Oliver got very quiet, not shedding tears but shuddering very finely, as if he were earthen inside and loosely caked and
just about to shear. Fan saw how much he was resisting, and to bolster
him placed her hand beside his on the café table, the simple sight of
which seemed to calm him down, the two opposing forms differently
sized but too similar in the proportions of the fingers to the palm, the
chafed, uneven rises of knuckle, the way their thumbs turned a little
too far inward, for their being anything else but true kin.

DURING THE NEXT COUPLE OF WEEKS, FAN GREW EVER
ingrained into the life of the Cheungs, such that it felt to them that
she had always been a part of their family. They all kept saying how
much they loved her presence, her indulging play with the children,
how she helped Betty make design decisions and kept Oliver exercis-
ing, which relieved his stress. Even the helpers adored her, as she
never minded picking up after Josey or lending a hand with the
dishes. This all came easily to her, of course, being someone who was
raised in a crowded household in B-Mor, embodying for Betty and
Oliver all the reasons that they were expending astounding efforts
and sums on this project.

The effort was all theirs but the sums, we should now note, had
begun to dwarf what was actually in their accounts (especially given
that they'd just built what had been a new house), as the deal with
the pharmacorp had been agreed to in principle but with the minor
contractual details, as one can expect with ever-complicating lawyers, still being haggled over. Of course, none of this mattered, as
after word of the sale, every major Charter bank had come to the
Cheungs hawking huge bridge loans at rates so low anyone would
have jumped at the offers. Borrowed or not, a sizable new lode of

money is a powerful thing, as everyone knows, not just the quickest balm but a device of dreams, an imagination machine that churns out the exact products of your wishing, one right after the other, so that it's all one can do to keep up the conjuring. Maybe that's why in B-Mor it's always been so costly to borrow money (besides being nearly impossible to make a windfall), which we see now may be a boon, to keep us from pitfalls, of course, but also ever grounded. Our eyes on smaller prizes.

And if we understand Fan in this way, it makes sense enough that she did not prod Oliver and Betty on the question of Reg. She was well aware how all-consumed they were with the light-speed progression of the work, the two houses at this point appearing just like the architect's full-color renderings (though in truth the serial simulations barely preceded the stages of construction), the design finally set so that each house had three entrances (a primary and two flanking) and the simple window pattern of a B-Mor structure, one atop the other on each of the three floors, the façades now cased in real bricks that had been aged in specialized weathering barns. The interiors were coming along as well, Fan doing a daily walk-through with Oliver and Betty and their architects or foremen during the shift changeover of workmen in the late afternoon, ascending the central stair of each bay as it took them to the landings of a floor's four rooms that would soon be as plush as the trailers but were distinct compartments, the plan so unlike the overabundant airiness of the former structure. The difference here was that you could move through the various doors and openings between the bays, go up and down and across from wherever you were, the bedrooms and parlors repeated except for the very large kitchen and communal dining room in each house, which would be anchored by a long, rough-hewn plank table for up to sixteen (the pair being made right now, in fact, by a woodworker at Seneca Circus).

But even with everything moving at a breathtaking pace, Fan still tried to remind Oliver as often as she could to please follow up with this or that colleague or friend, and while he never seemed irritated by her requests or replied with any curtness, she couldn't help but wonder whether he was intentionally not taking their calls or deleting their messages or indeed had never gotten in touch with them at all. For while she didn't want to think it, from his perspective what benefit would it be to speed up this process of searching for her Reg? Whether they located him and could bring him here, or else found the whole hope was futile, either way would only serve to hasten the arrival of the moment when Fan must decide whether to stay with them or go. And as we recount her travails, it's not difficult to surmise that this is the basic form of the question, no matter where she was, in B-Mor or the counties or in the soft glove of a Charter: Why did she go? Why didn't she stay? What ill condition does she see?

It's funny to say, but maybe if she knew how interested we had become in her absence, she might never have gone.

Though there are signs. Here in B-Mor, where the autumn sun shines in its unmitigated fullness, we see the lengthened shadows of the gathered throng and are grateful for them, as it's this darkness that now mostly blankets the streets and makes them seem full, our numbers sadly dwindled. There's still noisemaking and chanting, a chorale breaking out here and there, if with a less strident song. It's the same with the postings, and the chattering in the mall, as if a certain diminishment had settled into our cells and ceded the keenest color, the keenest heat, as with the first fading leaves now twittering on the lean-branched trees. The only things literally growing are the oddly styled heads you come upon quite regularly of late, the shifting, sheepish eyes of those no longer keeping up their clean-shaven scalps, their renascent hair unruly and confused in its swirls.

We briefly followed one of these persons last weekend, an attractive young woman in her late teens or early twenties, good skin and clear, pretty eyes, being curious as to what she might be doing with that part of her day. We trailed her for an hour in the underground mall, where she browsed the sale racks of blue jeans and glamour tees, then visited a cheap jewelry kiosk where she was clearly acquainted with the clerk, purchasing a shiny accessory for her handscreen before meeting a neatly dressed (and normally coiffed) couple at a tea stall. They took tea and some cookies, and the two women seemed to have some laughs at the expense of the man, who took the ribbing well enough. Then the man noted the time and the couple quickly got up to leave, perhaps for a movie, inviting her to come along, but she declined, happily shoo-shooing them away.

She first checked her handscreen for a while, then put it away and simply watched the streams of people through the clear partition that separated the tables of the tea stall from the mall corridor, her expression difficult to read, neither bored nor wistful nor in any way intrigued. And yet there was something about her in that moment of regard that gave us pause. She was quite enrapt, we were certain, even as her face remained almost totally blank, just as a drinking glass remains unchanged when filled with water but of course is not at all the same.

For we know the moment, too: to have given over to the full onrush of a feeling, to have ridden up the wall of the curl and maybe, if we're reckless or brave enough, done the deed, essentially turning our insides out. And for a period—this young woman's lasting perhaps a few weeks—heady with the rich feed of new and unexpected hopes, we make a whole world of that feeling, such that we can hardly imagine how it was before, or could ever be again, so that the smallest things we say or do seem touched with a destined aura. We connect with you who lingers in our path. We forget that every fervor will subside.

The young woman paid her bill and left, and as she stepped on the escalator rising to the street level, someone said loudly enough for her to hear, What about Fan?

She turned and looked about, unsure as to who had spoken. She looked suddenly so stricken and wan, as if her very conscience had leaped out from her chest and cuffed her. The escalator delivered her to the top and she glanced about nervously before scampering away.

It was awful, for someone to have singled out this poor soul, this girl who had only enacted with earnestness and the wonder of a pup those things we couldn't bring forth or otherwise contrive for ourselves. We must picture her as feeling hounded all the way home, passing the old-timers in the parlor without even her usual blithe Hey, ba, going up to the room she shared with two sisters but who were fortunately away and with unknowing irony doing just as we do in our secret night, our heads gravely cradled, towing rough fingers through the strands.

So what about our Fan? What was her disposition as she stood on the new street the bulldozers had graded between the houses and filled with gravel, bawdy-storied crews having installed drainage and laid out the formwork for the sidewalks? Betty had instructed the architects to consult Fan whenever possible, telling the almost identically dressed and spectacled trio (two men and a woman) that what it felt like out here was as important as in any room of the houses. This is where Josey and the twins and their cousins and their pals would spend much of their most cherished time, racing about, as Fan had described, in a game of tag using the stoops as safe bases, or playing soccer with the curbs as sidelines and ragged grow-house jumpsuits dropped down as goals, or simply sitting enervated beneath the mean summer glare, squinting and dry mouthed, waiting for the ice cream man to putter by on his three-wheeled scooter with its rear icebox full of treats (there was no such vendor here in the Charter but certainly one could be arranged). It was all being knit together before Fan's eyes, its imminence convincing her at least of the generous vision and spirit of these newfound kin, and perhaps engendering something deeper in her, too, those feelings none of us who are truly living can always master and which thus grace us, if also leaving us vulnerable.

It turns out, though, that Fan was more vulnerable than she could know. For Oliver was indeed taking all his colleagues' calls, and calling them all back, and then pushing to be referred to others who might be better positioned and connected to those who might actually know something. At first it was squarely annoying how difficult it was to find out almost anything about this Reg, by every account a thoroughly ordinary low-level facility worker, Oliver's frustration in fact boiling over during a call to a lab friend, when in an arrogant fit of pique he accused the fellow of indolence for not coming up with more useful results. But soon enough, as it grew clear how the channels of his always reliable school and medical network were seemingly being blocked, Oliver became intrigued. The more resistance or obfuscation or dead-ending he encountered, the more it sparked his mind with a deepening fascination, a fascination that soon altered his approach, such that he saw the problem as one of not just exerting pointed social pressures or unpacking certain linkages but embracing the phenomenon of a complex and special aberration, upon which he would apply the force of his research methodologies, structuring and casting his inquiries to probe certain notions and to isolate and test corollaries to see how they led back to a former line or else suggested a new one.

He mentioned none of these activities to Fan, in part telling himself that to do so without a ready or even provisional means of finding Reg would be irresponsible, and maybe downright cruel (despite the fact that he admired Fan for being Fan, which is to say the kind of person who would keep the right perspective on such qualified information). The other part was less generous; for soon enough, one of these lines, Oliver concluded, confirmed at least this: that while really no one could or would say where this Reg was, including someone very high up in the directorate, it was clear he'd become a primary object of curiosity for the very pharmacorp that was buying Asimil. This made perfect sense, if what he was now hearing back about the boy was true. There was Asimil and there was Reg; a life of serial therapies, or maybe none at all. The former would be astronomically expensive. But which was actually more valuable in the end? If he were running the pharmacorp, he would be running the numbers, having it penciled out, but regardless he'd want Reg in his hands, for sure (he'd easily confirmed that both his parents had died of C-illnesses and that Reg was an only child), to determine what in his makeup was leading people to believe he was C-free forever, although how, without his whole life having been lived and studied, could you ever be certain? Maybe you'd have to keep him forever.

Another week or so went by. By now the hardscape was completed, the sidewalks set and lined with granite curbing, and the roadway paved in the same light gray hue of our very own streets, and then laced with just enough mica to emit the slightest glitter. The young gingko trees were planted and staked. In fact, they decided not to roll out much sod on the double property but instead put in a large playground for all the children of the neighborhood to use, even if there weren't that many. Oliver had a street sign made up and affixed to the top of a black-painted steel gaslight post set at the head of the drive, the old-style letters embossed and hand-painted: BETTY'S LANE. Inside, the houses were nearly completed, with the installation of cabinetry and appliances and electronics and the finishes of the floors. All the rooms had already been painted or papered, the bedrooms laid in with carpeting.

Fan's rooms in her bay's three floors—all twelve of them, not including the baths—were painted in white. As with the other rooms in the houses, Betty had multiple scenarios for various beautiful and elegant color schemes for her walls and trim from which to choose, a mix of paints and wallpapers, curtains and rugs and throws, but Fan asked to have it done in plain white, the default, bulk white paint contractors used in the service people's dorms and public restrooms, which was the same white paint the originals in B-Mor had been given truckloads of long ago and that we never stopped using. She chose it for the sake of familiarity but also because the selecting of all those very particular colors seemed to her a tacit acceptance of a future in which she could not quite promise she would be.

Betty, clearly, had no such conception, instantly agreeing to Fan's request with the idea that it was a classic look, clean and simple, and she even went so far as to have all of Fan's furniture covered in the same flat white, if knocked down with the slightest touch of gray so everything wouldn't be so severe and polar, which turned out to be absolutely right. Fan was at once her au pair, her incredibly capable and independent helper, her sweet little sister, and Betty was now comfortable enough with her to ask more questions about Reg, what he looked like, what he enjoyed eating, his favorite pastimes, all, of course, so she could get a feel for what it would be like when he was here on the "block." They were in her soon-to-be bedroom suite, surrounded as if in snow. Betty was also naturally curious as to how they'd met, what she and Reg liked to do together, even mischievously inquiring, as a close girlfriend might, about the more romantic details, such as whether he was a good kisser. Fan had never really talked about such things before, but we know she felt comfortable enough with Betty, too, and perhaps slightly dazzled by the woman's openness and obviously generous heart, that she found herself divulging how Reg had her sit on his right whenever possible because of the small, hairy mole on his left cheek that he was terribly self-conscious about, even with her.

Oh, he sounds so sweet! Betty cried, and soon they were giggling about Oliver and how he couldn't walk by a mirror without furtively checking the state of his biceps or abs with his new toning regimen of weight lifting and swimming, the latter of which he started up again after taking Josey for her first swim lessons and deciding to do laps while she was being coached. In fact, Betty went on and told Fan how strange it was to have him around all the time, to be reminded of certain of his habits and traits, like his secret vanity, or his addiction to sour jellies and iced coffee, which apparently he steadily fed himself with during his hours at the medical center and lab, and had seriously cut back on now, though who could tell.

It seems it is nice for you, too, Fan observed.

Of course you've noticed, Betty said, smiling. It's been not just nice but wonderful. Maybe you think it's funny that I'm calling him Liwei, but for me everything feels different. He's still Oliver through and through, I know, but now he really spends time with Josey and wants to bathe the twins every day and for the first time I think since we were in school we're watching movies together again in bed at night, with popcorn and wine. We're not even having to talk that much if you know what I mean, she said, her eyes twinkling. We're having fun, even stupid fun. Some real joy. We still argue plenty and he drives me crazy with how he has to think everything through a dozen squared times but I guess that's gotten us where we are. Right? This is truly the place we should be.

Fan did not demur, nor try to judge whether Betty wholly meant what she said or was more hoping she was. It didn't matter, because, as we know, it is "where we are" that should make all the difference, whether we believe we belong there or not, and as such is the ground on which we will try our best not to feel trapped, or limited, or choose those paths that merely assuage our fears. By this standard, Betty was alive, and so was her Liwei, and Fan could finally now believe that in the near course of time Reg's whereabouts would be revealed; for she was only human, too, we have to remember, simply a girl with a love who was lost, and if the iron ordeals she endured these past months had made her batten down her longing, in the comfort and relative calm of Betty's Lane that ache had begun to bristle, steadily untwine.

With the project nearing completion and their having far less to manage, they took short excursions during the day. When Josey returned from preschool just past midday, they all climbed into the Cheungs' buslike new van and went to town to lunch and shop or visit the children's museum or zoo before heading to their newly joined private fitness club where Oliver and Josey swam in the full indoor pool while on the deck Fan watched the twins along with one helper, the strapped-in babies loving the sounds and splashing of the water. The club had set up several treadmills in a connecting room with a waist-high wall, to afford an open view so parents could watch their children swim, and Betty slowly walked on one of these while she caught up on some of her evening programs.

This is just how they were situated one Saturday afternoon, Fan passing a rattle back and forth with one of the twins, the helper, Pinah, engaging the other, Josey paddling somewhat frantically in the nearest lane toward the swim instructor, though making her way across the pool, with Oliver motoring back and forth in a far lane, when several groups of men in warm-ups and swimming caps with goggles strapped to their foreheads walked out to the deck. Among them was Vik Upendra, Fan recognizing him immediately even with his back turned, for his extra-long limbs and the way he wildly flapped his arms to loosen them, rather than shaking them like the others did. Apparently, they would later learn, there were seasonal club league swim meets, this being the autumn competition for under-forty men. At this point Betty had also seen him, as she was no longer paying attention to her treadmill screen, and when Vik finally turned and saw Betty, Fan could see the instant falter in his face, like any boy excited for a day's swim but who had arrived to a completely drained pool. His arms, which had been stretched high, dropped down slowly and he began to walk toward her, keeping his eyes on her, even as she was minutely shaking her head and looking down at her screen, not wanting to meet his eyes. But Vik stood directly in front of her, and although Fan couldn't hear him for the din of the indoor pool and the whining jogging machines, she could see very clearly that in so many words he was telling her that he still loved her and that she was doing all she could not to tell him the same.

On the other side of the pool, Oliver was still swimming and would have kept his head in the water for many more laps, but he must have noticed all the new adult swimmers crowding; he didn't make his turn. He hung on to the wall instead, still wearing his dark goggles, his gaze settling immediately on Vik and his wife. He just watched them talk, or Vik talk. There was nothing else for him to do. Finally Betty begged him to please stop doing this now and Vik, seeing there was nowhere to go, relented. He walked to Fan on the near side of the pool.

How are you? he said, his pleasing face all broken into parts.

I'm fine, Fan said, her own chest heavy. I hope you will be, too.

Thank you, he answered. Then he slowly walked to the far end with a dignified deliberateness. When he reached the last two lanes, he donned his goggles and then dove into the pool in the next-to-last lane. He smoothly swam the length, freestyle, heading toward where Oliver was now treading at the wall, and when he got there, he didn't stop or slow but made a flip turn and reversed, kicking hard away. Oliver followed him in his own lane, by the half point catching up to Vik. They kept pace with each other for the rest of the length, their speed more steady than anything else, as if they wanted to be going side by side, as if the eyeing each other were building up their strength.

Then, near the wall, Oliver swam beneath the lane divider and into Vik's lane, and when they both flipped and turned, they were still neck and neck, but now flying. The commotion and sight of two swimmers racing in the same lane was now drawing the pool's attention, such that people were collecting along the four sides to watch them go, crowding and leaning over one another, including Fan and Pinah the helper, so they could see these two, the long man and the short man, the gliding strides and the pistons, their arms sometimes tangling or even striking the other on the shoulder, the cap, the torsos jostling and pushing each other against the divider, riding up over it. There was a race to win but neither knew how long the race was, they just kept eating up lengths until Vik, longer and more fit for having been swimming all these years, began to pull away, one length becoming two, becoming three, until it was no longer a race anymore, Vik flipping and turning against a straggling Oliver and then turning again, clearly keen on reaching and lapping him.

By this time Betty was shouting for Oliver to stop, to get out of the pool. When Oliver saw Vik closing, he made a furious kick, perhaps for propulsion, but it caught Vik in the nose and instantly bloodied him. There was a guffaw from the spectators, both swimmers now treading in the pinking water. Vik held his face and saw the blood and then fell upon Oliver, the people around now yelling, Betty screaming, with some of the spectators so riled they either stepped in or jumped in themselves or were pushed in from behind, so that others might see the swimmers fighting, though lifeguards and some swim team members had already jumped in and separated Vik and Oliver.

Fan couldn't see any more for the bigger people blocking her view, but she did notice Pinah through the scrum, or rather she saw the pinned dark hair of Pinah's head, suspended a foot below the surface of the water. Her arms flanked wide. Fan jumped in and crouched at the bottom and then shot them both up with a fierce boost of her legs, the plumpish woman much heavier than Fan would have ever thought. Some people on the deck pulled Pinah out and a lifeguard started working on her, Fan watching from the water as she caught her breath at the pool ladder. Luckily the guard got Pinah to cough and hack and start to breathe again quickly, as she'd been under for only a few seconds.

Fan climbed out quickly, panicking for a second, but saw the twins still secured in their bouncers, if now crying. But she didn't want to pick them up for how soaked she was, her loose sweatpants and T-shirt now clinging to her. Then she saw a toweled, totally spent Oliver being hugged by Betty at the other end of the pool. Betty was fiercely whispering to him, perhaps beseeching him. Whether he was, in fact, listening to her, Fan could not tell. All she knew was that he was staring at her with the deadest eyes, the hollow of the feeling making her instinctively pull the wet fabric from her belly.

LOOK AT THE FISH.

Our best B-Mor primes. Look at the eyes, luminous and clear. Even on ice, the scales are tiled tight to one another, the points of the fins unbroken, unclipped. Peel forward the gills and see the darkest cherry red, as if there's blood hotly pushing through its robust, meaty body. The mouth is closed but not clamped in any grimace, saying instead this with a tranquil set of jaw:

We are in good order.

Take us up.

We are ready to be chosen.

And choose them they do. For the rumors are done. Any remnants of the months-long scare about the wholesomeness of our fish are now very few, to be found in only the most phobic quarters, such as those flats and villas where they parse every morsel and sip and likely never enjoyed them anyway. The rest, however, are back at the fish shops all across the Association, queuing as before and with their unyielding Charter scrutiny selecting the ones they deem the brightest, finest, the most pure. They have absolute confidence in their ability to discern and analyze and perhaps well they should, given where they are. They fully believe in themselves, and it doesn't matter if our fish are of unsurpassed quality, virtually identical in size and composition, and raised in such a way as to make it almost impossible, if not ridiculous, to try to choose among them. And yet they do, studying the displays like they were buying gemstones, and while there are no jostling scrums like at a special clearance or sale in B-Mor, when someone else picks the very one they've identified as theirs, the one they'd determined was destined to best nourish and block any rogue unknittings in their cells, they can't help but get there just a bit earlier the next time.

The result has been a heady rise in the price per kilo of #1 primes, enough, in fact, to get us near the record levels reached during the last big boom, when it seemed no Charter could go for more than a couple of days without a fillet on his plate. All the facility tanks are full again with every stage of them, from specks of fry to the stoutest matureds, the concrete floor of the grow houses tickling the feet with the constant vibrato of the filter pumps running around the clock, the air heavier, moister (though it truly can't be, given how engineered everything is) with the enriched quality of the reprocessed effluent dripping onto the plant beds. These are growing as dense as ever, so that you can hardly see a coworker weeding directly on the other side, merely hearing the threshing of his gloved hands against the stalks.

And from all this flush being there's a scent that is at once off-putting and sweetly alluring, too, whiffs of faint rot and newest life columned together and vented through the roof so that the surrounding households of B-Mor must be dreaming of every earthly hunger, of filling themselves with whatever goodness may be at hand. Or are their lights burning later, sometimes into the wee hours of the morning, to feed newly roused desires?

The rest of us have no such wafts carrying across our paths, and yet here we are in the mall-going throng, like everyone else pursuing our day's own trivial ends but feeling drawn in, too, by the wider pitch and tow. There's no specialness or majesty in this, there's nothing different from what has gone on here since the originals set themselves up, we descendants doing what we should be doing, work-day or free-day, in the households or in the parks, contracting ourselves for best use and the welfare of the run of times to come. Nobody knows the future. So when we chat on the stoops, say, before the evening chill finally drives us in, of the lady on the next block who attempted to circumvent the usual regulations and produce her own designer line of fashion slippers in her attic using a platoon of counties peddlers as cheap labor, or of the man who was caught sitting at night—totally unclothed—high up in one of the largest trees in the park because he simply wanted, he said, a better view of the stars, we rib one another and chuckle and maybe even argue about the state of our settlement, though with no more of those uneasy skips or pauses, no more throaty, dire tones. We speak and abide one another and then we go in.

For what is there to worry about now? With the relative quiet prevailing, the directorate, or some other body, we can't be sure, has reversed some of the more disheartening measures of recent times, foremost being restrictions on health clinic visits, which are still limited (as they should be, given the realities of the times) but at a more reasonable frequency, and the qualification for Charter promotion (back up to 2 percent), as well as certain smaller things that indeed make a difference day to day, such as suddenly better pricing for our own excellent produce and fish. There's even talk of the schools using more of our goods in preparing the children's *bento* lunches, rather than random broccoli and potatoes of vaguest origins and from suppliers long unnamed and unknown, though this remains to be seen.

Finally there has been an unprecedented round of new, if modest, public works as well, something they're promoting as Keep It Up, which has employed at very decent pay small armies of recently retired folks and unemployed younger people, who are now sweeping the streets and sidewalks, clipping shrubberies in the parks, power washing and then painting faded or graffiti-tagged buildings and walls, as well as a hundred other sundry projects meant to bring up the luster of our good place. You see them on their snack breaks, maybe a group of eight or ten of them sitting on the picnic benches near the noodle and kebab stands, all wearing the same asparagus green jumpsuits with lighter green caps (inevitably one of the youths sporting it sideways) and while not talking much as they eat (they wouldn't know one another), older and younger at least joking or sharing a taste of this or that with enough ease and good feeling to suggest that they're in this together, communing as they labor, this enduring snapshot of what makes us who we are.

And if you put all of this together, if you collect these happenings and projects and promotions, you would have to say that they comprise again the typical habit of our lives here in B-Mor before this period of disturbance, which, from really anyone's perspective now, would appear to have passed. It's like a dream irrepressibly vivid and captivating when it was happening but now nearly impossible to remember, not just its details but the very fact of it. We just slept through it is the sensation. Rested the whole of our night. Of course, there are some who must know we did not make passage serenely in a void. Some of us still tap our fingers to the rhythms of those street-filling chants, or can see, when no one else can, the shape of the signs still ghosted in our minds, now blotted by layers of clean fresh paint. It's not common, not at all, but every once in a while someone will rise up from a chair in an eatery or tea shop or step from the movie theater line and face the blithe crowd with half-open arms and without having to utter a word say to all: So what is this?

What is this?

What is this?

Naturally, nobody will acknowledge her. Everyone becomes a wall. And the person, solo in a room, sits back down. The act and moment are gone.

And yet it happens that some of us, like spies in a perilous land, will meet a certain gaze; and once we do, that recognition can soften the most wary eye and make us want to exchange all kinds of notations again, even the more improbable tales and rumors, to report everything we know of our Fan, who we're sure can somehow hear us a little better now. It's not that we can ever help her or lend her more courage. We simply wish her to know that we are here, and not unsatisfactory, and that in this regard she can please pay us no great mind.

For it was important that Fan keep everything out in front of her. After the scuffle at the fitness center pool, they all went back to Betty's Lane, and while there was a certain heightened state in the new household—this coinciding with their move from the trailer into one of the new houses—with Oliver and Betty perfectly okay as they all breakfasted at the huge kitchen table, at least until, say, Josey or someone else would make some innocent comment, or after nothing was said at all, when Oliver would abruptly rise and retreat to his study. For a few seconds nothing would happen and then Betty would trail after him, and because of the particular acoustics of the center stairwell shafting the house top to bottom, you could hear them even behind the closed study door rasping at each other, Oliver usually the aggrieved party and Betty the remorseful, though midstream their roles would often switch, and switch back. Josey and the babies, of course, paid little or no attention, preoccupied as they were by screens and toys, the helpers trying anything they could to coax them to eat.

Soon enough Oliver and Betty would return to the table, both looking a bit abraded, and resume whatever they had been doing, usually Oliver checking the markets and Betty reviewing her to-do lists for the day, which included calling her parents, who hadn't quite yet moved in, as they had gone on a thirty-day cruise with other older Charters, this one around Cape Horn; they logged in every other day, waving and blowing kisses to Josey and the babies from the windswept balcony of their stateroom. Otherwise there were few incursions from the outside world, this pattern of Oliver and Betty repeating itself daily, their ascents and descents, until one morning Betty didn't follow him, and he didn't return, at least not until after the dishes were cleared, the lessened tension and casual regard they had for each other surely signaling a calmed new stage. But this more orderly state was somewhat unsettling, too, as are most accommodations in matters of the heart, and if Fan didn't exactly think their marriage was in jeopardy, she did wonder if some other thing or element had now lodged itself between them, their desire for happiness nourishing a fast-growing buffer all around it so that it would hardly be noticed. Fan was still quite young and her love for Reg was unsullied and the only thing giving her self-pause was that on the night before he vanished she had decided on her own to invite risking the condition she was in now. Yes, it was youth's first passion, yes, as Reg might dorkishly croon, they were "burnin' like wildfire," but in truth Fan made the cold decision in that moment to invite a part of her beloved Reg forever, whether he might wish her to or not. Why did she? Nothing was threatening their future. Again we are sure it was out of love, only love, that she'd told him not to worry. And if there was any secondary reason to be with him again, perhaps it was her hope that she could simply show herself to him, and thus tell him what she'd done.

And which, Oliver informed her and Betty one day on returning from a meeting with a prominent village friend, might happen quite soon, for there'd been a breakthrough lead: Reg was indeed being "studied" at a directorate research facility, one in fact very close to B-Mor. He asked Fan if she knew why he would be examined like this, and of course, Fan had no idea. She truly could have no idea, and never did. Reg was special but no doubt mostly, if not only, to her. In any case Oliver was optimistic, describing how the pharmacorp was applying pressure on their behalf, using its considerable leverage with certain directorate members so that they would allow him a visitation, if not his outright release.

Betty took this news as excitedly as Fan did, promptly taking her the next day, as the best big sister might, to the boutiques in the village to find just the right outfit for the visit. Unlike Miss Cathy, however, Betty didn't have a preconceived (and squarely daft) conception of what Fan should wear, pretty much liking everything the salesladies brought out for Fan to model, from the designer-jeans-and-blouse look to something more sophisticated, such as a smart cocktail dress, and nixing them (as long as Fan agreed) simply because they didn't quite fit the bill of a reunion with one's beau. They tried to figure out what each outfit would say to him on first glance, the bright yellow sundress declaring, *I'm very happy!* or the knee-length cashmere sweater dress murmuring, *I've longed for you,* or the more formal lacy white gown announcing, *We shall never part again.* Fan made sure to ask for sizes that would be loose-fitting and comfortable, saying she disliked snug clothing. It was all good fun and Fan found herself giggling along with Betty as she popped out from behind the changing curtain, but in the end Fan chose the outfit that she felt most comfortable in, a set of athletic stretch pants and top and zip-up jacket, all in matte black.

You look great, Betty said, if with eyebrows slightly raised. Very sleek. But why so dark and serious?

Fan explained that this was the closest thing to how Reg most often saw her, which was when she'd just climbed out of the tanks.

Ah, I see, Betty nodded. You want him to feel he's at home.

Yes, Fan said, although that wasn't quite right. For really she wanted him to think, *Here's my Fan.*

They each got a pair of black athletic slip-ons (Betty decided to get the same outfit as Fan, in her size), and afterward they had to stop at the fitness center before going home to empty Betty's locker. The Cheungs had decided to quit the club, not to blame it for what had happened but simply to get past the unpleasant memory and association. They weren't going to join another club; given all the new space they had, they were now planning instead to put a swimming pool in the basement of one of the houses.

Liwei wants a full gym with weights and cardio, too, Betty said, fiddling with the combination wheel on her locker. Plus a romper room for the kids, for when it's bad weather.

That would be fun for them, Fan said.

It will be, as long as everything goes the way it's supposed to. The architect is drawing up plans. But I've been worrying about it. We're going to have all the money we'll ever need, but only when the deal goes through. Only God and I know how much we've spent in the last month! Many times more than we have, that's for sure. There's no reason why the deal shouldn't happen, but every time I ask Liwei when it's going to happen, all he says is that the lawyers are the problem. The lawyers! That they just keep bickering over the tiniest details.

Fan said that she'd heard him complain about that.

But you know what I did yesterday? Betty said. I thought, What could they be fighting about that's so important? Liwei isn't even going to run the lab anymore or have any say, he's giving up all control, so what's there to argue about? So I called a friend who works at the law firm we hired and asked her if she could find out what the remaining issues were and you know what she told me?

Fan shook her head.

She told me there were issues before but of course none now. I said, Why "of course"? Because the contract was agreed to more than a week ago, she said. Liwei apparently was in to sign it. Liwei didn't tell me he did, but we were fighting a lot then and I can understand how it slipped. Anyway, my friend said now we're simply waiting for the countersignature. But for some reason they're taking their time. They don't seem to be in any hurry. Of course, you don't need to know about such things, but it's all a little worrisome, don't you think?

Fan agreed it was, to which Betty gave a great sigh, though in a strange way the corroboration seemed to make Betty feel a little better, too, and after she deposited her sneakers and toiletries in the plastic shoe bag she'd brought with her, she set the bag down on the narrow upholstered leather bench that ran between the polished wood lockers.

Could I ask you something? Betty said, taking Fan's hands in hers.

Sure.

When you were out there, in the open counties, I assume you weren't all alone, because that would have been too hard and dangerous, yes?

Yes.

But you must have felt very alone anyway, right? I know you left of your own free will but putting that aside, you must have felt at times that you'd lost everything. Your household and your clan and your friends. Your work in the tanks. The many other things you surely enjoyed. And of course, your Reg. All the things that had made you you, made you Fan, there was none of it. It was all gone, and maybe, in your mind, gone forever. Was it like that?

Fan didn't immediately answer.

And when it was like that, Betty went on, her beautiful eyes disked wide and dark, it must have been frightening, so frightening. I can hardly imagine, but did you feel something else, too? Something on the other side of all that? I've been feeling very funny of late. It's nothing like what you probably experienced but I can't stop feeling it. I can only describe it as this amazing and cavernous emptiness I'm floating at the center of and that I found completely terrifying at first, like I wanted to die, but now I'm not so sure. There's something about it that drives me crazy. Do you know what I mean? Do you know what I'm talking about?

We know any feeling, even if identical in physical sensation, can never quite tell the same story in another. Still, Fan did understand the feeling, though she told Betty she wasn't sure, not wanting to say that she'd always had it, even when she was back in B-Mor, even when she held Reg's hand tightly in hers while they were walking in the park. She was as free as she had believed, and always had been. Only in leaving was it confirmed.

Betty had wanted to stay out a little longer, maybe even take a ride somewhere, make it an entire girls' day, but it was nearing dinnertime and Liwei would be anxious to get the evening meal going. With the project now essentially done and the pool and gym plans just now in development, he and Betty had more than ample time to devote themselves to those aspects of home life they considered vitally important, from the nurturing of Josey and the twins, to best environmental practices regarding their household's resource use and waste, to of course what the family ate. Eating was obviously elementary, it was what people did most of in their day, literally taking in the world, and in this area Liwei took a particularly intensive interest, not so much from a gastronomic angle about how things should taste but rather with the idea that each of them—even the babies—should take part in the production of the meal, from the selection of the ingredients at the village market to the chopping and measuring and cooking (the babies given a strong whiff of everything, from ginger slices to cinnamon sticks, after which they'd sometimes cry), the idea being a holistic appreciation through mindful exertions that would result in the best chance for well-being. Frankly, it was often a bit of a circus, the meals never coming out quite right because everybody at every stage had to take her turn, and it was fortunate they still had enough helpers about to mop up the rampant messes, especially if Josey got ahold of the mixing bowl.

It was not difficult for Fan to see that these intricate domestic efforts Oliver and Betty were now directing themselves toward were a constructive means of siphoning off energies that might otherwise go toward arguing or stewing or avoiding each other in the big but now more compartmentalized house. And she assumed this: Betty was still in regular touch with Vik. As far as she could tell, they didn't meet in person, they couldn't possibly, for how busy and full the Cheungs' house schedule was, and with the family being almost always together. But Betty had a second handscreen that slipped out of her handbag in the car and which Fan found beneath her front passenger seat and replaced, Betty zipping up her bag even as she drove. She was grateful that Betty had not divulged any more to her, too, as it would have dragged her anew into the ethical quandary that was finally rendered moot after the incident at the pool. For although she did not know him very well yet, Oliver was Liwei and Liwei was her blood and his pitiable position made her feel she still knew too much, her chest giving the smallest heave whenever just the three of them were together, usually after putting Josey on the preschool shuttle.

The funny thing was that Fan was spending much more time with Oliver than with her, perhaps to limit the chances that Betty, wine-soaked, might want to engage in a certain heart-to-heart, perhaps to figure out if she truly liked him, or could ever feel for him what she did for the others of the household back in B-Mor, that somehow remarkably uncomplicated love that one need rarely express or demonstrate. The Cheungs as well as their friends believed deeply in demonstrations, the minute-by-minute acting out and temperature taking of respect and admiration and devotion, though with Fan, Oliver seemed to be reverting to what he must have been like when he was back with the clan, the two of them now hardly much talking at all while they were busy in the kitchen, or listening to the architect explain the details of the newest plans, or watching Josey do her little-girl cartwheels across the shiny new street, her rear arcing higher than her legs.

He didn't have to tell Fan he was enjoying or appreciating her company, for if he was or not, it didn't seem to matter as much as his simply being with her, or if not near her, having a clear notion of where she was. It was enough for him to walk into Josey's room and see them playing dolls, and he wouldn't even nod or say hello, just noting it as part of how his people were lodged in the house. Nor had he spoken of what happened at the pool or did he seem to have noticed anything unusual about her after she came out of the water. For isn't that what we like best about being in our household, having a picture of auntie and uncle up there in the garret, and cousins out in the front, and a brother and nephew across the hall, not having to dwell too much on who they are but instead pointedly feeling their array, the same sense our primordial predecessors must have had when returning at dusk and gazing up into the umbrella tree. It's not always a perfectly wonderful feeling but it is ours, going forward and back.

Of course, where Fan was on Betty's Lane will be viewed by some as a most unnatural version of our plan, given how swiftly (if sometimes not so smoothly) their realm was realized, and operated not via equally shared labors but through the pressured application of unbounded wealth; but we must point out, too, that at least Oliver and Betty had, in their exactingly purposeful Charter mode, thought everything through, selecting in and out the best and worst of our ways, which can only be to their credit, and our tradition does not naturally demand that they bear the consequences of such over-reaching control. Most times nothing happens. People do get away.

And when they don't, maybe it's just the turning of the Earth, such that some bit of light plashes across their path too early or too late. For we think for Oliver and Betty it was like that. One day Oliver gathered everyone including the helpers to relate some disappointing news, namely that they could not yet go forward with the basement pool and gym project because of certain zoning restrictions, telling only Betty that it was, in fact, because the bank was reviewing their credit lines, which were now temporarily suspended. All Fan knew was that he somehow looked grayer in the temples, grayer in the cheeks, and although he'd position himself as ever in the middle of the kitchen chaos, he picked lifelessly at his plate, downing only his unsweetened iced coffees, one right after the other, generally appearing badly dispatched enough that Betty had begun to sneak extra cream and whey protein into the drinks, which fortunately he didn't seem to notice. Each new day that passed, two of them, three, then five or six, without word from the law firm of the contract being signed seemed to increase the time he spent up in his study, saying he was going over their financial accounts, though of course the conclusion was always instantly the same. They were running low on money, and there was no money coming in. The last few pieces of furniture and decorative items and artworks were still being delivered morning and afternoon, but a telling sign was that their wrappings and packages were no longer being opened, Betty having instructed the helpers simply to leave them for now, that she'd do it herself later. In fact, Betty now often lingered up in Oliver's study after bringing him something to eat, and it was soon left to Fan to decide what she and the kids and the helpers would do with their day, what they would eat, when they'd retire, even when they'd arise. Betty had had the helpers set up a cot in Oliver's study so that he could simply fall asleep, usually near dawn, in something other than his desk chair, Betty herself often staying up with him. It was usually completely silent up there, but sometimes there'd be a fit of arguing in the middle of the night, loud enough to wake one of the twins. Most often it was midday when they'd finally come down, usually Oliver before Betty, as his thirst for his drink would rouse him.

But then one morning, just after Fan put Josey on the shuttle, they came down together, both showered and neatly dressed, Oliver in a crisply pressed shirt and flannel slacks and Betty, to Fan's instant notice, wearing the outfit matching the one she had for reuniting with Reg.

We did it, Oliver said, raising his hands. Betty was covering her mouth.

The contract? Fan said.

Yes! they both said. It went through!

The helpers started hopping and clapping, and Fan did, too.

But then Oliver nudged Betty, and she gasped: And also Reg!

Fan didn't know what to say.

Go up and change, Fan, Betty told her, tears in her eyes.

It's a long drive to where he is, Oliver said. So let's get ready. We'll want to leave soon.

WHAT HASTY PREPARATIONS we make for our future. Think of it: it seems almost tragic, the things we're sure we ought to bring along.

We pack too heavy with what we hope we'll use, and too light of what we must. We thus go forth misladen, ill equipped for the dawn.

But not so our Fan. She wasn't a prophetic one, as we know, or always ever ready, nor was she chosen, at last, to lead anyone but herself. For at every turn, whether she bore a full satchel or one slim or nothing at all, she stood resolved, her boldness not one that simply pushed her forward but rather fixed her, solid, on the very spot she found herself. *Where you are.* Did this make her impervious? Heroic and wise? Not at all. She was as subject to chance and malice as the rest of us. She could only entertain hopes for the future. But we know very well that there was a quality about this rootedness, which, unlike the rest of us, she never bemoaned or fought or disbelieved, that every person who met her couldn't help but recognize with a gentle trembling.

Betty accompanied Fan upstairs. Despite Oliver's advice that they should soon get on the road—only he was going to go with her in the livery car, as it might end up an overnight or maybe two, with Betty staying back with the kids—she suggested Fan take a soaking bath, after which Betty said she would paint her nails and help her with her hair, which was still in a simple bob. Maybe they would get the curling iron out, or even give Fan a wave, one of the helpers likely having a box of instant perm. While the tub was filling (and seasoned with several scoops of Betty's fancy lavender-scented salts), Fan packed a small overnight bag, a blouse and nice sweater and a pair of jeans Betty had recently bought for her. That was going to be all but Betty thought she should take along a few more outfits, in case they allowed her to see him through several days. So Pinah brought up a much bigger bag, this one with wheels, and after merely half filling it with the various options of what they'd laid out on the bed, Betty went ahead and larded on other pieces from Fan's closet, leaving just enough room for a toiletries bag.

You never know what you'll feel like, Betty said, telling her that even if it was only another day's visit, she'd have plenty of choices for what she might like to wear. Really, who could tell until right then!

This seemed reasonable enough, of course, though while she lay in the slightly too warm bath, her head propped on an air pillow, Fan must have felt that something was amiss, that Betty was being a bit too indulgent, even for her. Had they changed their mind about her and Reg residing there? Had it been just their sentimental dream? If this was so, we are sure, she would tell Reg that she was only grateful for their company, for their care and aid, and that she would miss Josey and the twins and the helpers, too, for all the good mayhem and laughter, and that she did not regret a moment along Betty's Lane. No need to linger.

So she rose from the tub and peeked into the bedroom and was surprised to see that Betty was still sitting on the bed, awaiting her while messaging on her handscreen. Betty quickly put it in her pocket when she noticed Fan. They did her nails, finishing them plainly with a clear lacquer, and they decided in the end that Betty should simply give her ends a trim, so that she would look fresh and neat. In fact, after the cut and the lightest dabbing of blush Betty applied, she looked as fit and fine as ever, perhaps never so much life arisen in her face. While Pinah and now another helper, Violet, took down her bag, Fan changed into the special outfit, and when she came out, Betty took her hand and they regarded themselves in the mirrored doors of the closet passage, the two of them looking like any sister divers back in B-Mor.

Are you ready? Betty asked her.

Fan nodded.

They went down the stairs together. The front door was open and through the clear pane of the storm door they could see Pinah and

Violet letting the bag bump down each stoop step to the sidewalk. Betty now said she had to call about a furniture delivery and that Fan should wait outside. Her car was coming any minute.

Besides, she said, I despise good-byes, even for just the briefest trips.

Shouldn't I wait? Fan said, glancing upstairs, where she knew Oliver was still packing and changing.

He'll be down very soon. Oh, look, here it is.

A silver sedan with darkened windows rolled up, and out from it emerged a squat, burly driver in a shiny blazer that pinched at his underarms.

Okay, no good-byes. I'll see you very soon, okay?

Okay, Fan said. Very soon.

Still, Betty opened her arms, beckoning her, and Fan let herself be taken in. And it was surprising how Betty gave her the deepest hug she'd ever felt, from Reg included, like the woman would sooner perish than let her go. But then she did.

Now hurry.

The very notion, we fear, Fan was thinking herself as she skipped down the stoop. Now hurry back toward B-Mor. Now hurry to sweet Reg. For if there is ever a moment when we are most vulnerable, it's when we're closest to the idea of the attained desire, and thus farthest from ourselves, which is when we'll tread through any flame.

While Pinah and Violet pecked her on the cheek, the man hefted the big bag with one hand into the trunk of the sedan. She looked back at the door and Betty was gone.

Miss Fan? the driver said, and when she acknowledged him, he said *Please* and took her by the arm and guided her to the rear door. *Please*, he said again as he felt her begin to resist, his stiff fingertips pressing a nerve of her elbow she did not know was there. She heard mewls of panicked confusion from Pinah and Violet. Her knees almost gave way.

Please!

Before she could speak, she was in the cave of the car, propping herself up in the backseat, her eyes not yet adjusting. It smelled just cleaned. They were already rolling forward, just turning out onto the real street. And they passed another silver sedan, oddly enough, on its way into Betty's Lane. Fan realized there was a second person in the front, who now ordered the driver to speed up, to go as fast as he could.

I like your outfit, he said, turning to her now.

It was Vik. Gentle-eyed Vik. It's a good one for traveling. But the question now, little one, is where would you like to go?

Where indeed.

Where would you go, dear Fan?

Where would you have Vik direct the car, as Betty had asked him to, unable as she was to abide her husband's plan? For Liwei was going to deliver you not to anywhere near us and Reg but to the pharmacorp, in the hope that someone bearing Reg's legacies would be fair exchange for their final purchase of his work. Or at least that was his intention. Could he have done it? Truly tendered you so? We know that at the very moment the guard post's gate bar was lifted and you flew out, Oliver had stepped down the stoop himself with his own overnight bag and was ushered into the car. But there he found only Betty in the backseat and knew immediately what she had done. Did they fight? Did they cry? Did they speak of love and doom? All we know is that they remained inside, and the car did not soon move.

The other one, we will have to dream, traveled swift and wide and far. It went in a direction away from us, you knowing now that you must be left somewhere you'd go unnoticed and undisturbed, at least for a good long while. For that time would be coming; there could not be any more travails. So perhaps you went north, where people wouldn't think to look, or south for a winter's warmth, or maybe westward, that ready route, drawing you forth to reach another sea.

But sometimes, we're sure, you're much closer than we know, waiting out word of Reg in some modest but nice place, maybe like the one Mala spoke of. We can almost see it now, small but tidy, emptied of its household save for a black-clad girl, the brightest shape we know.

Don't hurry, Fan.

Stay put for now.

We'll find a way.

You need not come back for us.